THE
WATCHER

Also by Brian Freeman

Immoral
Stripped
Stalked

Write to Brian Freeman at brian@bfreemanbooks.com
or join the mailing list at www.bfreemanbooks.com

THE WATCHER

Brian Freeman

headline

Copyright © 2008 Brian Freeman

The right of Brian Freeman to be identified as the Author of
the Work has been asserted by him in accordance with the
Copyright, Designs and Patents Act 1988.

First published in Great Britain in 2008
by HEADLINE PUBLISHING GROUP

1

Apart from any use permitted under UK copyright law, this
publication may only be reproduced, stored, or transmitted, in
any form, or by any means, with prior permission in writing of
the publishers or, in the case of reprographic production, in
accordance with the terms of licences issued by the
Copyright Licensing Agency.

All characters in this publication are fictitious
and any resemblance to real persons, living or dead,
is purely coincidental.

Cataloguing in Publication Data is
available from the British Library

ISBN 978 0 7553 3527 5 (hardback)
ISBN 978 0 7553 3528 2 (trade paperback)

Typeset in Sabon by
Palimpsest Book Production Limited, Grangemouth, Stirlingshire

Printed and bound in Great Britain by
CPI Mackays, Chatham ME5 8TD

Headline's policy is to use papers that are natural, renewable and
recyclable products and made from wood grown in sustainable
forests. The logging and manufacturing processes are expected
to conform to the environmental regulations of the country of origin.

HEADLINE PUBLISHING GROUP
An Hachette Livre UK Company
338 Euston Road
London NW1 3BH

www.headline.co.uk
www.hachettelivre.co.uk

For Marcia

That's my last Duchess painted on the wall,
Looking as if she were alive.

Robert Browning,
My Last Duchess

Who Killed Laura Starr?

By Tish Verdure

4 July 1977

When I arrived home near midnight, I could still hear the whistle and pop of fireworks in the neighborhood. The slashing rain had finally diminished to drizzle and fog, and the streets were alive with illegal celebrations. Starbursts opened like hazy flowers over the trees. Sparklers hissed. Bottle rockets screamed. The summer night smelled like candy and burnt-out matches as I stood in the yard and watched the rainbow of lights around me. In the next block, I heard kids whooping as if they were bloodthirsty Indians. I felt wet and wild myself.

When I looked up, I saw that Laura's upstairs window was dark. There were no signs of life.

I crept into our house through the screen door and tracked damp, bare footsteps across the kitchen floor. I was quiet. I didn't want my father to hear me and ask me questions about where I had been and what I had done tonight. My mouth could lie, but not my face. If he saw me, he would ask me about Laura, too. Where was she? Who was she with? I didn't want to risk a repeat of last night.

Dad and Laura. Bitter argument.

I took the stairs two at a time, bolted into my bedroom, and locked the door behind me. I felt dreamy. Maybe this was what it was like to be on drugs. Without turning on the lights, I peeled off my soaked clothes down to my dirty skin. My thighs were bruised and sore. I

1

was sticky down there, where some of it had leaked out. My body ached inside, but it was a good ache. A first-time ache.

My independence day.

Oh, God, the pill! I couldn't forget that, not tonight. I rummaged through my underwear drawer and found the pink plastic container I kept hidden in the back. I thought about taking two, just to be sure, but that was stupid. I also thought about throwing open my bedroom window and shouting to the world: CINDY STARR IS NOT A VIRGIN! Really stupid.

I pulled on clean panties, jumped into my pajama bottoms, and slipped a Fleetwood Mac T-shirt over my head. I didn't take a shower or brush my teeth. I lay down on top of the blankets with my eyes wide open. No way I was going to sleep tonight. I was too full of Jonny.

I had dropped him off at his house after we left the park. His mother was waiting up for him. She doesn't like me, but I know what she's been through since she lost Jonny's dad. It was that way with my dad, three years ago, when my mom died. Mrs Stride is terrified of losing her son, like Jonny is the last thing that reminds her of her husband. And I'm a threat. She knows I love him. We're going to get married, I don't know when, but we're going to get married. I'm going to take him away from her.

Too many things in my head!

I sat up in bed and pushed my long hair back behind my ears on both sides. I needed to talk to someone. I don't have a million girl-friends, because there's always too much to do at home to be out spending time with friends. I thought about going downstairs and calling Jonny again, just to hear his voice one last time, but he was probably in bed by now, and his mother would answer, and that wouldn't be a good thing at all.

I decided to talk to Laura. The truth is, I don't do that a lot.

You have to understand that Laura and I have always been close, but not really *close*, you know? I'm seventeen, she's eighteen. It's just the two of us, but we're like magnets that push each other apart. I'm the funny one, the athlete, the flirt, and Laura is moody, mysterious, and scared of boys. Being opposites as sisters isn't such a good thing. You're always looking in the mirror and thinking about what you don't have.

2

It's been hard for Laura since Mom died. She and Dad scream at each other all the time. Mostly, they argue about God. Laura stopped going to church after Mom's accident, like it was God's fault that we lost her. Dad tells her she's going to hell for turning her back on Jesus. Yeah, he really says stuff like that. Dad has always been a starched-shirt-on-Sunday Christian, even more so these past few years without Mom. He talks about God punishing him for his sins. I think it was just a drunk driver.

Me, I found out who I was after we lost Mom. I know how that sounds, but I had to take over, do the cooking, do the cleaning, keep the house together. I decided that you have to pick a direction in life, and that's that. I'm going to go to college, marry Jonny, become a physical therapist, and help people recover from serious injuries. You know, like Mom never got a chance to do. Laura is jealous that I'm so sure of where I'm going.

I made up my mind to talk to her. I got out of bed and slipped down the hallway to her room. You can't really be quiet, because the floorboards screech like witches. I tapped gently on her door.

'Laura?'

On most nights, the yellow lamp beside her bed glowed until very late, and I would find her with a book under her nose. Tonight there was no light under the door. When she didn't answer, I turned the knob carefully and went inside.

'Laura?' I said again.

She wasn't there. She hadn't come home yet. I switched on the light, which made my eyes squint and blink. Her room was the way it always was. Laura was messy. Clothes on the floor. Albums stacked on her dresser by the record player. Posters of Carly Simon and Linda Ronstadt, both a little crooked where they were taped on the wall. Books everywhere. Virginia Woolf. Sylvia Plath. Gail Sheehy.

Where was she?

I thought back to the evening in the park. Laura and I drove up there together. I was meeting Jonny after his softball game, and he and I were going down to the lake to swim. I knew tonight was going to be the first time for us. I'd been planning it for weeks.

The thing was, before Jonny showed up, Laura was acting weird. She was saying scary stuff I didn't understand. Then she asked me if

I could keep a secret. I said sure, I could keep a secret forever if I needed to, which was true. But she never got a chance to tell me what it was. Instead, she went off by herself onto the trails. It was night. The rain was pouring down.

I never should have let her go.

I told myself that everything was OK. Laura had a rendezvous with a boy. Just like me and Jonny. That was why she was late tonight. I almost left her room, but then I saw something on her bed, and I realized I was wrong.

The letter was just like the others that had arrived anonymously over the past two months. Laura told me they had stopped. Why did she lie? I unfolded the piece of paper and stared at the grainy black and white photograph and what was scrawled across the page in red ink and almost sank to my knees and threw up.

As I held it in my hand, I remembered something else from the park. Before the storm broke, before Jonny found us, Laura kept saying that someone was hiding in the woods.

Watching her.

I knew I had to go back.

I flew downstairs with my car keys. I was still wearing my pajama bottoms and T-shirt. It was now past one in the morning, and most of the fireworks outside had long since burned down to scorched black patches on the grass. I drove my dad's Opel Manta, and the streets were empty, so I went fast through the gray glow of the fog. It took me fifteen minutes to make my way back to the wilderness refuge near Tischer Creek. I didn't recognize any of the cars in the matted weeds. The park was sprawling, and I was sure that there were kids hiding under the cover of darkness, doing what Jonny and I had done earlier.

I had no idea where to find her. I shouted, 'Laura!'

I thought I heard whispering. I began to get scared and feel foolish and stupid for being here on my own. I pumped my arms and ran into the center of the muddy ground we used as a softball field and spun in circles, trying to see into the trees and trails through the mist. I heard thousands of crickets chirping madly. The grass underneath my feet was spongy and wet. I almost never wore shoes during the summer.

'Laura!'

The dark silhouette of a heron with its giant wingspan and odd, dangling legs flew lazily over my head. I had flushed it with my shouting. It swooped toward the cool water of the lake and disappeared. I headed the same way, searching for the break in the trees that led to the south beach, where Laura and I had waited for Jonny a few hours earlier.

I never made it that far. Thirty yards away, I came upon something in the grass.

Laura's shoe. A pink Converse Flyer.

I picked it up, looked around for the other shoe, and didn't see it. I hunted in the field for anything else that belonged to her, but all I saw were cigarette butts and beer bottles. I knew I had to go into the woods to find her. Near where I was standing, holding her shoe, I saw a trail that tracked north along the lakeshore, in between the birches. Some kind of unspoken bond between sisters told me that was where she had gone.

When I followed it, the trail swallowed me up. The moon vanished. I took careful steps, not wanting to make noise when I didn't know what was ahead of me. I didn't shout Laura's name anymore. The path was covered in a crackling bed of pine. Rain dripped down through the covering crowns of trees. Wind snickered through the trees and landed like a warm, wet breath on my neck.

Long minutes passed. I didn't usually come this way, so the path was unfamiliar. My mind made up scary stories about what was in the woods near me. I had no idea how far I had gone or whether I should have taken one of the criss-crossing trails that led uphill away from the lake. If anyone was two feet away, I wouldn't have known it. This was the kind of place where monsters felt real.

I saw a pale break in the darkness ahead, where the trees thinned. There was a part of me that wanted to turn and go back. I didn't want to see this secret place and what was hiding there.

Somehow I knew. I just knew.

I heard water tap-tapping on wet sand. I emerged from the woods into a clearing eighty feet across, a notch in the forest where the lake swooshed onto a ribbon of beach that bubbled toward the trees in a half-moon. Gold streaks were wavy on the lake. I could see very clearly after the darkness of the trail.

My hand shot to my mouth and caught myself in mid-scream.

I ran.

'Laura,' I whispered, my voice strangled.

It was worse than anything I could have imagined. I saw the aluminum baseball bat beside her body, shiny and glistening and sticky. I smelled copper. I sank to my knees, my arms outstretched, my hands quivering in the air. My lips murmured like I was saying a prayer, and a whimper rumbled out of my chest.

'Oh, no, no, no.'

She was all red. Red everywhere. Like she was drowned in wine. Her beautiful golden hair was the color of garish lipstick. Crimson fangs dripped from the wings of the butterfly tattoo on her naked back. Mosquitoes littered her skin, some living, some dead, trapped in the pool and unable to fly from the feast. Her face was toward me, cheek in the mud, but there was no face anymore, no smile, no soft brown eyes, nothing that had ever been my sister. Life had been hammered out of her blow by blow. I tried to imagine the fury that had done this and couldn't conceive of a heart so black.

I put a tentative hand on her arm. Her skin was already unnaturally cold. My hand came away like I had dipped it in finger paints.

That was when I heard it. Branches snapping. Movement. Breathing. Not from Laura, but from the black forest. I scooped up the baseball bat and scrambled to my feet. My fingernails dug into the leather grip. I wound up fiercely, ready to swing.

Someone was behind me . . .

PART ONE

INDEPENDENCE DAY

One

Lieutenant Jonathan Stride shielded his eyes as the glass door shot a laser beam of sunlight at his face, and when he could see again, he realized that the woman who had stepped out onto the patio was his late wife, Cindy.

For an instant, time slowed down the way it does on a long fall, while the buzz of conversation continued around him. He forgot how to breathe. The enigmatic smile he remembered from years ago was the same. When she lifted her sunglasses, her brown eyes stared back at him with a familiar glint over the heads of the others in the restaurant. She was in her late forties, as she would have been if she had lived. Small, like a faery, but athletic and strong. Suntanned skin. An aura of intensity.

It wasn't her, of course.

More than five years had passed since Cindy died of cancer as he sat beside her hospital bed. The pain of her loss had retreated to a distant ache in a corner of his soul. Even so, there were moments like this when he saw a stranger, and something about her brought it all back. It didn't take much, just the look in her eyes or the way she carried herself, to stir his memory.

This woman was looking back at him, too. She was small but a couple of inches taller than Cindy, who had barely crossed five feet four on tiptoes. Her blonde hair fell breezily around her shoulders, and her sunglasses were now tented on top of her head. Her earrings were sapphire studs. She wore a blue-flowered summer skirt that hung to her knees, baby blue heels, a white blouse, and a lightweight tan leather jacket with a braided fringe. She balanced one hand on a narrow hip as she watched him. The lacy ties of her jacket dangled between her legs.

He knew her from somewhere.

'Your five seconds are up,' Serena Dial told him.

Stride broke away. 'What?'

Serena sipped her lemonade and eyed the woman in the leather jacket as she was shown to a table on the patio. A gust of wind blew off the lake and rustled her own silky dark hair. 'You get a free pass to look at any woman for up to five seconds. After that, it officially becomes flirting.'

'She reminded me of someone,' Stride said.

'Sure she did.'

Serena was an ex-cop and now a private investigator. She and Stride had shared a bed for almost two years.

Stride turned to his partner in the Detective Bureau, Maggie Bei, as if consulting an Olympic judge for a ruling. 'Is this five-second thing commonly known?' he asked.

'Absolutely,' Maggie said, with a wink at Serena.

Stride knew when he was on the losing end of an argument. 'OK, I was flirting,' he admitted.

Serena stretched out her arm lazily and used the back of her hand to caress Stride's cheek, which was rough with black and gray stubble. She sidled her long fingers through his wavy hair and leaned forward to plant a slow kiss on his lips. She tasted like citrus and sugar.

'Most animals mark their territory by urinating,' Maggie remarked, with her mouth full of a large bite of her steak sandwich. She batted her almond-shaped eyes innocently at Serena and grinned.

Stride laughed. 'Can we get back to work?'

'Go ahead,' Serena told him. She swiped a French fry from Maggie's plate and bit into it while baring her teeth.

'What's the latest on the peeper?' Stride asked Maggie. He stole a sideways glance across the restaurant at the other woman and noticed that she was doing the same thing to him from over her menu.

'He struck again on Friday night,' Maggie replied. 'A sixteen-year-old girl in Fond du Lac noticed a guy in the trees outside her bedroom when she was getting undressed. She screamed, and he took off.'

'Did she get a look at him?'

Maggie shook her head. 'She thought he was tall and skinny, but that's it. It was dark.'

'That's nine incidents in the last month,' Stride said.

'It's summer. Time for the perverts to come out.'

The calendar said 1 June. It was late Sunday afternoon, but the sun was warm and high over the steep hillside on which the city of Duluth, Minnesota, was built. It wouldn't be dark until after nine o'clock. After the usual long, bitter winter, the tourists were streaming back on the weekends to watch the ore boats come and go through the narrow channel that led out into Lake Superior. The Canal Park area, where the three of them sat on the rooftop patio of Grandma's Saloon, teemed with lovers and children feeding noisy gulls by the boardwalk. As tourists and locals collided, and the weather got warmer, Stride and his team got busier. Crime was creeping up for the season but, so far, it was nothing more than the usual run of thefts, break-ins, drunks, and drugs.

Plus a peeping Tom with a fetish for blonde high school girls.

Stride had overseen the city's Detective Bureau, which handled major crimes in Duluth, for more than a decade, and he had steeled himself to human behavior that defied all rational explanation. Sexual abuse. Meth labs. Suicide. Homicide. The peeper had shown no inclination to violence, but Stride didn't minimize the danger of someone who liked to watch young girls undress in their bedrooms. It was a short trip through the looking glass to molestation and rape.

'He's been stalking the south side, right?' Stride asked.

Maggie grunted affirmatively and pushed her black fringe out of her eyes. She was a diminutive Chinese cop who had worked side by side with Stride since he took over the major crimes unit.

'Yeah, all the reports have been south of Riverside,' Maggie said. 'He's crossed the bridge into Superior a couple times, too.'

The great lake that loomed over Stride's shoulder narrowed into the jagged bays and harbors of the St Louis River as it wound southward between the cities of Duluth and Superior. On the scenic drive along the river, Duluth broke up into small towns like Riverside, Morgan Park, Gary, and Fond du Lac. None of the towns was large enough to afford its own police force, so the Duluth Police stretched its enforcement coverage all the way along the river's twisty shore.

'You know what it's like down in the river towns,' Maggie said. 'People leave their shades up and their windows open. For a peeper, it's like a cat with a goldfish bowl. Lots to look at.'

'Do we have any leads on an ID?' Stride asked.

'Nothing yet. We have no description and no idea how old he is. We're working our way through the sex offender list, but no one looks like an obvious suspect.'

'How about a car?'

'We've had reports of a small SUV – something like a CRV or a Rav4 – near three of the peeping locations. Maybe silver, maybe gray or sand. No one in the area would claim it. That's as close as I've got to a lead.'

'What about the victims?' Stride asked. 'How does this guy find them?'

'The girls range in age from fourteen to nineteen,' Maggie said. 'They go to different schools, and I haven't found any overlap in their social lives. They're all blondes, though. I don't think this guy is just going from house to house, trying to get lucky. We'd have caught him by now if he was simply trolling through backyards. When he hits a house, he already knows there's a girl there with the right look.'

'Has he made any attempts to get inside?' Serena asked.

Serena wasn't a member of the Duluth Police, but she was a former homicide detective from Las Vegas. In addition to being his lover, Stride considered her one of the sharpest investigators he had ever worked with. He and Maggie consulted her unofficially on most of their cases.

'No, he just watches,' Maggie said. 'The girl's window was open in several of the incidents, but he stayed outside.'

Serena stole another fry from Maggie's plate. 'Yeah, but he might be getting his courage up. Along with other things. Peeping's a threshold crime.'

'That's what I'm afraid of,' Maggie said. 'I want to catch this guy before he moves on to bigger things.' She glanced at the opposite side of the restaurant patio and added, 'By the way, boss, you're about to understand why women adopted that five-second rule.'

'What do you mean?' Stride asked.

Then he looked up and understood.

The woman in the braided leather jacket, the one who reminded him of his late wife Cindy, was coming over.

'You're Jonathan Stride, aren't you?' she asked.

Stride pushed his chair back and stood up. He was over six feet tall and when he looked down at the top of her head, he saw silver roots creeping into her blonde hair. He took her offered hand and shook it. Her long nails dug into his palm. 'Yes, that's right.'

'I'm sure you don't remember me, but we were in high school together. I graduated a year before you and Cindy did. My name is Tish Verdure.'

Her voice had a seductive, breathless rumble. Her clothes smelled of violet perfume covering cigarette smoke. She was perfectly made up, but under the foundation, age and nicotine had carved winding paths into the skin around her brown eyes and above her forehead. Even so, she was very pretty, with a tiny, tapered nose, a pale pink oval at her lips, and a pointed chin.

Stride remembered her name but nothing else, but it explained why she had looked familiar to him. 'It's been a long time,' he said in an apologetic tone.

'Don't worry, I knew Cindy before the two of you ever met.'

'I don't recall Cindy ever mentioning you,' he said.

'Well, back then, I was Laura's best friend.'

At the sound of Laura's name, Stride felt a rush of memories storm his mind. Himself and Cindy, naked in the water, making love. Ray Wallace checking his gun. The huge black man, Dada, escaping on a train car. Most of all, the whooshing sound of a baseball bat in Peter Stanhope's hands. It may as well have been 1977 again.

Serena cleared her throat loudly. Stride burst from his trance.

'I'm sorry. Tish, this is my partner, Serena Dial, and this is my colleague on the police force, Maggie Bei.'

Maggie waved with half her sandwich without getting up. Serena stood, dwarfing the other woman, and Stride felt the air blow cold like dry ice between Serena and Tish. They didn't know each other, but with a single glance, they didn't like each other.

'Do you live in the area?' Stride asked.

Tish studied Lake Superior with wistful eyes. 'Oh, no, I haven't been back to Duluth in years. I don't really have much of a home base. I'm a travel writer, so I'm on the go most of the time. When I stay put, I live in Atlanta.'

'What brings you back here?' he asked.

'Actually, I was looking for you,' Tish told him.

'For me?' Stride asked, surprised.

'Yes.'

Stride exchanged glances with Serena and Maggie. 'Maybe you should sit down and tell me why.'

Tish took the empty chair at the table for four, facing the lake. She slid a leather purse off her shoulder and put it on the table in front of her. She pulled out an open pack of cigarettes. 'Can you smoke outside at restaurants here?'

'I wish you wouldn't,' Serena told her.

'I'm sorry,' Tish said. 'I know I should quit, but smoking's one way I handle my nerves. The other is drinking. Not very smart, I guess, but what can you do?'

'I'm a reformed smoker myself,' Stride said.

'Well, I don't mean to be such a mystery,' Tish told them. She smiled at Maggie and Serena, but the two women wore stony masks. Tish ignored them and focused on Stride. 'First of all, I want to tell you how sorry I am about Cindy's death. I know the two of you were a real love match.'

'It was several years ago, but thank you,' Stride said.

'I would have come to the funeral myself, but I was in Prague on a story at the time.'

Stride felt suspicion poking like a spring seedling out of the ground. 'That's kind of you to say, Ms Verdure, but you knew Cindy back in high school. I don't think anyone would have expected you to go to her funeral twenty-five years later.'

'Oh, Cindy and I stayed in touch,' Tish said.

'I'm sorry?'

'Not very often, but we wrote to each other now and then.'

'Really.' He didn't say it like a question. He said it for what it was – disbelief. He added, 'Do you mind showing me some identification?'

'Not at all.' Tish dug in her purse for her wallet and extracted her driver's license, which she handed across the table. The silence from

14

the other three people didn't appear to bother her. 'I understand how odd this is, me showing up after all these years,' she continued. 'Cindy and I wrote to each other at the hospital where she worked. It was only the occasional postcard or Christmas card, that kind of thing. For me, it was nice having a little connection to my life back here. I left Duluth after graduation and never came back, but that doesn't mean I forgot about it. And of course, whenever I wrote to Cindy, it made me feel a little closer to Laura. Do you know what I mean?'

Stride studied the Georgia driver's license carefully and confirmed that the name Tish Verdure and the photo matched the woman sitting across from him.

'Who's Laura?' Serena asked.

Stride felt as if a scab were slowly being pulled away from a deep wound. 'She was Cindy's sister.'

Serena's eyebrows arched, with a look that said unmistakably, *why haven't you told me about her?*

'Laura was murdered,' Stride went on. 'Someone beat her to death with a baseball bat. It was 4 July 1977.'

'Did they catch the guy who did it?' Serena asked.

'No, he got away. Because of me.'

He didn't say it in a way that invited questions. Serena opened her mouth and closed it again. Maggie pushed the food around on her plate, not looking up.

'Maybe you should tell me why you're here, Ms Verdure,' Stride said. 'And what you want from me.'

'Please, call me Tish.' She leaned forward with her elbows on the table. Her brown eyes were dark and serious. 'In fact, I'm here because of Laura. It's obvious that her death still weighs on you. Well, it does on me, too. She and I were very close in high school.'

'So?'

'So I'm writing a book about Laura's murder.'

Stride's weathered face wrinkled into a scowl. 'A book?'

'Exactly. Not just about her death, but about the people around her. How their lives changed. It's a non-fiction novel, sort of an *In Cold Blood* thing, you know? I mean, look at you. You're the man in charge of the city's major crimes unit. Your wife's sister was killed when you were all of seventeen, and the case was never solved.'

'I think this conversation is over,' Stride declared.

'Please, wait.'

'I won't be part of a book about Laura,' Stride told her. 'I have no interest in dragging up that part of my life again.'

'Just hear me out.' Tish held up her hands. 'It's not just a story about Laura's death. There's more. I want the book to be a catalyst to reopen the investigation. I want to solve the case. I want to find out who murdered Laura.'

Stride folded his arms. 'You?'

'That's right. Look, I'll do it on my own if I have to, but I want your help. What's more, I think you *want* to help me. This is a chance to put this case behind you once and for all. Cindy told me what kind of person you are. How every death takes a piece out of your soul.'

He was angry now. 'Ms Verdure, don't you think I would have reopened this case years ago if I thought there was more to be done? Laura's murder was never unsolved. We know who did it. He got away. He disappeared.'

Tish shook her head. 'I don't believe that's what happened. I don't think you do, either. There was a lot more going on in Laura's life that summer. It was easy for the police to pass it off on some anonymous vagrant, a *black* vagrant. Talk about your stereotypical bogeyman. No one wanted to deal with the fact that it was probably someone close to Laura who killed her.'

'Do you have a suspect in mind?' Stride asked.

'Well, you could start with Peter Stanhope.'

Serena's head snapped round at the mention of Stanhope's name. 'Peter was involved?' she asked Stride.

'Yes, he was the prime suspect for a while,' Stride admitted.

'Why didn't you tell me any of this before?' Serena asked.

Stride was silent. Peter Stanhope was an attorney from one of Duluth's most influential families, but more importantly he was one of Serena's clients as a private investigator.

'I've done my homework,' Tish continued. 'Randall Stanhope had the police in his pocket back then, and it wouldn't have been hard for him to shift the focus away from his son. Somebody needs to take a close look at Peter Stanhope.'

Serena pushed her chair back with an iron screech and stalked away from the table.

Maggie watched her go, then leaned forward, shaking her head. 'Look, Trish.'

'It's Tish.'

'Tish, fish, knish, whatever. Let me give you a reality check. You can't go around making accusations about anyone, let alone a rich lawyer like Peter Stanhope, without evidence. You can't expect the police to help you.'

'Unless you've got something new to add to the investigation, we can't do anything,' Stride added. 'Even if we wanted to.'

'I do have something new,' Tish said.

Stride's face was dark and suspicious. 'What is it?'

'I know Laura was being stalked.'

Who Killed Laura Starr?

By Tish Verdure

20 May 1977

Laura showed me the letter today. I caught her reading it on her bed when I went into her room, and I saw what it was before she could hide it. I could tell she was upset. I wondered how long she had been staring at it before I came in.

The note was written on ruled white paper, the kind we use in school. The edge was jagged where it had been torn out of a binder. Someone had used red lipstick to scrawl the message.

WHERE DO YOU WANT IT, BITCH?

'What the hell is this?' I demanded. 'Where did this come from?'

Laura snatched the note out of my hand. 'Someone put it in my locker.'

'Do you know who?'

'I have no idea.'

I wanted to see it again, but Laura hid it away in the drawer of her nightstand before I could ask.

'You have to tell someone about this,' I said.

Laura ignored me. She hummed along to a Hall and Oates song on her record player. 'Sara Smile'. Her fluffy blonde hair jiggled as her shoulders swayed, and she rubbed her index finger nervously as if she were trying to wipe away a stain. She acted as if, by putting the note away, it didn't exist anymore.

'Laura,' I chided her. 'This is serious. If you won't tell anyone about it, then I will.'

She wagged her finger at me. 'Oh, no, you won't, little sister. I don't want to make a big deal about this. You know what boys are like. It's just a joke. It would make it worse if I acted like I was scared.'

I didn't think it was a joke.

I flopped down into Laura's white beanbag. I knew there was no point in trying to change her mind, because she didn't call me 'little sister' except when she was being stubborn. Most of the time, Laura liked the fact that I was the one in charge of the house. I could boss her around when it came to chores, and she didn't care. She was like a sailboat drifting on the lake, letting the wind decide where she would go and not really minding where she ended up. Me, I revved my motor and followed the shore.

I stared at her on the bed. She wore a V-necked white T-shirt and cut-offs with a thick black belt. She was much prettier than I was. She had the curves and the boobs and the big Farrah hair. Jonny told me last week that my face was much more interesting than Laura's, because it wasn't symmetrical and perfect like hers was. He thought that was a compliment. I told him he needed to do better.

My own hair is so dark it's almost black, and I keep it straight as an arrow, with a perfect part down the middle. I have a sharply angled nose, like a little shark's fin jutting off my face. My irises are so large and dark that they crowd out the whites of my eyes. I have two little peaches for breasts.

Hey, I knew who the guys went for. It was Laura, not me. Maybe that's why Laura was much less comfortable with guys than me. She kept her distance. She rarely went out on dates. During the winter, she went to the movies with Peter Stanhope a few times, but she broke it off when he wanted to get into her jeans. As far as I knew, Laura was still a virgin. Not that she would tell me that kind of thing.

'You haven't been around much lately,' I said. For more than a week, Laura had been disappearing after school. Coming in late or staying out all night. Acting quiet and brittle. Twice I've heard her crying in her room.

'So?'

'So are you OK?'

Laura shrugged. I didn't really expect her to tell me anything. We didn't confide our secrets in each other. Even so, I wasn't going to let it go. She could pretend all she wanted, but I knew something was wrong. You had to look for little things with Laura. When our mother died, the only hint about what was going on inside her head was when I found a ceramic statue of Jesus, in pieces, underneath her window.

I looked for a clue. Something different. It didn't take me long to realize that she had flipped a photograph face down on her nightstand. When I saw that she was still tugging at her finger, I noticed something else, too. No silver ring on her index finger, just a pale white band of skin. Laura saw where my eyes had gone, and she sat on her hands to cover them up. I knew there was no point in asking her about it, so I went another way.

'Who have you been hanging out with?' I asked.

Another shrug. 'I've been over at Finn's a lot.'

'You and your lost causes,' I told her.

That was the wrong thing to say. Her eyes flashed at me with annoyance. Even so, I was right. Laura had a weakness for people who were damaged. She always believed she could find a way to lift them up. It was one of her best qualities, but Laura was too naïve, too trusting. I must have gotten the cynical genes, because I don't think people ever really change.

Finn was a good example. He lived across the bridge in Superior with his older sister, Rikke Mathisen, who was Laura's favorite teacher at our high school. I knew Finn only because Laura brought him around now and then. He was an addict. Always into drugs. Creepy eyes staring at you when he thought you weren't looking. Miss Mathisen knew Laura was a soft touch, and she thought Laura could help Finn battle his demons. So Laura spent hours over there. I thought it was a mistake, but you couldn't tell her anything.

I opened my mouth to push Laura again about what was wrong, but she cut me off with a question of her own. Out of the blue.

'So have you slept with Jon yet?' she asked.

I made sure her bedroom door was closed, so my father couldn't hear. 'No.'

'But you're gonna, right?'

'Yeah, over the summer, I think. He knows I want to. But I told him I didn't want to have sex until we were so close it felt like we were having sex already.'

'I like that.'

'Plus, I have to start taking the pill.'

'You could use condoms,' she said.

It was the strangest conversation she and I had ever had, because it was such a normal sister-sister kind of thing. We just didn't talk like that. But I knew what she was doing. She had changed the subject from her to me.

'I don't want to,' I said. 'If I'm going to have sex, I want to really feel it, you know?'

Laura laughed. 'No, I don't know.'

'Are you on the pill?'

'Don't need it.'

'Oh.' I didn't know what to say next. 'I've got a job for the summer.'

'Yeah? Doing what?'

'Waitressing at that new place by the bridge. Grandma's.'

'Good for you.'

'They need people. I can get you in there if you're thinking of sticking around.'

That was as close as I had come to asking flat out if Laura was planning to leave home after she graduated next month. For months she had told Dad she was going away as soon as school was out. Travel. Work. See the world. Now I wasn't so sure. No ring.

'I don't know what I'm going to do yet,' Laura said.

I got out of the beanbag. 'I'm going for a run,' I said.

'Have fun.'

I decided to stick my nose a little further into her business. 'Listen, I really think you should tell someone about that note. Whoever this creep is, he sounds dangerous.'

Laura slid open her nightstand drawer and looked inside. The letter was on top. I saw the lipstick through the thin paper. 'He's just some freak,' she said. 'I'm going to throw them out.'

She took the note and tore it over and over until the pieces were the size of confetti. Then she sprinkled them into her wastebasket.

I felt uneasy. 'Them? Are there more?'

'Yeah.' Laura shrugged.

'How many?'

'I don't know. Ten maybe.'

'Ten? When did this start?'

'A few weeks ago.'

'Do you still have them?'

She nodded.

'I want to see them,' I told her.

Laura sighed theatrically, as if I was making a big deal over nothing, and dug inside the drawer. She came out with a small stack of papers tied together with a rubber band. She pulled them apart and spilled them onto the blanket.

I couldn't believe what I saw.

Some were written in lipstick like the other one. All of the messages were obscene and violent.

I'm going to fuck you.

Keep your door locked.

Are you going to be alone tonight, whore?

There were photographs, too. Whoever had done this had cut them out of porno magazines. I saw black and white shots of men with huge penises and women servicing them with their mouths. More messages were scrawled on the photos.

You'll suck mine, too.

Is your ass still a virgin?

'Are you crazy?' I nearly screamed at her. 'You have to go to the *police* with this.'

'I don't want to make things worse. School will be done soon, and he'll stop.'

'You don't know that.'

'Come on, he hasn't done anything. He's just trying to creep me out. He's like some peeping Tom trying to get under my skin. Well, I won't let him.'

'Do you have any idea who's doing this?' I asked again.

'No. I talked to a few guys, you know, to see if they'd heard anything. I thought maybe he'd be bragging about it to his buddies. But nobody knew who it was, or if they did, they wouldn't tell me.'

'Did you tell Dad?'

'Are you kidding? He'd flip. And don't you dare breathe a word, little sister. Somehow it would wind up as my fault.'

While I watched, Laura began tearing up all of the notes and photographs. I wanted to stop her. I told her I thought she was making a big mistake, but Laura shredded and ripped and tore until she had a small mountain of remnants that she slid off her bed into the garbage.

'So much for that,' she said.

Two

Stride and Tish left Grandma's Saloon together. Tish lit a cigarette when they were alone on the concrete pier that jutted out into Lake Superior. Her muscles unwound. She tilted her chin and exhaled a stream of smoke like a sigh. The breeze caught and dispersed it, but Stride could taste the ghost of smoke in the air, and he had to jam his hands in his pockets to beat down the craving.

She leaned against the wall bordering the canal. Stride was next to her. The deep, narrow channel led from the lake to the inner harbors of Duluth and Superior. A century-old lift bridge, resplendent in gray steel, rose and fell over the canal when the boats came. On the opposite side of the bridge was the area known as the Point, a tiny finger of land jutting out like a natural shelter for the harbor. Stride and Serena lived there, in a lakeside cottage that dated back to the 1890s. The city side of the bridge was known as Canal Park, and it had become a haven for restaurants and hotels in the last twenty years. Tourists came to Canal Park to watch the big boats because it was like seeing living dinosaurs from the city's past. Once upon a time, Duluth had been an industrial boomtown, whose economy was linked to the fate of hundreds of great ships carrying iron ore. The downtown area was filled with old Victorian mansions that were reminders of a time when the city was rich from mining and shipping. Not anymore.

'I can't believe how this area has changed,' Tish said. 'When I was a kid, there was nothing but old factory buildings down here. Now it's like Coney Island.'

'Yeah, there's a lot of money in Canal Park, but it doesn't trickle down,' Stride told her. 'They're building condos to lure people up from Minneapolis, but the city is struggling. Like always.'

'You live out on the Point?' Tish asked.

Stride nodded.

'Nobody lived out there in the old days. The Point was where kids went to smoke dope and have sex on the beach.'

Stride laughed. 'It still is.'

Tish zipped up her leather jacket. The early evening breeze off the lake was cool. 'I forgot that the summers aren't hot here.'

'We're counting on global warming,' Stride said. 'In a few years, we'll be the new Florida.'

'You sound cynical.'

'You can't live your whole life in Duluth and not be a little cynical,' Stride said. 'Everyone here is always looking for the next big thing, but no one wants to admit that our time is past. Back when you and I were growing up, shipping was already on the way out. Nothing ever really took its place. The politicians keep selling dreams, but most of us have learned to tune it out and get on with life.'

'There's a big world out there,' Tish said.

'Yeah, well, don't get me wrong. I love this place. I tried to move away once, and I had to come back.'

Tish nodded. 'I know. I read up on you. You've been a cop your whole life. You've been in charge of the Detective Bureau for more than ten years, and you could probably be the police chief if you wanted, but you like it on the street. A couple years ago, during an investigation into the disappearance of a teenage girl, you quit your job and followed a cop named Serena Dial to Las Vegas. That didn't last long. A few months later, you were right back in Duluth, and Serena came with you.'

'Is this all research for your book?' Stride asked.

'Yes,' Tish admitted. 'Plus, I was curious about you. I felt like I knew you through Cindy. I wondered what happened to you after she died.'

'Let's make one thing clear,' Stride told her. 'Anything I say is off the record. OK? I only agreed to talk with you because you're right, Laura's death still bothers me. But nothing I tell you goes into any book unless I give you the green light.'

25

Tish frowned. 'That ties my hands.'

'You're right, it does. You probably don't work with sources when you're writing travel essays, but this is how it goes in the real world. If you want my help, then you'll have to hope I say yes at the end of the day.'

'You don't trust me, do you?' Tish asked.

'No.'

She threw the cigarette at her feet and crushed it. 'I understand,' she said. 'I was naïve coming here, figuring you'd open up to me. I keep forgetting. Cindy knew me, but you didn't.'

Stride said nothing. He didn't know what to think about Tish. He didn't hear any guile in her voice, but he didn't believe that Cindy would have carried on a relationship with a woman from their teenage years and never told him about it. Even so, he found himself liking Tish. Maybe it was because she reminded him of Cindy, and maybe it was because he sensed that her passion about Laura wasn't faked. This was about more than a book. This was personal to her. He wanted to know why.

'What can I do to make you trust me?' Tish asked.

'You can start by telling me your story,' Stride said.

'What else can I do?' she said, smiling.

He didn't smile back.

Tish sighed and studied the hills of the city, where the streets climbed from the water like terraces on the face of a cliff. 'You're right, the city hasn't changed much in thirty years. All the old buildings, all the old houses, are still there. I could close my eyes and be a kid again.'

Stride heard a tremor in her voice. 'Is that not a good thing?'

'Not really. Most of the places I go, people complain about too much change. Nothing's the way it used to be. I guess I expected Duluth to be different, too. I wasn't ready for the memories to hit me in the face.'

He waited.

'Back then, I couldn't wait to get out of Duluth,' Tish continued. 'I left the city the day after I graduated from high school.'

'What year was that?'

'It was June of nineteen seventy-seven, the month before Laura was

26

killed. I moved to St Paul, got a job, got an apartment. I never wanted to see Duluth again.'

'Why were you so anxious to get away?'

Tish hesitated. Stride watched her carefully, wondering if she was about to lie. He had interviewed suspects for years, and most of them got that same look on their faces when they made up a story. It was as if they needed those few seconds to play the lie out in their heads to see if it hung together. He expected a generic lie from Tish that didn't tell him anything about her life. *I was a kid. I was born to run.* Something like that.

She surprised him.

'Look, I was screwed up, OK? My mom was killed when I was eleven. For the next few years, I bounced around the city in foster homes. I was an angry girl. I felt homeless. I don't blame it on any of my foster parents. They did their best, and I didn't make it easy for them.'

'What about your father?' Stride asked.

'He wasn't in the picture. Mom got pregnant when she was only twenty-two. She sold perfume in a department store back then, so she met a lot of married men. When I was a kid, she told me that she dated a handsome Finnish sailor who came to the city one day on an ore boat. To me, that sounded romantic. She didn't bother explaining the truth. It wasn't until much later that I realized what a coward I had for a father.'

'I'm sorry.'

'Don't be sorry for me,' Tish said. 'Mom was the one who had it tough. Being single and pregnant in the nineteen fifties was like having the plague. She got run out of her church. Got fired from her job. She was out of work for months before she landed a teller position at a bank. We were always scratching to make ends meet. But she was great. Very proud. Very independent.'

'I'm sure it was hard to lose her.'

'It was.'

Stride knew a little of how she felt. He had felt homeless himself when his father died. He was sixteen. If he hadn't been rescued when he met Cindy a few months later, he might have wound up a lost child, like Tish. Bitter. Lonely. Looking for escape.

27

'Anyway, I try not to dwell on it,' Tish said. 'That's just how it was. I've lived a pretty amazing life, and that wouldn't have happened if I had had a normal childhood. We all pay our dues.'

'What did you do after you left the city?' Stride asked.

Tish leaned on the wall of the pier and stared down into the chocolate-brown water. 'If you're running away from Duluth, St Paul isn't far enough to get away, so I decided to go someplace warmer. I went down to the Caribbean and did odd jobs, buzzing from island to island. Eventually, I wrote an article about my experiences, and I sold it to a travel magazine in the UK. That was what got me started. I began to do more articles, and I built relationships with other magazines around Europe. They started paying me to go all over the world, so I did.'

'Sounds nice.'

'It was. I did it for a long time. Then I met someone, a photographer who worked with me on a piece from Tallinn in Estonia. We fell in love. That was how I wound up in Atlanta. We both got jobs at the *Journal-Constitution*. It was great for a while, but it didn't work out. I mean, we're still friends, but we realized after several years that we weren't going to make it as lovers. So I started traveling again, but my heart just hasn't been in it. That was when I decided to take some time off. When I did, I realized I was thinking a lot about Laura.'

'Laura died a long time ago,' Stride said.

'I know, but some wounds never really heal.' Tish slid a silver chain away from her neck and let it swish against the white silk of her blouse. She fingered a slim ring that dangled on the end of the chain. 'See this ring? Laura had one just like it. We got them together at the Grandstand at the State Fair. That was the summer before she died. It's cheap, but I like to keep it with me.'

'You two were close?'

Tish nodded. 'Inseparable.'

'So how come I don't remember seeing the two of you at Cindy's house?'

'Oh, that. You were never a teenage girl.'

'Meaning?'

'Meaning we had a fight. That was probably around the time you

28

and Cindy got together. We didn't talk to each other for a few weeks. It was May, not long before school let out. I went to the Cities right after that.'

'What was the fight about?'

'I don't remember. Something stupid.'

This time, Stride thought she was lying.

'How did the two of you meet?' he asked.

'We were both in Rikke Mathisen's geometry class in our junior year,' Tish said. 'Laura and I sat next to each other. It was like we were kindred spirits. Laura was restless, like me. She had lost her mom too, and her dad was a piece of shit, so she could relate to what I was going through.' She hesitated. 'I'm sorry, I guess I shouldn't have said that. He was your father-in-law.'

Stride shrugged. He and William Starr had never been close. The man had dealt with the tragedies of his life by taking his anger and his Puritan guilt out on everyone around him. Except Cindy. He knew better than to tangle with his youngest daughter. Cindy had pretty much run her dad's life for the next fifteen years after his wife's death, until William Starr succumbed to cancer. Just as Cindy would do ten years later. Stride finally understood how easy it would have been to end up like his father-in-law, when he lost his own wife in the prime of her life.

'I think Cindy was a little jealous of me in those days,' Tish said. 'You know as well as I do that Cindy and Laura were never really the same after their mom died. Cindy took over, and Laura let her, but that's not the same as being sisters. So when I came along, it was like I was the sister Laura had been looking for. Cindy never said anything, but I don't think she liked it. I was always there. I slept over a lot. Laura and I shared everything. We were going to run away from Duluth together, see the big wide world, you know?'

'Except you moved away, and Laura didn't,' Stride said.

Tish's face clouded over. 'Yeah.'

'What happened?'

'I told you, it wasn't important.'

'No, you told me you didn't remember,' Stride said.

Tish looked at him. 'You're right, I don't.'

She was still lying.

'Anyway, we were past it,' Tish went on. 'I wrote to her when I moved to St Paul, and she wrote back, and we became friends again, just like before. Laura was going to join me in the Cities. She never got a chance, though. She was killed before she could get away. I guess that's why it's gnawed at me all these years. It wasn't supposed to be that way. She and I were supposed to escape together. Instead, we let some silly argument come between us, and she stayed behind. And she never made it out.'

She made it sound as if Duluth were a war zone, and Laura had been a soldier trapped behind enemy lines.

'When did the stalking begin?' Stride asked.

'During the spring. Late April, early May.'

'Did Laura have any idea who was doing this to her?'

Tish shook her head. 'No, but it must have been someone at school. Most of the notes wound up in her locker. She thought it would all go away after graduation.'

'It didn't?'

'No, the letters and photos started arriving by mail after school let out. Laura told me about it when she wrote to me in the Cities. I was scared for her.'

'Why did you bring up Peter Stanhope's name? Do you have any reason to believe he was the one who was stalking her?'

'He was one of the last people to see her alive. I know he was a suspect in the murder.' She added, 'Does your girlfriend have some kind of relationship with Peter Stanhope?'

'He's a client,' Stride said.

He didn't tell her that the relationship went deeper than that. Stanhope had asked Serena to be a full-time investigator at his law firm, and Serena was wrestling with the decision. Stride thought she was planning to say yes.

'Is that going to be a problem?' Tish asked.

'Peter's rich and powerful. That's always a problem.'

Tish shrugged. 'I'm not afraid of him. Look, I know that Peter was after Laura. They dated for a while that spring. Peter was looking for another conquest. If Laura had put out, that would have been the end of it.'

'But she didn't?' Stride asked.

'No way. Peter was hot for sex, but Laura didn't want to do it. So she broke it off. He took it badly. You know how rich young punks like Stanhope can be. They think they can have whatever they want because their daddies have money. He wanted Laura, and he was furious when she turned him down. The letters started arriving not long after that.'

'That's not enough to make a connection,' Stride said.

'Well, I know what Peter was like. He came after me before Laura, and I didn't want anything to do with him. He got nasty when I told him no.'

Tish shivered as the sun sank below the crest of the hill. Long shadows accompanied a damp chill off the water.

'Listen, Tish,' Stride said. 'I'm going to tell you a couple things, but like I said before, it's off the record. OK?'

Tish nodded unhappily.

'I need to hear you say it,' Stride said.

'Yes, this is off the record.'

'Good. You have to remember that I know this case inside and out. I lived it back then with Cindy and with Ray Wallace, who was the cop in charge of the investigation. When I took over the Detective Bureau, I went through the file page by page. I reviewed all the evidence, because I had my doubts, too. I didn't find anything new that pointed at Peter or at anyone other than Dada – the man I confronted near the railroad tracks.'

'So what did you find?' Tish asked.

'First, there was a fingerprint report. There were prints on the base-ball bat that matched Dada's.'

'Except it was Peter Stanhope's bat,' Tish said. 'I read about that in the paper. His prints must have been on the bat, too.'

'Yes, but his prints made sense. Dada's prints didn't.'

'Laura was being stalked,' Tish insisted. 'Someone had been pursuing her for weeks. That wasn't a stranger. It was someone who knew her.'

Stride put a hand lightly on her shoulder. 'The police knew about the stalking.'

'Are you sure?'

'Cindy told them. I was there when she told Ray. Look, Cindy thought the same thing you did, that whoever had been pursuing

Laura was the one who killed her. She even had one of the notes that this guy sent her. A porn photo with a warning scrawled on it.'

'So?'

'So there weren't any fingerprints on the photo,' Stride said. 'It wasn't helpful.'

'That was then. Don't they have better techniques for raising prints now? Maybe there's still something there.'

Stride nodded. 'We have much more sophisticated techniques for that kind of thing, but what we don't have is the photograph. It's gone, along with the other crime scene photos they took back then. So's the bat. Somewhere along the line, much of the physical evidence from the case was lost.'

'Son of a bitch!' Tish exclaimed. 'Don't you think that's suspicious?'

'You're talking about a case from thirty years ago. Things get misplaced.'

He didn't tell her his own suspicion that Ray Wallace was the one who had made the evidence disappear.

Tish walked away. They were near the lighthouse at the end of the pier. She climbed the steps and leaned back against the chapped white paint of the light tower with her arms folded. Her purse was slung over her shoulder. Stride followed her up the steps.

'I'm sorry,' he told her.

Tish looked up at him. 'Can I trust you?'

'What?'

'You said you don't trust me. Can I trust you?'

'I think you can. There will always be things I have to keep confidential, but I won't lie to you.'

Tish unzipped her purse. She slid out a small, clear plastic bag that contained a yellowed envelope. He could see block handwriting, and even without taking it in his hand, he saw the name written on the front.

LAURA STARR.

'Here,' Tish said. 'Physical evidence.'

'What the hell is this?' Stride asked.

'It's one of the stalking letters that Laura received. She sent it to me while I was living in St Paul.'

'You've had the letter all this time, and you never told anyone?'

'In the old days, I didn't think it mattered,' Tish said. 'Then I put it away and forgot all about it. I was clearing out old boxes in Atlanta a few months ago when I moved out of my partner's apartment, and that's when I found it again. Don't you see? This changes everything. That's when I started thinking about the book again, because I knew I had something that could reopen the case.'

Stride did see.

The letter to Laura wasn't a note that had been pushed through a school locker. Whoever sent it to her had put it in the mail, using a stamp and licking an envelope. Even thirty years later, that meant one thing.

DNA.

Three

Clark Biggs watched his daughter squirm on the living room floor with her legs tucked underneath her. Mary picked up her colored blocks and carefully stacked ten of them one on top of the other, until she had built a rainbow tower. When she was finished, she beamed at Clark with the biggest, most beautiful smile he had ever seen, the kind that made his heart ache every time he saw it. Then she toppled the tower by blowing on it like the big bad wolf, giggled at him, and began setting up the blocks again. She could do it over and over and never tire of the game. She was like every other five-year-old girl in the world.

Except Mary was sixteen.

To anyone looking at her, she was a typical teenager. She had a curly mop of blonde hair and eyes that Clark thought of as Caribbean blue. Her face was round and bright. She was almost six feet tall, with a stocky frame. A big girl. She could have been a runner or a wrestler. It seemed so wrong and unfair that she kept growing into a pretty young woman while remaining trapped in the mind of a child. Clark lay awake nights blaming himself and God for the accident in the water. He consoled himself with the belief that Mary would be perpetually happy, perpetually innocent, without the awkwardness, pain, doubt, and self-consciousness of becoming a real teenager. It was little comfort.

'It's bedtime, Mary,' he murmured.

She pretended not to hear him. She kept playing with her blocks and humming a tune to herself. Clark realized it was the theme song

34

to a television show they had watched earlier in the evening. He was always amazed at the things that made it inside her brain, when so many other things did not.

'Bedtime, Mary,' he repeated without enthusiasm.

Mary stopped and frowned. Her lips turned downward like a clown's. He laughed, and she laughed, too.

'Five more minutes,' he said.

Clark hated Sunday nights. At ten o'clock, Mary would go to bed, and he would be alone in the small house for another hour while he watched TV and poured himself a last beer. In the morning, his ex-wife Donna would come by the house, and they would silently make the exchange. Mary would cry and go with her, and Clark would cry and watch her go. Then he would pour coffee into a Thermos, silently wrap up a turkey sandwich for his lunch, and head off to his construction site on the Duluth harbor, knowing that the house would be empty when he returned home. Five long, lonely days awaited him. During the week, it was as if he were in a trance, waiting for that moment on Friday evening when Donna's SUV pulled up in front of his door, and Mary ran up the sidewalk to get folded up in his arms. His beautiful girl. His baby. He lived for the weekends with her, but they were over almost as soon as they began, leaving him right back here, dreading her bedtime, feeling his soul grow cloudy at the thought of a week alone.

'Come on, honey,' he told her, his voice cracking.

Clark got off the sofa. Mary got her big bones from him. He was burly and strong. He had worked construction since he was eighteen, and after twenty years laboring outside through bitter cold and ninety-degree summers, he woke up every morning with his muscled body stiffened into knots. In his twenties, he could take a hot shower and come out refreshed and limber. Not now. Pain dogged him through his days.

Mary bounded up and held out her hand. He took it to lead her to her room. Her skin was pink and soft, and his own skin was like leather. She knew he was sad on these nights, and she tried to cheer him up by making faces. He smiled and let her think it was working, when the truth was that nothing could lift him out of depression at these moments.

35

'Blocks, Daddy,' she said.

'Yes, honey, I'll take good care of your blocks. They'll be here for you next week.'

Her bedroom was at the rear of the small house, with two windows looking out toward the woods at the back of the lot. Mary danced into the bathroom to brush her teeth. It was dark, and Clark went up close to the bedroom windows and studied his reflection in the glass. Puffed-up brown pouches sagged under his eyes. His sandy hair was too long; he needed to cut it, which he usually did himself to save money. His jeans were fraying. He could poke a finger through the left pocket to his skin. He wore a NASCAR T-shirt and a camouflage baseball cap.

'Meeeeeeee!' Mary shouted, flouncing into the room and jumping onto the squeaky frame of her bed. She slept in a twin bed that was too small for her, but she didn't mind that her feet dangled off the end. There was barely room for Mary among the beanbag animals she collected. She wore a frilly nightgown that came to her knees. That was one thing that worried Clark whenever Mary was out in the world without him. She had no concept of sexuality, but her body said otherwise. She looked like a normal, healthy, attractive girl. She had no embarrassment, and she often stripped off her clothes and wandered around the house naked and couldn't understand why Clark insisted she stay dressed.

'That was quick,' Clark said. 'Did you really brush your teeth?'

Mary nodded seriously.

'Really?' he repeated.

She folded her arms tightly and nodded again, her whole body quivering like gelatin.

'OK,' he said.

Clark turned off the overhead light but left the lamp lit by her bed. Mary liked the room bright throughout the night. He checked her windows and locked them, because otherwise, Mary had been known to climb outside and run through the backyards of the neighborhood. She didn't sleep well. She might close her eyes for an hour, and then she would get up, and Clark would hear her bouncing an inflated ball against the bedroom wall. If he wasn't too tired himself, he would get up and play with her, until finally she grew drowsy again. Sometimes she simply curled up on the floor, and he would pull the blankets off the bed and cover her.

He tucked her into bed. Her eyes were bright. 'Good night, Mary.'

'I love you, Daddy.'

'I love you, too, honey.'

The ache in his stomach at the thought of her leaving in the morning was so great that he couldn't say anything more. He kissed her forehead and as he closed the door, he saw her waving her hands at the ceiling, as if she could see the stars from her bed and conduct them like an orchestra.

Clark returned to the sofa and finished his beer and opened another one. He thought about seeing Donna in the morning when she came to collect Mary. Donna lived across the bridge in Superior and worked as a legal secretary. Clark was in Gary, living in the white concrete block house that had once belonged to his parents. For five years, he had shared Mary with Donna from a distance, and for five years, he had hated the arrangement so much that it felt like a disease inside him.

It wasn't Donna's fault. The bitterness between them had long ago died into loneliness. They had married young and tried to make a go of it, but the pressure of raising Mary together had destroyed them. They each loved their daughter, but Mary demanded so much that they had run out of energy to love each other. Donna thought they should try again. She had made noises about making a fresh start. Two weeks earlier, when she had come to his house to drop Mary off, she had stayed there all evening, the three of them together like in the old days. After Mary went to bed, they had drunk wine, and laughed, and wound up sleeping together. They were kids again, the way it was before Mary, before the divorce. The sex felt warm and familiar. But when he awoke, he was alone. Donna couldn't face him. That told him all he needed to know.

He knew he should go to bed, but he didn't get up from the sofa. He watched television until his eyes began to blink shut, and his head fell forward on his chest. He slept heavily, as if he had been drugged by exhaustion and alcohol, and had no sense of time passing.

Clark woke up to Mary screaming.

A terrible, wailing, nightmare scream.

He was instantly awake, but he was disoriented, unsure what was real. At the end of the hall, in shadows, Mary's door flew open and banged against the wall. His daughter was silhouetted against the pale light in her room.

'Him him him him him!' she shouted.

Clark dove over the back edge of the sofa and pushed himself off his knees, shaking his head to drive the sleep from his brain. He spread his arms wide. Mary bolted for him and grabbed his body so hard he nearly spilled over onto the carpet. Her skin was wet with sweat and fear. Her blue eyes bulged, and her nose flared as she sucked air into her lungs. Clark felt her fingernails digging like knives into his back. She held him with such fierce strength he could hardly breathe.

'Mary, what is it? What's wrong, baby?'

'Him him him him him him him!'

'Oh, Mary, it's OK, it's OK, there's no one there.'

'NO NO NO NO NO.'

Clark stroked her hair and sang to her under his breath. She trembled like a bird. This had happened the previous weekend, too. She had had a bad dream and imagined there was someone in her room and refused to go back in there for the rest of the night. Mary didn't know what was real and what was not. When she imagined something, it was the same as if it was really there.

'Shhh,' he murmured over and over.

She cried into his shoulder. He grabbed a fleece blanket from the sofa and wrapped it around her, covering her. Her tears were damp on his neck.

'Come on, I'll show you it's OK,' he told her. 'I'll show you that no one's there.'

'No, Daddy, no, him him him him.'

'Oh, I know, I know, but it was just a dream, honey, that's all it was.'

Mary shook her head while it was buried against his chest, and then she looked up with a panicked face, put her mouth against his ear, and whispered so clearly it made him shiver: '*Window.*'

Clark felt chilled.

His fists clenched, and adrenaline made him alert. Clark's eyes streaked to the living room windows, which he had left open. They looked out on dark squares of night. The curtains breathed with the wind. He smelled pine and rain. He didn't understand what had happened, but for Mary to use a word like that meant something important.

Clark lifted Mary off her feet. She was heavy, but she wrapped her arms around his neck and let herself be carried to the sofa. He laid her down among the cushions and kissed her and looked deeply into her eyes, trying to understand her, trying to make her communicate with him. He always cherished the idea that there was a place somewhere in both of their minds where they could come together and erase the canyon that her disability put between them. He just wished he could find it.

'I'm going to close the windows now, Mary. I'll still be in the room.'

She pulled the blanket over her head. He went to the four windows that looked out on the front yard and slammed them shut and locked them. He saw spatters of rain on the glass. He went back and slowly peeled the fleece down from half of his daughter's face.

'Did you dream that someone was in your room, honey?'

She said again: 'Window.'

'Did you see something outside?'

'Him him him him him.' She pulled the blanket up again, hiding.

'You stay right here, honey. Daddy will take a look.'

Clark returned down the dark hallway to Mary's room. It was past midnight. He turned off the lamp by her bed, and with the room black, he went to the window and looked out at the back lawn and the woods a few feet away. He didn't see anything. He stayed there for several minutes, watching, but nothing moved outside.

When he returned to the living room, he found that Mary was asleep again, with her blonde hair messily sticking out of the blanket. He could see half her face, which looked peaceful and angelic. His own heart was racing, and he knew he would be up into the early hours. He sat down beside her, caressed her cheek with one callused finger, and was rewarded with a sigh. She made little noises of happiness.

Clark eased himself off the sofa again without disturbing her. He was nervous, and he wasn't sure why. Children had bad dreams, and that was that. Even so, he had never heard Mary use such a specific word. *Window.*

He retrieved a heavy flashlight from the kitchen and went to the front door and let himself outside. He locked the door behind him. When he stepped down off the porch, drizzle spat on his face. The leaves murmured with the night breeze. He switched on the yellow beam and waved it around the yard, seeing everything that should be there and nothing else – the weeping willow, the swing tied to the branch, the three old cars he scavenged for parts, the long grass that needed to be mowed. He stepped silently and carefully toward the rear of the house. He held the flashlight in a tight grip and led the way around the corner with the light.

Clark examined the backyard carefully. He didn't come back here often, except to push the mower around every few weeks. There was only a narrow strip of lawn, and behind it, the dense stand of birches and their white bark peeling like paint. He stared into the woods and had the strangest feeling that someone invisible was staring back at him.

He shrugged. His mind was playing tricks on him.

Clark went over to Mary's window and shone the light on the sill. He realized that he could stand here with half his body above the height of the window, and if the light was on, he could stare inside and see everything.

He turned the flashlight down to his feet.

Near his own boots were damp indentations in the grass, and behind them, he now saw a track of other footsteps, running away and disappearing into the protection of the trees.

Four

Stride swung into the driveway of their cottage on the Point at midnight. There was no garage, just a muddy patch of ground where they parked. During the winters, they strung power cords from the house to plug in the vehicles and keep the engines warm through the frozen night hours. He squeezed his Expedition into a gap near the fence beside Serena's Mustang and got out. Light rain tracked him as he tramped through the grass and up the steps of their front porch.

The lights were off inside, but when he opened the door, he saw a fire glowing in the fireplace on the opposite side of the living room. The log had burned down to ash and embers. A ballad by Patty Loveless played on the stereo. Stride heard Patty singing about a woman dying and going up to the stars. He had listened to that song over and over when Cindy was dying, and even now, it made his heart break.

Serena sat in a lotus position on the floor, her eyes closed, her face calm. She had taken up yoga as part of her recovery plan from burns she had suffered during a fire a few months earlier. The mental intensity of the exercises also helped her manage the memories of abuse she carried from her childhood. It seemed to be working. She was more at peace with herself than at any time since they had met.

Serena was totally different in appearance from Cindy. She was tall and full-figured. She had shoulder-length dark hair, but it was fuller and wavier than Cindy's. Her face had a high forehead and emerald-green eyes. Her skin glowed, but he could see the damage where her legs had been badly scarred. She was healing from the fire – she could

41

run again without her legs or her lungs giving out – but she had come to accept that her body would always be flawed now. Not perfect. Not forever young. It was the devil's bargain that everyone made with age, but Serena had put it off longer than most. She had covered herself up after the fire, even to Stride, but she was wearing shorts again, not caring if people saw. She had also gained a few pounds over the spring, when she couldn't work out with the intensity she had in the past. She was dieting to shed them, but Stride didn't care. He thought she looked voluptuous.

Her eyes opened as he took a seat in the leather chair near her. She carefully unfolded her legs and stretched them. Above her shorts, she wore a black bra over her full breasts. Her hair was tied into a ponytail behind her head.

'It's late,' she said.

'Yeah, sorry, time got away from me.'

'Were you with her?'

He didn't hear any jealousy in her voice, but he wanted to reassure her anyway.

'No, I left Tish down at the boardwalk hours ago. I went over to the police archives and pulled the material on Laura's murder and began going through the file again. The next thing I knew, it was almost midnight.'

'She got to you, didn't she?' Serena asked.

'I guess she did.'

'What do you think of her?'

Stride rubbed the brass studs of the red leather chair under his fingertips. 'She's keeping things from me. I don't know what, but I don't like that.' He added, 'I can tell that *you* don't like her.'

Serena shook her head. 'You're wrong.'

'Come on. I saw your hackles go up.'

'No, it's true. *She* doesn't like *me*. Big difference.'

'How can you tell?'

'Women know, Jonny.'

He wasn't about to argue.

'Was there anything in the police file?' Serena asked.

'No, but Tish had something new.'

He told her about the letter Tish had given him and about the

42

possibility that they could find DNA on the postage stamp or the flap of the envelope.

Serena digested this and then studied him with thoughtful eyes. 'I'm surprised you never told me anything about Laura and her death. We've been together a long time now, Jonny. Is there a reason you didn't want to share it with me?'

He didn't know what to say, because he wasn't sure why he had kept the story to himself. That week in July had changed him so profoundly, in so many ways, that he was never the same person again. He had realized during that week that he was going to spend the rest of his life with Cindy. He had decided during that week, as he got to know Ray Wallace, that one way to fight back against death was to become a cop. He had also discovered how much it hurt to make mistakes and that some mistakes could never be erased. When he thought about who he was today, he could draw a straight line all the way back to that summer. Even so, he had never been able to talk about it. He rarely talked about the passions that drove him. He realized that in the two years he had been coaxing Serena to share secrets about her past, he had rarely spent any time sharing secrets of his own.

Serena saw in his silence that he wasn't ready to say anything. She didn't push him. Instead, her face softened into a teasing smile.

'Guess what I did this evening?' she said.

He cocked his head with a silent question.

'I went to the library and found a copy of your high school yearbook from nineteen seventy-seven,' she told him.

'Oh, no,' he said.

Serena leaned closer and whispered, 'Nice hair.'

'I kept it long in those days.'

'You and Shaun Cassidy.'

'It was the nineteen seventies, for God's sake. It was the decade that taste forgot.'

'No, no, I like it. What a heartthrob you were. So intense. And those eyes! What did Cindy call them? Pirate eyes? I can really see it, Jonny. Smoldering, brooding, the future wounded detective.' Serena covered her mouth and started laughing.

'You've been spending way too much time with Maggie,' he told her.

'I saw a picture of Cindy, too. I've never seen a photo of her when she was young. She was amazing.'

'Yes, she was.'

'She had such an interesting face.'

'I told her that once, and she almost decked me.'

'No, really, with those big eyes and that sharp nose, and with the raven hair, she was something to look at. I see why you fell for her. I mean, Laura was a typical teen beauty, but Cindy was distinctive.' She let the silence linger, and then she added, 'So tell me about Laura. What was she like?'

'I didn't really know her all that well,' Stride admitted. 'She wasn't home a lot when I was around. I always thought she was one of those girls who was uncomfortable being as pretty as she was. She didn't like the stares from the boys.'

'Were she and Cindy close?'

'No. Not really. They weren't enemies the way sisters can be, but they both led their own lives. Cindy really regretted the distance between them after Laura was killed. She thought she had missed out on having a sister.'

'I saw Tish in the yearbook too,' Serena told him. 'She's not lying about her relationship with Laura. I spotted them together in three separate photos, and they were hanging on each other like BFFs.'

'Score one for Tish,' Stride said.

'Except you never saw them together, did you? You didn't know Tish. Why not?'

'Tish says she and Laura had some kind of fight, and she moved to St Paul by herself after graduation. That would have been in May and June, when Cindy and I began dating.'

'Did Tish say what the fight was about?'

'She claims she doesn't remember but that it wasn't anything important. I think she's lying on both counts.'

'So what was it?'

'I don't know, but what do teenage girls usually fight about?' Stride asked.

'Boys.'

'That's my guess.'

'Do you have any idea who it was?'

'Tish says that Laura dated Peter Stanhope for a while. She all but accused him of being Laura's stalker.'

Serena frowned. 'Peter.'

'Sorry, he was up to his neck in this case,' Stride said.

'Why didn't you tell me? I knew you weren't happy when I started doing work for Peter's law firm, but I didn't realize you had this kind of history with him.'

'It was thirty years ago. I've barely spoken to him since then. People change.'

That was a lie. Stride didn't think anyone really changed. He wasn't crazy about the idea of Serena taking a job at Peter Stanhope's law firm, but he also wanted her off the streets. Somewhere safe. The fire that had nearly killed her during the winter hadn't been an accident. Her career had put her in the path of a stalker, and Stride found himself struggling with his anxiety whenever she was back on the street. Serena was a former homicide cop from Las Vegas, which was one of the toughest beats he could imagine. Her background made her fiercely independent. Even so, he understood now the emotions that Cindy must have felt whenever he left the house and the fear that would have flitted through her brain whenever she picked up the phone. For the spouse of a cop, the call could come anytime.

'Can I tell Peter about Tish and her book?' Serena asked.

Stride shrugged. 'If Tish keeps digging, Peter's going to hear about it sooner or later. You can tell him. For now, I'm not involved.'

'Do you really think that Peter could have killed Laura?'

'I don't know. It's possible, but no one wanted to go down that road back then.'

'Because of Peter's father?'

'Yes.'

'Who worked the case?'

Stride rubbed the scar on his shoulder where a bullet had violated his flesh. The wound twinged like a reminder. 'Ray Wallace.'

Serena let out a slow breath. 'You think Ray gave Peter a free pass?'

'Maybe.'

'I think you should tell me exactly what happened that night,' Serena said. 'Don't you?'

'Yeah.' Stride steepled his fingers and stared at the fire and didn't say anything more.

'I could read the police file if you want,' Serena said. 'Or talk to Maggie. But I'd prefer to hear it from you.'

Stride ran his hand through his wavy hair, the way he did when he was tense. He thought about the long hair he had worn back then. And about Cindy's fingers running through his hair while they were in the water.

'Cindy and I felt guilty for a long time,' he told Serena.

'About what?'

'About leaving Laura alone that night.'

'You couldn't possibly have known what would happen.'

'Yes, but it was dark, and it was raining, and kids had been drinking, and we just let Laura go off into the woods. It was stupid. We should have stayed with her.'

Serena waited.

'A few of us were playing softball that night,' Stride continued. 'I was there. So was Peter Stanhope. Cindy was supposed to meet me afterward, and the two of us were going to hang out by the lake. I didn't even know that Laura would be with her, but she and Cindy stopped by the field while we were playing, and then they headed off by themselves. I was a little pissed. I didn't want Laura around.'

'Why not?'

'That was supposed to be the night. *The* night. Cindy and I were planning to have sex for the first time.'

'Oh,' Serena said, drawing out the word. 'Now I understand.'

'So I wasn't exactly thinking with my brain.'

'I'm sure.'

'The thing is, Cindy and I talked about it later, and we knew something was wrong, but we didn't care.'

'What do you mean, something was wrong?'

Stride frowned. 'Someone was in the woods that night.'

Who Killed Laura Starr?

By Tish Verdure

4 July 1977

I heard a growl of thunder beyond the trees, as if the storm were an animal getting closer. The path was dark, and that meant the sky over our heads had turned black, shutting out light through the trees. I felt the thick air like a weight on my chest when I breathed. You could almost see humid haze hanging in a cloud over the trail. My skin was dewy with sweat, and my long hair clung to it like vines. I wore a bikini top, shorts, and bare feet.

Laura was jittery as she walked beside me. She kicked impatiently at the dirt with her pink Flyers. Her eyes darted back and forth into the woods, as if she expected to catch someone spying. She wore jeans and a blue checked shirt with the sleeves rolled up past her elbows. Her backpack was slung over one shoulder. She twisted the silver ring on her finger.

'I hope the rain holds off for the fireworks,' I said.

Laura looked up at the tops of the trees. She made a noise in her throat and didn't reply.

I knew the Fourth of July parties would be washed out. It would be night in less than an hour, but before then, the deluge would begin. The air was perfectly calm now. Nothing moved. The brown birds that normally hopped around us in the dirt, looking for crumbs, had taken shelter. Every birch and pine looked as if it were holding its breath.

The summer storms always came quickly. One moment it would

47

be still, and then in an instant the wind would come alive, bending the young trees. The heavy clouds would sag open, gushing out rain. The night would turn to day in flashes as branches of lightning cracked from the ground to the sky.

Laura stopped on the trail. I gave her a questioning stare. Her lower lip trembled, and her eyes were frightened.

'What is it?'

She didn't say anything. The trees around us were already a black parade of soldiers. I followed her eyes, but I didn't see anything in the shadows.

'What?' I repeated.

'Someone's there,' Laura said.

I looked again. I took a couple steps closer to the trees. I didn't smell anything but pine, like Christmas in July.

'Are you sure?'

'I heard someone,' she insisted.

I thought she was wrong, but it was easy to feel like you weren't alone in the park. There was a bigness about it. It felt primitive, like we were miles from the city. People came here to do secret things. You never knew who was around.

'Come out!' I shouted. 'Hey!'

A violent rustling shook the brush, and Laura and I both jumped and screamed. We scrambled away, nearly falling. A wild turkey lurched out of the woods, wings flapping excitedly. He was a quivering bundle of striped brown feathers with a cherry-red neck, who beat his way across the path and buried himself in the tangle of leafy bushes.

Laura hugged the strap of her backpack tighter to her body. My heart galloped. It was silly, but it's the kind of thing that pumps you with adrenaline and leaves you feeling keyed up. When the turkey was gone, we kept walking, but Laura continued to turn every few steps and look nervously behind us.

I could hear boys' voices ahead of us as we got closer to the softball field. We had parked near the field an hour earlier. I wanted to sit and watch Jonny play, but Laura didn't want to hang around the boys, and I didn't blame her. They had beers at every base, and several of them were already drunk. We were the only two girls around, and they didn't take their eyes off us when we arrived. Some girls preened and puffed up at attention like that, but Laura wilted and wanted to run.

Even now, as we reached the end of the trail that looped back to the field, she hung back.

'Let's go down to the lake,' she said.

'Why don't we wait until the game's over? Then Jonny can come with us.'

'No, I know the two of you want to be alone.'

That was true. I felt bad, but I wanted Jonny to myself that night. Him and me. Out in the water and then on the beach together. Still, I didn't want to leave Laura by herself.

'It's OK. You can stay with us.'

'Say it like you mean it,' Laura replied. She finally smiled.

'No, it's just—'

'Don't worry, I'll leave when you guys get together. Let's go.'

'I need to tell Jonny where to meet us.'

I led the way out of the woods. Laura folded her arms over her chest and followed tentatively behind me. The voices and laughter got louder. There were a couple dozen boys in a rough diamond in the field, some playing, some sitting in the dirt near the parking lot. Cars were parked haphazardly in the weeds behind them, beside a winding road that led down from the highway. The field was nothing but grass and brush, small enough for a solid hit to pitch the ball into the marshland. Over the cattails, I could see a creek winding toward the lake.

The sky was like charcoal to the west. Bursts of lightning made the clouds glow, and I could smell rain. Somewhere nearby, on one of the other trails that made a web through the large park, I heard firecrackers.

I saw Jonny playing first base. The trees ended at the edge of the softball field, and Laura and I came up behind him. He turned as he saw the other boys waving to us. Some of them made catcalls. There were empty beer bottles thrown aside everywhere.

Jonny had a serious face, but it softened when he saw me. Whenever I was with Laura, I was used to being invisible, but Jonny looked at me as if he didn't see anyone else. I'd like to tell you what the connection

49

was between us, or why it happened so quickly. The truth is, I have no idea. Sure, he's handsome. Tall and lean, still a little short on meat and muscle, like most boys. He's got that long, wavy hair that looks untamed. And those amazing eyes. That was what I first noticed, his eyes, which are dark and deep. I could see everything in them. Pain. Loss. Black humor. Seriousness of purpose. He is so intense that I just have to cut him down to size every now and then, and he doesn't seem to care when I wound his ego.

Right now, he is searching. I understand, because that was me, after my mom died. I was fourteen then, and I spent a lot of time searching, wondering where to go, what I would do, who I would become. I feel as if I've found my answers, but Jonny only lost his dad nine months ago, and he's still looking. He grew up wanting to go to sea like his dad, but not anymore. His mother won't let another Stride step on board an ore boat. I don't think Jonny wants it now either. It's like the lake betrayed him when it took his father. Now the lake is an enemy.

I don't know what he will do, but when he figures it out, I know he'll pour his whole heart and soul into it. Like he's poured his heart and soul into me.

Jonny shouted something to the pitcher, who held the ball and waited for him. He came off the base and jogged up to us. He wore shorts and sneakers. His chest was bare. He kissed me.

'Hi.'

'Hi.'

We were awkward around each other, because we both knew what we were thinking. It's exciting, unsettling, and unnerving when you know you're going to do it.

'We're going down to the lake,' I told him. 'Meet us there, OK?'

'Yeah.'

'Will you be long?'

'No, we're almost done, and the rain will probably wash us out in a couple minutes anyway.'

'OK, love you.'

'Love you, too.'

Jonny kissed me again. He waved at Laura, but I could see him wondering if the two of us would be alone. Part of me wanted Laura to stay, because I was nervous about what was going to happen. Part of me couldn't wait to jump off the cliff.

We continued by the side of the field to where another trail led down along the creek toward the lake. The eyes of the boys followed us. They made jokes. Laura stayed on my left and stared at the ground.

I noticed Peter Stanhope among the boys. He was coming up to bat next. We had to pass within a few feet of him, and he leaned on his bat and watched us the whole way, his head swiveling to track us, his eyes gleaming. Laura didn't look up at all, but I could tell she knew he was there. It was Laura he wanted. He didn't say a word to either of us, but we felt him. Peter had a presence, because he was so sure of himself. He wasn't as tall as Jonny, but he was beefy and strong. He had bushy blond hair, parted in the middle, swept back in two waves. He chewed gum relentlessly, and his lips were always parted in a perpetual smirk that dimpled his cheeks. His skin was ruddy and freckled.

Most of the girls chased after him. They wanted a ride in his Trans Am. They wanted to swim in the Olympic-sized pool in his father's backyard. Peter went from one girl to the next, doing what he did with Laura, pushing them to have sex. Most said yes. Rumor is, he even bedded down a couple of the married teachers at school. That's the way life is when you're a Stanhope. The word 'no' isn't in your vocabulary. Peter's father, Randall, owns a big mining operation in the harbor. People are afraid of him. He's the kind of man who can get what he wants by picking up the phone. So Peter lives that way too. Taking the things he wants.

I resented him, because we never had much money in my house, and I figured anyone with that much money probably got it by stepping all over other people. I also didn't like the way he treated Laura. I was never sure why she went out with him. But he didn't care what I thought. I was nothing. He looked right through me, and I could see him stripping off Laura's clothes in that horny brain of his.

'Come on,' I said to her.

We hurried out of the field. It got dark again as we entered the forest. Laura glanced behind her, as if Peter might be following us.

'He's a creep,' I said.

Laura didn't say anything at all.

The stream tumbled over stones beside the path. We walked beside it for ten minutes until the creek split out of the trees into a furry brown nest of cattails, where we could see the midnight-blue waters of the lake pooling at the shore just past the weeds. We both ran out onto the beach. My toes bunched the sand as I headed for the water, where I splashed in the foam. A handful of ducks lifted off noisily.

'You want to swim?' I asked Laura.

'I don't have a suit.'

'So?'

She shook her head.

I came out of the water and sat down in the sand. Laura slid the backpack off her shoulder and sat down next to me. We didn't talk. I watched the black stain in the sky grow as it blew closer. The north side of the lake was already obscured by nightfall, and the line where the water became the trees was impossible to distinguish. There was another beach on that side and more trails that wound down from the other end of the park.

The warm breeze turned cooler. Laura sat with her hands around her knees, staring at the water.

'You and Dad really went at it last night,' I said.

Fights weren't new between them, but this one was worse than usual.

'I don't want to talk about it,' Laura said.

'What was it about this time?' I persisted.

'Nothing.' She looked away, shutting me down. Her legs twitched. She twisted her neck to stare over her shoulder, and I thought she might get up and run away.

'What's wrong?' I asked.

'Nothing's wrong,' she said.

'You sure?'

Laura shrugged. 'Life's weird.'

'How so?'

'I don't know. Just weird.'

'You're pretty weird, too,' I told her, smiling.

She didn't smile back at me.

'Sorry,' I said. 'It was a joke.'

'That's OK.'

I felt a spatter of raindrops on my skin.

'Seriously, what's wrong?'

'I'm just thinking about stuff.'

'Like what?'

Laura hugged her knees together. The drizzle ran like tears on her cheeks. 'Do you think you could ever kill someone?' she asked.

I stared at her. 'What kind of question is that?'

'I mean, do you think only an insane person could do it?'

I tried to read her face, which was a mask of shadows. I realized it wasn't rain. She was crying.

'You're scaring me, Laura. What is this about?'

'What if Dad were abusing me?' she asked. 'Could you kill him?'

I felt a chill. 'Oh, my God, did something happen between you two?'

Laura shook her head. 'No, it's not that.'

'Then tell me.'

'It doesn't matter now.'

I was afraid she had opened up to me as much as she ever could. 'Laura, please.'

'I just wish everything weren't so complicated,' she said.

'Like what?'

'I don't know. Everything.' Laura looked at me. 'Can you keep a secret?'

'Of course.'

'Even from Jon?'

'If I have to, sure. What is it?'

She didn't tell me. She never got the chance. This time, we both heard it. Something snapped in the woods behind us. We spun around, and I heard Laura suck in her breath. We couldn't see anyone, but someone was there.

'Jonny?' I called.

No one answered.

'Wait here,' I said.

I didn't shout this time. I charged the woods, sprinting through the sand onto the trail, where I skidded to a stop. I listened but heard only the wind as it landed with a frenzy, kicking the forest to life. I made a slow circle, my eyes narrowing as I tried to penetrate the darkness. I stared where I thought I had heard the branch break and was rock still.

I knew I wasn't alone.

I heard a shout from Laura, and when I turned back toward the beach, I could see that the rain had come. It was sheeting down. Lightning sizzled, and the forest shook with thunder. The noise covered everything else. Whoever was near me could use the storm to escape.

I waited a few more seconds, and then I smelled something odd and sickly sweet above the freshness of the rain. Marijuana.

Five

Tish Verdure nursed a gin and tonic and studied the row of ageing high school sports photos hung above the booth in the downtown bar. One was a group photo of a state championship hockey team. Another was an action shot of two tall white boys fighting over a basketball lay-up. In a third, she saw a cheering section of baseball players in a stadium dugout, with bats strewn around them on the ground. Some of the photos were from her vintage in the 1970s, and she saw faces that looked familiar. For all she knew, some of the boys were in the bar right now. She wouldn't recognize them today.

The waitress, a bored UMD student in a Rascal Flatts T-shirt, told her that one of the men at the bar wanted to buy Tish a drink. Tish waved her off without giving the man a look. It wasn't the first time tonight. Men assumed that a single woman in a bar was on the prowl, when all she really wanted was to get drunk. She knew she drank and smoked too much. It was a way to get through the days and nights.

Tish wondered if she had made a mistake by coming back. Stirring up her life wouldn't accomplish anything, and she was already lying about her past. Stride knew it – she could see it in his eyes when he looked at her. A part of her wanted to pack up and go before things got worse, but she owed it to Laura to be here. She owed it to Cindy, too. She had foolishly made a promise to her, and she couldn't put off any longer her need to honor it.

She paid her bill. It was one in the morning. She left the bar through the crowd of smokers outside the door and strolled past dark store-fronts toward her rental car. Rather than get in, she continued past

55

it, down the sharp slope of Second Avenue toward the corner. She stood by a parking meter on the curb and stared diagonally across the street, where a crumpled piece of newspaper blew up against a brick building like a tumbleweed. The ground floor of the building housed a wireless phone store behind its big windows. Neon glowed brightly in the display.

Back then, when she was a child, the same space had been a bank office. The bank where her mother worked as a teller.

Tish had been in school when it happened. The policeman who came to get her had a black mole on his cheek and breath that smelled like burnt coffee. He took her to the station and put her in a white room, and then a woman in a flowery dress came in and told her. That was it. She slept with strangers that night.

'I'm home, Mom,' Tish murmured to the air.

She turned round, leaving the old bank building behind, and stalked briskly to her car. The fresh air had burned off some of the alcohol clouding her brain. She drove north out of downtown through streets largely empty of traffic. The lights stayed green. She turned right at 21st Avenue, crossed over the freeway, and curled round a sharp curve to the cliffside road that led to the condominium she was borrowing. She parked under the trees at the end of the street and got out. She lit a cigarette and stood there, smoking, letting it burn down. The lake twinkled below her. The birches were silhouettes with a thousand arms, moving and alive. Behind her, the freeway overpass rumbled on its stilts like a concrete giant. She felt strange. As if eyes were watching her. That was how Laura must have felt. Tish shivered, but she finished her smoke before crushing out the butt in the street and continuing to her front door.

She stopped. Froze.

One of the miniature square panels of stained glass in the door was shattered, letting out a square of white light. The broken pane was near the deadbolt.

Tish backed up, listening. Everything was quiet. She looked behind her, feeling a stab of panic. The sensation of being watched had fled. She was alone now, but she felt violated. With her cell phone, Tish called the police. They told her a car would be there soon. Knowing that help was close by gave her the courage to return to the door, which was unlocked, and nudge it open. She took a cautious step into the foyer, listening for anything that would betray a stranger. She breathed the air, trying to smell an echo of whoever had been here, but all she detected was a lingering paint smell from the work that had been done on the place before she arrived.

Nothing was disturbed that she could see. Nothing taken. But she had only been in town for a few days, enough time to get up her courage to see Stride, enough time to visit the north beach in the park. A pilgrimage to feel Laura's spirit again.

All she had in the condo was her suitcase and some food.

Tish waited for a long time by the front door, and when she was convinced she was alone, she went to the bedroom. Her papers were strewn over the bed, not the way she had left them. Her clothes were in and out of the drawers. The closet was open, and so was her suitcase. Tish caught her breath and immediately went to the case and unzipped the netting over the main compartment and found the hidden pocket inside. She reached in as far as she could and exhaled with relief.

The letter from Cindy was still there. Untouched. So was the clipping about the robbery.

She returned to the living room to sit down and wait for the police. It was obvious that no matter how little time she had been here, someone already knew she was back.

Someone already wanted her gone.

Stride lay in bed on his back and stared at the ceiling. The bedroom window was open, and he could hear the surf on Lake Superior where it assaulted the shore on the other side of the sand dune. The narrow strip of beach was only steps from their back door. Tish was right that hardly anyone had lived on the Point year-round in the old days. Cottages like this one were mostly summer getaways then. Today, it was prime real estate. The old houses were being torn down and replaced by castles and condos. Anything on waterfront anywhere was gold. He liked it better when he and Cindy had first moved out here, and people wondered why anyone would want to live in the eye of the Superior storms. Stride wasn't always sure himself, except that the lake was so vast that he sometimes felt as if he were staring at eternity.

Serena sat cross-legged on the bed, watching him. The lights were off. Sometimes, when he closed his eyes, he expected that he would open them again and see Cindy sitting there, in the same pose, a crooked smile on her face. As if all the time that had passed had been in his imagination. He wasn't really closing in on fifty years old. He wasn't really bruised by death and loss. He was a teenager. A new cop. A young husband. Everything that was going to be lay ahead, not behind.

'You know what I remember about that night?' he told her. 'Other than me and Cindy, I mean. I remember the bat.'

Serena didn't say anything. He could see it like a video clip on a loop that played over and over in his head. Close up. That bat going round and round.

'It was Peter's bat. One of those aluminum ones. Bright silver. He never let anyone else use it. I remember him taking practice swings at home plate and hearing the whoosh of the bat. I can still see that bat in his hands. All I can think about is that, not long after, someone used that same bat to beat an innocent girl to death. A girl who would have been my sister-in-law. Someone hit her and just kept swinging and swinging.'

'If it was Peter's bat, how did it get into someone else's hands?' Serena asked. She spoke so softly that she was almost whispering.

'You're assuming it did.'

'Well, you said someone else's fingerprints were on it.'

'Yes, that's true,' he admitted. 'Someone else had it. Someone who killed Laura. That was the only explanation that made sense to me all these years.'

'How did the bat wind up at the murder scene?'

Stride remembered. He saw the bat again in his mind. Close up. In the field.

'The rain came,' he said. 'We all went running. The storm was severe. Everything turned black. It sounded like a train, the way a tornado does. I went to the woods to find Cindy and Laura down by the lake. Peter was on second base, and he took off as the storm hit. As I ran for the trail, I saw Peter's bat lying in the weeds. He must have forgotten all about it. So anyone could have picked it up. There were a lot of guys with us in the field.'

'But?' Serena asked, hearing him hesitate.

'But I remember thinking that Peter was going to come back for that bat.'

Stride was distracted, watching Cindy and Laura go. He was anxious for the game to be over. He could still taste her lips, which always tasted the same way, like a cherry Popsicle. When they kissed, they were connected, electricity passing between them. He had an erection, thinking about what they would do later. If they really did it. If she really meant it. He could tell she was nervous. He wondered if she had brought Laura with her as a shield, so that she had an excuse not to go all the way. As the two girls disappeared into the trees, though, he saw Cindy look back at him, and her face told him that nothing had changed. She wanted him. She was waiting for him.

He glanced at the black sky. Time was short. He hit the pocket of his mitt impatiently. Dave McGill was at the plate, and he kept tipping foul balls that dribbled to the edge of the field, where Raymond Anderson, who was the catcher, had to retrieve them. Stride thought they should call the game right now. He could taste rain, and he already felt the sky leaking drops onto his face. No one else paid any attention.

McGill finally struck out. Peter Stanhope took his place, swinging his silver bat theatrically, sporting an arrogant grin. Stride didn't really know Peter, other than by reputation. They weren't friends. They didn't hang out together. The only thing they had in common was baseball. The longest conversation he could remember having with Peter was about Rod Carew.

Peter swung violently and missed. Strike one.

Stride saw a bright flash and imagined Peter's bat, held high over his head, attracting the current like a lightning rod. Less than five seconds later, thunder washed across the field in a drum roll.

Peter swung again. Strike two. His face contorted in effort and frustration. His jaw worked his gum furiously. He was a good hitter, but over-eager, always looking for the home run on every pitch. He struck out as often as he connected. On the third pitch, though, his aluminum bat swatted the ball with a loud ting, and the ball lofted over Stride's head into the outfield, where it dropped for an easy single. Peter loped to the base. He bent down and picked up a half-full bottle of Grain Belt and swigged it empty, then tossed the bottle toward the weeds. He wiped his mouth with the bottom of his red tank top.

'So it's you and Cindy Starr, huh, Stride?' he said.

'That's right.'

'You know, her sister is the real prize.'

Stride didn't reply.

'Laura's the one with the tits,' Peter continued. 'Half the guys here got boners when she walked by. Why aren't you going after her?'

'Because I like Cindy.'

'Yeah? What's she like?'

'Why do you care?' Stride asked.

'I'm not hot for her, if that's what you think. I just wondered if the princess act runs in the family.'

'What the hell does that mean?'

'I mean that Laura walks around like some kind of ice queen,' Peter replied. 'Somebody needs to thaw her out.'

'Shut up,' Stride said.

'So how about Cindy? Is she a frigid queer like her sister?'

Stride threw off his baseball glove and shoved both bare hands against Peter's chest. Peter stumbled backward, lost his footing in the damp grass, and landed on his ass in the mud. Stride stood over him, fists clenched and cocked, ready to fight. He heard shouts from some of the other boys in the field. The pitcher dropped the ball; the batter threw the bat away; they all began to converge on Stride.

Peter laughed and got up, brushing dirt from his skin. He waved them away. 'Hey, it's OK, I had it coming.'

Stride watched carefully, expecting a sucker punch.

'Don't sweat it,' Peter said. 'I like to see how far I can push people before they push back. It's a little lesson I learned from my dad.'

'Apologize,' Stride told him.

'Yeah, all right. I'm sorry. That do it for you? You need to lighten up, Stride.'

Stride ignored him. The game continued. The batter at the plate struck out, and another took his place. One inning to go, and it was over. He could barely make out the action on the field, as the night drew closer and the dark clouds massed.

'You seen The Deep yet?' Peter asked.

Stride grunted. He and Cindy had seen it the previous weekend.

'Saw it three times,' Peter said. 'Fuck, Jackie Bisset in that T-shirt? Holy shit. I wish porn actresses looked like her. I saw Teenage Sex Kitten *downtown last week. What a bunch of losers. Pimples and no tits.'*

At the plate, Gunnar Borg punched a ground ball past the pitcher that took a jagged leap as it bounced off a half-buried rock in the field. Stride bounded to his right and scooped up the ball. He yanked it out of his glove and prepared to toss it to Nick Parucci at second for the out. Then he saw stars. Peter Stanhope ran over him, slamming Stride's body into the dirt with his right shoulder and jarring the ball out of his hands. Stride recovered quickly and grabbed the ball out of the grass again, but by then Peter was standing on second base, grinning, and the other runner was at first.

Stride's right side was black with dirt. He felt as if someone had hit him with a shovel.

'Don't mess with me, Stride,' Peter called.

Stride fired the ball back to the pitcher, turned on his heel, and marched back to first base. Gunnar Borg laughed.

At that moment, the sky finally opened up.

The wind blew in, and with it, the rain bucketed down. The pelting drops felt like needles. Lightning came, like flashbulbs popping, and the boys sprinted for the cars parked haphazardly in the weeds. Stride ran too, but in the opposite direction, toward the woods and the lake. Toward Cindy. The field was already sodden, a river of mud. Stride saw beer bottles, a fallen baseball glove, and empty bags of chips. Peter Stanhope's aluminum bat lay where he had thrown it as he ran for first base. Stride heard shouting a hundred yards away and then the roar of car engines. Headlights streaked across the field. Horns honked.

The downpour followed him into the forest. Rain beat down on a million leaves. His long hair was plastered against his skin. He ran, but it was too dark to see where he was going on the path, and he put a foot wrong and stumbled, cutting his knee. It stung, but the rain washed away the blood. He wiped moisture out of his eyes and pushed through the branches where a bent tree hung over the trail. The spindly twigs slapped back and scraped his face.

He smelled scorched wood and thought that part of the woods close by might be on fire. When the next flash of lightning struck, he could see the orange streak reflect on the surface of the water and see the silvery curtain of rainfall beyond the trees. The lake wasn't far. He hurried.

Then Stride heard something strange.

Whistling.

It was so close that someone had to be standing almost at his shoulder. He turned and pushed his way through the brush lining the path and broke through into a tiny clearing. A campfire had been built there. A few warm embers remained, throwing up smoke where the rain had doused them. That was the burning smell he had noticed. He didn't see anyone in the clearing, but then a shadow large enough to be a bear detached itself from one of the birch trees and approached the dying fire. Instinctively, Stride retreated. The man didn't see him at first. He was a huge black man, at least six foot five, with dreadlocks down to his shoulders and an oddly colorful beret of red, green, and gold. His limbs were as thick as some of the larger tree trunks, with well-defined muscles. He wore a white T-shirt and loose-fitting black pants that had the same tri-colored stripe as his hat.

Stride recognized him. They called him Dada. He was one of the vagrants who hung out near the railroad tracks during the warmer months. Dada was whistling, not like a nervous man in a cemetery, but like a cardinal at winter's end. Free. Loud. Stride backed up silently, but Dada saw him. Their eyes met. The music from his mouth stopped. Stride saw the man's lips curl into a smile, revealing white teeth against his coal skin. Dada didn't look afraid or surprised. He laughed as Stride made his way back to the trail without saying a word. His laughter lingered in Stride's ears, growing fainter as the storm drowned it out.

He continued toward the lake, making his way by feel as he slogged through the trees. Water streamed down his face. Mosquitoes harassed him, and he squashed them with his fingers. He didn't know how many minutes passed before the path opened onto the sandy clearing and his eyes could see what was ahead of him.

He found Laura first. She had taken cover under one of the older pine trees, its outstretched branches forming a green roof over her head. Her clothes were soaked. She clutched her backpack against her chest and gazed across the dimpled water. She looked bottled up, anxious. When he touched her shoulder, she screamed, then clapped her mouth shut.

'It's just me,' he said.

'You scared me to death.'

'Where's Cindy?' he asked.

Laura pointed. He looked out onto the beach, and there she was. She had taken off her shorts and was in her bikini, dancing in the rain. That was Cindy. A water sprite. A free spirit.

'Hey,' Stride shouted.

Cindy stopped when she saw him and bounded up the beach in her bare feet. 'Hey, you.' She threw her arms round his neck and kissed him. Her skin was wet and soft. Her long hair fell across his face.

'Do you want to go home?' he asked her. 'We weren't counting on a storm.'

'No, no, let's stay,' she insisted.

'Are you sure?'

'Yes. Really. I want to, Jonny.'

Laura slung her backpack over her shoulder and put her thumbs in the pockets of her jeans. She gave the two of them a strange smile. 'You guys be good, OK? I'm going to go.'

Cindy looked torn. She bit her lower lip. 'No, you better not, Laura. Not by yourself.'

'I'm fine, little sister.'

'Stay with us. It's OK.'

'You two don't need a chaperone. Not tonight. I told you I'd leave when Jon got here.'

'We'll go with you,' Stride said. 'All of us.'

'Yes, we'll all go,' Cindy said.

Laura hugged Cindy hard. 'You two stay. Don't worry about me.'

'No way. How will you get home? You can't get a ride now. I'm sure everyone left when the storm hit.'

'I can hike up to the highway and catch a bus.'

'No, no, no, that's crazy. Come on, we're all going.'

Laura detached herself from her sister and put a hand on Cindy's chest. 'Look, I'm not being noble. I love you, but I have to go.'

'Not *alone*,' Cindy repeated. 'I won't let you go alone.'

'I *won't* be alone,' Laura said.

'Not alone?' Serena asked. 'She was meeting someone?'

Stride nodded in bed. 'That's what she told us.'

'Who?'

'Peter Stanhope said it was him. He told the police that he and Laura were dating.'

'Did you believe him?'

'His story fit the facts, but Laura told Cindy she had broken it off with Peter because he was pressuring her for sex. Tish told me the same thing.'

'Unless Laura didn't want anyone to know that they were seeing each other.'

'Yes, that's true.'

'What happened next?' Serena asked.

Stride listened to the waves outside the window. The old house rattled in the wind. 'I don't know. That was the last time I saw Laura. Something happened to her in the softball field, where her shoe was found. But that's not where she was killed. She took another trail from the field and wound up on a beach on the north side of the lake almost a mile away. That's where Cindy found her.'

'So Peter's bat wasn't found in the softball field where you last saw it?' Serena asked.

'No. It was on the beach by the body. Someone took the bat, followed the trail from the softball field to the beach, and killed Laura there. And there was something else, too.'

'What?'

'No one knows about this,' Stride said. 'It was never released to the press. I only found out when I took over the Detective Bureau and pulled the file. The police found semen near the body.'

'Laura had sex that night?' Serena asked.

Stride shook his head. 'Not in the body. Near the body. In the woods near the beach where Laura was murdered. Whatever went down that night, someone was there watching. Either he killed her, or he saw who did.'

Who Killed Laura Starr?

By Tish Verdure

What do I remember about that night?

I remember the two of us alone, after Laura left to follow the trail back to the field. Me and Jonny. I know it was wrong to let her go, but back then we were all blinded by our desires. Any one of us could have made a different decision. If we had, the night would have gone another way. I try not to dwell on it. Life happens the way it's going to happen. So does death.

I remember us walking hand in hand out of the shelter of the trees. The rain came in sheets, but there was no more lightning, no more thunder, just wind and water. It sounds romantic, but it was funny, actually. We were laughing. We blinked our eyes and gulped air like fishes, as if we were breathing under a waterfall. We shivered in the cold. The wind whipped us around like dolls.

I remember saying, 'Let's swim.'

I had to start. If Jonny had reached to remove my clothes, I would have let him, but he would never do that. I unhooked my bikini top in back, let the straps slide off my shoulders, and saw my white breasts come free in the darkness. My long, wet hair covered them. I pushed my hair out of the way so he could see me. My pink nipples and the little bumps around them were swollen. I took his hand to make him touch me, and I showed him how, guiding his fingers with mine, caressing and rubbing the way I liked it. When we kissed again, I remember the feel of our wet, bare chests pressing together.

I remember stepping back and staring at my feet as I peeled my bikini bottoms down and feeling nervous and self-conscious when I

65

was finally naked in front of him. I couldn't look into his eyes. I felt an urge to cover myself, which was stupid. I remember finding the courage to look up, spread my arms wide, and say, 'Now you've seen the whole deal.'

I couldn't help but laugh. He was transfixed. His face was in awe. 'You're beautiful,' he told me.

I was, but how can you not be beautiful when you're seventeen? I wasn't a model, but I was the girl he loved. I remember folding my arms over my breasts and saying, 'Your turn.'

He had it worse than me. Guys do. I was intensely curious, without wanting to show him how much. He stalled. He fumbled with his shorts. When he got them off, his underwear was even whiter than my sun-starved breasts. It jutted out because of his erection. He looked nervous like me as he went the rest of the way, and it took him even longer to meet my eyes again.

I remember wanting to reach out and touch it, but I didn't.

'Are we ready for this?' he asked.

'You sure look ready.'

'That's not what I mean.'

'I know what you mean.'

No, I wasn't ready. I was scared to death. I knew he was, too. But I wasn't going back.

I remember us swimming. We waded out naked into the dark lake, with the rain cascading over us. The lake bed under our feet was a slippery mix of sand and stones. The water wrapped around us and rose up to our necks. You feel so exposed and vulnerable like that, naked and submerged, with the whole sky stretching over your head. You think strange thoughts about what might be in there with you. I remember yelping as a fish brushed my stomach, swimming between us, and then of course I realized it was not a fish at all, and it was a good thing Jonny couldn't see my face turn red.

I remember floating, my small breasts like little snowy peaks above the water line. Jonny held me. His hands explored. It felt good.

I remember finally touching him and watching his eyes close and his mouth fall open.

We could have stayed out there all night, postponing what both of us really wanted to do. Out in the lake, we were in a kind of frozen world, nothing behind us, nothing ahead. The splashing rain and the whistle of the wind blocked out every other sound. There was no moon to glisten on the surface, just complete darkness. I was blind to reality. Blind to the violence I had let my sister walk into.

I remember us lying on our backs on the beach. No stars. Fog and mist rising like clouds out of the low lands. The rain no more than spatters on our skin now. Hungry mosquitoes starting to wake up, buzz, and hunt for blood. If we didn't do it now, it wouldn't be tonight.

I remember him on top of me. I felt crushed and didn't care. Our kisses were urgent. We were both clumsy. I remember my legs spread wide like wings. We were laughing and struggling. I helped him, and somewhere after the pressure and pain, somewhere after our hands, feet, and knees found their right places, we both realized that we were really doing it. There was this little pause in the middle when we caught our breath and our eyes met with a kind of amazement. Then I felt his muscles all bunch into one, and I wrapped my legs tight around him, and I watched his face as it happened.

I remember we stayed like that for a very long time. I remember sweat and rain. When he withdrew, I showed him with my hands how to touch me, and I watched him watching me right up to the moment when our fingers working together pushed me over the top, and I closed my eyes, and it happened to me, too.

I remember thinking that in the morning, the world would be a very different place.

And God help me, it was.

PART TWO

TALKING TO STRANGERS

Six

Maggie was already awake when the phone rang at three in the morning.

She sat with her feet propped up on a kitchen chair and a cup of oolong tea getting cold on the table beside her. She wore a flowered silk robe. Every downstairs light was blazing, making it look as if she had thrown an all-night party and forgotten to send invitations. Light was the only way to give the house any warmth at all. Maggie called it her Dark Shadows house. It reminded her of the cheesy Gothic soap opera from the 1960s she had seen in reruns. Outside, the vanilla stone towered four stories, with ornamental molding along the roof lines like an ocean wave. A hodgepodge of arches and bays made it look like a Lego castle designed by a child. Inside, there were curious little rooms everywhere and dusty lace hung in the windows.

As a single person, she rattled around in it. Even when she was married, she had never liked the dark way the house felt at night. Maggie liked modern, bright, open spaces, with everything made of chrome and glass. The house was on the market now, and she was waiting for an uptick in housing sales to net her an offer. Once the house was sold, she had her eye on a downtown condo.

Maggie found herself up in the middle of the night several times a week, battling nightmares. The previous year had been the worst of her life, culminating in the murder of her husband in January and the cloud of suspicion that fell over her regarding his death. She still regretted her mistakes and secrets, which had temporarily strained the relationship between herself and Stride and put not only herself, but

71

Serena, in the hands of a brutal stalker. In the daylight, it was easy to forgive herself. The nights were another story.

She had a laptop in front of her, and she tapped her way through adoption websites. For months, she had been wondering about adopting a child, but the time and bureaucracy of the formal process intimidated her. She wasn't sure if she could wait years, only to be disappointed. She had made inquiries with a number of international adoption agencies, but their replies weren't encouraging. She was a naturalized US citizen; she had sought asylum from China after the uprising in Tiananmen Square, which essentially ruled out the possibility of adopting a baby from China. Being Chinese, however, she faced racism from countries which had no interest in turning over a white baby to an Asian mother. Her personal characteristics also worked against her, even in the US. She was unmarried. She was over thirty-five. She worked in a job where her personal safety was always at risk. The only thing on the plus side of the ledger was that she had inherited millions of dollars from her late husband's business. Money always talked.

Maggie closed the laptop when the phone rang. It was Max Guppo.

'Sorry to get you up,' he said.

'I was up.'

'You said you wanted to know as soon as he was spotted again.'

'The peeper?'

'Right. I'm down in Gary. A retarded girl saw him outside her bedroom. I'm here with the father. His name is Clark Biggs.'

Maggie took down the address. 'I'll be there in an hour.'

She took five minutes to shower, then pulled on a black T-shirt, jeans, and a pair of square-heeled lace-up boots. She didn't bother drying her hair, but let it fall in wet, messy bangs. A diamond stud winked from her tiny nose. She grabbed a burgundy leather jacket from her closet as she left the house and piled into the yellow Avalanche in her driveway.

Maggie sped down the hill onto I-35 and headed through the jumble of freeway overpasses that led south out of the city. The harbor sparkled in a swath of moonlight as the clouds raced past on her left. She accelerated to 85 miles an hour through the industrial zone, where plumes of steam belched into the air, forming white dragons against the black sky. Lingering raindrops tapped on her windshield. She veered off the interstate at Highway 23 and followed the fifteen-mile stretch of worn-out towns that tracked the path of the St Louis River. Low mountains loomed beyond the road, swarming with evergreens and birches. She could see green tracks carved into the hills, which turned white with snow and became ski slopes in the winter. They weren't exactly black diamonds, but if you were into downhill skiing, you didn't have many alternatives in a state as flat as Minnesota.

Clark Biggs lived in a town called Gary, which was one of the many small communities that had lost their way in the superstore generation. Its main street looked like a movie set out of the 1950s. Its brick buildings were mostly abandoned. Paint flecked away on old signs advertising Coca-Cola and Miller High Life. Between every building was an empty lot with weeds growing through cracks in the concrete. The bars were the new economic backbone of these towns, and they kept the Duluth Police busy every night after midnight.

Clark's small house was west of the highway and almost directly across the street from the town's elementary school. The development butted up against a densely wooded area of parkland. Maggie drove past the development in order to scout the crime scene and found herself in a trailer park on the opposite side of the woods. The forest encroached on the mobile home community from all sides, and it wouldn't be hard to park a car unnoticed and then duck into the trees and disappear.

She did a U-turn and returned to the development where Clark Biggs lived. The streets were wide, and the lots were large and flat, occupied by one- and two-story matchbox houses with detached garages. Tall, bushy oaks offered plenty of shade. It was the kind of neighborhood where cars and trucks didn't get traded in; they simply sat on the lawn, rusting. Many of the houses had fenced yards, but not the Biggs house, which was open and all on one level. It was painted white, with a block of five concrete steps leading up to the front door. The roof was missing a few of its red shingles. The large yard featured soaring pine trees and a weeping willow, and directly behind it, the yard spilled into the forest. The grass was long.

For a peeping Tom, it was a prime choice. A quiet area. Ground-floor windows. An easy sprint back to the woods. This was a neighbor-hood where the biggest worry was Dad losing his foundry job or brother Jim getting cut in a bar fight after midnight. No one thought about pulling the shades and curtains. There was no one around to watch.

Maggie parked on the street, and Guppo met her outside. He was in his fifties and not much taller than Maggie, but the stretch dress pants needed to accommodate his girth could have doubled as a parachute. A few strands of greased black hair labored to reach across his skull.

Guppo filled her in quickly.

'What about these footprints that Biggs found?' Maggie asked.

'There's not much we can do with them,' Guppo said. 'The rain mushed the prints by the time we got here.'

'Did the peeper head right into the woods?'

Guppo nodded. 'We followed the trail to the trees, and we lost it there.'

'There's a trailer park on the other side of the woods,' Maggie said. 'We need to talk to the people there. Kids, too.'

'You don't want me to wake people up over a peeping Tom, do you?'

'No, tomorrow is soon enough. I want to know if anyone saw strangers, cars, anything unusual. Find out how many people knew this girl, too. I want to know how this guy finds them. She's another blonde, isn't she?'

'Yes.'

'Pretty?'

'Well, yeah, but not in an adult way. She's like a child.'

'OK.'

Maggie hiked up the steps. Her big heels made a clip-clop noise. The screen door was unlocked, and she rapped on it with her knuckles and let herself inside. The house smelled like McDonald's food. The carpet in the living room was worn and gray. The furnishings showed their age with nicks and scratches.

'Mr Biggs?' she called.

Clark Biggs emerged from the shadows of a hallway on her left. He had his finger over his mouth to quiet her.

'Mary's finally sleeping.'

Maggie nodded and introduced herself. She quickly assessed Clark, who looked like a typical Minnesota blue-collar worker. Big and strong, a pot roast and Budweiser guy. Unlaced boots. Old clothes. Long, sandy hair with a ridge where his baseball cap had been. She could see sleeplessness and worry in his face.

They took seats on the tattered sofa.

'How is she?' Maggie asked.

'Scared to death,' Clark said bitterly. 'What kind of freak does that to a sweet little girl?'

'I understand how you feel,' Maggie said. 'My sergeant tells me that Mary is mentally handicapped, is that right?'

Clark nodded. 'She suffered a traumatic brain injury as a child that left her severely retarded.'

'What happened?' Maggie asked.

'A few other kids held her too long underwater as a game, if you can believe it. Physically, she's a normal sixteen-year-old girl, but she's barely at kindergarten level for learning.'

'I'm so sorry.'

'Don't feel sorry for me, Ms Bei. Mary is the best thing that ever happened to me, and I don't give a shit whether she's five years old going on forty. I would do anything for her.'

'Of course.'

Maggie decided that she liked Clark Biggs. She had a weakness for men who hid behind a brusque mask. Mary was the center of Clark's universe, despite the pain, expense, and hardship that her disability must have caused him over the years. Guppo had told her that Clark was divorced, and she imagined that taking care of a girl like Mary had proved to be more than their marriage could endure. He didn't look like a man who complained about it. He just went about his life.

'The other police officer said this man has done this before,' Clark said. 'Is that true?'

'We think it's the same man, yes. There have been nine reported peeping incidents on the south side of the city and in southwest Superior. The girls are all blonde teenagers, like Mary.'

'You mean he *chooses* them?'

'We think so, yes.'

'Who is this son of a bitch?'

'That's what we need to find out. Can you tell me if you know any of the other victims?' She rattled off the list of names from memory.

Clark shrugged. 'Katie Larson. That's Andy's girl, right? They live in Morgan Park?'

'Yes.'

'I know Andy from church. Katie babysat for Mary a couple times. That was two or three years ago. I don't know any of the others.'

Maggie jotted down the relationship in her notes. There had been ancillary connections among some of the other girls, too. Two of them were on the same soccer team. Two got their hair cut at the same place. Three went to the same high school. Nothing constituted a trend that tied any of the other girls together.

'Does Mary go to school?' Maggie asked.

Clark nodded. 'She attends a special school in Superior for developmentally disabled children. My wife takes her there during the week.'

'You and your wife are divorced?'

'Yes. I have Mary on the weekends. Donna takes her during the week.'

His face twitched. It was a sore subject.

'May I have Donna's address and phone number? I'll need to talk to her.'

Clark recited them. 'I haven't called Donna to tell her what happened. She's coming by in the morning. I want to let her know in person.'

'I won't talk to her until you do.'

He nodded.

'I'm sure Sergeant Guppo asked you some of these things already, but please bear with me,' Maggie continued. 'Have you noticed any strangers near your house recently? Have you seen any parked cars in the neighborhood that you didn't recognize?'

'Not that I can remember.'

'Has anything unusual happened involving Mary lately? Or has your wife mentioned any problems with her during the week?'

Clark shook his head. 'Nothing out of the ordinary.'

'Does Mary interact with many other girls outside school?'

'No, she's mostly with Donna or me.'

Maggie nodded. 'I'd appreciate it if you could write up a list tomorrow of the people that Mary regularly comes into contact with. Men and women. People at school. People at your workplace or your wife's workplace, if she ever goes there. Anything like that. Because of her condition, Mary's universe is substantially smaller than the other girls who have been peeped, which may make it easier for us to find an overlapping connection with the other victims.'

'I'll get you a list,' Clark said.

'This is an awkward question, Mr Biggs, but can you tell me more about Mary's intelligence level? Do you think she would recognize the man who peeped her? Or could she pick him out of a line-up if she saw him?'

'She's not stupid,' Clark snapped. 'She's just disabled.'

'I wasn't trying to offend you. I just want to know if she could be a witness for us.'

'I don't know whether she saw this guy's face, but Mary remembers things. If she saw him, and you show her a bunch of pictures, she'll pick him out. I'll never let her inside a courtroom, though, if that's what you're thinking.'

'I understand. Would you mind if I had an officer bring a photo book of registered sex offenders in this region, for Mary to look through?'

'I don't know if I want to traumatize her like that,' Clark said. 'If she sees him in there, she's going to be scared.'

'That may be the only way to find him.'

Clark sighed. 'OK. I want to be there, though.'

'Of course.' Maggie added, 'I'd like to come back and talk to Mary, too, if you don't mind.'

'She'll be with Donna. You'll have to clear it with her. I have to tell you, I'm not too crazy about the idea. You're not going to get anything from her, and I don't like her talking to strangers.'

'I promise I won't get her upset.'

'That's not a promise you can keep,' Clark said. 'She's a big girl, but she's a child. She's scared of things she doesn't understand.'

'May I see her?' Maggie asked.

'What, now?'

'Not to talk to her. I just want to see what she looks like.'

Clark frowned. 'I don't want to wake her up.'

'I'll be very quiet. I'd like to see her room, too.'

Clark relented and led her down the hall. For a big man, he walked quietly on the old floorboards. He inched Mary's door open and peered inside, then let Maggie squeeze into the room in front of him. Mary was asleep and snoring gently. Her father was right – she looked like any other teenage girl. Other than Mary being blonde, Maggie didn't see any physical characteristics that she shared with the other victims. She was heavier than most of the other girls. Her hair was the curliest of any of the others. She was lying on her stomach, with the blankets kicked halfway down her body. Her nightgown had bunched up, and her lower back was exposed. Maggie noticed a tattoo of a butterfly on her spine.

She silently checked out the windows. With the night light shining, she wasn't sure if Mary would have been able to see much outside. Maggie didn't feel confident about getting any results from the photo array of local sex offenders.

She returned with Clark Biggs to the living room.

'I notice your daughter has a tattoo,' Maggie said.

'So?'

'I was just surprised.'

'Mary loves butterflies. Her mother thought she would like having a tattoo of one. They did it without telling me.'

'Would you have objected?'

Clark frowned. 'No, I guess not, but I've got tattoos, and I know it hurts like hell to get them. Even so, Mary was thrilled with it. She likes showing it off by lifting her shirt, though. She shows it to everyone. I don't like that.'

'What do you mean, everyone?'

'If someone drives by, and she's in the yard, she lifts her shirt. If someone comes to the door, same thing. I can't make her stop.'

'I understand. I think that's all for now, Mr Biggs.'

'I hope you nail this bastard. I'm going to sleep on the floor in Mary's room until you do.'

'There's really no need for that,' Maggie told him. 'I know it was an awful experience for Mary, but it's over.'

'Until the next time,' Clark said.

'I don't think you need to worry about a next time. This peeper keeps changing targets. We're trying to catch up with him by figuring out how he picks his victims.'

'Bullshit,' Clark snapped.

Maggie arched her head in surprise. 'Excuse me?'

'I mean, he's done this to Mary before. What's to say he won't come back again?'

'You're saying this isn't the first time Mary saw this man?'

Clark shook his head. 'I think it happened last week, too.'

'Why didn't you tell me this before? Why didn't you report it?'

'I didn't think there was anything to report,' Clark said. 'I thought Mary had a bad dream. I thought she imagined it. But now that I think about it, the way she was shouting, "Him! Him!" I think it was because the guy came back.'

The guy came back.

That was a first, as far as Maggie knew. None of the other victims had suggested that the man might have been watching them before. Of course, maybe he got lucky. Maybe they didn't notice.

Maggie didn't think so, though. This was new behavior. New and frightening.

She didn't like it.

Seven

Serena drove west along the Point on Wednesday morning. After several days of rain, the clouds had blown out across the lake, leaving the city sunny and warm. In the calm harbor on her left, she spotted the rust-colored superstructure of an ore tanker shouldering through the deep water toward the lift bridge. She swore. She was running late already for her meeting with Peter Stanhope, and she knew that she would have to spend ten minutes now waiting for the boat to clear the canal and make its way to the open water.

As she expected, the bridge was up. Hers was the fourth car in line. She parked, rolled down her window to let in a humid breeze, and picked up a paperback by Louise Penny. When you lived on the Point, you were always prepared for delays at the bridge. Serena read several more pages of *Still Life*, until she saw the giant ship gliding under the bridge span. The boats always seemed to clear the bridge with only inches to spare, and they were an impressive sight, vast and silent. When the ship and the bridge exchanged farewell blasts of their signal horns, Serena turned her Mustang back on, and a couple of minutes later she headed through Canal Park toward the city center.

Peter Stanhope's law firm occupied the top two floors of the Lonsdale Building, in the commercial sector of Superior Street, among the banks, brokers, lawyers, and government workers that made the city tick. The façade was made of elegantly carved, copper-colored brick, with a roof line that resembled a Doric column. The building was smaller than the other high-rises around it and dated back to 1894. Peter could have chosen taller and more modern surroundings in the glass tower of the bank building one block east, but he had explained to Serena that he wanted his office to have a link to a more glamorous past, when the city, like his father, was rich and prosperous.

Serena found a parking meter and hurried across Superior Street between traffic. She wore black pinstriped dress pants that emphasized her long legs, pointed-toe heels, and an untucked turquoise silk shirt. Her black hair was loose and fell around her shoulders. She carried a slim burgundy briefcase and felt as if she were dressed to be a ladder-climbing corporate executive. It was a strange feeling. When she was a Vegas cop, she had worn tight jeans and sleeveless T-shirts and hung her shield from her belt.

She took the elevator to the top floor at ten minutes after ten o'clock. She was panicked about being late, but she relaxed when the receptionist told her that Peter was tied up in another meeting and was running at least twenty minutes behind schedule. She took a seat on the sofa, then got up again and paced restlessly in the waiting area.

The lobby furniture was antique and expensive. Black and white photographs adorned the wall, showing Peter's father and the postwar buildings, ships, and train cars of Stanhope Industries. Serena saw more modern memorabilia, too, including framed newspaper headlines of the major litigation victories of Peter's law firm. They had won forty million dollars in punitive damages from a Twin Cities manufacturer over a defective heart stent. Almost twenty million dollars following a school bus accident that left one child dead. And so on. Peter and his team of associates were personal injury lawyers with a vengeance.

Serena wondered, not for the first time, what she was doing here. She was a homicide detective. A private investigator. She had a hard time imagining herself working for a law firm, even though the work would not be all that different from what she did now. She would still interview victims and witnesses. She would try to find sources inside corporations to uncover things that their executives wanted to keep hidden. It was still investigative work. She worried that the job wouldn't be as exhilarating as her time on the street, but her experiences over the winter had worn down her physical and mental willingness to put herself in constant danger. For at least a year or two, she wanted to take a step back and rethink her life.

The opportunity had come out of the blue. Two months earlier, Peter Stanhope had read an article in the Duluth newspaper about Serena's background as a detective in Las Vegas. He called her with a freelance assignment to uncover evidence of fraudulent billing practices at a Twin Cities hospital. Over the course of the next six weeks, Serena built relationships with two nurses and an accountant, who turned over papers that allowed Peter's lawyers to pinpoint their discovery request and fast-track settlement negotiations. Peter was so impressed that he called Serena the following week to ask her to join the firm as a permanent employee.

She had been confused by Stride's reluctance when she told him about the job offer, because she knew he wanted her to find a less risky line of work. Now that she knew his background with Peter, she understood. Her own excitement had soured too.

A paralegal escorted Serena to Peter's office at 10:45. The corner suite was at the rear of the building, with a sweeping view toward the lake. Like the rest of the firm, Peter's office was decorated as if the year was 1950. On some level, Serena thought, Peter was trying to live up to his father's legacy. It couldn't be easy living in the shadow of an industrial giant. Serena thought it was interesting that after Randall Stanhope died, the first thing Peter had done was sell the family business.

Peter came around his desk and shook her hand firmly. 'Serena, I'm sorry to keep you waiting,' he said. 'This is what's called "lawyer time". We are perpetually late for everything except court dates. It's an occupational hazard.'

'That's all right,' Serena told him.

He gestured at the round oak conference table near the window. 'Please.'

They both sat down. Serena noticed a photograph over Peter's shoulder of Randall Stanhope and his son, who was about ten years old in the picture, standing on the span of the aerial lift bridge over the ship canal near the Point. Peter saw her staring.

'That's one of the few photos of me and my father together,' he told her. 'Randall didn't spend a lot of time with me. Anyone who says those were simpler times doesn't know how hard he worked.'

'I'm a little surprised that you're a lawyer now and not CEO of Stanhope Industries,' Serena said.

'I saw the writing on the wall,' Peter replied. 'The big money in steel was long gone and never coming back. Too much foreign competition. When Randall died, I figured I would let someone else run the company into the ground. Which they did.'

'So you decided to become a lawyer?'

'Yes. Randall's probably turning in his grave. He hated lawyers. To me, though, litigation is the ultimate competition.' He added, 'Would you like some coffee?'

'Sure.'

Peter retreated to his desk to phone his secretary.

This meeting was only the second time that Serena had met Peter Stanhope in person. Peter didn't hide his money. His suit was cut out of a charcoal fabric that glistened in the light. His shoes were like mirrors. He wore an amber-colored silk tie with a matching pocket square, a Tiffany watch, and silver cufflinks engraved with his initials. In her heels, Serena was about two inches taller than Peter. He was handsome, though, with a stocky, muscular frame. He had a strong chin and sunburnt nose, and freckles dotted his face. He wore glasses that made two tiny copper circles around his eyes. His thinning silver hair was swept straight back. Like Stride, he was in his late forties.

Serena always found that intelligence was in the eyes, and Peter's eyes were smart. He carried himself with polish and confidence, like someone at ease in his own skin. Even so, you couldn't have so much wealth, or so much success, and not have arrogance ooze through in your demeanor. Every now and then, Peter smirked, and Serena saw the cocky boy peek out from his soul. She knew that lawyers were experts at wearing masks, and she wondered who the real Peter was, the savvy professional or the arrogant teenager. Probably both.

'Have you thought about the job?' he asked as he sat down again.

'I have, and I'm still thinking. I hope that's OK.'

'Of course. Take all the time you need, but not a minute more. I want you with me. You could do great work here. Plus, the compensation would be a lot more than you ever made as a detective or a PI.'

'That wouldn't be hard,' she said wryly.

'You told me you needed to talk to me. I assume you have some questions?'

'I do, but not about the job.'

'Oh?'

'I wonder if you remember a girl named Tish Verdure,' Serena said.

Peter rocked back in his chair and pursed his lips. 'Tish Verdure. I'm pretty sure there was a girl in my high school named Tish.'

'There was.'

'Well, what about her?'

'She's back in town. She's writing a book about the murder of Laura Starr.'

Peter's face darkened. 'I take it you've been hearing stories about my teenage years.'

'That's right.'

'Stories that make you wonder if you want to work for a man like me.'

'Yes, that's true,' Serena admitted.

Peter let his chair fall forward, and he leaned across the table. 'Well, I appreciate your candor, and I'll try to be candid too. First of all, let's get one thing clear. I'm not going to apologize for who I am or who I was. I was an asshole in school, and a lot of people will tell you I still am. That probably includes many of the women I've dated.'

'That's pretty much what I heard.'

Peter shrugged. 'I'm not surprised, but I don't care what anyone else thinks. Look, Randall had more money than God back then, and I thought it gave me a free pass to rule the world. I was smart, but I didn't do squat. I slept with every girl I could. I was an arrogant son of a bitch.'

'Are you trying to win points for honesty?'

'Not at all. I told you, no apologies. This is me.'

'You know that my partner is Jonathan Stride,' Serena said.

'Of course. I didn't know Lieutenant Stride well back in school, and I don't know him very well now. But the things I remember probably don't give him a very high opinion of me.'

'You could say that.'

'OK, but here's where I draw the line. I did not kill Laura Starr.'

'Who did?'

'The police thought it was a vagrant.'

'Is that what you thought?'

84

'All I know is that it wasn't me.'

'She was killed with your baseball bat.'

'That doesn't prove a thing. The bat was lying in a field for anyone to pick up.'

Peter's secretary knocked on the door and came in bearing a small silver coffee urn and two china cups. She poured out and left without saying a word. Serena tasted the coffee and recognized the dark flavor of Starbuck's.

'So I take it that this writer, Tish, has her sights set on me,' Peter said. 'She wants to nail me for the murder.'

'You're certainly on her list.'

'You know, bad publicity doesn't bother me. I get my share all the time. I just hate to see old gossip used against me.'

'I'm not sure you can pass it off as gossip,' Serena said. 'Stride tells me that you were a suspect. Some people think that Ray Wallace deliberately steered the investigation away from you.'

'Ray was a problematic figure as a cop. We both know that.'

'A few years later, he was forced to resign as chief of police because of a bribery scheme involving Stanhope Industries,' Serena pointed out.

'That was long after I sold the company.'

'Yes, but Ray's relationship started with Randall. Your father.'

'All I can tell you is that if Ray helped me behind the scenes, there was no need for him to do so. I was innocent.'

Serena frowned. Peter was convincing, but selling stories to a jury was his job. 'Tell me what you remember about Tish Verdure,' she said.

Peter sipped his coffee. 'I remember that she and Laura were thick as thieves. Both of them blonde, very cute.'

'Did you date Tish?' Serena asked.

'Sure, I took a run at her. I took a run at every blonde with great tits back then. I still do. Tish said no. Shut me down cold.'

'You?'

Peter grinned. Serena saw the cocky boy flash in his eyes. 'Amazing, huh? Well, Tish was a weird girl. Laura was pretty much her only friend. No dad, and then her mother got shot. Tough life.'

Serena held up her hand. 'Wait a minute. Tish's mother was shot?'

'That's right.'

'What happened?' she asked.

Peter pursed his lips. 'She was a teller at a downtown bank. There was a robbery that went bad. The mother was a hostage who didn't make it out.'

'When was this?'

'Oh, I don't remember. Long before high school. Tish probably wasn't even in her teens when it happened. I only knew about it because kids talked a lot. Everyone wondered why Tish was so closed off, and the rumor mill spread the word about her mother pretty quickly. Like I said, she was a weird girl.'

'But you asked her out anyway.'

'I was a slave to my libido,' Peter said. 'Some things don't change.'

'Who did you go after first? Tish or Laura?'

'Tish, actually.'

'And when she said no, you went after her best friend?'

'Something like that.'

Serena shook her head. 'You're right, Peter. You were an asshole back then.'

'I never said I wasn't.'

'Did it bother you when Tish turned you down?'

'Not really.'

'I don't imagine too many girls turned you down.'

'That's why it didn't bother me,' Peter said, with a little smile.

'I heard Tish and Laura had a big fight that spring. Could they have been arguing about you?'

'About me? I can't imagine why.'

'Except you were dating Laura by then, right?'

Peter stared at Serena. He took another drink of coffee. 'Right.'

'So maybe Tish didn't like Laura hanging out with you.'

'If she did, I never heard about it.'

'How did you meet Laura?'

'We were in Miss Mathisen's geometry class together in our junior year. So was Tish.'

'Tish told us that Laura broke up with you after a couple dates because you wanted sex and she didn't.'

'Is that what she said? Well, she's wrong, but it was a long time ago.'

'Is there any reason Laura would have wanted to keep your relationship a secret?'

'I have no idea, but you were a teenage girl once. Isn't that the kind of thing that teenage girls do?'

'Sometimes.'

Serena wanted to ask more about the night Laura was killed, but she knew she had pushed Peter as far as she could. The rest was in Jonny's hands. He was the cop, not her. Not anymore.

'I appreciate your letting me ask you all these questions,' she told him. 'I'm still a detective at heart, I guess.'

'That's why I want to hire you.'

'I know. I'll get back to you very soon about the job.'

'I may be in touch even sooner than that,' Peter said.

'Oh?'

'I have another freelance job for you.'

'What's that?' Serena asked.

'Well, if Tish pursues this book, it could start causing me problems in the media. They'll drag up old lies again. I need your help.'

'What can I do?'

'You can find out who killed Laura,' Peter told her. 'Or barring that, you can prove it wasn't me.'

Eight

Tish was late.

Stride sat on a stone bench amid the rose gardens of Leif Erickson Park. He ate a roast beef sandwich and inhaled the floral aroma of thousands of red, yellow, and white roses surrounding him. Nearby, a white gazebo overlooked the lake, on a bluff adjacent to the boardwalk that followed the cliff's edge and wound down along the shore to Canal Park. At lunchtime, with a huge blue sky overhead, the park was crowded with people picnicking in the grass and admiring the flowers.

He saw Tish park on the opposite side of London Road and get out of a navy blue Honda Civic. She waited while a package delivery truck passed her and then crossed the street to the park. She waved at Stride and followed the cobblestone path through the garden to join him.

'Hi,' she said breathlessly, sitting down. She had no lunch with her, but she carried a white takeaway cup of coffee. She wore sunglasses, and she was dressed in a white Georgia T-shirt and gray sweatpants. She wore Nikes with no socks.

'Hello, Tish.'

'Sorry I'm so late. I was at the city engineer's office, and I had to wait for their copy machine.'

'What did you need there?' Stride asked.

'Aerial photos of the city from the late nineteen seventies.'

'For the book?'

Tish nodded. 'I wanted to see exactly what the terrain looked like back then.'

'The Duluth paper ran a story about you and your book today,' Stride said.

'Yes, I thought it might flush out more people who remember what happened back then. There aren't too many still around.'

'A heads up would have been nice,' Stride said. 'I'm getting calls.'

'I'm sorry. You're right. I didn't think about that.'

Stride took another bite of his sandwich and didn't reply. He saw the delivery truck that had passed Tish return down London Road in the opposite direction and pull into a no-parking zone across from them.

'I heard about the break-in at your condo,' Stride said.

'The cops who showed up thought it was just kids.'

'Probably,' Stride told her. 'They may have seen you move in and figured they could make a quick score. Those lakefront condos usually go to people with money.'

Tish shrugged. 'No such luck. I'm doing a spread on Duluth for a Swedish magazine, and the condo managers let me use an unsold unit for the summer. That's one of the perks of being a travel writer.'

'We're still looking into the break-in, but it sounds like nothing was taken.'

'Right. My laptop was in my car,' Tish said. She added, 'I don't think it was kids, though.'

'No?'

'I think someone's trying to scare me off.'

'Because of your book?'

'Yes. I suppose you think that's paranoid.'

'A little,' Stride admitted. 'It's been thirty years, Tish.'

She didn't answer.

'Tell me about the life of a travel writer,' he said, changing the subject. 'It sounds glamorous.'

'Not as much as you might think. Sometimes I feel permanently homeless. Whenever I fall in love with a place, I leave.'

'What was your favorite place?'

Tish blew on her coffee and then took a sip. 'Tibet. I love the mountains, but I couldn't live there.'

'Why not?'

'Heights,' Tish said. 'I hate heights. I always have. I had to cross this rope bridge over a canyon, and I swear they had to sedate me and pull me across on my ass with my eyes closed.'

Stride laughed.

'What about you?' Tish asked. 'What are you afraid of?'

'Me? I don't know.'

'Come on, there must be something,' Tish said. 'Or do tough guys like you never get scared?'

'I'm afraid of a lot of things.'

'Like what?'

'Loss.'

She looked at him. 'You mean like losing Cindy?'

'I mean like losing anything. I hate endings, goodbyes, funerals, everything like that. The end of books. The end of movies. The end of vacations. I like it when things keep going, but they never do.'

'How about you and Serena?' Tish asked.

'What about us?'

'Will the two of you keep going?'

Stride frowned. 'Why do you care? Do you need to flesh out our characters in your book?'

'No, it's not that. I think a lot about you and Cindy, so I wondered if Serena made you happy.'

'She does.' He was curt.

'I'm sorry, is that too personal?'

He shrugged. 'I'm a Minnesotan. We talk about the weather and the Twins, Tish. That's as personal as I get.'

'Oh, I forgot,' Tish said. She added, 'Beautiful day.'

'Yeah.'

'How about those Twins?'

'This could be their year.'

'You're right, this is much better,' Tish said, smiling.

Stride winked and finished his sandwich. He crumpled the wrapper into a ball, got up, and deposited it in a wastebasket twenty yards away. He returned and sat down next to Tish again.

'Are you expecting a package?' he asked her.

'What?'

He nodded at the delivery truck parked illegally fifty yards away.

'The driver in that van is watching you. He was following your car when you arrived.'

Tish stared. A face appeared in the window of the truck and then disappeared. The man had wraparound sunglasses and a shaved head.

'Can't you do something?' she asked.

'I can write him a parking ticket.'

Tish put down her coffee cup and stripped off her sunglasses. Her face was tense.

'Do you recognize him?' Stride asked.

'I don't think so.'

'He knows we've spotted him.'

The truck engine started like the growl of a tiger. The delivery truck jerked away from the curb and continued north on London Road. Tish watched it until the van disappeared behind a row of brick buildings.

'Do you still think I'm paranoid?' she asked.

Stride wasn't sure. 'Have you noticed the truck before?'.

'Now that I think about it, I may have seen it a couple times in the last few days.'

'It may be nothing, but I'll do a check with the delivery company,' he said.

'Thanks.'

'I haven't been ignoring you these past couple weeks,' he added. 'I didn't want to call until I had something more to tell you.'

'Do you have results back on the DNA tests?'

Stride nodded. 'I got them from the lab this morning.'

'And?'

He shook his head. 'I'm sorry. There was no match. We collected DNA from the flap of the envelope on the stalker letter that was sent to Laura, and we were able to get a good sample. When we ran it against the state and FBI databases, we came up empty. Whoever he is or was, he's not in our files.'

'Damn.'

'It was a long shot.'

'Let me ask you this,' Tish said. 'Would Peter Stanhope's DNA be included in a database somewhere?'

'I doubt it.'

'So it could be his DNA, and we just don't know it.'

'Sure.'

'Can't we get a court to compel him to provide a sample of DNA?' Tish asked.

'Not without probable cause,' Stride said. 'We would need to have something specific to tie him to the murder.'

'Laura was killed with his bat,' she protested.

'That might get us a DNA sample if the crime happened last week and if we still had the bat. After thirty years, no judge would grant a motion with what we have today.'

'You mean, because Peter Stanhope has more money than God.'

'Frankly, yes. I'm sorry, Tish, but there are certain realities to face here.'

Tish watched the calm blue water on the lake. A light breeze rippled through her hair. 'I can't believe there's nothing we can do. There has to be a way to get a DNA sample from Peter.'

'There's something else,' Stride said. 'More bad news.'

'What?'

'This can't go in the book.'

'OK, what is it?'

'We have additional genetic material from the crime scene. There was semen found near the body. The police kept that fact secret.'

'You still have the sample? It's still intact?'

Stride nodded. 'I ran the DNA from the semen. It's not the first time I've done that, but we add thousands of people to those databases every year. It didn't make any difference. There was no match.'

'Can you compare the semen to the DNA from the stalker note?' Tish asked.

'That's the bad news.'

'What do you mean?'

'I did compare the two samples. The DNA on the stalker note doesn't match the semen where Laura's body was found.'

'That's not good,' Tish agreed, frowning.

'No. Even if we could get a match to the stalker's DNA, it means we've got *someone else* at the murder scene. The county attorney wouldn't consider bringing charges against anyone unless we could identify the person who left that semen behind.'

'Do you have Dada's DNA?'

'No.'

'So it could have been him. We know he was in the woods that night. He could have seen whoever killed Laura.'

'More likely, he killed her himself,' Stride reminded her. 'Remember, Dada's prints were on the bat. Besides, it's all speculation. We don't know who Dada was or where he went. After thirty years, he's probably dead now. Life expectancy for vagrants like him isn't long.'

'Do you remember anything that might help us track him down?'

'You know as much as I do. He was a Rasta. Dreadlocks, tam, the whole works. He probably wouldn't look anything like that today.'

'He wasn't old, though, was he?' she asked.

'No. Early twenties, maybe.'

'So he could still be alive.'

'You'd stand a better chance of finding Amelia Earhart.' Stride heard the cough of an engine and glanced at the street. 'He's back,' he said.

'Who?'

'The delivery driver.'

The same truck they had spotted earlier parked on the opposite side of London Road, near Tish's Civic. This time, the driver's door opened, and a man climbed down. He crossed the street and headed straight for them. He was tall and extremely thin, with pencil legs. He wore the delivery company's uniform – short-sleeved button-down shirt, shorts, and white tennis shoes.

'Do you recognize him?' Stride asked.

Tish bit her lip. 'No.'

As he came closer, Stride saw signs of age and dissipation in the driver. He looked like a heavy drinker. He was in his forties, but his skin was mottled across his bald scalp, and blood vessels had popped in his cheeks and nose, leaving a rosy web. When he pulled off his sunglasses, his pale blue eyes were rimmed in red. His blond eyebrows were trimmed short. He had a long, narrow face.

'Tish?' the driver said, ignoring Stride. 'Is that you?'

She hesitated. 'Yes, it's me.'

'I heard you were back in town.'

'Have we met?' she asked.

93

'It's me. Finn Mathisen. I know it's been a long time. I don't look like I did back then, but who does, huh? Remember, I had big curly hair?'

'Oh, Finn, sure, I'm sorry,' Tish said. She sounded as if she really did know who he was now. 'How are you?'

'I'm getting by. I told Rikke you were in town, and she said I was crazy. But here you are.'

'Yes, here I am,' Tish said.

'I heard about the book you're doing.'

'That's right.'

'I was wondering if we could have lunch or dinner sometime. You know, talk about Laura and the old days. I'd really like that.'

Tish hesitated. 'Sure, why not.'

'Do you have a cell phone number or something?'

'Of course.'

'Hang on,' Finn said. He pulled a pen out of his pocket and clicked it open. Stride saw him write TISH on the back of his hand. 'Shoot.'

She rattled off her number, and Finn scribbled it on his skin.

'I'll call you,' he said.

'OK.'

'You look really good, Tish.'

'Thanks.'

Finn retreated to his truck without saying anything to Stride. He drove away, waving to Tish through the open window as he did. Tish gave a half-wave in return.

'Old friend?' Stride asked.

'Laura's friend more than mine.'

'He looks like he's had a hard life.'

'Yeah, it wasn't very good back then, either. His older sister, Rikke, was our math teacher. She asked Laura if she'd be willing to tutor him. Finn was into drugs in a big way. Very screwed up. Their parents were both dead.'

Stride nodded. 'I remember Rikke Mathisen. She was one of those Nordic blonde teachers, very attractive. The high school boys all had crushes on her.'

'I didn't really like her, but Laura did,' Tish said. 'I was pretty independent, but Laura still wanted a surrogate mother. I thought Rikke was being nice to Laura just to get help for Finn, and that bothered me.'

'Why?'

'You saw him. Finn had big problems. Laura wanted to rescue everyone, but she was pretty naïve. I told her not to spend so much time with him.'

'Did you tell her the same thing about Peter Stanhope?' Stride asked.

'Yes, I did.'

'Except she didn't listen.'

Tish shook her head. 'She did. Laura dumped Peter. He's lying about the two of them dating secretly.'

'We have no way to prove that.'

'We can prove it with Peter's DNA,' Tish insisted. 'If you had that, you could prove that he was stalking Laura by matching it to the note.'

Stride didn't like what he saw in her face. 'Let me give you some advice, Tish. As a cop. If you want to write a book, then write a book, but if you try to put yourself in the middle of a police investigation, you could wind up in a lot of trouble. So don't do anything stupid.'

Nine

Stride checked his voicemail on the drive back to City Hall and found an urgent message waiting for him from the new county attorney for St Louis County. He parked in his usual spot behind the building, but rather than head directly to his office in City Hall, he headed for the courthouse instead and took the elevator to the fifth floor. The glass doors to the county attorney's office were immediately on the right as he exited the elevator.

He asked the receptionist to tell Pat Burns that he was outside.

Pat was new to the job. The previous county attorney, Dan Erickson, had resigned in the wake of a scandal during the winter. Stride and Dan had been enemies for years, and he was pleased to see him gone. The county board had taken several months to name a replacement but had finally turned to Pat Burns, who was the managing partner in the Duluth office of a large Twin Cities corporate law firm. She practiced in white collar crime and had spent several years in the US Attorney's office in Chicago before moving to Minnesota. She was tough and smart.

Stride wondered why a lawyer earning a partner's income in a corporate law firm would give up hundreds of thousands of dollars a year to prosecute rapists and child pornographers, but he knew the answer boiled down to one word. Politics. Like everyone else whose backside graced a county attorney's chair, she had her eyes on higher office. That didn't bother Stride, but it meant that every prosecutorial decision was viewed through the lens of fundraising and vote-getting.

He waited twenty minutes before Pat's door opened. She was reading a legal-sized file folder and looked up at him over half-glasses. 'Hello, Lieutenant, come on in.'

He had been here once before on a courtesy call two weeks earlier. At that point, the office still looked as it did when Dan Erickson was the county attorney. Since then, the masculine touch had been erased. Dan's heavy furniture was gone. Pat preferred glass and Danish maple. The paint was fresh and brightened the room with a peach color. The old carpet had been ripped out and replaced with a light frieze. The whole room smelled of renovation, like a new house.

'Very nice,' he said.

'Thanks. I kept Dan's bottle of Bombay, if that's what you're into. Me, I prefer Chardonnay.'

'Nothing for me.'

'Do you mind if I indulge?'

'Not at all.'

'I practiced in London for two years after law school. I started out with the European habit of wine over lunch, and I've never been able to break it.'

She put the file folder down on her desk and took off her reading glasses. She opened a stainless refrigerator, pulled out an open bottle, and poured white wine into a small bell-shaped glass. She took a sip and then waved him toward a desert-colored microfiber sofa on the wall. Above the sofa, on a wooden shelf, was a modern steel sculpture on a cinder block base.

He was wearing jeans, a sport coat, and black boots, and felt underdressed. Pat wore a tailored cream-colored pants suit with a low-cut jacket and a white shell. A necklace of interlaced metallic squares dangled above the faint line of her cleavage. Her brown hair was short and coiffed, like an ocean wave breaking over her forehead. She was tall and slim, and Stride knew from her bio that she had turned forty years old in January.

Pat sat on the opposite end of the sofa and crossed her legs. She balanced her wine glass on her knee and inclined her head toward the file folder on her desk. 'The widow of that golfer who got killed by lightning last month is suing the county,' she told him.

'How is that our fault?' Stride asked.

'It's not, but a new theory of legal liability is born every day.'

'Golfers are walking lightning rods,' Stride said. 'We fry one or two every summer that way.'

'Exactly. He was on a county golf course, and the wife's attorney says we had insufficient procedures in place to provide shelter from an inevitable and predictable threat.'

'How about a caution sign with a picture of Ben Franklin?' Stride asked.

'Don't give them any ideas,' Pat replied, smiling. She added, 'Anyway, let's move on to police matters. Is Maggie making progress on the peeper case?'

'Not so far. He hasn't struck again since the incident involving the disabled girl in Gary a couple weeks ago. We're keeping an unmarked vehicle near her house for several hours each night in case he comes back.'

'Is that likely?'

'The father thinks he peeped her once before. He may have a special interest in this girl.'

'Keep me posted on this case,' Pat told him. 'Families don't get too upset when drug dealers kill each other, but they feel vulnerable when perverts are peering in the window at their daughters.'

'Understood.'

'I'd like to set up a monthly status meeting with you,' Pat added, 'so we can go over outstanding cases. OK?'

'Of course. I'll set it up with your assistant.'

'I'm not trying to tread on your turf, but I like to know what's in the pipeline. I don't want to be surprised by headlines or get sand-bagged by reporters.'

'I understand,' Stride said. 'If anything happens, either K-2 or I will call you directly to keep you in the loop.'

K-2 was the departmental nickname for Deputy Chief Kyle Kinnick.

'I appreciate it,' Pat said. She added, 'Peter Stanhope called me this morning.'

'Oh?'

'He's concerned about this reporter, Tish Verdure, and the book she's writing about an unsolved murder back in the nineteen seventies. There was an article in today's paper.'

'That's right,' Stride said.

'This is the kind of thing I need to know about *in advance*, Lieutenant.' She didn't snap at him, but her voice was cool and direct. 'Particularly if someone like Peter Stanhope is involved. I don't like to be blindsided when a major campaign contributor calls me to talk about a murder investigation, and I don't know anything about it.'

Stride nodded. 'You're right. I apologize. I should have called you when I first met Tish and heard about her project. Candidly, I didn't think that—'

Pat cut him off with a wave of her hand. 'Never mind. I don't want explanations or excuses. It's done. I just want us to be clear for the future, OK?'

'Absolutely.'

'Now you can tell me about this case. I gather you knew the victim?'

'She was my wife's sister.'

'Oh, I see. I'm sorry. Tell me what happened.'

Stride sketched out the facts of the case and retraced the investigation for her. He also told her what he knew about Tish's book and about the DNA tests he had run in the past several weeks.

Pat sipped her wine and listened carefully to the story. 'Peter was asking if we had any plans to reopen an active investigation of this case.'

'I don't think we have enough evidence to do so,' Stride said. 'So far, nothing changes the original theory of the crime, which is that Laura was killed by a vagrant. Tish hasn't come up with anything to disprove or discredit that idea.'

'But you're running tests on physical evidence.'

Stride nodded. 'That's true. If we had made a DNA match and found out who was stalking Laura, or whose semen was near her body, that certainly would have changed things. We'd have new questions to ask and potentially someone with new information.'

'Except from what you say, one of the key pieces of physical evidence is missing,' Pat said. 'Namely, the murder weapon. We also don't have any idea how to find this vagrant after thirty years, or whether he's even still alive. I don't know how we would go about bringing a case against anyone under those circumstances.'

'Agreed,' Stride said. 'We've got a lot of suspects and a lot of reasonable doubt.'

'That means we need to be extremely careful about allowing speculation to make its way into the media. I don't want anyone tried in the press when we have no intention of bringing charges in court.'

'You mean Peter Stanhope,' Stride said.

'I mean anyone.' Pat paused. 'Look, Lieutenant, I'm a practical person. You and I both know that money talks. If I could prove Peter Stanhope was guilty of something, would I throw the book at him? Absolutely. Do I want you to avoid spreading rumors about him if we can't prove he's guilty of anything? Absolutely. I'd say that about any suspect, but yes, I'm going to be extra careful when it comes to someone who is a friend and supporter. That's life.'

'I'm well aware of that.'

'I have no idea what Peter Stanhope was like as a teenager or a young man. All I can tell you is that my firm has been on the other side of his in litigation, and my partners spoke highly of his professionalism.'

'Understood.'

'So let's set some ground rules. First, be extremely cautious with what you tell Tish Verdure. We don't know her. She's a journalist and potentially a loose cannon. The last thing we need is her turning this into another Martha Moxley case, all right?'

'Fair enough.' He didn't mention that he had just come from a meeting with Tish and that he had already shared something with her that he probably shouldn't. The existence of semen near Laura's body.

Pat held up two fingers. 'Second, we both know that this case could blow up in our faces no matter what we do. If Tish gets someone in the New York media to take an interest, we're going to get hounded with queries. This could wind up on *20/20* or *Cold Case*. National press.'

'What do you suggest?' Stride asked.

'I suggest you make sure you know this case inside and out. OK? Go back over everything. Make sure you're able to answer any question that comes up. Revisit the entire investigation, but be discreet.'

Stride hesitated.

'What is it?' Pat asked.

'I have some concerns that the original investigation may have been compromised.'

Pat nodded. 'You mean Ray Wallace.'

'Yes.'

'Ray was before my time, but I've heard stories. He was a big problem.'

'Ray was a good cop, but he crossed the line,' Stride said. 'He may have leaped too quickly to a theory of the crime that exonerated Peter Stanhope. He may have made the murder weapon and the original stalker letter disappear.'

'Well, if Ray screwed the pooch, we should know about it before Tish or someone else gets there ahead of us.'

'Of course.'

'One last thing,' Pat said.

'Yes?'

'At some point, I may pull the plug. If all we're doing is chasing our tail, and it's obvious we're never going to have enough evidence to put someone on trial, then I'm going to shut this down. I'm sorry, I know this girl meant something to you and your late wife. But if we don't find anything new, then you and Tish are both going to have to live with the idea that the case will always be unsolved.'

Who Killed Laura Starr?

By Tish Verdure

5 July 1977

The three of us were in our living room on Tuesday afternoon. It was me, my dad, and Jonny. The house had never felt so small. I hadn't slept at all, and the walls felt like they were closing in, and the ceiling was coming down on top of me. I couldn't breathe. The room was baking hot and so sticky that you broke into a sweat without doing anything at all. We all sat there, not saying a word, watching the dusty stream of sunlight through the front window. Jonny held my hand, and I buried my head in his shoulder. Tears of anger and regret streamed down my dad's face. His face was beet red. He had blamed Laura for living when my mom died, and now he blamed her for dying like she did. He had lost another one.

My dad. He was never a big man, and year by year he seems to shrink. His dark hair, which was so full and thick when I was a little girl, is mostly gone now. His clothes don't fit, but he won't let me buy new ones, so his white dress shirts balloon at his shoulders. He sits in his recliner in the evenings and reads his leather Bible by the dim light. No ambition anymore. Just crushed dreams and a tug of war with God. I remember how he used to come home from Wahl's in his sharp pinstripe suits, like a man on top of the world, a man going places. He was going to run that department store someday. That's what he told Mom. Now other men have climbed over his shoulders, and Dad writes newspaper ads for white sales. At fifty, he looks sixty. You just don't realize how one person depends on another, and when

102

they're not there, it's like going off a bridge, and you're falling and falling.

I went to Jonny's place. After. In the middle of the night. He answered the door, and I looked a sight, crying, dotted with blood. He called the police, because I couldn't do it. They came and took us back there, and I led them through the woods to the body, but I couldn't go out to the beach. I couldn't see it again. Even the big, tough cops couldn't believe what had been done to her. Things like that don't happen. Not here in Duluth.

They asked me a lot of questions in a police car parked back in the weeds and had me repeat over and over what I did and what I saw. I think they could have done that for hours, but Jonny stood up to them and insisted that they take me home. I needed to tell my dad. I needed to stand under the shower and wash away the blood. They took pictures of me first, though, flashbulbs popping in my face out there in the woods. They scraped blood from my skin. I realized that they thought maybe I had done this myself. That I had killed her. I didn't understand how anyone could think that. I told them I was innocent. I'm not sure they believed me.

'I'm so sorry, Dad,' I murmured.

I felt a need to take this on myself, for his sake. I never should have let her go.

Dad didn't look at me. 'God's punishment is a terrible thing.'

'You know I don't want to hear that.'

'I told Laura she was sinning,' he said.

I wanted to scream at him, but I didn't. I bit my tongue. This was how he dealt with grief, how he explained awful, random things. He had become so hard and unbending over the years. As if standing straight made any difference at all when you were in the path of a tornado. As if lightning somehow distinguished between good and evil.

Dad bowed his head and started crying again. I sighed and looked up into Jonny's dark eyes. He kissed my head. We had both grown older overnight, in a lot of ways.

I heard a knock on the front door. 'I'll get it,' I said.

The man on the doorstep had bushy red hair and a matching mustache. He wore oversized wire-rimmed glasses over pale blue eyes.

I figured he was in his mid-thirties. He was medium-height, but heavy and strong, with fingers like thick pork sausages. He wore a plaid sport coat and a white dress shirt that bulged out over his belt. No tie. Open collar and a fuzz of red chest hair. He wore flared denims and muddy dress shoes. I saw splotchy stains on his shoes. I wondered if it was blood.

'I'm Detective Inspector Ray Wallace,' he told me. 'Duluth Police.'

'Come in,' I said.

Wallace walked with a limp. He followed me into the living room, and I sat down next to Jonny again. Wallace introduced himself to my dad, who didn't get out of his recliner. Wallace's eyes shot around the room as he pulled out a dining-room chair and sat down. You just know when somebody is smart, and Wallace was smart.

'I'm very sorry for your loss, Mr Starr,' Wallace said.

My dad used a handkerchief to blow his nose and then folded and replaced it in his pocket. He laid his hands on his knees and didn't say anything.

'I'm trying to find out exactly what happened to her, sir,' Wallace continued.

Dad still didn't say a word. He stared blankly into the dust.

'I didn't do it,' I blurted out, filling the silence.

To a cop, that must be like lighting up a big sign that says, I did it! I did it!

Wallace smiled with his lips, not his teeth. His mustache wriggled like a red worm. 'No one is saying you did, young lady.' He looked at Jonny. 'And who's this?'

'I'm Jon Stride. I'm Cindy's boyfriend.'

'Nice to meet you, Jon. Why don't you head on home now, OK?'

Jonny pushed himself off the sofa and shook Wallace's hand. There was something different about him right then, something I'd never seen before, something mature and attractive. I could see them sizing each other up like men do. 'If Cindy says she didn't do it, you can take that to the bank. And I'm staying. I was there last night.'

Wallace got a little glint in his eyes. 'Suit yourself.'

Jonny sat back down.

I said, 'It's just that they were taking pictures, and I had blood on me because I stepped in it, and I picked up the bat because I thought I heard someone in the woods.'

'You picked up the bat?' Wallace asked.

'Yes.'

'So we'll find your fingerprints on it?'

Oh, hell. 'Yes, I guess so.'

'OK, that's good to know. It's Cindy, right?'

'Yes.'

'Did you get along with your sister, Cindy?'

'Yes, of course I did.'

'Because sisters have been known to fight from time to time.'

'Sure, sometimes, but never anything serious.'

My dad stirred from his gloom and interrupted. 'What's this all about, Wallace? You're out of your head if you're accusing my daughter.'

Wallace adjusted his glasses on his face with his thumb and index finger. 'I'm not accusing anybody, Mr Starr. I'm just gathering information.' He turned back to me. 'Cindy, do you still have the clothes you were wearing last night?'

'Yes.'

'Did you wash them?'

'No, they're in a basket.'

'We're going to need those, OK? I'll have to take them with me.'

'OK, sure.'

'And shoes.'

'I wasn't wearing shoes.'

'Ah.' Wallace pulled a Polaroid snapshot from his shirt pocket. 'This is you last night, right?'

'Right.'

'There's some blood around your hands and on your legs and feet.'

'Yes, I know. I told you, I stepped—'

Wallace shook his head. 'It's OK. Don't worry. The lab people tell me whoever did this would have been drenched in blood. I mean drenched. Head to toe. Not a little around the edges.' He looked at William Starr. 'I'm sorry, sir, I don't mean to be so graphic. What I'm saying is that we already concluded that it was very unlikely that

105

Cindy was involved. But I like to see people's faces before I draw my own conclusions.'

'If you want to blame anyone, blame me,' Dad announced.

Wallace shifted, and the wooden chair squealed. He looked curious. 'What do you mean, sir?'

'I mean, first it was my wife and now my daughter. They're both dead. It doesn't matter who held the bat. It was God who killed her.'

'I don't believe God kills eighteen-year-old girls,' Wallace said.

'You're wrong. He does it all the time. Every day. Sinners get punished.'

'I see.' Wallace's voice became flat and cold. 'Mr Starr, your neighbors overheard you shouting at Laura the night before she was killed.'

I saw Dad's fingers tighten on the Bible in his lap.

'Yes, we argued sometimes.'

'What was the fight about?'

'I wanted her to stay on God's path.'

'But she didn't?' Wallace asked.

'Not always.'

'In what way?'

'That's between me and Laura,' Dad snapped. 'How can you ask me that when God is deciding the fate of her soul right now?'

Wallace didn't like that answer.

'Mr Starr, did you know Laura wasn't home last night?'

'Yes. I went to her room around ten o'clock, and she wasn't there.'

'What did you do?'

'Nothing. I went to bed.'

'Did you know where Laura had gone?'

'No.'

'Did you stay up to wait for her?'

'Yes, but I fell asleep.'

'Were you home all night?'

'Of course, I just told you that.'

'Did you talk to anyone?'

'No.'

Wallace nodded. 'Mr Starr, did you ever hit your daughter?'

Dad bolted out of his chair, trembling. His white shirt fluttered. I hadn't seen him move so quickly in years. 'How dare you!'

Wallace didn't shrink. 'You heard the question, sir.'

'Never,' my dad insisted.

'Sometimes fights get out of hand.'

'I never touched her.'

Wallace eyed me. It was as if, without saying it flat out, he wanted me to tell him yes or no. Pass the secret silently between us. He wanted to know if it was true, if Dad had ever struck Laura. Or me. I met his gaze.

'My father wouldn't do that,' I said.

Wallace nodded. That was enough for now. I told myself that I was right, because I knew my father had never lifted a hand against me, and I didn't believe he had ever done so to Laura. Even so, I couldn't get Laura's voice out of my head.

What if Dad were abusing me? Could you kill him?

I said nothing about that.

Wallace kept his attention on me. 'Cindy, you've gone over with my men what happened last night. I'm going to ask you to repeat some of it for me.'

'Sure,' I said.

'I know you've been through hell, and I know how hard this is for you.'

'Thank you.'

'Please tell me again exactly what you did last night and everything that happened right up until the time when the police responded to the call. Don't leave anything out.'

So I told him.

Well, I told him some of it. There were things I left out. About me and Jonny that night. And other things, too. Jonny chimed in along the way, about Peter and the baseball game, about the storm, and Peter's bat lying in the field. I could see Wallace's mind working furiously whenever Peter Stanhope's name came up, like part of him was with us, and part of him was somewhere else. I wasn't stupid. We were practically accusing the son of one of the richest men in the city of murder. A cop hears that, and he looks for a place to run. Wallace found that place right away. A black man in the woods.

'So you and Laura thought someone was watching you,' he said when we were done.

107

Nothing about the stalker note. Nothing about Laura and Peter dating and then breaking up because Peter was demanding sex. Nothing about the bat, or the threats against Laura he made during the game.

'Yes.'

'It couldn't have been Peter Stanhope, though, right? Because he was still in the baseball field with Jon here when you heard somebody.'

Jonny and I looked at each other. We both nodded.

'You're sure it was marijuana you smelled?'

I glanced at my dad. 'I've never used it, but I know what it smells like.'

'Did you see this black guy that Jon talked about?'

'I didn't see anyone.'

Wallace looked at Jonny. 'You must have seen this guy, this vagrant, in almost the same place where the girls were. Right?'

'Within a hundred yards or so,' Jonny said.

'OK, tell me more about this guy with the dreadlocks.'

'They call him Dada.'

Wallace wet his lips with his tongue. 'Whoa, whoa here, you know who this guy is? You've seen him before?'

Jonny nodded. 'He hangs out by the tracks in the harbor. Where the trains head south.'

'What were you doing down in that area?'

'It's somewhere to go,' Jonny said.

I knew why he went there. It was his private spot, his getaway, his place to think. Jonny told me he liked to hike down there, among the wanderers who came and went, eluding the police and the railway security. In his head, Jonny felt like a traveler too. Homeless.

'OK, so who is this guy?'

'I first saw him a month ago. He was in the woods down near Raleigh Street, where it heads out across the Arrowhead Bridge. The others are scared of him, because he's so big. They think he's some kind of ghost.'

Wallace snorted. 'Ghost.'

'Most of the guys down there are a little crazy. They see someone like Dada, it's easy to believe almost anything.'

'Is he violent?'

'I don't know. I've only seen him a couple times.'

'Can you show me where you saw him?'

Jonny nodded. 'Yeah, I think so. He moves around, though. They all do.'

'If he killed a girl, he probably took the first train south,' Wallace said. 'My guess is he's long gone.'

He stood up. His right leg, the one that limped, looked stiff. He rubbed his knee, and I saw him grimace in pain.

'I think that's all for now,' he said. Then he looked at Jonny. 'I could use your help, Jon. Do you have time to come with me?'

Jonny looked at me, and I nodded.

'Sure.'

Wallace cinched up his slacks over his stomach. I was disappointed. He was leaping at the idea that some stranger did this, even though Laura had been receiving threats for months. Even though Peter Stanhope's bat killed her. Money talks.

'So you're going after this man Dada?' my dad asked.

He believed it too. Everyone did. No one wanted to think about the alternative, because it was too complicated. Too scary.

'Nope,' Wallace said. 'I mean, we will, but not yet.'

I stared at him, surprised. But maybe I shouldn't have been. After all, he was smart.

'The first thing I want to do is get the truth out of Peter Stanhope,' Wallace said.

Ten

Ray Wallace.

For years, he had been Stride's best friend. His mentor on the police force. It was as if, in the restless months he spent after losing his father, he had been waiting to find someone who could give him a new direction. Later, Stride discovered that when you put someone on a pedestal, they're almost certain to break when they fall.

He still remembered the first question he had asked Ray when they walked out the door of Cindy's house on 5 July 1977.

'So what's with the limp?'

Ray stopped with his hand on the driver's door of his Camaro. 'Vietnam,' he said. 'I took a bullet in the knee.'

'Oh, man.'

'Yeah, it was a bitch, but you know what? After something like that, it's hard to get bent out of shape about any of the bad stuff that life throws at you.'

Stride would remember that comment for years.

Right up until the moment that Ray shot him.

'I like the way you stood up for your girlfriend, Jon,' Ray said as he started the car.

'Cindy didn't do anything wrong,' Stride told him.

'I think you're right, but she's not giving me the whole story, either.'

'She's not a liar.'

'I didn't say she was, but there's a difference between lying and leaving out part of the truth, you know?'

Stride was silent.

Ray steered with one hand, with his elbow balanced on the Camaro's open window. He sucked cold coffee under his red mustache with the other hand.

'Do you think you'll figure out who killed Laura?' Stride asked.

'I hope so. I'll tell you right now, though, it won't be easy. From what you say, there were a lot of people in the woods. That means a lot of suspects and a lot of crap for a defense lawyer to throw around in court. Unless someone saw something, we might never know the truth. And the fact is that truth is as slippery as ice sometimes.'

Warm summer air blew through the open windows. The car engine roared as Ray stepped on the gas.

'I have to make a stop first,' he said.

He drove along the lakeshore on London Road until he reached the Glensheen Mansion, where he turned into the mammoth estate's main driveway. Stride saw several police vehicles parked inside. Ray shut down the engine and got out, then leaned back through the window of the Camaro.

'Wait here for a couple minutes, OK?'

Stride saw Ray approach another detective who was standing with two or three uniformed officers in the middle of the driveway. The huge red brick mansion with its three distinctive peaks was visible through the trees. Ray lit a cigarette. Stride could hear the murmur of conversation but couldn't make out the words. He guessed what they were talking about. A week earlier, the heiress to the Congdon mining fortune, Elisabeth Congdon, and her live-in nurse had both been found murdered inside the mansion. One suffocated, one bludgeoned. The papers said the motive was robbery, but Stride had already heard rumors floating around the city that the murders might have involved a member of Congdon's family and an estate worth tens of millions of dollars.

Fifteen minutes later, Ray got back in the car.

'Money,' he said. 'It makes the world go around.'

'Did you arrest someone?'

Ray winked and looked pleased. 'Keep an eye on the papers.'

He turned the Camaro around. 'It's not a good year for the filthy rich,' Ray said. 'In May, they found that woman in Indianapolis.

Marjorie Jackson. Shot in the stomach and five million bucks stashed around her house. I mean, can you imagine keeping your money in your vacuum cleaner bag? Now we lose Mrs Congdon. Sometimes you wonder if it's really worth it, having all that dough.'

'Like Randall Stanhope,' Stride said.

Ray nodded. 'Yeah.'

'I think Peter killed Laura,' Stride told him.

'Yeah? Why is that?'

'It was his bat. I think he attacked her in the softball field, and she managed to get away, and he chased her up to the north beach.'

'Say you're right,' Ray said. 'How do you prove it?'

'Maybe someone saw him.'

Ray spilled coffee on his pants, and he dabbed at the stain with his fingers. 'Maybe, but we need to find a witness first, and that witness has to be willing to testify against the son of one of the richest men in the city. Don't kid yourself. Most witnesses won't do that.'

'So you're saying we can't touch him?'

'I'm not saying that at all. But sometimes you know in your head that someone is guilty, and you still can't make a case. Oh, and keep your opinions to yourself, Jon. When we're inside the house, don't speak unless I tell you to speak. Got it?'

'Sure. Why do you want me along anyway?'

Ray smiled. 'Three reasons. First, I want Randall to think Peter is just another witness, not a suspect, and having you there will help me sell that idea. Second, I think Peter is less likely to lie if you're in the room, because he's not sure what you saw.'

'And third?' Stride asked.

'Third, I don't want anyone to think I gave Peter a free ride because of his daddy's money. You're my backup, Jon. Welcome to the police force.'

It was the kind of estate that reeked of old money. Robber baron money. The house and its grounds were surrounded by a fence made of iron spikes, with intermittent stone columns that matched the mottled fieldstones of the mansion. The brooding estate itself was a quarter-mile inside the fir trees, nearly invisible from the road. Ray stopped at the two-story gatehouse and announced himself at the intercom. A minute later, an iron fence swung silently open. He drove through the trees and parked under the mansion's porte cochère.

Stride had never been this close. He glimpsed fountains in the rear. Trimmed globe bushes. A fenced tennis court. The Tudor estate towered above him in sharp peaks, dozens of chimney stacks, and red Duluth stone. Most of the chambered windows were swathed in thick curtains.

'Did Randall build all this?' Stride asked.

Ray shook his head. 'No, this is turn-of-the-century stuff. Before income taxes, know what I mean? For a while in those days, Duluth had more tonnage running through its harbor than New York. We were number one. A handful of families like the Stanhopes and the Congdons got very, very rich.'

'And now?'

'Now they're doing everything they can to hold on to it.'

A maid greeted them at the door and showed them to a library on the other side of the vaulted foyer. Stride felt self-conscious, wearing shorts and a white baseball jersey. His sneakers slipped on the marble. Inside the library, he noticed squared beams stretching the length of the ceiling, wheat-colored wall coverings, and an Oriental rug over-laying a hardwood floor. One wall featured hand-carved bookshelves, lined with old volumes of ship's logs from the 1800s. He saw oil paintings of old men in suits.

'Maybe I should go,' Stride said.

'Don't be intimidated,' Ray replied. 'These people belch, fart, and have bad breath like everyone else.'

They heard laughter from the doorway and smelled cigar smoke.

'Do I? I guess I should never have had the puttanesca for lunch.'

It was Randall Stanhope.

Stride had never seen him in person, only on television and in photographs in the newspaper. He was smaller than he expected, no more than five foot eight. He had trimmed gray hair, boxy black glasses, and like the paintings on the wall he wore a three-piece dark suit. In his left hand, he held a lowball glass filled with ice and an amber-colored drink. In his right hand, he pinched a cigar between his thumb and index finger.

'You're Ray Wallace, is that right? The chief has told me a lot about you. Says you're an up-and-comer in the department. I like that.'

'Thank you, sir.'

'Who's the boy?' Stanhope asked, fixing his blue eyes on Stride.

'This is Jon Stride,' Ray said. 'He was in the park with Peter last night. He's helping me re-create what happened that led to the death of this young girl, and I thought Peter could fill in some details where Jon wasn't around.'

Stanhope smiled. 'You're a baseball player, like my son.'

Stride nodded. 'That's right.'

'Well, good.' Stanhope turned to Ray. 'I hear they're about to pick up Elisabeth Congdon's son-in-law for the murders at Glensheen. Quick work.'

'That's actually not public yet, sir.'

'Oh, I know, but the mayor called me. Nasty business.'

'Yes, sir.'

'But I know that's not why you're here.'

'No, sir. Is Peter in the house? I'd like to ask him a few questions.'

'Absolutely. I was horrified to learn about this girl's murder. Brutal thing. Naturally, Peter will tell you everything he can. This girl was a friend of his, and he's anxious to help you find out who killed her.'

'I appreciate that,' Ray said.

'Tell me something honestly, Detective. You don't for one moment consider my boy to be a suspect, do you?'

'I don't really have enough information to consider anyone a suspect, sir,' Ray replied.

Stanhope smiled. Ray smiled back.

'The sheriff was right in calling you a smart man, Detective.'

'Thank you, sir.'

'I've talked to Peter in detail about this incident myself. I believe he can help you identify the guilty party.'

Ray's eyebrows shot up. 'He saw who killed Laura?'

'Not the crime itself, but when you hear his story, I think you'll feel as I do.'

'I'd like to talk to him.'

'Of course. Peter!'

Peter Stanhope sauntered into the library. He had been waiting outside. His blond hair was washed and combed. He was close-shaven. He wore dress pants, a white shirt, a tie, and a tweed blazer. Stride

114

noticed deep scratches on Peter's broad, freckled face and a misshapen purplish bruise on his forehead. Peter's gait was stilted and stiff. He shoved his hands in his pockets and grimaced in pain.

Behind Peter, the same maid who had answered the front door entered the library silently and handed Randall Stanhope a large cardboard box. She left, and Stanhope passed the box to Ray.

'Peter's clothes from last night,' Stanhope said. 'Unwashed. Plenty of mud and grass stains, but as you will see, no blood, other than, perhaps, a little of his own. I anticipated that would be one of your first concerns, so I made sure we preserved the evidence.'

Ray crooked a finger at Stride, who peered into the box. He took a quick glance at the clothes and nodded. The clothes in the box were the same clothes Peter had been wearing the night before.

'What happened to you, Peter?' Ray asked.

'Someone kicked the shit out of me, what does it look like?' Peter snapped.

'Peter!' his father interrupted sternly. Stanhope turned to Ray. 'I'm sorry. Peter is very upset about what happened.'

'Of course.'

'You see, Peter and Laura were lovers.'

Stride opened his mouth to protest, then clamped it shut. Ray folded his arms and studied Peter, who was leaning uncomfortably against the bookcase. 'Is that true, Peter?'

Peter shrugged. 'Yeah.'

'For how long?'

'A couple months.'

'Her sister told me that Laura broke up with you after a couple dates. She said you were pressuring Laura for sex, and Laura said no.'

'I hear yes a lot more than I hear no.'

'That's not an answer.'

'Laura wanted to keep it a secret. Her and me. She didn't want anyone to know.'

'Why is that?'

'Who knows? Girls are weird that way. Maybe she didn't want everyone asking her for favors, you know? When people hear my last name, they want stuff.'

'So what happened last night?'

Peter glanced at Stride. 'There was a big storm up there. It washed out the ball game, and I went running for my car. I waited there until the rain had mostly stopped, and then I went back into the field.'

'Why?'

'I knew Laura would be coming.'

'Did the two of you arrange to meet? Was this a date?'

'We didn't plan anything in advance, but I saw her in the field with her sister. She gave me a look. I knew what she meant. She was telling me to hang around, so we could get together.'

'A look?' Ray asked.

'Yeah, a look.'

'OK, go on.'

'I heard her coming, so I surprised her. Came up behind her. She freaked out for a minute, because she didn't know who it was. That was when she scratched me.' He touched his face.

'She scratched you by accident?'

'Exactly.'

'Then what?'

'Then we started making out. I mean, when she realized it was me, she was really sorry. She said she had heard someone in the woods earlier, and she was scared. Then we started kissing, and we lay down in the grass, and, well, you know.'

'No, I don't know,' Ray said.

'We were going to have sex.'

'Right there in the softball field.'

'Sure.'

'And did you?'

Peter shook his head. 'No. We were rolling around in the grass, and we were starting to get our clothes off, and that's when it happened.'

'What happened?'

'This guy attacked us.'

'What guy?'

'I don't know who he was. Some big black guy.'

'What did this guy do?'

'He hit me with my baseball bat.'

116

'How did he get your bat?'

'I left it in the field. He must have picked it up. He hit me in the back. The doc says I've got some broken ribs. Then he yanked me off Laura. I mean, he picked me up like I was a rag doll. This guy was strong. Laura screamed, and I saw her run for the woods, trying to get away. He started after her. He still had the bat in his hand. I got up and took a swing at him, and he punched me in the head with his fist. Knocked me out cold, flat on my back. That's all I remember.'

Ray looked at him. 'What happened when you woke up? How long were you out?'

'I don't know. Fifteen minutes maybe.'

'Where was Laura? Where was this black guy?'

'They were both gone.'

'Didn't you look for her?'

Peter shuffled his feet. 'No.'

'This girl is your lover, and some guy chased her into the woods, and you woke up and just left?'

'I panicked. I was scared to death.'

Randall Stanhope interrupted. 'I'm sorry, Detective. Obviously, my son should have made efforts to see if his girlfriend was safe. I'm very disappointed in his behavior.'

Peter's eyes flashed with anger. 'Hey, what could I do? If I'd gone after him, I'd be dead now too. Is that what you want?'

'Shut up, Peter,' his father told him.

'Let's get back to this man who assaulted you,' Ray said. 'What else do you remember about him?'

Peter shrugged. 'He was big. Like a bear. I think he had dread-locks.'

'Have you ever seen him before?'

'No.'

Ray nodded. 'Jon saw a black man matching this description in the woods that night.'

'Ah,' Randall said. 'Well, that's good. Another witness. Do you think you'll be able to find him?'

'Jon says he's a vagrant who lives down by the tracks,' Ray said.

'Oh, so you've seen him before?' Randall asked Stride.

Stride nodded.

117

'Isn't that lucky,' Randall said. 'Detective, I hope you can apprehend him. Of course, I know that these people are often desperate itinerants. I wouldn't be surprised if he's long gone by now. He must know that the police will be on his trail.'

'No doubt,' Ray said.

'Do you need anything else from Peter right now?'

Ray shook his head. 'Not for the moment.'

'That's good. Do you have another minute, Detective? I'd like to share something with you privately.'

Ray rubbed his mustache and nodded at Stride. He tossed him the keys to the Camaro, which Stride caught in mid-air. 'Wait outside for me, OK, Jon? I won't be long. Play the radio, if you like.'

Stride and Peter left the room together. The waning sunlight gathered through the high windows in the vault of the foyer, but where the two boys were, the room was filled with dusty shadows. Stride heard a clock ticking. A gamey smell of venison rose from the downstairs kitchen. Peter escorted him silently to the front door; there was a frozen tension between them.

'You weren't dating Laura,' Stride said.

'What are you, a cop? Leave it alone.'

'Did you kill her?'

'No, I didn't, you asshole. Get the hell out of here.'

Peter yanked the heavy door open. Stride shoved past him and heard the door slam as soon as he had cleared the threshold. He kicked at the loose gravel, then bent down and picked up a loose rock and hurled it into an oval duck pond. He walked past Ray's Camaro and found a black, wrought-iron bench in the gardens, where he sat down, his long legs stretched out. He waited. Silhouettes of birds flitted among the fir trees. The air outside was humid, and he began to sweat. Twenty minutes later, the front door opened again, and Ray came out alone. Ray lit a cigarette and strolled over to the bench.

'Hey, Jon, sorry that took so long.'

'No problem.'

Ray exhaled a cloud of white smoke. 'So what do you think?'

'I think Peter is lying.'

'Maybe,' Ray said. 'But his story about this guy Dada tracks with

118

what you saw. You didn't spot this guy until after the storm hit and you left the softball game, right?'

'Right.'

'Any chance Peter saw him hanging around before the game?'

'Not likely,' Stride said. 'I was already in the field when Peter arrived, and I didn't see Dada anywhere around there.'

'So Peter must have seen him after you did. After the storm. When Laura was coming back to the softball field.'

'I guess so,' Stride said.

'Do you think Laura could have been hiding her affair with Peter?'

Stride frowned. 'I think Cindy would have known.'

'Sisters don't always tell sisters everything.'

'Well, yeah, that's true. Cindy and Laura weren't best pals or anything. But Peter didn't make it sound like he was dating Laura when he talked to me during the game.'

'That could be him keeping it secret.'

'Maybe.' Stride wasn't convinced.

'Anyway, can you stay with me a while longer? I could use your help again.'

'Sure,' Stride said.

Ray reached inside his sport coat and withdrew a long-barreled revolver. He opened the chamber and checked it. Stride could see the silver jackets of bullets loaded inside. Ray spun and locked it with a solid click and shoved it back in his shoulder holster.

'OK then,' Ray said. 'Let's go get Dada.'

Eleven

Donna Biggs pulled off Highway 23 near the river overlook at Perch Lake Park. She shut off the car and sat silently by the water, which was drenched in the orange glow of the dying sunlight. The river here was broken up by narrow swirls of land, like chocolate ribbons dropped into vanilla cake batter. From the bank at Fond du Lac, it was a cool hundred-foot swim with the stars overhead to the beaches and birch trees of the nearest island. She remembered midnight skinny-dipping here as a teenager, when a dozen or more kids would steal off from the fishing pier to drink, smoke weed, and have awkward sex in the sand. She and Clark had hooked up for the first time on one of those nights.

Mary tugged at her sleeve, demanding attention. 'Mama?'

Donna knew what her daughter wanted. They had made a ritual of these stops on Friday nights. A few final peaceful moments together before the lonely weekend. 'Would you like to sit by the river for a while?' she asked.

Mary's head bobbed vigorously.

'Come on then.'

They were only a few miles from Clark's home in Gary. She was late dropping Mary off, and Clark had already called twice, wondering where she was. Usually, Donna had Mary at his house in time for the two of them to go to dinner, but tonight, she had had to work late, and she stopped at McDonald's to get Mary some chicken nuggets and French fries because she was hungry. Donna herself didn't eat at all; she felt tired and nauseous. By the time she had packed Mary's bag and got on the road, it was after eight o'clock.

Mary clambered out of the car and ran in her gangly way toward the water.

'Careful, honey, not too close,' Donna called.

She stretched her legs and took a seat on an old wooden bench. When she looked through the maze of trees to her right, she squinted into the sinking sun. On her left, a narrow dirt trail climbed away from the river. Thin green vines and white flowers dangled over the path, blowing off pollen dust in the warm breeze. Honey bees buzzed near her face, and she shooed them away with a flip of her hand.

Mary chased a Monarch butterfly with orange and black wings. The fluttering insect dotted up and down, and Mary held out a finger, hoping it would land there. She ran back and forth, following it until the butterfly disappeared over the water.

'Come sit by me, sweetheart,' Donna told her.

Mary plopped down heavily on the bench. Donna wrapped an arm around her big girl's shoulder and pulled Mary's head into the crook of her neck. She kissed her blonde curls and poked a finger into the girl's cheek. Mary giggled. They were an odd mismatch of mother and daughter. Mary got all her tall, heavy genes from Clark. Donna was small, at least six inches shorter than Mary and fifty pounds lighter. She knew it looked strange, this oversized teenager clinging to the tiny hand of her mother. Mary was still a child. Donna was the one who had gotten older and more conscious of the burden of being a parent. It was one thing to care for a child when you were twenty-five and something else altogether when you were almost forty.

Donna was still dressed for the office. She worked as a legal secretary in a small Wisconsin law firm, where they insisted she wear business suits and keep her sandy hair fashionably styled. The salary and benefits were good, though, and the firm gave her flexibility when Mary needed special care. She had worked there for five years, ever since she and Clark split up. Security was a trade-off for the long hours and loneliness in her life.

'Did you see that?' Donna asked, pointing at a splash in the water and the widening ripples. 'That was a fish.'

'Fish!' Mary said.

121

'Would you like to be a fish?' Donna asked. 'You could swim under-water and make friends with turtles. Maybe you could even be a mermaid with a big fish tail. Wouldn't that be funny?'

'Fish!' Mary said again.

Donna smiled. She held Mary's hand, and they sat watching the hawks circle above them and the boats come and go lazily on the river. They counted birds in the trees. Donna picked a wildflower and let Mary pluck the petals. Half an hour passed as easily as the water at their feet, and the sun eased below the trees. Golden sparkles on the water became shadows.

It was time to go. Clark was waiting, and it wasn't fair to be so late. He missed Mary.

Donna missed Clark, too. She kept waiting for her love for him to die out completely, but instead, it was the bitterness of their break-up that had begun to seem distant and unimportant. They had both been desperate, unable to cope with Mary together. When she saw him now, she found herself drawn all over again to his courage and his solemn manner. She had even allowed herself to stay over a few weeks ago, to climb back into their bed. They hadn't talked about it. She had slipped away in the morning before Clark awoke, not because it felt like a mistake, but because she was scared that Clark didn't feel the same way.

'Hey! Mary!'

Someone shouted a far-away greeting from the highway behind her. Donna looked back and saw a teenage boy about Mary's age, hurtling down the sharp hill on a bicycle. He waved madly at them, his face cracked into a grin, his black hair twisting in the currents of air. She recognized him, a neighbor boy from her years in Gary, who lived two blocks away from their old house. He was an adopted Korean child, squat and strong. He loved Mary and had played with her growing up. As they got older, he was one of the few boys who didn't make fun of her retardation.

Mary saw him, too. 'Charlie! Charlie!'

Charlie veered across the highway. His wide backside hung over the bike's banana seat. He yanked back on the handlebars, hiking the front wheel off the road, showing off the way boys do. Mary squealed with delight. Donna heard the skid of rubber as Charlie braked hard.

The bike slowed, and tread burned off onto the highway in a black streak.

Through the screech of the tire, she also heard rocks scraping on the ground. Loose gravel.

Her breath caught in her chest before she could shout a warning. The bike's front tire rose higher, like a whale breaching, and the back tire spilled out underneath it. In the next instant, it was airborne. Charlie flew, too. The bike bounced, clanged, and made circles as it crashed on the pavement, its spokes spinning like tops. Charlie's hands and legs stretched out in an X in mid-air. He soared and snapped down head first, bone on asphalt, and even fifty yards away, the sound popped through the brittle air like a firecracker.

He lay still in the middle of the highway.

'Charlie!' Mary wailed.

Donna bolted upright. She stood, paralyzed, her face swinging back and forth between Charlie and Mary. Her instinct was to run and help, but her instinct was also never to leave her daughter alone. She bent down and grabbed Mary's face between her hands and spoke softly but firmly. 'Mary, you sit right here. Do not move, OK? Do not move. Sit right here. Please, baby, I need you to understand. Show me you understand.'

Mary's eyes were filled with confusion and glassy tears. She didn't move.

'That's good, baby, you sit right there, you don't move.'

Donna sprinted for the highway, fumbling with her cell phone and punching the numbers 911 as she ran. Her work clothes felt clumsy. Her blouse came untucked from her skirt. She lost her balance as her high heels tripped her up, and she swore and kicked them off. Rocks chewed at her nylons and cut her feet. When she reached Charlie, she murmured a prayer as she watched the blood spreading like a cancer under the boy's head. She craned her neck to stare up and down the highway, which was dark now in the deepening twilight. There were no cars approaching from either direction. She spotted a silver Rav4 parked on the shoulder a quarter-mile to the north, but she didn't see anyone inside. She was alone.

Donna saw Mary. Still on the bench. Her thumb in her mouth.

She heard the 911 operator in her ear and was relieved to hear

123

another person's voice. She took a breath and swallowed down her panic. She tried to remember exactly where she was, but the names of the streets and towns didn't come. For an instant, she could have been anywhere on earth. Then the location burbled out of her brain, and she stuttered, trying to relay it. The operator was annoyingly calm, asking her the same questions over and over, making Donna repeat herself.

'I need help!' she insisted. 'Get me some help!'

The operator finally told her what she wanted to hear. The police were on their way. An ambulance was on its way. Everyone was coming. Stay with him.

Donna heard moaning at her feet. Charlie was waking up, trying to move his limbs.

'No, no, stay still,' she murmured. She didn't know if he heard her. She got on her knees on the highway and took his hand. It was limp. He didn't squeeze back. 'Stay still.'

His eyes were closed. He tried to turn his head, and she put her lips next to his ear. Her hand was in his blood. 'Don't move. Stay right there, Charlie. Help's coming.'

She listened for the sirens. Where were they? She took another glance up and down the highway, looking for headlights, afraid that the cars wouldn't see her and Charlie in the gloom until it was too late to steer around them.

Her cell phone rang. She answered it with sticky fingers and heard Clark's voice.

'Where the hell are you? This is so damn unfair, Donna.'

Words spilled out of her mouth. She couldn't slow them down. 'Clark, get down here, get down here now!'

'What's going on? Is it Mary?'

'Just come now, I'm on the highway south of town. Come right now!'

God bless him, he didn't ask any more questions. The phone was dead. He was already gone and on his way. When you needed him, Clark always came through. That was why she had loved him for so long.

All she had to do was wait. Wait for the sirens. Wait for Clark.

Crouching on the ground, she couldn't see the bench by the river

124

where Mary was sitting. She didn't want to call Mary's name and risk her wandering into the road. She laid Charlie's hand on the pavement. 'I'm still here,' she told him.

Donna stood up.

'Oh, my God!' she screamed.

The wooden bench was empty in the shadows. She didn't see Mary anywhere. Donna tore at her hair. Blood smeared on her face. She looked everywhere, at her car, at the trees, at the path that disappeared up the river bank. 'Mary! Mary!'

She screamed over and over, but she didn't see her beautiful girl.

'Oh, God, someone help me! Help! Mary!'

A baby rabbit no bigger than Mary's fist poked its nose out of the goldenrod and hopped into the middle of the dirt trail. Mary wanted to hold it so she could feel better. She had held a rabbit before, and its fur was soft on her fingers and its warm little body made her happy. She got up and crept toward the path, laying each foot down softly and quietly. The rabbit watched her come. Its big dark eye blinked at her. Its nose smelled her. The animal took two more hops, turning its white puffball tail toward Mary. They began a little dance, Mary taking a step, the rabbit taking a hop, as if they were playing with each other.

'Bunny,' Mary cooed. 'Here, bunny.'

She followed it up the trail. She looked down at her feet, not at the trees or the river, and not at the highway, which soon disappeared from view behind her. She didn't notice it was getting dark. The bunny led her away, a hop at a time, and when it finally shot north on the trail and disappeared, Mary ran, trying to catch it. She called out for the bunny in a murmur and hunted in the brush. It was gone, but when she jumped into a patch of wildflowers, she flushed another butterfly, which floated just out of her reach. She forgot about the rabbit and followed the butterfly instead.

She forgot about Charlie, too. And Mama. She didn't think about being alone, because the butterfly was with her. It wasn't until the butterfly soared off into the treetops that Mary stopped and looked around her and realized that no one was close to her anymore. It was nearly dark inside the trees. She could see the river down the bank

125

below her, but the dancing dots of sunlight were gone, and the water looked black. Mary stood in the middle of the trail, not knowing what to do. She bit her lip and blinked. Tears dripped down her cheeks.

'Mama?'

She didn't dare speak loudly. She didn't know who would hear her. She wished the bunny would come back. Somewhere below her, awfully far away, she thought she heard Mama's voice. Mary didn't know how to find her, and she was afraid that Mama would be angry at her for running away. She had done that before, and Mama always got upset, although she hugged her hard.

Mary wanted a hug right now.

She heard noises in the woods. Her eyes grew wide. She hoped it would be Mama, or Charlie, or Daddy, and that they had come to get her and take her home. She took a step backwards and laced her fingers together over her stomach. It was hard to see anything at all now, just shadows that were like the night outside her bedroom window. She looked up, wanting to see the sky, but the branches drooped like arms over her head, and she didn't like it at all. The noises got louder. She cried harder and whimpered.

'I'm sorry.'

The trees moved. They were alive. Mary saw a man climb out of the trees, not even ten feet away from her. He reached out his hands toward her the way a monster would, but it wasn't Charlie, or Daddy; he was a stranger, and she couldn't speak, she couldn't scream, because she wasn't supposed to talk to strangers. Not at all. Not ever.

She didn't want to look at him. She thought if she closed her eyes, he would go away, like a bad dream. But when she did, and she opened them to slits, he was still there, and he was coming closer. When he was close enough for her to see his face, her mouth fell open in a terrible O, because this man was worse than a stranger.

He was the man outside her window.

The man who scared her.

'Him him him him him him him!'

He said something to her. He moved toward her, his grasping arms outstretched.

'No no no no no!'

Mary ran, falling as she did, then getting up and crying. She didn't look behind her. She never wanted to see the man again, never wanted to see his face, never wanted to feel him watching her, never wanted to find him outside her window. She wanted Mama and Daddy to make him go away. She wanted to wake up and be in her bed.

She couldn't see anything in front of her as she ran. She didn't know where she was. She knew only that the world was going down, that the branches and brush grabbed at her like the hands of monsters, that she heard animals breathing and snorting.

The ground under her feet became a dark pool of quicksand.

Water.

She was in water. She was in the river.

And then there was no ground under her feet at all, and she was sinking.

Twelve

Stride slid open a small cubbyhole inside the cabinet of his desk. The drawer was empty except for a photograph, which Stride removed and held at the corner between his thumb and forefinger. The picture was more than ten years old. It showed two men, dressed in suits, standing in front of a brick fireplace at the Kitch, which was the private club where the movers and shakers of Duluth sipped martinis, ate red meat, and decided the city's future. Stride was the man on the left. Next to him was Ray Wallace, with an arm around Stride's shoulder and a smile as big as the lake. It was the night Stride had been named to lead the city's Detective Bureau. Ray was the police chief.

He could see paternal pride in Ray's eyes. There was nothing fake about that glow. Ray had guided every step of his career from his earliest days on the police force. That night at the Kitch, Ray told him that the only thing that would ever make him happier was the day he could hand the keys to the chief's office to Stride as he retired.

Two years later, Ray drilled a bullet through Stride's shoulder.

He used the same long-barreled revolver he had kept in pristine condition since his own days as a detective, the same gun he had used to hunt Dada. While Stride watched, bleeding, from the floor of Ray's cabin, Ray took that revolver, put the barrel in his mouth under his droopy red mustache, and blew out most of his brain through the back of his skull.

Looking back, Stride knew he should have seen the signs. He could see them in the photograph as he stared at it. Ray was heavy. His cheeks were florid from the four Scotches he drank at dinner. Age wore on him. He had trappings of wealth he never should have had, like the watch on his hand, the bottle of champagne at dinner, the spring vacation to Aruba, and the pearls around his young wife's neck. Back then, Stride had never *wanted* to see the signs. He had refused to allow them into his mind, until a whistleblower from Stanhope Industries laid out all the papers for him at a Twin Cities hotel, and Stride could see twenty years of bribery and corruption with only one name to explain it all away. Ray.

Stride hired a forensic accountant who followed the paper trail to Ray and to a handful of senior executives at Stanhope. The mayor and county attorney would have been content to let Ray resign and slip away quietly, but the media got their teeth in the story, and Ray was staring not only at disgrace and bankruptcy, but at jail time, too. When Ray's wife called Stride from their cabin near Ely, Ray was threatening to kill all of them. His wife. Their two kids. Stride went up there alone, wanting to talk Ray out of it, man to man, detective to chief. He thought he had a chance of making it all end peacefully when Ray let his wife and kids walk safely out the door. He only realized later that this was between himself and Ray, that Stride's betrayal was like a son taking down a father. Ray wanted Stride to be there when he killed himself.

'You don't still blame yourself, do you?'

Stride saw Maggie in the doorway of his office. The rest of the Detective Bureau was dark behind her; it was after midnight. She strolled inside and sat down sideways in the upholstered chair he kept in the corner. Her short legs dangled off the ground. She had a can of Diet Coke in one hand.

'I've been down that road too many times,' Stride said. 'There's nothing I would have done differently.'

Maggie and Cindy had been the two people in his life who helped him climb out of a well of depression after Ray died. Without Maggie, he doubted that he would have gone back on the job after his shoulder healed. He had been ready to quit, but Maggie had nagged him about open cases until he realized that he still loved being a cop, with or without Ray.

'There's one thing I don't understand,' Stride said.

'What's that?'

'I still wonder why Ray never tried to corrupt me. He was on the take all those years, but he never once asked me to cut a corner for him. He never asked for my help.'

'He knew you'd say no,' Maggie said.

'Do you think so? If Ray had come to me when I was a young cop and asked me to look the other way on something, do you think I wouldn't have done it? No way I would have said no to him.'

'Maybe that's the point, boss.'

'What?'

'You were the one thing Ray was really proud of,' Maggie told him. 'He wasn't going to mess you up the way he was messed up. He didn't want you to wind up like him.'

Stride laid the photo down on his desk. 'Maybe you're right.' He looked up at her and added, 'Why are you here so late?'

'I saw your light.'

'Any more news on the adoption front?'

'Not yet. I still can't make up my mind.'

'You know what I think. You're a natural.'

Maggie shrugged and didn't say anything more.

'Were you on the scene in Fond du Lac?' he asked.

Maggie took a long swallow from her can of soda. She draped her head back and stared at the ceiling. 'Yeah.'

'Did the girl make it?'

'No. She was dead when they pulled her out of the water.'

'How about the boy? The one on the bicycle?'

'Lucky. His vitals are good. The docs think he'll pull through.'

'How are the girl's parents?'

Maggie shook her head. 'They're both wrecks. Mary was everything to them. Taking care of her destroyed their marriage, but they lived and breathed for that girl.'

'I hope the mother doesn't blame herself for leaving the girl alone,' Stride said. 'It was a terrible accident. There was nothing she could have done.'

'I'm not so sure it was an accident.'

Stride balanced his elbows on his desk. 'What do you mean?'

'Donna Biggs thinks the peeper was there. She thinks that's what spooked Mary and made her run. When she went into the water, he took off.'

'Is there anything to back it up?'

'Donna swears she saw a car parked just up the hill from where she was. She says it was a silver Rav4, which tracks with the reports of a mini SUV near several of the peeping scenes. No one got plates, of course.'

'That's not much.'

'Donna also saw a man get into the Rav when she was running up the trail after she heard Mary scream.'

'Can she recognize him?'

'No.'

'Is there any physical evidence?'

'We'll be searching the woods between the trail and the spot where the car was parked.'

'I don't want to sound like a pessimist, but even if you find this guy, it's going to be a tough road to prove he was responsible for Mary's death.'

'If he tried to grab her, and she wound up dead as a result of his actions, we can make a manslaughter case out of that.'

'I know, but with what evidence?' Stride asked.

'The peeping history with the girl. The car. Any physical evidence we can find. Mary's scream. Hell, who knows what souvenirs this guy kept? Maybe when we find him, he'll have pictures. If I can put a few of the pieces together, Pat Burns can make a jury see the light.'

'You sound like this case is personal,' Stride said.

Maggie nodded. 'I saw the girl when she was sleeping at her house. She was sweet. I told her father he didn't have anything to worry about, and now the girl winds up dead. We were staking out Clark's house and Donna's apartment, but it looks like he outsmarted us. Donna says she stopped at this park every Friday night before she dropped Mary off at her ex-husband's place. He must have been following them.'

'Or the mother is wrong.'

'I don't think she is.'

Stride trusted Maggie's instincts. 'Go with your gut,' he said.

He picked up the photograph from his desk and studied it again.

He was having a hard time shrugging off the past. 'You know, I've always believed that Ray's death was one more ripple effect from Laura's murder,' he said.

'How so?'

'I think the connection between Ray and Randall Stanhope started back then,' he told her. 'That's when Ray got corrupted.'

'You don't know that.'

'No? After we interviewed Peter, Randall asked Ray to stay behind. Then Ray came out a while later, and the two of us went after Dada. It wasn't until years later that I realized what must have happened.'

'You think Ray and Randall did a deal,' Maggie concluded.

Stride nodded. 'Exactly. Ray didn't go there with me to catch Dada. He went there to kill him.'

It was twilight. Ray drove onto the gravel shoulder within sight of the Arrowhead Bridge. The twin spans of highway jutted like wings at the arch, leaving the passage open for one of the rust-red ore boats arriving from the Soo. The water was black and windswept. The two of them got out of Ray's Camaro and leaned against the hood near the front bumper. Cool drops of rain burst on the windshield. Ashen clouds massed overhead, inching from the high hills toward the lake.

Ray slapped his pack of cigarettes and offered one to Stride, who took it. He coughed when the smoke hit his lungs. Ray smiled at him. The breeze rustled his red hair.

'So this is the area where you saw Dada?'

'Yeah.'

'Rough area for a kid to be walking around. You should think twice about coming down here by yourself, you know?'

'I'm all right.'

Ray gestured down the railroad tracks. 'You know those guys?'

About a hundred yards away, Stride saw two twenty-something men in jeans, with no shirts, swigging beer and strolling across the muddy ground, kicking at stalks of wild wheat. Pyramids of taconite and stripped tree trunks rose around the tracks like mountains. One of the men finished his bottle of beer and laid it sideways on the track. When the next train came, it would shear the bottle in two.

132

Stride had come across bottle halves all over this area. Some of the men used the bottoms as soup bowls.

'No, I've never seen them.'

Ray stubbed out his cigarette on the ground. 'I'm going to talk to them.'

'Let me come with you,' Stride said.

'I'm sorry, Jon. If things get ugly, I can't have a teenager in the midst of it.'

'Except I know the area.'

'I know you do. Right now, though, I need you to let me handle this myself. OK?'

Stride shrugged. 'Yeah, OK. I'll hang out here.'

'Good.'

Ray hitched up his pants and set out along the dirt road toward the tracks. Stride climbed onto the hood of the car and watched him go. Ray got within fifty yards of the two men before one of them looked back and spotted him. They both took off. Ray cursed loudly and chased them, but with his limp, he couldn't run fast or far. The two men cleared a shallow hill and disappeared from sight. It was five minutes before Ray crested the same hill and was gone.

Stride was alone. He felt the ground vibrate with the rumbling thunder of a train gathering speed out of the rail yard. A snake of red and green train cars, littered with graffiti and overflowing with iron ore, shuddered along the tracks, growing closer. Stride slid down the roof of the car and crossed the asphalt highway. On the other side, a shallow slope led to a cluster of oak trees where a creek twisted lazily toward the harbor water. Stride skittered down the hill and hiked to the tracks. He waited for the train engine, which followed the coast of the water as it headed south. The train was long. Dozens of cars shouldered by him. He smelled ore dust, which was as tarry as a cigarette in his lungs. The cars banged, hummed, shimmied, and jolted.

It took ten minutes for the entire train to pass. When the caboose wiggled past him, the giant noise diminished, getting further away. He watched it go. He realized his skin was damp with rain.

'Who's your friend?'

Stride jumped. He spun round and found Dada behind him. A dead

133

oak tree loomed behind the black man, and its spindly branches seemed to grow out of his head. Dada dwarfed him, and Stride wasn't small.

'Is he a cop?'

Dada was six inches away, and Stride wanted to back up, but he didn't. This close, he could see that Dada was young. Maybe twenty. He wasn't wearing his colorful beret. His ropes of matted hair sprouted off a high forehead and dangled like wriggling worms to his chest. The whites of his eyes were stark against his dark skin. He had arched, devil-like eyebrows.

'I said, is he a cop?'

Dada's voice was surprisingly smooth, almost hypnotic.

'Yes,' Stride said.

'Is this about that girl?'

'Yes.'

'They think I killed her?'

'They want to talk to you,' Stride said.

Dada swung a dented canteen by the silver chain on its cap, and then he lifted the trunk to his lips and took a swallow. He wiped his scraggly beard.

'Talk? A white girl gets killed, and a black man is seen with her, and all the police want to do is talk?'

Rain fell harder around them. Water beaded on Dada's head and face. Stride heard the drops slapping on the earth.

'Did you do it?' Stride asked.

'What do you think?'

Stride stared at him. 'No, I don't think you did.'

'Then get out of my way. There's another train coming. It's time for me to go somewhere else.'

'I can't do that,' Stride said.

He felt the ground shake again with the earthquake of a train getting closer. Every minute, another long dragon left the harbor.

'You're brave to stand there, but you're a fool if you think you can stop me.'

'Just talk to him,' Stride said. 'Tell him what you saw. Without you, they're never going to solve this case.'

'Did you know the girl?'

'She was my girlfriend's sister.'

134

'I'm sorry.'

'Tell me what you saw.'

A train whistle screamed. The rain sheeted down and dripped from Stride's eyelashes.

'That girl had secrets,' Dada said.

He laid a paw on Stride's shoulder and shoved him effortlessly aside. A train engine growled by behind them, dragging rusted gray boxcars. The grinding of steel wheels on the track unleashed an awful squeal. Stride had seen baby pigs castrated. It sounded like that.

He threw himself at Dada, but it was like tackling a tree trunk. Dada angled an elbow sharply into Stride's chest and jabbed once, like a single blow from a hammer. The air fled Stride's lungs. He was knocked backward onto his ass and sat in the mud, struggling to breathe. Dada was steps away from the shuddering train cars. Stride scrambled to his feet and dived again, aiming low. He launched his upper body against the black man's ankle. Dada's foot scraped across the wet ground, and then Dada toppled and fell. The canteen spilled from his hand and rolled.

'Tell me!' Stride shouted.

Their skin was streaked in mud. The train cars clattered past them only ten feet away, deafening and huge. Stride clawed for a hold on Dada's wrist, but Dada climbed to his feet, carrying Stride with him. Stride chopped at the man's neck. The blow did nothing. Dada shooed him away like a fly, pushing him backwards, but Stride charged again and hung on, hammering the man's kidneys with his right fist. Dada's knotted muscles were like a punching bag, absorbing the blows.

'Stupid boy,' Dada said.

He hit Stride across the mouth. His silver ring sliced Stride's face. The punch felt like a metal shovel swung into his teeth. Stride staggered two steps and crumpled backward into the weeds. He coughed and tasted blood. When he bit down, his jaw didn't align, and one of his molars dangled as if held by a thread. He wanted to get up, but his eyes sent his brain jumbled images of what was in front of him. Pain throbbed and beat against his skull.

He heard something. A crack. A sharp metallic ping.

A voice.

'Stop!'

135

It was Ray. He was shooting.

Stride struggled to all fours. His mouth hung open, blood trailing from both sides of his lips like a vampire. He shook his head, trying to rearrange his blurred vision. When the picture cleared, he saw Dada sprinting for the train as it accelerated. On the highway, near the Camaro, Ray held his revolver in both hands and fired again.

The bullet ricocheted off one of the boxcars.

Dada grabbed the rung of a steel ladder and swung a leg gracefully onto the bottom step. The last few cars in the huge centipede wriggled past. Stride saw Ray limping, trying to run, failing. The train left them both behind. Dada shrank in his eyes, lost in the growing darkness, vanishing, escaping.

Stride crawled a few inches, felt the world spin again, and then passed out.

'Well, you are just so cool,' Maggie told Stride with a smile.

'It wasn't my finest moment,' he admitted.

'How did Ray feel about Dada getting away?'

'In retrospect, I think he was relieved. He knew that Dada was long gone once he got on that train. We were never going to see him again. Everyone got what they wanted. Ray. Laura's dad. Peter Stanhope and his father. They could all believe that we knew who killed Laura, and he had left town for good. It could all go away, go underground. And that's what happened.'

'But did Dada kill Laura?' Maggie asked.

'Ray had the lab check Dada's canteen for fingerprints, and they compared them with Peter's bat. There was a match. Dada had his hands on that bat, which tracked with Peter's story. There weren't any other witnesses.'

'That was enough for Ray?'

'That was enough for everyone. Even me. Until now.'

Who Killed Laura Starr?

By Tish Verdure

I never believed the story about Dada. I couldn't say anything, though. My dad needed closure, not an open wound. The police wouldn't listen. They barely pretended to search for Dada around the country, because no one really wanted to find him. If he came back, questions would be asked, and the answers were better off buried with the body.

It's easy to believe in evil. Easy to spot it. The black devil came to town, and he picked one girl to sacrifice, and then he rode the dirty train back to the wilderness. That's the kind of fable they used to tell us in church. People around here like to think that good and evil are as easy as black and white. Good people wear the cross. Bad people don't. Bad people are strangers. It's so much harder to accept that evil could be living among you. Your neighbor. Your teacher. Your friend.

The stalker? No one wanted to know about him. Dada wasn't the one on the school grounds, slipping vile notes into Laura's locker. He wasn't mailing threats to her. It didn't matter. If Dada killed her, why look for a stalker? If Dada killed her, the city was safe again. Parents could stop holding their breath. Kids could make out in the park. That's what we all wanted.

So I let it go, even though I knew it was a lie. Even though I knew there was a killer among us. I didn't know his face, but I was sure I knew who he was.

Someday I hoped the truth would come out, but that wasn't up to me.

Jonny took it hard. He felt as if he had let me down. He took the

137

blame on himself; he had let Dada escape. The doctors worked on his jaw, but his face always looked imperfect after that, slightly flawed. I liked it. It made him human. He looked older, too. Tougher. Like the scar on his face from Dada's ring was a reminder that you could fight and lose, but you could never win if you didn't fight at all. I began to see the man I would live with. Love. Marry.

The strange thing is, I knew he was going to be a cop before he did. The experience with Laura, Peter, and Dada changed him. So did Ray. I never told him that I didn't trust Ray, not ever, not for a minute. But Jonny had found someone's footsteps to follow, the way he once expected to follow his father's path. I always thought he would be a better cop than Ray, because Ray was in it for himself. Jonny was different. He was in it because something had been taken from him that year, and this was a way to get it back.

Not that he ever would. When you lose some things, they're gone for good.

Life goes on, for better or worse, but sometimes in the silence, your mind travels back. I never really got past that summer. We never talked about it again, but I carried it with me every day. I knew he did, too.

I never went back to the park. To the lake. I didn't want to be reminded. Even so, there would be days when I drove along the highway that skirted the wilderness refuge, and I would stare down into the nest of trees, and I would be seventeen again. In my bare feet. The baseball bat in my hands.

If only I could tell Jonny the truth about what happened that night.

PART THREE

THE WITNESS

Thirteen

Clark Biggs looked stiff and uncomfortable in a straight-backed wooden chair pushed against the living-room wall. His hands sat limply in his lap. His eyes were fixed on a bookshelf across the room. Maggie followed his stare to a picture frame with a photograph of Clark and Mary in the backyard. They were playing in the fall leaves. Mary tossed colored oak leaves in the air, her smile big and wide, her blonde curls flying. In the photograph, Maggie could see the contentment and pride hiding behind Clark's solemn eyes. Today, that happiness had been vacuumed away, leaving his heart empty.

'Mr Biggs?' she asked again softly.

He broke out of his trance. 'I'm sorry, what?'

'I was asking if you had ever seen a silver Rav4 parked around the neighborhood, or whether anyone you know owns a vehicle like that.'

'Oh.' He put his hands on his knees and studied the faded pattern in the carpet at his feet. 'No, I don't think so.'

'Neither do I,' Donna Biggs said. 'I'm sorry.'

She sat beside Maggie on Clark's sofa. Every few seconds, she stole nervous glances at her ex-husband, as if she were struggling with her desire to comfort him. Donna's eyes were red-ringed and moist.

'The bad news is that there are hundreds of vehicles like that in the Duluth and Superior area,' Maggie told them. 'That's a long list. However, we're cross-referencing vehicle ownership with criminal records to see if we can narrow down the suspect pool. We're also going back to the other neighborhoods where the peeper struck to re-interview people who may have seen something, now that we have a specific vehicle type. We'll also be checking the vehicle ownership records against the list of people and organizations you've given us, to see if there's anyone who was part of Mary's life.'

'No one who knew Mary could have done this,' Donna said.

Clark bobbed his head. 'Yes, it was a stranger. If it was anyone she knew, Mary's reaction would have been different.'

'I understand, but we have to cover every angle,' Maggie said. 'Remember that this could be someone who had little or no direct contact with Mary. Peepers and stalkers often develop elaborate fantasies about their victims based on nothing more than their physical appearance or a minor encounter. To a girl, it may be no more than saying hello to a clerk at a store. To a maladjusted mind, that simple conversation can trigger an obsession.'

'Mary was a child,' Donna protested. 'Who could possibly think of her that way?'

Maggie sighed. 'Mary was also a pretty girl.'

'She was vulnerable,' Clark said. 'How could you leave her alone, Donna? How? Tell me that.'

Donna's cheeks turned bloodless and white. 'What could I do, Clark? I mean, for God's sake, what could I do?'

'You call 911, and you sit there with Mary. That's what you do. She was your responsibility.'

'And leave that boy bleeding in the street?'

'You should have locked Mary in the car.'

'There was no time! I didn't have time to think!'

Maggie put a hand on Donna's knee. 'Mr and Mrs Biggs, I know you're both upset, and I understand. Whatever you both think, you are *not* to blame. Mrs Biggs, you almost certainly saved that boy's life, and you had no way of knowing that anything like this could happen to Mary. Mr Biggs, I know you're devastated, but the best thing we can do right now is try to find the man who terrorized your daughter and make sure he doesn't do this to anyone else. OK?'

Clark Biggs got out of his chair and paced. Some of Mary's plastic blocks were littered across the living-room carpet. He bent down, picked up one of the blocks, and squeezed it inside his meaty fist. His eyes were closed. He was unkempt, with dirty hair and blond stubble on his face.

142

'Mr Biggs?'

'I know. I'm sorry.'

'That's all right,' Maggie said.

'Why did it have to be water?' Clark murmured.

'Oh, Clark, please don't,' Donna said.

'Was God pissed off that we saved her the first time? Did He think she hadn't suffered enough? How could He put her back in the water? Tell me that, how could God let her die in the water?'

Maggie expected to see tears on Clark's thick cheekbones, but his sun-cracked face was dry, and his eyes were empty. On the sofa, Donna moved to go to her ex-husband, but then she stopped herself. Maggie could see that the love between them wasn't dead, but they may as well have been on opposite edges of a canyon, with no way to cross.

'Did you find anything in the woods?' Donna asked quietly. 'You said they were going to search the woods for clues.'

'I wish I could tell you we had more luck,' Maggie replied. 'We found some trash on the path, in the trees, and on the side of the highway, but nothing with any obvious connection to the peeper or his vehicle. Later, when we identify him, it's possible that something we found will help us place him at the scene.'

Clark let Mary's block fall out of his hand. 'When you find this man, will you charge him with murder? Will he have to pay for what he did to Mary?'

Maggie hesitated. 'That's not my decision. The county attorney will make that call, based on the evidence we gather. I assure you, I will do everything possible to make a case that we can bring to trial. I want to see justice for Mary.'

Donna shook her head sadly. 'If you can't find corroborating evidence, then it's just my word, isn't it? I work in a law office, Ms Bei. I know that's a problem.'

'Why is that a problem?' Clark asked. 'If Donna says she saw him, then she saw him.'

'But I didn't *see* him,' Donna said. 'I saw a car and a man I can't identify. I know how defense lawyers work. They'll say it could have been anybody. Or they'll say I made it up.'

'Made it up?' Clark asked. 'What the hell does that mean?'

'I was the only one who saw the Rav on the highway, Clark. They'll say I felt guilty because I left Mary alone, and I was just trying to protect myself by blaming someone else. They'll say I knew about the peeping, so I used it as a convenient excuse.'

'That's bullshit,' Clark said.

'It's way too early to be thinking about any of this,' Maggie said. 'Once we identify this man, we're likely to find much more evidence in his house and car. If we can find something that ties him to Mary, then your testimony will carry a lot of weight with a jury, no matter how much smoke a defense lawyer tries to blow at them.'

She tried to sound convincing, but she knew Donna was right. Stride was right, too. The most they were ever likely to do was convict the man of interference with privacy. A two-year felony for peeping on minors. Two years was a lousy trade for losing a daughter.

'The first thing we have to do is find him,' she added. 'This man stalked Mary. Somewhere, somehow, their lives intersected.'

'You said it could be as simple as Mary saying hello to someone on the street,' Donna said. 'If that's true, how will we ever narrow it down?'

'Well, we have to hope it wasn't quite that simple,' Maggie told her. 'Mary wasn't the first girl he peeped, but something about Mary was special. He hooked onto something about her that made him come back to Mary. The question is what. Her physical appearance isn't really distinctive compared to the other girls. If you lined them all up, you wouldn't pick out Mary as being different.'

'She was mentally handicapped,' Donna said.

Maggie nodded. 'Yes, but you wouldn't necessarily know that just by looking at her. I think there had to be some kind of interaction between Mary and this man, however minor. I'll talk to the people at Mary's school again, but if the connection didn't happen there, then the chances are that you were with Mary when it did happen. Because she was hardly ever alone, am I right?'

She knew as she said the words that she had accidentally jabbed another needle into Donna's guilty conscience. The one time she had left her daughter alone, Mary died. Donna wiped her eyes.

'Yes, you're right,' she said. 'We were always with her.'

'Mr Biggs, you told me that you think the peeper was at Mary's bedroom window the week before the incident you reported. That was also a Saturday night, correct?'

Clark nodded.

'Do you think that was the first time?'

'That was the first time Mary saw him,' he insisted. 'I'm sure of that.'

'I'm trying to nail down a timeline here,' Maggie said. 'I'd like to know when this man first met Mary. So I'd like you both to think hard about the days just before that Saturday. I want you to remember if anything unusual happened during that period.'

'I'll check my calendar at work,' Donna said. 'Mary was with me until Friday evening.'

'Nothing happened on that Saturday,' Clark said. 'Mary and I were home all day. I ordered a swing set, and it was delivered that morning. After I set it up, I couldn't get Mary off the swing for the rest of the day. The two of us spent all afternoon outside, and then I grilled hamburgers for dinner.'

'Did anyone stop by the house while you were outside? Or did you notice any unusual activity? People circling the neighborhood?'

Clark shook his head. 'I keep a close eye out for that kind of thing.'

'Mary was sick for a couple days that week,' Donna added. 'She didn't go to school on Wednesday or Thursday. I had to take her to the doctor's office.'

'Did you see anyone new while you were there?'

'Yes, there was a male nurse in the lab we hadn't met before. Mary liked him.'

Maggie jotted down the name of the clinic in Superior where Mary's doctor was located. 'That's good,' she said. 'That's exactly the kind of information I need. If you remember anything else like that – any kind of casual contact Mary had with a stranger – please let me know immediately.'

Donna and Clark Biggs both nodded.

'Tell me, Ms Bei, do you think that – well, is this man violent?' Donna asked. 'Did he intend to do some kind of harm to Mary?'

Maggie knew what she was thinking. Maybe, somehow, it was better this way. Death by drowning was a better fate than to be kidnapped by a predator. God was actually being merciful.

'I just don't know,' Maggie replied. 'He hasn't shown any inclination to violence yet, but that doesn't mean he wouldn't have crossed the line eventually. He still may.'

'It doesn't matter what his intentions were,' Clark growled. 'He killed her. This pervert killed my little girl.'

Fourteen

The lake breeze made the water choppy out beyond the lift bridge. Dozens of seagulls placidly rode the swells. The small harbor tour boat bobbed in the white-tipped waves, and Tish Verdure held on hard to the red steel railing near the bow. She zipped up her leather jacket to her neck, but the cold made its way inside her clothes. Beside her, Finn Mathisen swayed with the rolling motion of the deck. He looked as tall and lean as a flagpole. His tie-dye shirt billowed in the wind. He tilted his head back and finished his can of Miller Lite.

'You look really cold,' he said.

'Yeah, I guess I am.'

'Come on, let's go sit inside.'

He took her hand and led her back to the enclosed lower deck of the ship. Tish almost sang with joy when the door closed behind them, cutting off the wind and leaving her under the hot air vent from the boat's furnace. She shivered, warming up. Most of the other passengers were here, seated on benches by the windows, soaking up the view. Finn found an open stretch of bench on the starboard side, where the boat looked out on the lake, and the two of them sat down.

'I'm going to get another beer,' Finn said. 'You want something?'

'No, thanks.'

She watched him head up to the bar. His clothes looked a size too large, as if he had dropped weight since he bought them. He was in his late forties, like her, but he wore his age hard. She noticed a tremor in his hands. A yellowing in his skin. He was ill. She wondered if his shaved head was voluntary, or whether he had lost his hair to cancer treatment.

147

When he came back, he noticed her eyeing his bare skull. 'I was losing most of my hair anyway.'

'The shaved look is trendy now,' Tish said.

'You don't have to say that. I figured bald was better than having a forehead that went halfway up my head. My hair used to be so thick it was like an afro, but I started finding blond curls on my pillow in my twenties.'

He popped the top of his beer can.

'So how are you, Finn?' Tish asked.

Finn drank down half the can on his first swallow. He wiped his mouth with the cuff of his shirt. 'How am I? I guess you can see how I am.'

'I'm sorry.'

'Self-inflicted wounds,' he said. He held up the beer can. 'This is the enemy. Back then, I was mostly into grass and coke. Not that I have to tell you that, huh? I finally kicked drugs and took up alcohol instead. The docs say my liver is hoisting the white flag.'

'But you're still drinking.'

'If I'm going to die, I'll die happy,' Finn said. 'I've been in and out of rehab for years. I'd get sober for a while, but I couldn't kick it. A few months ago, they said the damage was permanent. So what the hell.'

'You shouldn't give up.'

'I don't think of it as giving up. It's more like suicide for dummies. If I had any guts, I would have killed myself years ago.'

'Finn, for God's sake,' Tish said.

'What, does that shock you? I'm sorry. Laura never wanted to see me as a lost cause either. She was the only one who ever tried to help me.'

'I wish you wouldn't talk like this.'

'Hey, at least I'm not blaming anyone but myself anymore. For years, I blamed my mother. Even after Rikke and I got out of North Dakota, I figured that I was who I was because of what my mother did to us. That didn't change anything, though, so I started blaming Rikke. It was all her fault that I couldn't stand on my own two feet. I even moved away for a few years. But after another stint in rehab down in the Cities, I realized the only person that fucked me up was me. So I came back here. Nothing changed.'

'How is Rikke?' Tish asked.

Finn downed the last of his beer. He was wobbly. He leaned forward and pressed his face against the glass window of the boat. They were in the ship canal now, heading back toward the harbor. The bridge was up, and Finn bent his neck back to look at the span suspended above them.

'She's like me. Bitter.'

'Is she still teaching?'

Finn swung his head back and forth. 'She left the schools years ago. She was fired for having an affair with a student. These days, you do that, you go to jail. Back then, they just swept that kind of thing under the carpet.'

'I'm sorry.'

'No, you're not. Laura liked Rikke, but you didn't.'

Inside the harbor, Tish felt the wavy rocking of the boat diminish. She saw the ribbon of land on the Point and thought about Stride and Serena living there. Ahead of them, she saw the towers of grain elevators and the giant docks for the ore boats. They looked darker and larger in the evening gloom.

'Why did you want to see me, Finn?' Tish asked.

He shrugged. 'I think about the old days a lot.'

'Sometimes I wish I could forget them.'

'I've forgotten way too much already. I've had blackouts all my life. Big gaps where nothing's left. Maybe it's better that way.'

Tish said nothing.

'I hear you're writing a book about Laura's death,' Finn continued.

'That's right.'

'Why would you want to do something like that?' he asked.

'Excuse me?'

'I mean, why dig up the past? Wasn't it bad enough as it is?'

'I guess I felt like I owed it to Laura,' Tish said.

Finn's hands twitched. He eyed the bar, but he stayed on the bench. 'You know I was in love with Laura back then.'

'No, she never told me,' Tish murmured.

'That's OK. I knew she didn't feel the same way. I never told her how I felt, because I didn't want to hear her say it. But like I said, she was the only person who ever gave a shit about me. Other than Rikke.'

Finn put his hands on top of his skull and squeezed. He closed his eyes and opened them, blinking rapidly.

'Are you OK?' she asked.

'Yeah. As OK as I'll ever be.' He added, 'What happened between you two?'

'What do you mean?'

'That May, Laura hung out with me a lot. You weren't around. She was really upset that you were gone. She needed someone.'

'Things happen between friends,' Tish said.

Finn nodded. 'Do you feel guilty for leaving her behind? I mean, maybe if you'd stayed, she'd still be alive.'

Tish felt as if she'd been struck. She opened her mouth to deny it, but she couldn't. 'Yes, I think about that.'

'Me, too. I wanted to be the one to save her. Instead, look how it turned out.'

'It's not your fault.'

'No?' He hesitated. 'Listen, there's something I need to tell you. There are some things I need to get off my chest.'

'About what?'

'Laura's murder.'

Tish held her breath. 'What is it?'

'A lot of it is missing, you know? Gone. I only remember bits and pieces. I was high, out of my mind, like usual. I just thought, maybe this would help you.'

'What are you saying?'

'I was in the park that night,' Finn told her. 'The night Laura was killed.'

Tish's two hands clenched into fists. 'What did you see? Did you see who killed her?'

'No.'

'Why were you there?' Tish asked.

'When I saw Laura and her sister in the park, I began following them. I was watching them down by the lake.'

Marijuana, Tish thought. 'Why follow Laura?'

'Because I loved her. I told you.'

'Were you stalking Laura? Did you send her those letters?'

'What letters? What are you talking about?'

She looked for guile in his face and didn't see any. 'Never mind. What did you see that night?'

'I saw her leave her sister and her boyfriend by the lake. I followed her along the trail until she got back to the softball field.'

150

'Then what?'

'Someone attacked her in the field.'

'Who?'

'I don't know. It was too dark. I couldn't see him. All I could see was the guy jumping her, pushing her to the ground. She screamed.'

'What did you do?'

Finn stared at his feet. 'Nothing.'

'My God, Finn, how could you? You just let it happen?'

'I thought about shouting for help, but I didn't want anyone to know I was there. Anyway, it didn't matter.'

'What do you mean?'

'While I was watching, I heard someone behind me. Someone came running when Laura screamed. I ducked into the woods, and this guy ran out into the clearing. It was a big black guy. I didn't know who he was.'

'What did he do?'

'He saved her.'

'How?'

'He picked up a baseball bat in the field and swung it into the guy's back. Then he pulled the guy off Laura and beat the crap out of him. Laura ran the opposite way, into the woods, toward the north beach. You know, where they found her body.'

'What did the black guy do?'

'He followed her.'

'With the bat?'

Finn shook his head. 'No. The bat was still lying in the field.'

'You're sure about that?'

'I'm sure. I saw the black guy throw it away.'

'Then what?'

'Then nothing. I don't remember any more.'

'Did you go home?'

'I told you, I don't remember,' Finn snapped.

'This is important,' Tish said. 'You have to think.'

Finn's face twitched. 'Don't you think I want to remember? After that, it's all black. I don't know what happened. I don't remember anything at all.'

Fifteen

Stride watched the face of the county attorney, Pat Burns, as Tish recounted Finn's story. Her brown eyes were intense and focused behind her half-glasses, but he couldn't see belief, disbelief, surprise, or worry. When Tish was done, Pat reclined in her swivel chair behind her desk. She considered Tish without saying a word.

'You're a writer, Ms Verdure,' Pat said. 'What's your interpretation of what Finn told you?'

Tish glanced at Stride, who was seated beside her in front of Pat's desk. 'I think this changes everything,' she said.

'How so?'

'Well, isn't it obvious? The whole theory behind Dada committing the crime was that his fingerprints were on the bat. Now we know why. It wasn't that he attacked Laura, it was that he rescued her by fighting off Peter Stanhope. Peter was trying to rape her. They weren't dating. There was no secret meeting planned. He assaulted her, and then this black man Dada broke it up.'

'According to Finn, Dada was the one who followed Laura toward the beach where her body was found,' Pat pointed out.

'Yes, but without the bat. That's important.'

Pat nodded. 'Isn't it odd that he would remember a detail like that so clearly?'

'He remembered it, that's the main thing.'

'So he says.'

'Are you saying he's lying?'

152

'I have no idea, but why didn't he come forward back then? Why wait thirty years to tell this amazing story?'

'He told me that he blacked out the entire night. For months, he didn't remember a thing. He didn't even remember being there. It's only come back to him in flashbacks. Recovered memories.'

'Recovered memories aren't very reliable. Juries don't like them.'

'Except his story fits the facts.'

'Yes, you're right. It does.' Pat looked at Stride. 'What do you think, Lieutenant?'

'I'd say that Finn was telling the truth, up to a point,' Stride said. 'His story about what happened in the softball field with Laura and Dada makes sense. His motive for coming forward now is another question. I also don't know whether he's telling us everything he remembers.'

'Why do you think Finn chose to come forward now?' Pat asked Tish. 'Did he say anything about that?'

'I think he felt guilty for keeping it secret for so long.' Tish hesitated. 'Also, I don't believe he's well.'

'You think he's ill? Is it serious?'

'He told me his liver was failing. He has a long history of drug and alcohol abuse.'

'The perfect witness,' Pat said, with a thin smile. She added, 'If you don't mind my asking, Ms Verdure, what exactly do you hope to accomplish by writing this book?'

'What do you mean?'

'Well, is your motive to make a lot of money? Is it to get publicity and headlines?'

'I want justice for Laura,' Tish said. 'That's all.'

'In other words, it's important to you that your book somehow "solves" this case.'

Tish nodded. 'Mark Fuhrman wrote a book about the Martha Moxley murder in Connecticut, and now someone's finally in jail for the crime.'

'I have to tell you, Ms Verdure, if that's your goal, you're setting yourself up for a big fall. I'm sure Lieutenant Stride has explained the challenges of conducting a prosecution on a case where we have so many missing witnesses and so much missing evidence.'

'Yes, he has,' Tish replied. 'But I'm bringing you material you've never had before. New evidence. New eyewitnesses. I want to know what you're planning to do about it.'

Pat folded her hands together. 'What do you want me to do about it?'

'I want you to seek a motion compelling Peter Stanhope to provide a DNA sample that the police can match against the evidence on the stalker letter and at the crime scene.'

'No,' Pat said.

'No? That's it?'

'That's it.'

Tish pushed the chair back and stood up. 'I can't believe this. We have a witness who proves that Stanhope was lying about what happened that night. If we can match his DNA, we can prove that he was stalking Laura. That's not enough?'

Pat shook her head. 'No, it's not. For one thing, Finn never mentioned Peter's name. He admits he couldn't identify the boy who was with Laura.'

'But Peter already placed himself with Laura in the softball field with his own statement. He never denied he was there. He blamed Dada for the assault, but Finn's statement proves that's not what happened.'

'Not necessarily. Finn says it was dark. He could easily have mis-interpreted what was happening between Laura and the boy in the field. He could have misconstrued Dada's actions, too.'

'You want to bury this because Peter is one of your political allies, right? I know how the game is played.'

'You don't know a thing, Ms Verdure,' Pat snapped. 'I'm not going to seek a motion based on fragments of recollection from a noto-rious drug addict who has remained silent about this case for decades. It would be an abuse of my authority, and no judge would even consider it. In addition, I'm not going to seek a motion because it would not further a prosecution in this case. Even if I could prove that Peter Stanhope was stalking Laura, I wouldn't have nearly enough evidence to sustain a murder charge. Until I am convinced we have something to prosecute, I'm not going to go out on a limb. Is that clear?'

'What kind of Catch-22 is that?' Tish asked. 'You can't get evidence unless you're ready to prosecute, and you'll never be ready to prosecute without evidence. In other words, you're going to do nothing.'

'I didn't say that.'

'It sure sounds like it.' Tish added, 'You know, I haven't talked to the national press yet, but maybe it's time I did.'

'If you bring in the national news media, you lose control of the story,' Pat replied. 'That's not going to help your book. Media pressure often has the opposite effect of what you intend.'

'I'll take that risk,' Tish said.

'Ms Verdure, you've given us a new angle to investigate in this murder, and we *will* investigate it. Just not the way you may want us to.'

'What do you mean?' Tish asked.

Pat gestured to Stride. 'Lieutenant, do you want to explain?'

'We're going to take a close look at Finn's story,' Stride told Tish.

'That's good. That's what I want.'

'But this isn't just about Peter Stanhope,' he added.

'What do you mean?' Tish asked.

'I mean that Finn put himself at the scene of the murder with his statement,' Stride explained. 'We had no idea he was there until now. He admitted to you that he was following Laura that night. So yes, I want to know what Finn thinks he saw. But the reality is, he just made himself a suspect, too.'

Sixteen

Stride took a left exit off the interstate and headed for the steep span of the Blatnik Bridge. The narrow crossing over Superior Bay was also known as the High Bridge, a nickname held over from the days when the second bridge between the cities of Duluth and Superior was the lowly Arrowhead Bridge. Ever since the Bong Bridge had opened in 1985, and the Arrowhead Bridge was torn down, the two bridges had provided identical clearance for ships, about 120 feet from the roadway to the cold waters of the harbor. But for locals, the Blatnik Bridge would always be the High Bridge.

Police on both sides of the bay hated the bridge. Fog, ice, and snow caused numerous accidents. Wind blew cars and trucks across the lanes. Jurisdiction was always a headache, because the state line cut right through the center of the bridge. And then there were the citizens who used the High Bridge like the Golden Gate, as a favorite spot for suicides. The Blatnik offered no pedestrian walkway, only a gravel-strewn shoulder and a three-foot concrete barrier. Leave your car at the height of the span, get out, and take a three-second journey to neverland.

Stride had seen the bridge from both sides, helping untangle wrecks on the highway in the fog and sailing under the bridge in Coast Guard boats as they trolled for bodies. To him, the bridge meant death.

He drove fast in the left lane, crossing under the blue steel arch of the bridge and descending into the decay of northern Superior. He made his way off the highway onto Tower Avenue, driving past shuttered storefronts, where the main street was a ghost town. The two cities were known as the Twin Ports, but Superior was the poor sister, its population declining, its economy staggered by industrial decline. No one made money here. No one built houses. They looked for work and staved off the wolf at the door.

Stride drove south, past the city's small retail strip into the low, empty land. He turned onto a dirt road that led across a series of railroad tracks. The home that Rikke and Finn Mathisen shared was on a two-acre lot at the end of the developed land, where the road ended in waste and fields. The grass on the square lot was long. Oak trees yawned over the three-story Victorian house. Blue paint chipped away from the siding.

He parked his Expedition across the street and got out. He was immediately adjacent to an unguarded railroad crossing, where nothing but a white X marked the tracks. Tilting poles of telephone wires paralleled the railway. Stride could see a train rumbling between houses a quarter-mile away. Its whistle blasted through the quiet in several staccato bursts. When it stopped, he noticed the calmer noise of wind chimes tinging from the Mathisen porch.

It was nearly eight o'clock on Thursday evening. On sunny summer nights, there would be more than an hour of light left, but the clouds overhead were thick and gray, making the dusk look like night. A steady breeze blew dust off the dirt roads. Hot, humid air came with it. Stride walked up the sidewalk, where green grass pushed between the squares of pavement. He noticed a driveway leading to a detached garage behind the house and saw a 1980s-era tan Impala parked in the weeds.

The wooden steps to the porch sagged under his feet. He went up to the front door and peered inside, seeing lights downstairs. When he rapped his knuckles on the door frame, he saw a tall, stocky woman emerge from the kitchen with an apron tied around her waist. She answered the door, and Stride saw an older version of the woman who had taught him math during his junior year in high school.

'Can I help you?' she asked, drying her hands on the flowers of the apron. Under the apron, she wore a collared white T-shirt and shorts. The windows were closed, and the air from the house was stale and warm.

'Ms Mathisen?'

157

'Yes.'

'My name is Lieutenant Jonathan Stride. I'm with the Duluth Police. You wouldn't remember me, but you were my math teacher for a year back in high school. That was longer ago than either of us would like to admit, I think.'

Rikke didn't smile. 'Police?'

'Yes, I was hoping to talk to Finn.'

'He's not here.'

'Do you know when he'll be back?'

'No.'

'Well, do you mind if I come in? I'd like to ask you a few questions too.'

Rikke didn't rush to invite him inside. 'You said you're with the Duluth Police? Shouldn't you have someone from Superior with you? This isn't Minnesota, you know.'

'I know, but that's not actually necessary,' Stride told her. 'This won't take long.'

Rikke shrugged and opened the door. Inside, the old house was decorated with worn throw rugs woven in diamond patterns and half a dozen clay pots of drooping philodendron plants. He noticed two skinny cats wandering across the wooden floors. A fine layer of cat hair had settled over the living-room furniture, and he caught a whiff of ammonia. He sat down in an uncomfortable Shaker chair. Rikke untied her apron and sat on the sofa opposite him. She picked at the fraying fabric and pulled white foam from the arm of the sofa. An orange tabby walked across her lap.

'What do you want?' she asked.

He tried to picture the twenty-something teacher inside her. Back then, she had been tall and fit, with wavy, flowing blonde hair and Nordic good looks. She had intense blue eyes and large circular glasses propped on her high cheekbones. Full, ripe breasts swelled underneath her white sweaters and defied gravity. Her fleshy, strong thighs bulged out of her jeans. She had a severe way about her in the classroom, like a dominatrix. They joked about it in the locker room. 'Teacher, I've been bad.'

Thirty years had taken a toll on Rikke. She was heavier, with cellulite dimpling her legs. Her blond hair was short and came out of a bottle.

Her face was rounded and jowly. She no longer wore glasses, but her eyes were as fierce as he remembered, like two globes of azure ice. He noticed that one breast sagged like a melting snowman across her chest, and where the other breast should have been, the fabric of her shirt puckered over empty space. A pink ribbon was pinned to the pocket.

'You taught algebra, didn't you? Or was it geometry?'

'Geometry.'

'But not anymore?'

'Not in a very long time.'

'I have it right, don't I? Finn lives here with you?'

'Yes, he does.'

'He's your brother?'

'That's right.'

'It's unusual to find a brother and sister who have stayed together so long,' Stride said.

'Finn's had a hard life,' Rikke replied. 'He's seven years younger than I am, and he's always needed someone to look after him.'

'Why is that?'

'Why do you care? Do you suspect Finn of having done something wrong?'

'Not at all.'

'Then why are you here?'

'Finn provided some information that's pertinent to one of our investigations,' Stride told her. 'Candidly, I'm trying to assess his credibility as a witness.'

'What investigation?'

Stride didn't reply.

Irritated, Rikke pushed the cat off her lap and pulled at her shirt. 'What do you want to know?'

'Tell me about his background. You said he had a hard life.'

'Finn and I grew up in North Dakota,' Rikke replied. 'Our father was killed in a car accident when Finn was ten. Our mother died five years later. I had just graduated with my teaching license at the time. I took Finn, and we moved here. I got a job. I bought this house with the money we got from selling the farm. I was hoping to give us a fresh start, but for Finn, the wounds went too deep. He spent years

159

on drugs. He's still drinking himself to death. Sometimes I think I should have kicked him out and let him stand on his own two feet, but I was the only family he had. I wasn't going to turn my back on him.'

'That can't have been easy.'

'I didn't say it was.'

'Do you remember a girl named Laura Starr?' Stride asked.

The muscles in Rikke's face tightened. Her cheeks bloomed with pink circles. 'Yes, of course.'

'A journalist named Tish Verdure is writing a book about Laura Starr's murder,' Stride said.

'So I hear. I read the papers.'

'Finn told Tish he was in the park the night Laura was killed.'

Rikke shook her head. 'Finn said that? No, that's not right.'

'You think Finn is lying?'

'He may be making up a story to impress this woman, but more likely his mind is pulling bits and pieces of things he's read about the murder over the years. Finn's mental state is highly unreliable, Lieutenant. Drugs and drink have fried his brain since he was a boy. He doesn't have a solid grasp on what's real and what's not, certainly not after so much time has passed. I assure you, he wasn't there.'

'It was a long time ago,' Stride said. 'How can you be so sure?'

'You think I ever let Finn drive back then?' Rikke asked. 'He never had a car. The only way he got anywhere was if I drove him. That night, we were both at home watching the fireworks.'

Stride leaned forward with his hands on his knees. 'Did Finn know Laura?'

'Yes, we both did.'

'I understand Finn was in love with her.'

'Finn? Puppy dog love maybe. Nothing more. Laura was one of my favorite students – a sweet girl, very pretty, very quiet. She wanted to be a counselor for teenagers in dysfunctional families. She was passionate about it. I encouraged her to spend time with Finn, because I thought it would help them both. To her credit, she really devoted herself to Finn. I think she made a difference with him, and I'm sure he was grateful to her. To him, that was probably love.'

'What else can you tell me about Laura?'

160

'You should probably talk to Tish about her,' Rikke said. 'The two of them were best friends for a while.'

'For a while?'

Rikke cocked her head. 'Yes, they certainly weren't friends at the end.'

'Oh?'

'God, no. They broke up very badly. Laura came to me in tears.'

'Did she say what happened?'

'She told me they had a fight.'

'What was the fight about?'

Rikke steepled her fingers together. She spoke slowly. 'It was about a boy. Tish was insanely jealous. She demanded that Laura stop seeing him.'

'Who was it?'

'Laura didn't tell me his name, but I always assumed it was the boy from that rich family in Duluth. The Stanhopes. I read in the papers after her death that Laura and Peter were seeing each other.'

Stride didn't like where this was going. It made him wonder again about Tish's motives in pursuing Peter Stanhope.

'Did Finn talk to you about Laura's murder after it happened? Did he ever say he knew something about it?'

'Of course not. Like I told you, he wasn't there.'

'I do need to talk to Finn,' Stride said, getting to his feet. 'How do I reach him?'

Rikke waved her hand dismissively. 'He comes and goes when he pleases. I'm not my brother's keeper. Call the delivery company, and maybe they can help you find him somewhere on his route.'

Stride nodded. 'I appreciate your time.'

Rikke didn't reply.

'You know, I do remember something from your geometry class,' Stride added.

'Oh?'

'I think it was called the parallel postulate.'

Rikke shrugged. 'If two lines cross a third and form less than two right angles, then eventually the two lines will meet if extended far enough. Why on earth do you find that so interesting?'

'It's something I find in most of my investigations,' Stride told her. 'Sooner or later, the lines always intersect.'

*

161

After Stride left, Rikke Mathisen stood at the living-room window that looked out on the street. Holding aside the lace curtain, she watched Stride retreat into the dusky gloom and climb into his truck. His headlights burst on like two staring eyes, and then gravel scraped as he sped down the dirt road back to the highway, jolting across the railroad tracks. She watched until the red taillights disappeared and kept watching as night fell outside like a black cloud enveloping the house. Her orange tabby cat rubbed against her legs and mewed, but Rikke didn't move. In the distance, coming from the northeast, a train screamed. Even at this distance, she felt its vibration under her feet. It didn't matter how long she had lived here. She heard every train.

Rikke turned away. Hung on the foyer wall by a steel wire was a mirror, framed in heavy brass, laden with dust. She caught a glimpse of her dark reflection, and her breath clutched in her chest, because it was her mother's face staring back at her like a mean-eyed ghost brought up from the earth. Fate was cruel. Thirty years had passed, and she had become the person that she and Finn had hated for so long. You can run and run, and when you think you've escaped, you realize that all along you've been running in a circle.

She switched off the downstairs light and felt her way with her hands, like a blind person, toward the mahogany steps that led upstairs. At the top of the stairs, she stared at the closed door in front of her. Finn's room. She jiggled the metal knob, but it was locked. He always kept it locked. He didn't realize that Rikke had a key. She let herself inside and turned on the light, not caring if Finn saw the glow from his bedroom window when he drove home. The room was messy. Soiled clothes were strewn across the bed and draped over the closet door. Crushed cans of Budweiser littered the floor like silver hockey pucks. She smelled urine from his sheets. He still wet the bed.

The top drawer of his black lacquer nightstand was open. She yanked it out and overturned the drawer onto the floor, where the contents rolled and clattered. She did the same with the bottom drawer. She got down on all fours and pushed through the pile of junk with her hands. Finn saved everything. Old cell phones and computer cables. Half-completed tax forms. Dried-up pens and pencils snapped in half. Thumbed porno magazines, bottles of lubricant, and rubber strokers crusted over with discharge.

An old photograph.

Rikke held it up and stared at it. The picture was four inches square, with a narrow white border, its colors faded and unnatural. She recognized Finn in the backyard of their house, sitting next to Laura at a picnic bench, with his arm around her shoulder. They were young and smiling. Laura wore a tank top. Finn was bare-chested, his blond hair curly and big. Rikke remembered taking the photograph. She held it, her hands trembling, then tore it in half, and tore it in half again, and again, until the pieces were too small to rip. She scattered them like pinches of coarse salt over the mess on the floor.

Back then, Finn had given up his room for Laura on those nights when she stayed over. She had slept here in his twin bed, while he slept on the sofa downstairs. Except when he would creep upstairs and watch. Rikke knew all about it. She had seen him hovering in the blackness of the doorway to his room, staring at his bed, where the stars glowed faintly and illuminated bare flesh. They never talked about it. Some things were just understood.

She went to his desk next, pulled out all the drawers, and poured them out like jugs of water. She sifted through the debris without seeing what she wanted, but she knew she would find what she was looking for eventually. She knew Finn. With her face sober and emotionless, she pulled all of his clothes off the hangers in the closet, pulled the board games down off the dusty shelf, and felt along the grainy surface of the wood with outstretched fingers. When she found nothing, she dragged the mattress off Finn's bed and then flipped the box spring off the frame.

Nothing.

She toppled the black nightstand to the floor with one hand. The lamp came with it, crashing and breaking. She bent over and peered at the underside of the nightstand and nodded grimly to herself.

There it was.

A bulging manila envelope was taped to the unfinished wood with duct tape that was losing its stickiness, because it had been pulled off and resealed countless times. Rikke grabbed the envelope. Slabs of tape came with it. She ripped the flap and extracted the dog-eared sheaf of papers inside. She went through each one carefully, studying every picture. They were grainy color photographs, printed on the inkjet on Finn's desk. Blurry images, taken at night. It didn't matter. She could see clearly enough what they were.

Teenage girls.

When she had seen them all, she shoved them back into the envelope. On the opposite wall, beside Finn's desk, was a metal trashcan. She emptied it of garbage and then put the envelope inside. She hunted for a box of matches amid the chaos she had created on the floor, then lit a match and dropped it inside the trashcan, where the wispy fire smoldered on the paper and grew in a widening torch of flame and smoke. The envelope and all the photographs curled into flakes of black ash that floated in the room like coal-colored snow. In the hallway, the smoke alarm honked in protest. Rikke ignored it.

When it was over, the metal inside was scorched. She took a ruler, got down on her knees, and hacked at the warm ashes, turning them into dust. Her skin was streaked with soot. She got up and wiped her hands on her shorts, leaving black fingerprints.

The computer was next. And the camera. They would all go in the river sometime during the middle-night hours. You couldn't erase things like that. Someone who knew what they were doing could always find them again.

Rikke heard a noise in the hall and looked up.

Finn was in the doorway.

Seventeen

Tish parked in an alley behind the Kitch, where it was dark except for a soft yellow glow from inside the club windows. A diagonal rain swept the street as she climbed out of her Civic. She unfolded an umbrella, held it at an angle like a flag, and splashed through the puddles in her heels around the corner of the building toward the high door. The four-story clubhouse towered above her, regal and imposing in red brick, like a rich man's mansion. Hollow-eyed Indian gargoyles guarded the entrance and stared at her disapprovingly. By the time she slipped inside, her white dress was speckled with rain spots. She flipped her hair, and water sprayed onto the wine-red carpet.

The sprawling main corridor was lined in dark wood and sconce lights and bore the club's logo in gold on the floor. Tish took a few tentative steps, expecting someone to stop her. Instead, the hallway was empty. She had never been here before, but she remembered people talking about the Kitch the way people on the east coast talked about Skull and Bones. The faces of members had changed in 125 years, but admission was still by invitation only. To Tish, it felt like a secret society for the privileged. A place built stone by stone on money and tradition.

On her left was a lounge with thick beams lining the ceiling and deep paisley carpet on the floor. A wood fire burned in a brick fireplace, and two leather recliners were carefully placed on either side of the hearth. She was cold from the rain, and she approached the fireplace, putting out her hands to warm them and feeling heat on her dress. As she dripped on the carpet, she noticed an oil painting on the west wall. It was of an old man with a familiar face, in a three-piece suit. His head was almost bald. He looked tough and prosperous. When she approached the portrait, she saw his name inscribed on a brass plate on the frame.

Randall Stanhope. Former president of the club.

'Can I help you?'

The voice came from behind her. Tish turned and saw a tuxedo-clad attendant in his fifties with a clipped mustache.

'I'm sorry,' Tish said. She squared her shoulders and gave the man an engaging smile. 'I'm supposed to be meeting Peter Stanhope here. Can you tell me where to find him?'

She had no meeting scheduled. Peter hadn't seen her in thirty years. But everyone told her that the Kitch was where he spent most of his evenings. Like his father.

'Mr Stanhope is in the pool room downstairs,' he told her. 'Would you like me to tell him you're here?'

'No, I'll just join him there.'

'Do you know the way?' the man asked.

'I'm afraid not.'

'Let me show you.'

The attendant led her downstairs, where the ceilings were lower and the walls felt as if they were closing in. Tish heard raucous male laughter. The pool room was smaller than she expected, with lapis color on the walls and in the checkerboard carpet. Half a dozen men in white shirts and loosened ties gathered around a pool table lined with burgundy felt. They drank Scotch from crystal lowball glasses.

The conversation stopped when they saw her. Tish recognized Peter Stanhope immediately. He had a custom pool cue in his hand and was bent over, taking aim on a shot down the table. He was the only man still wearing a suit coat. She was close enough to smell the alcohol on his breath and see the overhead lights shining in his silver hair. As she watched, he struck the cue ball with a sharp crack and thunked the solid purple four ball into the far pocket.

'Mr Stanhope?'

'Yes, George?' Peter asked. He looked past the attendant and sized up Tish.

'I believe you have a meeting with this woman.'

166

Peter straightened up and propped his cue against the table. He folded his arms and rubbed his sunburnt chin with his left hand. His blue eyes twinkled with curiosity behind penny-colored glasses. 'Do I?'

George's smile evaporated. 'Is there a problem?' he asked.

'I don't know,' Peter replied pleasantly. He eyed Tish. 'Is there?'

'My name is Tish Verdure,' she said quickly.

Tish heard a rumble of displeasure among the other men in the room. They knew who she was. Peter didn't react, other than to flick his tongue quickly across his upper teeth. 'Ah.'

'I was hoping we could talk.'

'I'm terribly sorry, Mr Stanhope,' George said, stepping in front of Tish. 'This woman told me she had a meeting scheduled with you. I'll see her out immediately.'

Peter waved his hand. 'No, no, it's fine, George. I've been anxious to speak to Ms Verdure, as it happens. Boys, carry on without me, all right?' He approached Tish and extended his hand. His grip was strong, and his fingers were smooth, except for the dust of pool chalk.

'Would you like a drink?' he asked her.

'Some red wine, I guess.'

'George, a bottle of the Alphonse Mellot pinot that I had last night, all right? Is anyone in 306 tonight?'

'No, sir.'

'Take it up there, will you?'

'Of course.'

Peter refilled his own tumbler from a half-empty bottle of Lagavulin and then took Tish's arm by the elbow. 'Shall we?'

He guided her to a turn-of-the-century elevator that was uncomfortably small. They were shoulder to shoulder. Peter didn't say anything as they rode upward. He just smiled, showing beautifully white teeth, and smoothed down his hair. She noticed his eyes straying over her body. When the doors opened, he led her to a room painted in cream, with an off-white sofa, an armchair, and a square glass coffee table. Through a doorway, Tish saw a queen-sized bed with an elaborately flowered comforter. She backed up.

'This is a bedroom,' she said.

'A guest room,' Peter said. 'Members outside the city stay here sometimes. Or men whose wives have kicked them out for the night. That's why I prefer the single life.' He added, 'Don't worry, I'm not going to assault you, if that's what you're concerned about. I just thought we would both like some privacy.'

'Leave the door open.'

'Whatever you want.'

Peter took the armchair and worked on his drink. Tish sat uneasily on the sofa, her knees squeezed together. A couple of minutes later, the attendant George entered the room with a balloon-shaped wine glass and an open bottle. He set them on the table in front of her and poured, then gave her an imperious look and retreated from the room, closing the door behind him.

'Do you want me to open it again?' Peter asked, nodding at the door.

Tish shrugged.

'Well, here we are,' he continued. 'It's been a long time. You're looking good, Tish. Do you mind if I call you that?'

Tish shrugged again.

'You were sexy then, and you haven't lost your appeal,' he told her, his eyes roving. 'Real beauty matures with age, don't you think?'

'If you say so.'

'It wouldn't kill you to repay the compliment,' he said.

'You know you look good, so why do you need to hear it from me?'

Peter laughed. 'Try the wine, Tish. It's excellent.'

Tish did, and it was.

'Are you trying to tell me you've changed?' she asked.

'We all change. You're different, I'm different.'

'It doesn't matter,' she said. 'I don't care who you are now or how much money you have. It's what you did thirty years ago that concerns me.'

Peter nodded. 'You think I murdered Laura. You think I took a baseball bat and beat her head in.'

'Yes, I do.'

'Well, I didn't do that. How can I convince you I'm telling the truth?'

Tish took another drink of wine. It was fruity and light as helium. 'You can't. I already know you lied back then.'

168

'Oh?'

'Finn Mathisen saw you,' Tish snapped. 'He saw you attack Laura in the field. The black man, Dada, he *saved* her. When Laura ran off, the bat was still in the field. It was still with you.'

'Finn Mathisen,' Peter murmured, shaking his head. 'I haven't thought about him in years. Him and his sister, Rikke. She was one of those tasty young teachers we all lusted after. Please, Tish. We both know what kind of witness Finn is. Pat Burns is never going to put someone on the stand who probably can't remember most of the nineteen eighties.'

'I don't care what kind of witness he would make,' Tish said. 'I'm writing a book, not doing a dance for a jury. What matters is that he's telling the truth.'

'Say he is. That doesn't mean I killed Laura.'

'Are you admitting you assaulted her?'

'I'm not admitting anything. However, even if I was stupid enough to think that "no" from a girl really meant "yes" just because my name was Peter Stanhope, do you think I would kill her over something like that?'

'Over not getting what you want? Yes, I do.'

'Well, you're right, I don't take rejection well,' Peter admitted. 'You said no to me, and I called you a queer. As I recall, I kissed you and grabbed your tits. I was a pig.'

'Yes, you were.'

'But I didn't kill you, did I? Because here you are.'

'Maybe you wanted Laura more than me.'

Peter's smile faltered. His full lips twitched.

'Maybe you were obsessed with her,' Tish continued. 'Maybe you were enraged that she didn't want you.' She met his eyes and whispered, '*Are you going to be alone tonight, you whore?*'

His fingers clutched the tumbler so tightly that she thought the crystal might shatter. 'I have no idea what you're talking about.'

But he did.

Tish knew that she was right. She swallowed down her loathing and drank more wine.

Peter stood up, stretching his legs. He caught his reflection in a brass mirror and dusted the broad lapels of his suit coat. His grin returned, more brightly than before. 'I always wondered if you were upset that Laura found me attractive.'

'She didn't.'

'You're wrong about that. All the girls back then were interested in me. You were the exception. Or were you just playing hard to get?'

'Oh, please.'

'Is that why you didn't like me dating your best friend?'

'Laura broke it off with you. She told me she did.'

'Ah, but are you sure she wasn't lying? Maybe Laura didn't want you to know what was really going on between us.'

'That's ridiculous,' Tish snapped.

'I wonder what you would have done if you'd found out the truth,' he said. 'I imagine you would have been very upset.'

'Are you finished?'

'I haven't even begun. Don't tangle with a lawyer, Tish.'

'I'm going to get you,' she insisted.

He laughed. 'You know that's not going to happen.'

She cringed, feeling on display as he watched her. His eyes glittered with lust that he didn't bother hiding.

'The sad thing is, I'm telling you that I think you're a murderer, and you still want to sleep with me.'

Peter sat down next to her on the sofa and took an oversized swallow of his Scotch. Their legs touched. 'True.'

'Are you that desperate?'

'I'm not desperate at all.'

'I picture you with a harem of twenty-something models,' Tish said.

'Sometimes.'

'So why come on to a woman in her late forties who thinks you're the devil?'

'I'm not the devil. I thought you were finally beginning to find me charming.'

'Hardly.'

'Believe it or not, I like women who are mature. Strong. Independent. I don't find many women who stand up to me.'

'So you're saying that having a woman accuse you of murder turns you on.'

170

'I've heard worse accusations than that.' He grinned. 'I think you're lying, Tish. You do find me attractive. You always have.'

'You find yourself attractive enough for both of us.'

'There aren't many women who get to reject me twice.'

Tish felt a shiver of fear. 'What does that mean?'

'Not what you think. I just mean you've managed to deflate my ego, not to mention my manhood, in two separate decades.'

'You'll live.'

'I already told you that I don't take rejection well. It just makes me more determined.'

'Do I need to scream?'

'Not at all. I wouldn't dream of ravishing a woman who doesn't want me to ravish her.'

'Good.'

'I'm going to kiss you, though,' Peter said. 'I think you owe me that.'

'I don't owe you anything.'

'So slap my face if you want.'

He leaned across the sofa. Tish stared into his eyes and didn't turn away. His lips were rough as they moved against hers. She felt nothing but responded as if she did. She put her hands around his neck and held him to her. He smelled like a man. She felt his fingers stroke her breast with a feathery touch, testing the waters. It was now or never.

Tish bit down on Peter's fat lower lip. Hard. Warm blood sprayed onto their faces, and she mashed her cheek against him and held on tight. Peter bellowed in pain and fought to disentangle himself. He shoved her away and leaped to his feet. His chin was a messy cherry river dripping onto his shirt.

'You crazy bitch!' he shouted.

'Get the hell away from me, Peter,' Tish told him calmly.

He ripped open the guest room door. 'You're out of your fucking mind.'

Tish watched him go as she dabbed smears of blood from her face onto the sleeve of her white dress.

She was thinking: *I've got you.*

*

171

Two hours later, a noise woke Tish out of a dead sleep in her condominium.

She bolted up in bed, the blanket bunching at her waist. She listened to sounds from the open window, where surf slapped at the base of the bluff. The air horn of a truck blared on the freeway. That was all.

She climbed out of bed and grabbed her robe from the closet. Her white dress was wrapped in plastic on the shelf.

She stopped. Waited.

A few seconds later, she heard it again. Sharp and musical. From somewhere outside came the sound of glass breaking.

Tish ran into the main room of the condo and hunted for her phone. The room was black with shadows. She was alone, no one lying in wait for her, no one charging out of the corners at her. She didn't hear the noise again.

A car peeled away on the street, its loud engine growing faint as it roared toward the curve leading back to the city. Tish crept to the front door and peered through the spyhole. Outside, the sidewalk and street were quiet. She opened the door carefully and watched tendrils of fog drift through the glow of the street light. When she stepped outside, sweat began to grow on her skin like a fungus.

Nothing moved.

The pavement scratched her bare feet. She took tentative steps toward the curb. When she saw her rental car, parked near the trees, she ran.

Half of the windshield was caved in, the other half frosted with starbursts of white glass. Scissor-sharp popcorn littered the seats. Jammed between the spokes of the steering wheel was a wooden baseball bat.

Eighteen

The asphalt in the parking lot of the delivery company where Finn Mathisen worked was wet, with steam rising from pools of water. Rain showers had dodged in and out of the city all day, leaving behind a moldy smell of worms. The humid air made Stride's black T-shirt cling to his skin, and the charcoal sport coat he wore over it felt damp. A line of sweat traced his forehead. It was Friday night. He wanted to go home and jump in the shower, but Finn was an hour late returning from his delivery route.

The parking lot was filled with cars left by delivery drivers for the day. Vans and trucks backed up to docks around him, loading and unloading. The company substation was less than a mile from the Duluth airport, making it easy to feed packages to outbound flights. He heard the thunder of a jet overhead, which he knew was the evening Northwest flight from the Twin Cities. It would suck up passengers and cargo and then roar back south.

A dirty yellow van rumbled off the highway. Stride caught a glimpse of the driver and recognized the narrow face and shaved head of Finn Mathisen. Finn didn't see him. Stride waited while Finn backed up his truck to an open dock and watched him clamber out of the truck, climb the steps of the platform, and disappear inside the building. Even from twenty yards away, Stride could see that Finn's uniform was soiled from a day in the heat. These were the days in Duluth that leached away everyone's energy.

Stride waited half an hour before Finn strutted out of the building's front door. He had showered and changed and was now wearing cut-offs that made his legs look like matchsticks and a gray tank top with gaping sleeve holes. He wore old sneakers with no socks.

'Finn,' Stride called.

He pushed off his Expedition and met Finn where the sidewalk ended and the parking lot began. Finn was three inches taller than Stride, but he looked as if he would blow away when the wind came off the lake.

'Who are you?' Finn asked. His eyes danced nervously.

Stride introduced himself. When Finn heard the word *police*, he shuffled his weight from one foot to the other and stared over Stride's shoulder at the row of parked cars as if he wanted to bolt. Mint breathed out of Finn's mouth like fire from a dragon.

'You got a date tonight, Finn?' Stride asked.

'Huh? No. What do you mean?'

'You've got sweet breath. Like you brushed your teeth fifty or sixty times.'

'I have halitosis, and I need to use those breath strips,' Finn said.

Stride nodded. 'It's funny, when traffic cops smell mint, they immediately think DUI. You wouldn't be late because you stopped for a couple cold ones at a bar, would you?'

Finn glanced back over his shoulder at the company door. 'Hell, no.'

'I've got a Breathalyzer in the car,' Stride told him. 'You want to have a go at it?'

'I wasn't drinking!'

'OK, Finn. Whatever you say. I have some questions for you.'

'Yeah, my sister told me you came by the house. She said you were asking about Laura's murder.'

'That's right.'

'I don't want to talk about it. It was thirty years ago. It was a shitty time in my life.'

'Is your life any better now?' Stride asked, eyeing the man from top to bottom. Tish was right. He looked as if he was dying.

Finn flinched. 'Yeah, all right, I've spent my life sitting in a park with God flying overhead crapping on me. Is that what you want to hear? I'm a loser.'

'What I want to hear is whether you told Tish the truth.'

'Man, what do you care? I mean, what are you after? Everyone from back then is old or dead.'

That was true. Stride didn't really have an answer. He hadn't asked himself why he cared so passionately about this case, thirty years after Ray Wallace called it solved. It wasn't about Tish. It wasn't about Pat Burns asking him to turn over rocks, in case the national press started asking questions. He had begun to realize that Laura's murder had changed the course of his life, and it was disturbing to discover that he knew much less about the case – and about Laura – than he had ever believed.

'If the guy who killed Laura is alive, then he still has a debt to pay,' Stride said.

'You don't need to be behind bars to pay a price. You think living with something like that for thirty years doesn't eat you up?'

'Is there something you feel guilty about?' Stride asked.

Finn swallowed hard. 'I just want to go home. I don't want to get involved.'

'Talk to me, Finn.'

'I already told the whole story to Tish.'

'I don't like getting stories second-hand.'

Finn rubbed sweat off his bald head. 'All right, all right.' He repeated his memories of the night Laura was killed in the park, which followed the story as Tish had recounted it. He skimmed over the details, but Stride let him continue without interrupting him. Finn ended with his claim that Dada had followed Laura into the woods, leaving the bat in the softball field.

'Is it possible you misunderstood what was happening between Laura and the boy in the field?' Stride asked.

'What do you mean, misunderstood?'

'Maybe they weren't fighting. Maybe they were making out.'

Finn shook his head. 'No way.'

'You're certain that the black guy, Dada, left the baseball bat in the field?' Stride asked.

'Yeah.'

'How can you be so sure?'

'I saw him throw it away, OK?'

'What else do you remember?' Stride asked.

'Nothing. I don't remember a thing.'

Stride watched Finn's eyes. The man was lying.

'You told Tish there are gaps in your memory,' Stride said.

'There are gaps in my life,' Finn replied.

'Sometimes people aren't sure what's real and what's a dream, you know what I mean? Are there things like that?'

'I said I don't remember, OK? Nothing means nothing.'

But it didn't. Finn was keeping something from him. Stride was sure of it.

'Why were you following Laura?' he asked.

'I liked her.'

'Did you follow her to the park?'

'No, she wandered by. Her and her sister.'

'Did you know someone was stalking Laura? Threatening her? Sending her obscene messages?'

'No,' Finn replied.

'It wasn't you?'

'No, I wouldn't do that. All I did was follow her.'

'You knew Laura pretty well, didn't you? Why not tell her you were there? Why spy on her?'

Finn opened his mouth and closed it. 'I don't know,' he muttered.

'Is that the best you can do?'

'I didn't – I mean, I just liked to watch her. I was embarrassed.'

Stride nodded. 'Is any of this story true, Finn?'

'What do you mean?'

'Your sister says you weren't in the park at all that night.'

Finn shook his head. 'Rikke doesn't think I can fight my own battles. I'm still just a kid to her.'

'So she lied.'

'Hey, she said we were watching fireworks, right? Well, you were there that night. It stormed. There weren't any fireworks.'

Stride remembered. Finn was right.

'Why would she say that?' Stride asked.

'To protect me.'

'Do you need protection?'

'Back then, yeah, I probably did.'

'Did you kill Laura?'

'No.'

'How do you know? You said you don't remember a thing. You

said Dada left without the bat, and the boy who attacked Laura was unconscious in the softball field. That leaves you and the bat, Finn. Maybe you picked it up. Maybe you did what you'd been doing all night. You followed Laura to the north beach.'

Finn squeezed his head with his big hands. His fingernails were chewed and bloody. 'No.'

'How do you know?' Stride repeated.

'Leave me alone,' Finn said. His yellowing skin burned crimson. He covered his eyes.

'I think Rikke lied for you because she thinks you killed Laura.'

'No.' His voice was muffled. Sweat dripped down his face like tears and spilled off his chin.

'How can you be sure?'

Finn clutched his fingers into fists and beat against his forehead. 'I'm not sure! Does that make you happy? I don't know! I don't remember! For all I know, I took that fucking bat and beat her into a pulp. OK? You try living with that. You try *not knowing* if you murdered a girl. See what that does to your life.'

He shoved his way past Stride and ran for his car.

As Stride watched Finn climb into his vehicle, he remembered talking to Rikke about geometry and realized he was seeing the parallel postulate at work again. He was watching two lines intersect.

Two lines he would have preferred remain parallel, never touching, so that the past didn't infect the present.

Finn drove a silver Rav.

Nineteen

There was no escape from the heat.

Even on the Point, which usually enjoyed a cool breeze off the lake, the evening air was stifling. Stride parked in the mud near his cottage. Heat radiated off the dirt, and the leaves drooped in the trees around him. Serena wasn't home. He didn't bother going inside, but instead climbed the shallow dune in order to watch the dusk descend on the lake. He and Serena kept two chairs in the sand at the crest of the hill, where they often sat to drink coffee in the mornings.

One of the chairs was occupied. It was Tish.

She didn't look at him as he took a seat next to her. Her eyes were locked in the distance, watching sailboats on the water. She had a plastic bag in her lap, which she protected with both hands, as if it were a child that might squirm away and fall. They didn't say anything. The lake was still, like pale blue china, and the line where the sky and the water met was lost in a sticky haze.

'I went to the wrong house,' she said finally.

Stride didn't reply.

'It was the house where you and Cindy used to live. The people there told me how to find you.'

'I haven't lived there in a long time.'

'I know,' Tish said, turning to study his face. 'Cindy showed me a photograph of your house once. I never forgot it. I recognized it as soon as I saw it. I guess I never really thought about all the time that had passed. Somehow I thought you'd still be there. Cindy, too. I suppose that sounds crazy.'

'No, it happens to me, too,' Stride said. 'But Cindy's gone. So is Laura. So are their parents. It's almost as if the whole family never existed.'

'Don't say that.'

'It's just the way it is.'

'I understand how you feel,' Tish said. 'I lost my mother. I lost Laura. In a strange way, when Cindy died, I felt orphaned again. Like she was the last link to my past and my family. But I'm not comparing my loss to yours.'

Stride said nothing.

'There's something I need to tell you about my book,' Tish said. 'I've written the early chapters in Cindy's voice. I tell the story through her eyes.'

Stride's face tensed with dismay. 'Why did you do that?'

'She was there. She was the witness.'

'You don't have a free pass into her life,' he snapped, his voice getting louder. 'Or mine.'

Tish looked flustered. 'I'm sorry. She's part of the story. So are you.'

'That doesn't give you the right to walk on her grave.'

'I'm not doing that at all. I swear.'

Stride shrugged. There was a weight on his chest.

'I didn't realize this would make you so uncomfortable,' she said.

'It's not just that.'

'Then what is it?' she asked.

'Nothing. Forget it. This isn't about you or your book.'

He wanted to say something more, but he didn't. He wanted to tell her how angry he was that his grief came alive every time he saw her. He wanted to confess to someone that he felt guilty, because he had allowed Cindy to slip back into the daily beating of his heart, where Serena belonged now. Instead, he pushed away his emotions and changed the subject.

'After what happened to your car, I'd like to keep an officer outside your condo overnight,' he told her.

Tish blinked. He knew she could hear the sudden coolness in his voice. 'So this time you don't think it's just kids.'

'I don't know, but I'd rather not take any chances.'

'OK, sure, whatever you want.'

179

Tish took the bag on her lap and passed it across to him silently. Stride looked inside and saw a white dress, neatly folded. 'This is for you,' she said. 'I'm not sure you'll understand what I did. Or why I did it.'

He grew concerned. 'What is this?'

'You'll find a sample of Peter Stanhope's DNA in a bloodstain on the dress,' Tish said.

Stride closed the bag and stared at the sky. 'What the hell did you do?'

'What I had to.'

'Son of a bitch, Tish, are you out of your mind?'

'Look, Peter is *guilty*, and you told me flat out that there's no way the courts can force him to give us a sample. So I took it. I hope I left a scar, too.'

'You just confessed to battery.'

'He started it when he tried to kiss me, the bastard. I know what you think, but I got us something we never had before. A way to confirm whether Peter was stalking Laura.'

Stride shook his head. 'It's not that simple. There's a reason why a court wouldn't compel a DNA sample. We don't have any probable cause. Even if we run the test and find out that Stanhope *was* sending Laura those notes, that doesn't change anything. It's not like Pat Burns is going to put him in front of a jury. It's not going to happen.'

'Are you saying you won't run the sample?'

'Do you think I just snap my fingers and get these things done? There's a backlog. There are other priorities. It's one thing to compare DNA in a stalker note against a database to try to break a cold case open. It's another to test one specific individual just because you've got it in your head that he's guilty.'

'Don't make it worthless, Jon. Tell me I didn't do this for nothing.'

'I'll talk to Pat Burns. That's all I can do.'

'I can't believe you'd ignore this,' Tish insisted. 'I can't believe you'd walk away from the one chance we have to find out what really happened. You heard Finn's story. Peter assaulted Laura that night. He was in the field with the bat after Dada rescued her.'

'Finn has no credibility. If there's one person whose DNA I'd like to run, it's Finn.'

180

'What are you talking about? You think Finn killed Laura?'

'I think it's a damn strong possibility. Finn is deranged, Tish. It's not a big leap to think he was capable of murder.'

'You're giving Peter Stanhope a free pass. Is it because of his money? Did you learn your lessons from Ray Wallace?' She stopped. Her eyes widened as she realized what she had said. 'God, I'm so sorry. Please forgive me.'

'No one gets a free pass from me,' Stride said.

'I know. I'm sorry.'

'You're the one who can't see past Peter Stanhope,' Stride said. 'There are plenty of other people who are hiding things about Laura. Including you.'

'Me?'

'Rikke said you were jealous of Laura's relationship with Peter.'

'Don't be ridiculous.'

'It looks to me like you're obsessed with him,' Stride said.

'This isn't about Peter. No one else was standing up for Laura, so I decided it was up to me.'

'Why?'

'She was my best friend.'

'So why were the two of you fighting that spring?'

'We weren't. We were past it.'

'What was the fight about?'

'I told you I don't remember. It was thirty years ago.'

'You're lying, Tish. Don't lie to a cop and think he won't know. Were you fighting about Peter Stanhope? Is that why you're so focused on Peter? It makes me wonder whether *you* had a motive to kill Laura.'

'That's crazy. You don't honestly think I would go through all this trouble if I had anything to do with her murder, do you?'

'Where were you that night?' Stride asked.

'I already told you. I was living in St Paul.'

'No, what *specifically* were you doing that night? Where were you? Who were you with?'

Tish shrugged. 'I have no idea.'

'That's strange. I'd think you'd remember what you were doing the night your best friend was brutally murdered.'

'You're making too much of this,' Tish said. She stood up, and the chair toppled backward into the sand behind her. 'Laura was killed by a stalker. You've got Peter's DNA. It's up to you now.'

'I have one more question,' Stride told her. 'And you'd better answer this one.'

Tish folded her arms in annoyance. 'What?'

'When did Cindy show you a photo of our house?'

Tish's mouth fell open. Stride thought she had slipped, that she had said something she never intended to share. 'I don't know. It was probably something she included with a Christmas card.'

'Stop lying to me. You said Cindy showed you a photograph. She didn't send it to you. She was *with* you. When was this?'

'A few months before she died,' Tish admitted.

'Where?'

'She visited me in Atlanta.'

Stride searched his memory. In those last terrible months, Cindy had begun to wrap her mind around the fact that she was dying, that the treatment options had finally run out. The only time he could remember her being gone was a weekend where she went off by herself, vanishing from his side for three long days. To make peace with the past, she said. She never told him where she went or anything about her trip. Back then, he had been afraid that she might commit suicide to spare him and herself the agony of a slow death. Instead, he now knew that she had gone to see Tish.

Someone she had never mentioned to him in her entire life.

Why?

'You owe me the truth,' Stride said.

Tish picked up the fallen chair and steadied it in the sand. She sat down again but didn't look at Stride.

'Cindy first wrote to me about fifteen years ago,' Tish said. 'It was shortly after her father died.'

'Did you know William Starr?'

'Enough to despise him.'

Stride nodded. He remembered the long weeks when Cindy had sat at her father's bedside while he waged a losing battle with cancer. William Starr had always been a hard man to like. Judgemental. Rigid. Obsessed with righteousness and punishment and all the while terrified

182

of going to hell for his own sins. Death has a way of softening even the toughest of men. Stride remembered Cindy holding her father's hand, listening to him weep, giving him absolution in a way that no priest ever could.

'Cindy had no illusions about her father,' he said.

'Neither did Laura. She loved him despite everything he did to her, but I knew he was a gutless piece of shit. He cheated on their mother, did you know that? Many times. Laura heard them arguing about it.'

'Why did Cindy contact you when he died?'

Tish hesitated. 'I guess when she lost him, it brought up all her old emotions about Laura. It's that aloneness you feel when your family is gone. So she thought of me. She knew how close Laura and I were, and she decided to rekindle a friendship with me.'

'Then what?'

'We wrote back and forth for years. Not often, but enough that we became close.'

'She never told me about you,' Stride said.

'Well, we had a bond because of Laura. Cindy and I both lost someone we loved. Neither one of us ever put it behind us.'

'Why the visit in Atlanta?' Stride asked.

Tish's voice was soft. 'Cindy knew she was dying. She wanted to see me. To say goodbye. And to tell me things. She told me everything that happened to her that night in nineteen seventy-seven. With Laura. With you. In the lake. Everything. Things she had never told anyone else before. That's why I chose to put so much of the book in her voice.'

Stride shook his head. He felt as if he were falling, fast and hard. 'Why would she do that?'

Tish took his hand.

'Because she didn't want me to let it go. She wanted me to do something. That's why I'm obsessed. That's why I have to see this out and do whatever it takes to get to the truth. Don't you see, Jon? That's why I'm here. I've resisted it ever since Cindy came to me, but I couldn't resist it anymore. Coming back after all these years wasn't my idea. Writing a book about Laura's murder wasn't my idea. It was Cindy's.'

Twenty

When Serena arrived home after midnight, she found the door to their attic hanging open. The unfinished space had an Alice-in-Wonderland feel to it, like crossing over into a different dimension. The stairway was built right into the cottage's great room, with five dark walnut steps leading up to a pair of narrow locked doors. Behind the doors, a single lonely bulb gave light, and the old wooden beams angled up to a high ceiling. Several more steps ended in another set of doors, where century-old paint flecked off the finish. Tonight the upper doors were open too. She continued to the attic level.

Up here, the heat gathered like a cloud during the warmer months; during the winter, it was frigid, and the old chambered windows collected frost. The space was wide open. The sharp peaks of the roof rose above her head. The unfinished floor was a landmine field of splinters and nail pops. Spider webs hung like draperies from the beams. There was nothing but unpacked moving boxes strewn on the floor. Someday, they had plans to convert the upper floor into a master suite and take advantage of its quirky angles and lake views, but for now, it was a dumping ground for remnants of both their pasts.

'Hey,' she said.

Jonny was seated on the floor in the middle of the attic. He wore only black boxers. His feet were bare, his hair damp and wild from the shower. The contents of two open boxes were scattered around him. She saw shoeboxes filled with photos, rubber-banded stacks of letters and postcards, and other paraphernalia from his first marriage that he had long ago packed away.

He didn't reply.

'God, it's hot,' she said. She sat down near him and reached for a stack of photographs that showed Jonny and Cindy on the strip of lakeside beach on the Point. Both were young. Jonny's hair was dark. One picture, slightly off center, had obviously been taken on self-timer, with the camera balanced on a tree stump. It showed the two of them kissing. The kind of kiss you felt down to your toes. Serena couldn't help herself; she felt a pang of jealousy. She put the photos back, not wanting to look anymore. She felt as if she had intruded on something sacred.

'You OK?' she asked.

Jonny looked lost. He didn't share his memories easily. Serena had made it a point never to push him, because she had spent years dealing with the ghosts in her own past, and she knew that you couldn't open up about them on anyone else's time. Every now and then, he opened a window to her. Only a crack. Only when he was ready.

He lay back, propping himself up on his palms. When he looked up into the shadows of the high ceiling, she saw dark stubble on his face. For a man in his late forties, he was fit and strong. His stomach was taut. He worked out ferociously, as she did. It was only a stall, of course. Age was catching up on both of them, in their skin, their eyes, their muscles, their hair, and their bodies.

'Did I ever tell you about the day I found out Cindy had cancer?' he murmured.

'No, you didn't.'

She could almost see his mind traveling back, retrieving the memory from among the cobwebs. She knew she was about to learn something important.

'I was investigating a girl's disappearance,' he told her. 'You remember the Kerry McGrath case? I was working on it sixteen hours every day. Cindy had been having unusual pain and vaginal bleeding, and so she had an MRI scheduled. I was supposed to go with her, but I totally forgot. She had to go alone. I didn't get home until nearly midnight, and I never even remembered the appointment. She was sitting on the bed, smiling at me. This fragile smile, like glass. I didn't notice. I was talking about the investigation, going on and on, and Cindy just smiled at me.'

'Oh, Jonny,' Serena said softly.

'It was like I never took a breath, you know? I was so caught up in it. And then finally, I looked at her, and I still didn't get it. I didn't have a clue what was wrong. So she said, still smiling, "It's not good, baby." Just like that. Her smile broke up into little pieces, and I knew. I knew what was coming. I knew that every plan we had made for the future had just evaporated. I looked at this little jewel of mine on the bed, and I watched her start sobbing, and I knew I was going to lose her.'

His voice caught. He closed his eyes.

Serena felt tears on her cheeks.

'I am so sorry,' she said.

He exhaled a long, slow breath. 'No, I'm sorry. This isn't fair to you.'

'You don't have to keep things from me,' Serena told him. 'It took me a long time to be vulnerable around you. I was so busy protecting myself that I forgot that you had demons of your own.'

'It's this case. It's brought it all back.'

'Is that a good thing?'

'I don't know. I spent years getting over Cindy. Now I feel like the stitches have been ripped open.'

Serena wondered whether to say anything. 'Is it making you question things?' she asked.

'Like what?'

'Me.'

She saw his face cloud over.

'Don't think that,' he said. 'That's not it at all.'

She thought he was trying to convince himself.

'There are days when I feel like I'm competing with a ghost,' she admitted. 'Someone who's always perfect, who's always young.'

'There's no competition. I apologize if I ever made you feel that way.'

'No, this is my problem, not yours.'

'It's not that this case makes me miss Cindy any more than I do already,' Stride told her. 'I always will, you know that. The hard part is that I'm learning things that make me question my whole life. Cindy was keeping secrets from me. I never would have thought that was possible.'

He told her about meeting Tish on the beach and about everything she had said to him. He gestured at the boxes. 'I've been through all of Cindy's old papers. There isn't a word about Tish anywhere. She

186

was hiding something, and for some reason she decided not to share it with me. I don't understand.'

'Don't be too quick to believe what Tish tells you,' Serena warned him. 'This woman has her own agenda. I'm worried that she's playing with your head, Jonny. I don't know what her game is, but I don't like it.'

'If she wanted to get me hooked, I'm hooked,' Stride said. 'All I can do is keep following the trail.'

'Just don't start doubting your past because of her. Maybe there's a reason Cindy never mentioned Tish to you. Maybe Tish is lying.'

Stride nodded. 'I know. I thought about that too, but there's a casualness in how she talks about Cindy. I really think they knew each other. She may be lying about other things, but not about that.'

Serena wasn't convinced. 'I think you should let this case go.'

'You're probably right, but I can't.'

'You're not going to get the satisfaction you want. Pat Burns is right, and you know it. This case isn't going to trial unless someone decides to confess, which isn't going to happen. So exactly what do you hope to accomplish?'

Stride began to gather up the leftovers from Cindy's life and put them back in their boxes. He handled each item delicately, as if it were an antique that might break apart in his hands if he was too rough. 'I'm not sure.'

He reached inside one of the boxes and extracted a leather-bound Bible, its covers rubbed and smooth. With a puff of his lips, he blew dust off it. Stride turned it over in his hands and then flipped through the tissue-thin pages. The corners were worn and well-thumbed.

'Did that belong to Cindy?' Serena asked.

'Her father.'

He tried to remember a time when he had seen William Starr without this Bible in his hand. It was always there, propping him up like a crutch.

'Cindy was different after he died,' he said.

'We all are.'

Stride nodded, but he didn't put the Bible down. 'This was something else. I saw a change in her. Back then, I thought it was grief, but now I realize it was more than that. It was Tish.'

Twenty-one

Maggie stopped in the town of Gary on Saturday afternoon to visit Clark Biggs, but the house was empty. His truck was gone. She left a handwritten note wedged inside the screen door and used her cell phone to leave a message on his answering machine. She was worried about him. This was the worst time, in the days after a child died. More than once, she had witnessed a double tragedy, where a child was killed and a parent committed suicide soon after.

At the highway, she turned south toward Fond du Lac, rather than heading north to the city. It was her day off, but she wanted to go back to the park where Mary Biggs had died. There was nothing more she could learn from the scene, but she often returned to places where crimes had occurred, as if echoes of what had happened, or what the victim saw, could still make their way into her brain. It was superstition, but she believed in it. It was also the perfect day to wander on the trails near the St Louis River.

The heat hadn't broken. The afternoon sun blistered the pavement. She kept her Avalanche ice cold as she drove, shivering in her spaghetti-strap top and white shorts. Her small feet barely reached the pedals. As she neared the gold reflections of the river at Perch Lake Park, she could see a flotilla of multicolored sailboats squeezed into the narrow inlets. Motorboats dragged teenagers through the waves in old tires. On the shore of the nearest island, she spied rows of near-naked bodies, their bare flesh baking on beach towels.

Maggie got out of her Avalanche and adjusted her burgundy sunglasses. She took a seat on the nearest bench, pulled her legs underneath her, and tilted her face to the sky, relishing the sunlight. When she opened her eyes, she realized that, like Mary, she was alone here. Everyone else had someone with them to share the day. Husbands had wives. Mothers had sons and daughters. Boys had brothers. Even the old men walking by themselves had dogs on a leash.

Maggie thought it again. She wanted a child. Someone to raise, take care of, and be with. It was easy to wish for something when you couldn't have it.

She pushed off the bench and headed along the dirt trail leading up the shore, past birch trees and lowland brush. This was the route Mary Biggs had walked, innocent and unknowing, from the safety of the little gray bench to a place where strangers and deep water took her away. From where she was, Maggie kept an eye on the highway. Donna Biggs, running to rescue her daughter, could have glimpsed a tall man through the trees as he climbed into a silver SUV, but at this distance, she wouldn't have been able to identify him. She knew that Donna was right, because she believed that Finn Mathisen had been here. Stalking Mary. Driving a silver Rav. But what she knew and what she could prove were two different things.

When she reached the point in the trail where Mary had run for the river, Maggie veered off the path into the woods. She knew the ev techs had been over this ground thoroughly, and she didn't expect to find anything they had missed. Even so, she wanted to put herself in Finn's shoes. Mary is screaming, running away. The noise terrifies him. He escapes back into the trees, heading for his car, pushing through spindly branches that claw at him, hearing his own breath and the squish of wet leaves beneath his feet. It isn't far, but it must have seemed far, wondering if he would be caught. Maggie saw the road ahead of her. She emerged from the trees, as he would have done, and found herself on the gravel shoulder of the highway. The silver Rav4 would have been parked right here.

He got in; his tires spun on the loose rock; he sped away.

Maggie stared down the curving stretch of road. She could see the flat area near the parking lot where the young boy had spilled off his bicycle. From there, Donna could see clearly up the slope. She would have seen the Rav parked here as she called out for help. It all must have happened quickly. Mary wandering up the trail. Donna noticing she was gone. The man spying on Mary, realizing she was coming closer, stepping out onto the trail to confront her. Mary wailing. Donna running to find her. Finn – if it was Finn – pushing through the trees.

Maggie realized that Finn couldn't have predicted that Mary would wander up the trail alone. That was a bonus. He knew that Donna and Mary came down to the park most Fridays and that they spent time sitting on the bench by the river. So the most he could have hoped for was to spy on her. Watch her. Where would the best place have been to do that? Maggie didn't think he would have risked sitting in his car, with traffic coming and going. He would have taken binoculars and staked out a spot near the trail, closer to where they sat.

She wandered down the slope, looking for a place where she could duck back into the trees. She kept an eye on the parking lot, as Finn would have done, trying to find a hiding place with the best vantage. Twenty yards away, she found a slim trail, where the foliage was beaten down, a shortcut for kids to hike and ride bikes off the highway on their way to the river. She followed it, certain that Finn would have used this route. Maggie reached the wider trail, the one Mary had used, and realized that if she continued down to the water, she would have a largely unobstructed view across the bend of the river toward the clearing where Donna and Mary sat, watching the birds fly.

Maggie scooted down the gentle slope to the water. There, she could imagine Finn tucked behind the brush, crouched down, binoculars in hand, zooming in on the pretty young face a hundred yards away. When she studied the area, however, she didn't see any remnants of someone lurking there. She would get the ev techs to come back and examine the spot in detail, but she wasn't optimistic.

Frustrated, Maggie retraced her steps up the slope. When she pushed her way back onto the main trail, she was surprised to find a man watching her, no more than ten feet away.

It was Clark Biggs.

'Oh!' Maggie exclaimed. 'Mr Biggs. I've been looking for you.'

Clark nodded but said nothing. His hands were jammed in his pockets. He hadn't shaved, and he looked as if he hadn't slept. Maggie thought that big men always took it hardest. The burly ones were used to thinking of themselves as strong, but when it came to something like this, a strong man was nothing in the face of disaster. His muscles didn't matter. His courage didn't matter.

'Why are you here?' she asked.

'Talking to Mary,' he said.

'I understand.'

'She loved the water,' he continued. 'It's so ironic, because the water is what killed her. I used to take her down to the Wisconsin Point, and we'd spend hours on the beach there. She hated to leave. It was her favorite place.'

Maggie said nothing.

'Tell me you found this bastard.'

'We're pursuing some promising leads, but I don't want to get your hopes up, because this could all come to nothing. But I do need your help.'

'Anything.'

Maggie took a breath. 'If you don't mind my asking, how are you? I can only imagine what you're going through. And your ex-wife, too. I know that families are often reluctant to get help, but there are people you can talk to.'

'I don't want that kind of help,' Clark said.

'If you should change your mind, call me. I can give you some names.'

'I know a little about you, Ms Bei. I know you lost someone close to you earlier this year too.'

'Losing a husband isn't the same as losing your daughter,' Maggie said. She didn't add that Eric's murder had come at a time when their marriage was largely over, when their love had wasted away to contempt.

Clark shrugged. 'Loss is loss. Just tell me, how can I help? I want to see this man rotting away behind bars where he belongs.'

Maggie reached into the pocket of her shorts and extracted an eight-by-eight postcard with six photos pasted in two rows. All the photos were from driver's license records. All the men were bald, in their forties.

'I'd like you to look carefully at this photo array and tell me if you recognize any of the men here.'

Clark took the wrinkled postcard from her hand and held it up at arm's length. Maggie watched his eyes as he studied each photo. He hesitated at the man in the upper right corner, then moved on. When he was done, he went back to that photo and squinted at it for nearly a minute. Finally, he tapped the picture with his finger.

'This one,' he said. 'I've seen him before. I don't know where, but I know I've seen him.'

'He's a delivery driver. On the Saturday that Mary first saw the man outside her bedroom window, this man delivered a package to your house. A swing set.'

Clark's fingers tightened on the card. Maggie didn't like what she saw in his eyes. She pried the card out of his hands and slipped it back in her pocket.

'So it's him,' he said.

'We're a long way from proving it, but we think so.'

'Does he drive a silver Rav4?'

'Yes, he does.'

'That should be it then, right? I mean, what else do you need? You've got the right car, and you've got him at my house. Can't you arrest him?'

'Nothing would make me happier, but we don't have enough evidence yet,' Maggie told him. 'We're going to be executing a search warrant, and we're going to question him thoroughly. Depending on what we find, we may be able to charge him with interference with privacy. In effect, that's the law against peeping Toms. However, we're a long way from a manslaughter charge, and to be honest with you, we may never get there.'

'So this guy harasses my daughter to death, and he gets a slap on the wrist.'

'Please, Mr Biggs. The investigation is still at an early stage. If this is the man who harmed Mary, I will do everything I can to see that he's punished for it.'

'Does he have a connection to the other girls who were peeped?'

Maggie nodded. 'He made deliveries to three of the other houses. That's significant, but not necessarily persuasive for a jury. We're looking for ways that he might be connected to the remaining girls, but we haven't found anything yet.'

Clark's face twitched. He snapped a branch from a tree overhanging the trail and broke it in half again and again, dropping the pieces on the dirt. He stared down at the river, where the reflection of the sun was blinding.

'I was hoping you could remember what happened when the swing set was delivered,' Maggie said. 'Did the driver have any kind of interaction with Mary? Did he see her?'

Clark closed his eyes and didn't respond. Maggie waited for him without speaking, and when Clark opened his eyes again, he nodded slowly.

'Mary and I were both outside,' he said.

'Did anything happen?'

Clark sighed. 'Yes. Mary exposed herself. She lifted up her T-shirt and showed him her breasts. She did that kind of thing all the time. She was just a kid, she didn't mean anything by it.'

'How did the driver react?'

'I apologized. He said it was no big deal.'

'Did he say anything else?'

'I don't think so.'

'Do you recall ever seeing this man around Mary before?'

Clark shook his head. 'No. I don't get many packages. He didn't act as if he knew who she was.' He swore and added, 'Is that really enough to set these guys off? I mean, could just seeing Mary's breasts turn him into a freak?'

'It happens,' Maggie said. 'To men like this, an innocent exposure of nudity by a girl, even accidentally, can trigger an explosive string of erotic fantasies. They literally build it up in their heads until they believe they have an actual relationship with her. It can become an obsession.'

'Son of a bitch,' Clark said. 'I was always telling Mary not to do it, but she didn't understand. She thought it was funny.'

'It's not your fault. Or Mary's.'

'Didn't this guy realize she was retarded? I mean, how can anyone think that about a little girl?'

Maggie didn't answer.

'Don't let him get away,' Clark told her.

'We'll do our best.'

Maggie turned to walk away toward the parking lot, but Clark stopped her with a hand on her shoulder. His grip was surprisingly tender.

'There's something else,' he said.

She turned back. 'What is it?'

'He saw her tattoo.'

'I'm sorry?'

'The driver saw Mary's tattoo. She was bent over, and her shirt rode up, and he saw the tattoo she had in the small of her back. Remember? You saw it. It was a butterfly. He was staring at it, and when I noticed, he looked away. He said something to her about it. Like how pretty her tattoo was. Mary loved that. That was when she flipped up her shirt.'

'A butterfly tattoo,' Maggie said. She did remember.

'Exactly. I don't know if it means anything.'

'It just might.'

Twenty-two

The interrogation room was small. From the door to the wall was barely six feet. When the door was closed, it felt as if the ceiling were coming down and the walls were squeezing against your shoulders. The fluorescent light was cold and sterile. You blinked when you looked up. You could smell each other's sweat, farts, and belches. There was one metal desk – it barely fitted inside – and one wobbly chair where the suspect sat, close to the ground. Stride sat next to Maggie on top of the desk, their hips touching. Finn squirmed in the chair, his long legs uncomfortably bent, like a spider's.

'So what is it now?' Finn said. 'I came down here like you asked. God, don't you guys have anything else to investigate? Have all the criminals gone on vacation? Shit, it was thirty years ago.'

Stride nodded at Maggie, who read Finn his rights.

'Whoa, whoa, whoa!' Finn exclaimed. 'What the hell is this? Are you arresting me for something?'

'Not yet,' Stride said.

'Do I need a lawyer?'

'I don't know. Do you?'

'Look, I was just trying to help Tish. I didn't have to say a word. Goddamn it, Rikke was right. I never should have gotten involved in this.'

'You're not under arrest,' Stride told him. 'We just want to make sure you understand your rights. You can call a lawyer if you want. You can walk out that door. Got it? We want to clear a few things

195

up, but that's up to you. Of course, it's going to be hard to clear things up if you're not talking to us.'

Stride saw blue veins in Finn's skull, twisting over his head like rivers.

'Yeah, sure, talk,' Finn said. 'I don't care. Can we open the door?'

'Maybe in a few minutes. This is the only room available.'

'How about some water?' Finn asked.

'This won't take long, and then we'll go and get some water and a little more air to breathe. OK?'

'I just want to get this over with.'

Maggie grabbed a manila envelope from the desk. She opened it and slid out a photograph, which she handed to Finn.

'Does this look familiar?' she asked.

The photograph was a close-up of a Monarch butterfly tattoo on a girl's back, life-size and detailed, with orange and black wings that looked as if they would flutter in the wind. The photo had been taken at the morgue. The girl was Mary Biggs.

'It's a tattoo,' Finn said.

'I didn't ask you what it was,' Maggie snapped. 'I asked if it looked familiar. Have you ever seen a tattoo like this before?'

Finn turned the photograph over and refused to look at it. 'No, I don't think so.'

'No? On Saturday, May the twenty-fourth, you delivered a package to a man named Clark Biggs in Gary. His daughter Mary was in the front yard. She showed you her tattoo.' Maggie slapped the photograph. 'This tattoo.'

'I don't remember. I deliver hundreds of packages every month.'

'This girl exposed herself to you. She showed you her breasts. Does that happen every month too?'

Finn smiled. 'You'd be surprised. Women answer the door, and a lot of times they're not wearing much.'

'This is funny to you?' Maggie asked. 'The night you delivered that package, someone was outside Mary's bedroom window, watching her undress. He was there again the next week. And on Friday night, he was on a trail with her in Fond du Lac. Terrifying her. Terrorizing her. Mary was just a little girl inside her brain. She didn't understand. She ran, and she fell into the river, and she drowned. A sweet, innocent girl. Dead.'

Finn's skin was the color of dirty dishwater. He stared at his feet. 'That's too bad.'

'Is that all you can say? Let's cut to the chase, Finn. Mary's mother saw you. She saw the silver Rav you drive, too.'

'It wasn't me.'

'You delivered packages to three other girls who have been peeped in their bedrooms in the last month.'

'I told you, I deliver a lot of packages.'

Maggie reached into the envelope for another sheaf of papers stapled together. She folded the first page back. 'This isn't the first time, is it, Finn? You've been watching girls for a long time. According to DMV records, you lived in the Uptown area of Minneapolis for three years in the late nineteen nineties. During that time, there was a string of eleven reported incidents of a peeper targeting blonde teenagers. The peepings started a month after you moved to the city. They stopped right after you left.'

'Minneapolis is a big city. That doesn't mean anything.'

'Fifteen years ago, you were fired from your job as a custodian at a school in Superior,' Maggie continued. 'I talked to the woman who was the principal back then. She said there were accusations that you had been going into the locker room at inappropriate times to watch the girls.'

'Oh, come on, like I'd be the first janitor who liked to sneak a peek now and then,' Finn said. 'I'm not saying I did, but what's the big deal? The teachers all do it too. It doesn't mean anything.'

'We're searching your house right now,' Maggie told him. 'There are officers tearing your place apart. What are they going to find, Finn? Photos? Maps? We're going over your car with a toothbrush, too. We'll find something that ties you to the girls you've been stalking.'

Finn's bald head glistened with sweat under the hot light. 'I think I should go. I thought you wanted to talk about Laura. I'm not saying anything else about stalking or peeping or whatever the hell you think I did.'

'You can go if you want,' Stride said. 'But you brought it up, so let's talk about Laura. She had a tattoo almost identical to the one that Mary Biggs had. Did Mary's tattoo remind you of Laura? Is that why you focused on her?'

'I'm not saying anything.'

'You told me you saw Laura and Cindy in the woods that night by accident. Then we find out about Mary Biggs and all these blonde girls with someone panting outside their bedroom window. You know what I think, Finn? I think you were *watching* Laura. I think you were stalking her. Sending her threats. I think you followed her to the park that night.'

'I didn't stalk her,' Finn replied. 'I never sent her any letters.'

'There's something else,' Stride continued. 'We never released this to the media. Someone masturbated at the crime scene where Laura was beaten to death. I guess the guy was so turned on by what he had done he had to jerk off. We still have the semen, Finn. What happens next is we get a court order to sample your DNA and we match it against the semen we found at the scene. I think we're going to get a match, Finn. I think you were at the murder scene that night.'

'I told you, I don't remember,' Finn said.

'Then let us help your memory. Give us a DNA sample right now. Let us run the test. Don't you want to know the truth?'

Finn looked at them, horrified. 'No.'

'You told me how hard it is to live your life not knowing if you killed someone. Maybe it will unlock your memory if you find out you were really there.' Stride paused and said, 'Or maybe you remember already, Finn. Maybe you know what happened that night.'

'I can't tell you anything. It's gone.'

Stride shook his head. 'It's not gone. It's still inside your head. You say you saw someone attacking Laura. Trying to rape her. Are you sure it wasn't you?'

'No! That wasn't me. It was someone else.'

'Who?'

'I don't know who it was. I couldn't see.'

'Then Dada broke it up. Laura ran into the woods. Are you sure you didn't follow her?'

'No,' Finn told them. He crossed and re-crossed his legs.

'You said you don't remember. Isn't it possible you *did* follow Laura into the woods? Toward the beach?'

'I wouldn't do that.' His eyes darted around, looking for escape.

'That night didn't end in the field. Someone went after Laura. Someone

198

took the baseball bat and chased her up to the north beach. Someone killed her. Beat her to death. Hammered her until she was almost unrecognizable. If I did that, I'd probably black it out, too.'

'Oh, my God,' Finn murmured.

'Or did you just *see* it? You're a watcher, right? Did you see who killed Laura? Because that's what we need to know. We need to know what happened.'

'*I don't remember.*'

Maggie leaned forward. 'You remember Mary Biggs, though, don't you? You remember what she looked like, right? Well, here's what she looks like now.'

She spilled a stack of photographs onto the desk. Autopsy photos. She picked them up one by one and pressed them into Finn's hands, watching him go blue, watching him swallow hard, watching his head bob back and forth like the ticking of a clock as he stared, unable to look away, at the swollen, lifeless remains of Mary Biggs, pulled from the water after she drowned.

'You killed her, Finn. You killed this wonderful girl.'

Finn squeezed his eyes shut.

'OPEN YOUR EYES!' Maggie bellowed at him. His eyelids sprang up in shock. She clutched a close-up photo of Mary's face, her skin puffed and pale. She shoved the photo so close to Finn that Mary's face was his whole world, and he couldn't see anything else.

'Tell me why,' Maggie said. 'Tell me why you did this to her.' Her voice softened. 'Look, I know you didn't mean to. Did you love her? Did you want a chance to tell her how you felt? But she didn't understand. She was scared of you.'

Finn gulped air like a fish. He swallowed hard as if something were in his mouth that wouldn't go down.

'Mary and Laura both deserved better,' Stride said quietly.

Finn was a rubber band that had been stretched until it was frayed and ready to snap. When Finn buried his face in his hands, Stride caught Maggie's eye. They both thought the words would spill out now, like a dammed-up river seeping through sandbags and finally bursting free. He would talk. He would confess. He would throw off the anvil that had weighed on his conscience. He would seek absolution for the secrets that had made his life so miserable that he

199

could only escape it into a numbed world of marijuana, cocaine, and alcohol.

'Let it go,' Maggie murmured.

Stride said, 'It's OK.'

Finn stared wildly at them. Tears ran from his eyes; mucus ran from his nose. He clapped a hand to his mouth, shoved them both aside with a stiff jerk of his arm, and bolted through the door, slamming it behind him. They heard the gasping, retching noise of his stomach spewing onto the marble floor of City Hall. When Stride opened the door again, the sweet stench of vomit made him cover his nose and look away.

Finn was gone.

Ten minutes later, the interrogation room still smelled of Finn's body. Stride leaned back on the desk until his head banged against the wall. Maggie jumped off the desk, took the chair in which Finn had been sitting, and propped her feet up.

Her cell phone rang. She slid it out of her pocket and answered. Stride recognized the voice of Max Guppo, the overweight detective who had been leading the search team at Finn Mathisen's house, along with cops from Superior. Maggie asked a few questions and then hung up. She didn't look happy.

'Nothing,' she said.

'Come on.'

She shook her head. 'They didn't find a damn thing to link him to the peeping cases. His room looked as if it had been vacuum-cleaned of anything potentially incriminating. The computer had no hard drive, for God's sake. Just a big hole in the tower. His shoes were all new. His clothes had been washed.'

'Rikke,' Stride said.

Maggie nodded. 'She knows what he's been doing. Maybe we can lean on her.'

'She's been covering for Finn for thirty years. She's not going to stop now. What about the car? The silver Rav?'

'Ditto. Cleaned and pressed. Even the tires had been hosed down.'

Stride sighed. 'So where are we?'

'I think we'll be able to make a charge of interference with privacy

200

stick. If we can tie him to the other victims, a jury will make the leap.'

'If.'

'He had to find them somehow. We'll track it down. Hell, he delivered to four out of the nine households where a girl was peeped. That's a big coincidence right there.'

'Big, but still a coincidence,' Stride said. 'If we can get six or seven, OK. Four's not enough. Even with the silver Rav. He has no priors. We'll never get the stuff from Minneapolis or his old janitorial job admitted in court. A defense lawyer can blow smoke and make a jury believe Finn is just a victim of circumstances.'

'And Mary's murder?'

Stride shook his head. 'You know that's going nowhere. We'll be lucky to pin the peeping charge on him. We can't put him at the scene with Mary, and even if we could, we can't establish what really happened.'

'At least we can charge multiple counts. He's done it ten times that we know of. If we get the right judge, we can go for two years a count.'

Stride put a hand gently on Maggie's leg. 'I know this case means a lot to you, Mags, but you're dreaming. With no priors? He'll get a year for everything and be out in three months. If he sees the inside of a jail at all. That's life.'

'That sucks.'

'I know it does.'

'What the hell do I tell Clark Biggs?'

'That we're still working on the case. We're not done yet. If we can get a DNA sample from Finn and can prove that he was at the scene where Laura was murdered, we can take another run at him. Maybe he'll confess. He might not go down for Mary's death, but if we put him behind bars for Laura's murder, that's some justice.'

'If,' Maggie said, mocking him.

'Yeah, yeah.' Stride rubbed his hands over his face and felt a bone-deep tiredness throughout his body. 'Think they've cleaned up the hallway yet?'

Maggie reached over and pushed the door open. 'Nope.'

'Shit,' Stride said. 'I have to wash my face.'

'Is that what guys say when they have to take a leak?'

'No, we say we have to take a leak.'

'Do most guys wash their hands after?' Maggie asked.

'You don't want to know.'

'Yuck.'

Stride laughed. He left the interrogation room and covered his nose against the pungent aroma of puke. The hallways were empty. It was evening, and City Hall was mostly deserted. He found the frosted glass door that led to the men's room, opened it with his shoulder, and started a stream of cold water running in the nearest sink on the long countertop. He bent over, splashed water on his face, and rubbed his skin hard. His fingers ran through his hair, leaving it wet and disheveled.

He smelled it before he saw it.

Blood.

His eyes were closed, and when he opened them, blinking, he saw the first toilet stall reflected in the mirror, its door ajar. Twin trails of fresh blood outlined the grout in the white floor tiles in ruby red squares. Stride ran for the stall and shoved the door open, making it bounce against the wall. Finn Mathisen was sprawled on the seat, his head lolling back, his mouth open and slack. His arms dangled uselessly at his sides, and a Swiss Army knife lay on the floor where it had spilled from his hand.

The blood on the tiles dripped from two jagged, vertical gashes Finn had carved into the veins on both wrists.

PART FOUR

ACT OF MERCY

Twenty-three

Serena spotted Peter Stanhope in the corner of the main room at Blackwood's. His table overlooked the calm lake waters through floor-to-ceiling windows. It was one o'clock, and the restaurant was crowded with the lunch rush. Peter drank a glass of red wine and checked email on his Blackberry with his other hand as she took a seat opposite him. She stared at his lower lip, which was swollen and purple.

He followed her gaze and shrugged. 'Tish.'

'I heard.'

'It was my own fault,' Peter said. He used his fork to separate a flaky piece of white fish, which he chewed gingerly. 'Even so, I never expected her to do something so crazy.'

'Not necessarily crazy,' Serena said.

Peter cocked his head with suspicion. 'What do you mean by that?'

Serena said nothing. Peter thought about it, and then he glanced around the restaurant and lowered his voice. 'This is about DNA? What the hell would Tish Verdure want with a sample of my DNA?'

'What do you think?'

Peter shook his head, as if scolding himself. 'That was stupid of me. I didn't know that Stride had any forensic evidence in Laura's murder.'

'You mean you thought Ray Wallace made it all disappear?'

'I don't like your tone, Serena. Not from someone who works for me. What sort of evidence do they have?'

'I can't tell you.'

Peter frowned. 'I could file a motion to stop the police from running any tests.'

'You could, but then it's all out in the open. In the press. People will wonder what you're trying to hide.'

'I already told you that I didn't kill Laura.'

'Then you have nothing to fear.'

'It's a little more complicated than that.'

Serena waited. Peter waved the waitress away from the table. He scowled and leaned back, folding his arms. 'What did George Bush say? When I was young and stupid, I was young and stupid.'

'You sent Laura those stalking letters,' Serena concluded. 'Didn't you?'

'OK, yes. You're right.'

'Why?'

'Why? I went out with Laura, and she shut me down. I thought she was playing games, stringing me along. I was pissed off. So I started sending her those notes. It was a joke.'

'I saw one of the notes. This was no joke.'

'Give me a break, I was seventeen years old.'

'Don't make excuses, Peter. You were terrorizing the girl.'

'Call it whatever you want. I didn't kill her.'

'This isn't just about sending ugly letters, is it? Finn was telling the truth. You attacked Laura that night in the softball field.'

Peter met Serena's eyes. 'I didn't attack her. I went back to the field that night to get my baseball bat. I bumped into Laura coming out of the woods. Yes, I tried to kiss her, and yes, I may have pushed things too far. I thought she was playing hard to get. That's all it was.'

'It sounds like rape to me,' Serena told him.

'I am not a rapist.'

'Yeah, rich boys never are.'

Peter's face screwed up in anger. 'I could have lied to you, and I didn't.'

'Really? What choice do you have? You've painted yourself into a corner. You already told the police that you and Laura were making out in the field. You admitted the two of you were together that night.'

'The smart thing for me would be to say nothing at all. That's what the lawyer in me says I should do.'

'Well, you've already started talking, so keep going. What happened after you accosted Laura?'

206

'The black guy broke it up. Knocked me out cold.'

'What happened after you woke up?'

'Laura was gone. So was the black guy. I had a splitting headache. I went home.'

'What about your bat?'

'I forgot all about it.'

'Was it still in the field?'

'I have no idea if it was or wasn't. I didn't look around for it. I didn't even think about the bat. I just wanted to get out of there.'

'What else can you tell me about that night?'

'That's it.'

'You don't know what happened to Laura?'

'I don't. As far as I know, the black guy killed her. That's what I've thought all these years.'

'Did you see Finn Mathisen that night?'

'No.'

Serena shook her head. 'As a cop, I wouldn't believe your story, Peter. You were stalking Laura. You were obsessed with her. You attacked her the night she was killed. And then you just walked away? And someone else went after her with your bat? You must think I'm a sucker.'

'Serena, I was no angel back then, but killing a girl? Not me.'

Serena got up from the table. 'I think we're done here.'

'That sounds like you're walking away from me. From the job.'

'I am.'

Peter reached into his wallet and dropped a fifty dollar bill on the table. 'Let me walk you out. I have something in my car that may change your mind. Call it a token of good faith.'

'What is it?'

'I have to show you.'

Serena shrugged and acquiesced. The two of them left the restaurant. In the parking lot, he pointed at a black Lexus near the rear of the lot. 'That's me.'

He took her arm as they walked.

'I heard about Finn's suicide attempt last week,' Peter said. 'Is he going to make it?'

'Assuming he doesn't try again.'

'Finn should be Stride's prime suspect, not me,' Peter said. 'He admitted being in the park that night and following Laura. Now he tries to kill himself when he's questioned.'

'Finn's a suspect, but you just put yourself back in the game because of those letters.'

'There's no game. Legally I don't have any concerns about what's going on. Pat Burns knows that. I'm sure Stride knows it too. There are chain of custody issues, evidence issues, witness issues. No one's ever going to charge me with a crime.'

'So what do you need me for?' Serena asked.

'My public persona is important to me. If this gets out in the press, and if suspicion continues to swirl around me, it will be extremely unpleasant for me and my business.'

They arrived at his Lexus. Peter ran his hand over the smooth finish.

'I don't know who killed Laura,' he continued, 'but if the media and the police are going to sink their teeth into anyone, I want it to be Finn. I want you to dig up everything you can about him. Find out about his background. Prove he's the kind of man who could kill a young girl. You're a detective. Investigate the suspect.'

'That's Stride's job,' Serena said.

'I'm not telling you to keep secrets from him. Whatever you find, you can share with Stride. But his hands are tied by police procedure and other cases. He also has Tish whispering in his ear that I'm guilty. I want someone on the playing field who's working for me.'

'I don't trust you.'

'I'm not asking you to trust me. If you find evidence that points to me, so be it. But you won't, because I didn't do it. Look, I know what kind of a woman you are, Serena. Once a cop, always a cop. You want to be in on this investigation, and I'm offering you the chance to dive into it. And get paid handsomely for your time.'

Serena wanted to say no, but Peter was right.

'Why Finn?' she asked. 'Why not ask me to take a look at the black guy? Dada?'

'Lawyers look for weaknesses. Finn's the weak link.'

'In other words, you'd prefer that Dada remains a mystery.'

'Anyone who's a suspect in this case wants Dada to stay a mystery,' Peter admitted. 'He's a get-out-of-jail-free card. As long as no one knows where he is, no can prove beyond a reasonable doubt who really killed Laura.'

Serena shook her head. 'I'd make a lousy defense lawyer. I'd always be wondering if my client was guilty.'

'Sometimes you don't want to know.'

'I do. I want to know.'

Peter unlocked the trunk of the Lexus. 'I told you I was going to take a leap of faith. This is how much I want you to believe me.' He reached inside the trunk and extracted a narrow box, about four feet long and six inches wide. The tape holding it closed was crusted and yellow. Serena saw a single word written on the box in black marker.

DESTROY.

'What is this?' she asked.

Peter handed her the box. It was solid and heavy.

'You were right about Ray Wallace,' he said. 'He conspired with my father to steer the case away from me. Randall wanted Ray to put it all on Dada.'

'What did Ray do?'

'He dropped the case. Later, he arranged for some of the key pieces of evidence to vanish from the police file. I think Randall figured someone might try to open up the case again someday, and he wanted a guarantee. So Ray destroyed most of the physical evidence. But not this. Randall insisted on keeping this himself. I think he knew it gave him leverage if Ray ever got a guilty conscience.'

'What is it?' Serena asked again.

'It's the murder weapon,' Peter said. 'It's the baseball bat. The one that was used to kill Laura.'

Twenty-four

The hospital ward was like a church, where every voice disturbed the silence. Even the noise of Stride's heels echoing between the walls felt as loud as fireworks. The corridor was dim. Most of the patients were sleeping through the late evening hours. He stopped at the nurse's station and was directed to a room near the end of the hallway.

He watched Finn Mathisen from the doorway but didn't go inside. The man's face, always pallid and yellow, looked like ash now. His eyes were closed. His forearms were bundled in white bandages up to his elbows. An intravenous line dripped fluid into the flesh of his right shoulder. He was stable now and almost ready to be discharged, but in Stride's eyes, he still looked like death. People in hospital beds always did.

If Stride had not gone into that bathroom, or if he had arrived even five minutes later, Finn would be dead. That didn't stop Stride from feeling guilty that he and Maggie had hounded Finn with their questions until he chose to escape by attempting suicide.

The question was, escape from what? From the guilt of stalking Mary Biggs to her death? Or from the guilt of beating Laura to death? Or both?

If Finn had succeeded, he would have taken the answers with him. Finn dying would have been exactly like Dada jumping on that train. The investigation would have shut down again, and suspicion would have landed like a bird of prey on Finn's dead body. Rightly or wrongly.

'What the hell are you doing here?'

Stride turned and found Rikke Mathisen behind him. She clutched a cup of hospital coffee in her hand, and steam curled out of the brown liquid. She was tall; they were almost eye to eye. Her face was hard with rage. She pushed past Stride into the hospital room and tugged the flimsy curtain, blocking Finn from Stride's sight.

'I said, what are you doing here?' she hissed again.

'I wanted to check on Finn.'

Rikke pointed her finger like an arrow out of the room. At the end of the corridor was a small waiting area, with dreadful orange sofas, out-of-date family magazines, and an overhead thirteen-inch television suspended from the ceiling. No one was there. The television was off. Stride went to the tall window and looked out on the main street of Superior below him. Rikke followed. She wore an oversized sweatshirt and jeans.

'You are not to come near him,' she insisted. 'You are not to talk to him. Is that clear? I've hired a lawyer. We are through with you, starting now.'

'How is Finn?'

'Alive,' she snapped.

'I hear he's going home tomorrow. I'm glad he's OK.'

'He's not OK.'

'I'm sorry about what happened.'

Rikke's eyes were two blue stones. 'Spare me. You knew perfectly well what kind of a man Finn is. He's an addict, for Christ's sake. An alcoholic. You deliberately went and pushed him over the edge. I hope you're proud of yourself.'

'It wasn't like that,' Stride said.

'You've put salve on your conscience by coming here, Lieutenant. Now go home. Get away from me and my brother.'

Rikke sat down, grabbed a dated copy of *People*, and flipped the pages savagely.

'You knew about Finn peeping teenage girls,' Stride said.

'I have nothing to say.'

'A girl died.'

'That's not Finn's fault.'

'I think you know it is. You destroyed evidence, didn't you? Our search team said someone burned papers in Finn's room. The hard drive of his computer was missing. If he's mentally ill, you're not helping him by covering up what he did.'

Rikke slapped the magazine shut. 'Finn does not belong in prison. He belongs with me. I can take care of him.'

'You can't control him,' Stride said. 'Isn't that obvious? He'll start all over again when he gets home. We both know it. What if another girl dies? How will you feel then?'

'Finn would never hurt anyone.'

'No? What about Laura?'

'I told you, he wasn't there that night. He had nothing to do with it. He was with me. At home.'

Stride shook his head. 'Someone masturbated near Laura's body. We still have the semen that was collected. If Finn was there, we'll be able to prove it.'

'I'm not letting you take a DNA sample from him.'

'We don't need one. Finn provided a large sample of his blood on the floor of the bathroom in the Detective Bureau.'

'You took his blood off the floor?' Rikke asked. 'What kind of barbarian are you? A man is dying, and all you can think about is your investigation?'

'My concern is with the victims,' Stride said. 'I'm going to test his DNA. We're going to find out that Finn was at the murder scene that night.'

'I'll talk to my lawyer. He'll put a stop to this rape of Finn's body. You're disgusting, do you know that? You're an animal. You don't understand what Finn has been through in his life.'

Stride squatted in front of her. 'Finn took the car that night, didn't he? When he came home, he was covered in blood. I think you did exactly what you did a few days ago. You covered up for him. You protected him.'

'I think you should go,' Rikke announced. 'I have nothing more to say.'

'Finn was in love with Laura. He was obsessed with her. That's how this all started.'

'You don't know anything,' Rikke told him. 'You should just leave it alone. Believe me, Finn's problems began long before Laura.'

Serena rang the doorbell and waited. The Honda Civic that Tish drove was parked in the driveway of the lakefront condominium. Masking

212

tape surrounded the edge of the windshield where the glass had been replaced. Across the street, Serena saw a Duluth police officer watching her from an unmarked police vehicle. She waved. He knew her.

It was after ten o'clock, but there were lights on inside the apartment. When there was no answer, she rang the bell again. This time, she saw Tish through the window as she came to the door. She wore a man's white shirt that draped to her mid-thighs. Her legs were bare. Tish opened the door, and tobacco wafted from her breath and clothes into the hot night air. The smell of smoke was mixed with the tart aroma of gin. Tish leaned against the doorway and picked at strands of her blonde hair.

'Serena Dial,' she said. 'What can I do for you?'

'I was hoping we could talk.'

Tish gave a casual shrug of her shoulders. 'OK.'

She turned away and wandered toward the rear of her condo. Serena came inside, closing the door behind her. The condo was sparsely decorated, without artwork on the white walls or curtains on the windows. The cream carpet under her feet was deep and lush, but the rental furniture was utilitarian. Serena saw a glass dining-room table that doubled as a desk, where Tish kept her laptop and research notes. The kitchen counter was clean except for an empty box from a Lean Cuisine TV dinner and two drained bottles of Schweppes tonic.

She followed Tish onto the balcony. Tish sat in a folding chair, with her legs propped on the slats of the wooden railing. She had a drink in her hand and a cigarette smoldering in an ashtray on the floor. Her shirt slipped down, revealing a triangle of white bikini panties. Serena leaned on the balcony, which looked out on the black expanse of the lake. There was almost no bluff below them, just sixty feet of air and then dark water. Everything was calm, without even a breath of wind to stir the heat around.

Tish flicked a mosquito off her forearm. 'I read about you,' she said.

'Oh?'

'I read about that guy who came after you last winter. You almost died.'

'You're right. So?'

'That must have been terrifying.'

213

'It was.'

'I don't think I would have survived an experience like that.'

'I don't like to talk about it,' Serena said.

'Sure, I understand.' Tish added, 'You know, when I first met you, I didn't like you. I'm not sure I would have liked anyone that Stride was with.'

'Why is that?'

'Loyalty to Cindy, I guess.'

'And now?' Serena asked.

'Now I see that there's a lot more to you than I realized.'

'How often does a girl get a compliment like that?' Serena said wryly.

'I just mean that when people meet you, I guess they don't always see past the face and the killer body.'

'This body has a couple more pounds on it than I'd like.'

'You don't have to be modest. Anyway, I shouldn't have prejudged you. I'm sorry.'

'Apology accepted,' Serena said. 'But I need to tell you something.'

'What is it?'

'Stride and I have a lot in common. He may not show it the way I do, but we're both damaged. Losing Cindy damaged him a lot.'

'I'm sure it did.'

'I don't like seeing that pain dragged up for him again,' Serena said.

'You mean me?'

'Yes.'

'You're honest.'

'What about you, Tish? Are *you* honest?'

'What do you mean?'

'I mean, did you really know Cindy?' Serena asked. 'Or are you making it up? Because as far as I can tell, there's no evidence that you ever even met Cindy. So if you're playing games with us, I'm telling you right now that I will make you regret it.'

'I did know her.'

'Then why did she never mention you to Jonny?'

'Even the most loyal of women has secrets.' Tish picked up her cigarette with two fingers. 'Don't you keep secrets about yourself?'

'Some,' Serena admitted.

'There you go.'

'If I keep a secret, there's a reason for it. Did Cindy have a reason to hide her relationship with you?'

'Maybe I asked her to.'

'Why would you do that?'

Tish swirled the ice in her drink and then drained the rest of it. 'You already told me there are places in your own past that you don't like to visit. Is it so hard to accept that I feel the same way? I wasn't ready to come back here and face my past. Cindy understood.'

'Are you ready to face your past now?'

'I'm here. It took me thirty years, but I'm here.'

'Did something happen back then between you and Peter Stanhope?' Serena asked. 'Is that what you're hiding?'

'No.'

'Then why are you so convinced that he's guilty?'

'You didn't know Peter back then. I did.'

Serena shook her head. 'If you were a cop, I'd say you've fallen in love with a suspect. Not love-love, not romance. It's easy when you're a cop to fixate on one suspect and wind up wearing blinders.'

'Maybe you're the one wearing blinders,' Tish said.

'Peter didn't try to commit suicide after being questioned about Laura's murder,' Serena reminded her. 'Finn did.'

'Finn was just a pathetic, mixed-up kid.'

'People like that are capable of anything,' Serena said. 'Including murder.'

'If Laura thought Finn was violent, she wouldn't have spent so much time with him.'

'Maybe she didn't know. Did Laura tell you anything about Finn's background?'

'She told me that something terrible happened to him back in Fargo, but I don't know what. That was when Rikke swooped in and rescued him.'

'Finn was in love with Laura,' Serena said. 'Love can be pretty twisted for someone like that. We know he was spying on Laura. He's been spying on young girls his whole life.'

'You mean the peeping incidents?'

215

Serena nodded. 'Stride and Maggie are certain that Finn is the peeper. He hounded one girl until she died.'

'That doesn't mean he killed Laura,' Tish said.

'You know what made that girl special? She had a tattoo of a butterfly on her back. Just like Laura did. He's still obsessed with her.'

Tish's eyes opened wide. 'Is that really true?'

'It's true.'

Tish brought her bare feet down onto the balcony and cupped her hands in front of her face as if she was praying. Then she shook her head. 'Peter is the one who attacked Laura,' she insisted. 'Not Finn. You don't know how vengeful Peter could be when he was rejected.'

'Are you talking about Laura or yourself?' Serena asked.

'Both of us.'

'Come on, Tish. What are you not telling me? What did he do to you?'

Tish's lips bulged with defiance. 'You mean other than pushing me into a closet at school and groping my tits and pawing my crotch? Peter was the kind of boy who took what he wanted even if you said no. He thought he was entitled. He hasn't changed a bit.'

'I'm not trying to defend his behavior,' Serena said.

'That's good, because he was nasty. Vicious.'

'How so?'

'After I said I didn't want to go out with him, he spread rumors about me all over school.'

'What rumors?'

'He told people I was queer. That made me very uncomfortable.'

'I'm sure it did,' Serena said. 'Teenagers are quick to believe that kind of lie.'

Tish watched the moths buzzing around the porch light and didn't say anything. She sucked on her cigarette.

Suddenly, Serena understood. 'Wait a minute, it wasn't a lie, was it? He was right. You're gay.'

Tish nodded slowly.

'Did you tell Peter?' Serena asked her.

'No, he had no idea it was true, but it scared me to death to have the rumor out there.'

'So you knew back then?'

'I knew.'

'Are you still in the closet?'

'I don't hide it, but it's not like I wear a T-shirt that says pink and proud.' Tish blew smoke out of her mouth.

'I'm sorry if this makes you uncomfortable,' Serena said.

'It doesn't, but you have no idea how ugly and hateful people get over homosexuality. The same people who tell me that Jesus loves me would stone me to death if they could.'

'Not everyone feels that way.'

'Enough do that I'm still careful about who I tell.'

'Is there someone in your life?'

Tish crushed her cigarette in the ashtray. 'Not anymore. I lived with Katja, a photographer I met in Talinn, for five years. She was getting too close, so I ran away. It wasn't the first time for me. Lesbian relationships crash and burn a lot. We get emotionally close, and then you put the physical attraction in the middle of it, and a lot of times it flames out.'

'Did Laura know you were gay?' Serena asked.

Tish's face glowed with dew from the humid air. 'We didn't talk about it.'

'Not even with your best friend?'

'You have to remember the times, Serena. It's bad enough today, but being gay was dangerous back then. This was when Anita Bryant was on the rampage about homosexuals. You didn't advertise being different. You kept the closet locked up tight.'

'What about Laura? Was she gay?'

'I told you, we didn't talk about it.' Tish stood up, shutting down the conversation. 'I think you should go.'

'If that's what you want,' Serena said.

'I do.'

Serena stood up too. 'Can I ask you about something else?'

'What?'

'What happened to your mother?'

Tish folded her arms over her chest. Her eyes were angry. 'If you're asking a question like that, you must already know.'

'I heard she was shot. She was a hostage who died in a bank robbery.'

'That's right. Why do you care?'

Serena wasn't really sure why she cared, but it was a detective's curiosity. 'When someone's life is touched by violence more than once, my instinct is to look for a connection.'

'There's no connection,' Tish insisted. 'The robbery has nothing to do with any of this. It was years before I even met Laura. My mother was in the wrong place at the wrong time.'

'It must have been hard to be left alone at that age,' Serena said.

Tish shrugged. 'It's hard to be left alone at any age.'

Twenty-five

Stride was stretched across the leather sofa in the great room of the cottage when Serena arrived home near midnight. He was sleeping, with a paperback novel still in his hand. One leg had fallen off the sofa, and his bare foot was on the carpet. Sara Evans sang on the stereo. Serena let him sleep while she undressed and got ready for bed. The windows were open, with the curtains blowing like sails, and the night air was humid and hot. She slept in a loose tank top in this kind of weather. Back in the living room, she turned down the lights, switched off Sara, and made herself a cup of pear tea, which she sipped in the love seat opposite Stride. Rose fragrance blew in from the bushes near the porch. Her eyes got lost in the shadows and felt heavy. When she put the teacup down, she leaned back into the folds of the sofa, and soon she, too, was dreaming.

In the mists of her brain, she was with Tish on a beach. A cool breeze kissed their bodies. She came upon Tish from behind, caressing the down of her neck. The bones of Tish's spine traveled like the graceful arch of a harp into the small of her back. Her flesh was young and soft, and Serena felt no guilt, only freedom, as they began to make love. Later, after they were done, she found herself in water, floating, alone. It was paradise, except for a strange, rhythmic thumping that wormed into the stillness of her world and unnerved her. Like a drumbeat or a heartbeat. She felt herself coming naked out of the water, and what she saw was Jonny, covered in blood, swinging a baseball bat with a sucking *thwack* over and over into a body on the beach. Killing Tish.

Serena started awake, gasping for breath.

Jonny was awake too, and staring at her. 'You OK?'

She shook the sleep out of her head and blinked. 'Yeah. What time is it?'

'Almost three.'

'I'm hungry,' Serena said.

'What would you like?'

Serena thought about her diet. 'Forty-six eggs.'

'Do you want those scrambled or fried?'

'Don't tease me. You think I'm kidding?'

Stride gestured at the narrow, heavy box she had left on the dining-room table. 'What's that?'

'I picked up something of yours at the lost and found.'

His eyes narrowed with concern and curiosity.

'The bat,' she said simply.

He looked at her. 'Stanhope?'

She nodded.

'That son of a bitch,' he said.

Serena knew he wasn't talking about Peter Stanhope. He was talking about Ray Wallace. Ray, who had sabotaged a murder investigation for money and power. Ray, who had handed over the murder weapon to a man he suspected of committing the crime.

Stride went to the table. He didn't touch the box immediately. Instead, he studied it closely, as if the cardboard, ink, and tape would talk to him. He bent down close to it, as if the smell of blood would still permeate the air. Then, using two fingers on each corner, he lifted it, measuring its heft.

'Peter called it a goodwill gesture,' Serena said. 'He didn't have to give it to me. He could have destroyed it.' She added, 'He admitted that he was the one who sent those threatening letters to Laura.'

'He admitted it because we'll find out anyway when we run the DNA, right?'

'Right.'

'Just when I'm convinced Finn is guilty, Peter elbows his way back onto the playing field,' Stride said.

'He says he's innocent.'

220

'Do you believe him?'

'I don't know, but I think it helps for me to stay close to him. He talks to me.'

'Did he say anything else?'

'Nothing I can share right now, but nothing you wouldn't guess anyway.'

'He assaulted Laura in the softball field,' Stride said. 'There was no date, no affair.'

'No comment.'

Stride put the bat down. 'Logically, everything points to Peter. She was killed with his bat, and he's had the murder weapon for years. If it weren't for Finn, I'd be certain that Peter killed her. Not that we'd be any closer to making a case.'

'Peter wants me to gather evidence against Finn,' Serena said.

'Are you going to do it?'

'I think so.'

'You may be helping the man who's really guilty.'

'I know.'

'But you can't resist the chase?'

'No,' she admitted.

'Rikke has shut Finn down,' Stride said. 'She's hired a lawyer. You can't talk to her.'

'I've got a different angle,' Serena said.

'Oh?'

'I want to go to North Dakota tomorrow. I want to find out about Finn's childhood. Tish said something terrible happened to him there. I'd like to find out what. Maybe that's the missing link.'

'Take Maggie with you,' Stride suggested. 'I'd like to have someone official on the trip.'

'You mean five hours each way arguing with Maggie about the radio station? We'll kill each other.'

Stride laughed. 'So take a private plane. Stanhope can afford it.'

'True.'

'We better get some sleep,' he said.

'To hell with sleep.'

Serena got up lazily from the love seat. She brushed her black hair back away from her face. Holding on to Stride's shoulders, she

221

straddled him on the sofa, with her knees on either side of his legs and her breasts near his lips. His hands slid behind her and cupped her buttocks through her panties. She put her hands on his face, bent her neck forward, and kissed him.

'I dreamed that you caught me sleeping with Tish and you beat her to death. You murdering bastard.'

'Tell me more,' he said.

'I don't kiss and tell.'

'You're a tease.'

'Do you find Tish attractive?' she asked him.

'Pretty, but not my type,' he said.

'Are you thinking about her or me right now?' she asked, pressing down with her hips.

'You.'

'Good answer.'

The phone rang.

'God hates me,' Serena said, rolling to her left and studying the caller ID screen on the receiver. 'Private call.'

'Wrong number.'

'Ignore it?'

'No, better get it.'

She groaned and picked up the phone. 'What?'

The male voice on the line was honey-smooth and deep as a foghorn. The caller asked for Stride. Serena punched the speakerphone button and held the phone to Jonny's mouth as she climbed back on top of him and worked awkwardly on his clothes.

'Stride,' he said impatiently. 'Who is this?'

'I'm a friend of a friend.'

'My friends don't call at three in the morning,' Stride snapped.

'I'm sorry for the time.'

'What do you want?'

'Do you know a man named Hubert Jones?'

Stride looked at Serena, who stopped what she was doing long enough to shake her head. 'No,' he said.

'He knows you.'

'Oh?'

'He wants to talk to you.'

'Have him call me at the office in the morning. My secretary can schedule an appointment.'

'You'll need to be on the road by then.'

'Excuse me?'

'Hubert Jones is flying in to O'Hare Airport in Chicago at noon. From there, he has an afternoon flight to South Africa via London. He'll be away in Johannesburg on an academic fellowship for nine months. If you want to talk to him, it has to be tomorrow. In Chicago.'

'Why would I drop everything to meet a man I don't know?' Stride asked.

'Like I said, he knows you. Look him up, Mr Stride. See what kind of a man he is. Then come to Chicago. And come alone, no other police, OK?'

'I'm hanging up,' Stride said. 'If Mr Jones wants to talk to me, he can call me at the office.'

'He said to give you a message,' the man interjected quickly.

'What is it?'

'He said to remind you that the girl had secrets.'

Stride didn't reply. Serena felt his muscles tense and his arousal vanish. The silence stretched out.

'Are you still there, Mr Stride?'

'Yes.'

'Does that message mean something to you?'

'You know it does.'

'Will you come to Chicago?'

Serena looked at Jonny, puzzled.

'I'll be there,' Stride said. 'Tell me when and where.'

The caller rattled off a meeting place at O'Hare, then hung up. Serena dropped the phone on the sofa and folded her arms over her chest.

'What's going on?' she asked. 'Who the hell is Hubert Jones?'

'I don't know, but I need to get to the office early to find out,' Stride said. 'Then I'm heading to Minneapolis to grab a flight to Chicago.'

'To chase a stranger?'

'To chase Dada,' he said.

223

Twenty-six

'I don't like small planes,' Maggie announced, strapping herself into the white leather seat of Peter Stanhope's Learjet 25. She tightened the seat belt until it nearly cut off the blood flow across her tiny waist. 'Does this thing have oxygen masks? I bet you have to use little nose plugs.'

'Relax,' Serena said. 'Pretend you're rich.'

'I am rich,' Maggie reminded her.

'So why don't you own one of these things?'

'Because I don't like small planes!'

Serena laughed. 'Don't be such a baby. This is better than driving.'

'The only reason we're not driving is because you don't want to argue with me about the radio station.'

'We still have to rent a car in Fargo,' Serena said. 'Dibs on country.'

'I have my iPod with me. We can listen to my Bon Jovi collection.'

'I have my iPod too. Martina.'

'Red Hot Chili Peppers.'

'Alan Jackson.'

'White Zombie.'

'Shania.'

'Oh, please,' Maggie scoffed. 'I don't listen to any singer with bigger tits than me.'

'Doesn't that pretty much rule them all out?' Serena asked.

Maggie stuck out her tongue.

Serena leaned her arm on the glossy wooden shelf beside her seat and stared out the window as the jet lined up on the Duluth runway. Beside her, Maggie squeezed her eyes shut and dug her fingernails into the armrest. The plane accelerated with a roar and lifted at a sharp angle into the breezy air. The climb was bumpy, with the jet's wings waggling like a shimmy dancer. Serena had flown in and out of Las Vegas so many times, riding the rocky thermals of the desert mountains, that turbulence no longer bothered her.

The plane headed straight west. Below them, she saw miles of forest dotted with jagged lakes, like the black footprints of retreating glaciers. Towns were thinly spread across the northern half of Minnesota. So were the roads and highways. Time passed quickly as the jet streaked over the land, crossing just south of the giant fingers of Leech Lake. Without clouds, Serena could see straight down. As they neared the western section of the state, the forested wilderness gave way to lush squares of farmland, ranging in color from muddy taupe to deep green, jutting up against one another like stripes in a flag.

They never climbed high enough to escape the unsettled pockets of air.

'This sucks,' Maggie told her.

'We'll be there soon.' Serena changed the subject. 'What's the word on adopting a kid?'

Maggie exhaled loudly through her nose. 'No one is very encouraging. Single Chinese chick cops need not apply.'

'You won't know until you try.'

Maggie peeled her fingers off the armrest long enough to push her black fringe out of her eyes. 'It's not just that. I'm not sure I'm up to the job of raising a kid by myself. I don't know if it would be fair to a kid. Plus, this thing with Mary Biggs really shook me up. Her parents threw everything into that girl. I don't know if I'm ready to love anyone that much. I'm not ready to risk what it would do to me if something happened.'

'You can "what if" yourself out of anything,' Serena said.

'Yeah, I know. Do you and Stride ever talk about it?'

'I can't have kids.'

'I mean adoption.'

'I think the window has closed,' Serena said. 'I grew up knowing my insides were messed up, so I never really developed the kid gene. Jonny says he's too old. I don't see it happening.'

'Do you think you're missing something?'

225

'Sometimes.'

'I feel like I'm missing something,' Maggie said.

'Then you should do it.'

The plane lurched as they descended into Fargo. On the ground, they rented a car and headed south out of the airport, past the university and through the square, tree-lined neighborhood streets toward downtown. They parked near the main library, which was located within a block of the curvy ribbon of the Red River, which served as the border between North Dakota and Minnesota and separated Fargo from its Minnesota twin, the city of Moorhead.

Inside the library, Serena asked at the help desk for Fargo phone books from the early 1970s. Soon after, the librarian deposited a stack of AT&T directories at the desk where the two women were waiting. The books smelled faintly of mildew. Maggie grabbed the volume for 1972 and groaned when she turned to the M pages.

'There are dozens of Mathisens in here,' she said. 'This place is like Little Norway.'

'Do we know the first names of Finn's parents?' Serena asked.

'Ole and Lena?'

'Yah sure. Dat's funny. God, I'm actually becoming a Minnesotan.' Serena peered over Maggie's shoulder at the list. 'Most of these people are probably dead or gone.'

'I'll call the Wisconsin DMV,' Maggie said. 'If we can get Finn's birth date from his driver's license, then we can look up his birth announcement in the local paper. That way we can get his parents' names.'

'Clever.'

Maggie pulled out her cell phone and dialed the DMV number from her directory. 'I'm on hold,' she said. She hummed for a moment and then added, 'So Ole brings home a vibrator for Lena on her birthday. And Lena goes, vat's dis for? So Ole says, vell, you stick dis between yer legs and use it to tickle your puddin'. And Lena goes, oh, dat's great, I already have somethin' like dat. Is dis thing called Sven, too?'

'You are a sick woman,' Serena said.

'Too true. Hey, hello, I need you to look up a birth date for me.' She rattled off her Minnesota shield number and Finn's name and address. A few seconds later, she scribbled a date on a piece of scratch paper. 'Got it, thanks.'

Serena read what Maggie had written. 'Twenty-second April 1959. I'll get the microfiche for the Fargo paper.'

Ten minutes later, they found a birth announcement for Finn Mathisen, sister to Rikke Mathisen, son of parents Nils and Inger. Nils was a feed corn farmer with a large plot of acreage west of the city. Maggie used her index finger to run down the list of Mathisens in the 1972 phone book.

'No Nils listed, but here's Inger,' she said. 'Same address.'

'I think the father died in a car accident when Finn was a kid.'

'So what are you thinking? We go out there?'

Serena nodded. 'Right.'

'Who the hell is going to remember them after thirty-five years?'

'Farmers don't leave home unless it's feet first or to hand the keys to a banker,' Serena said. 'Hopefully, a couple of Finn's neighbors are still around.'

'Do you have any idea what we're looking for?' Maggie asked.

'Not a clue, but I bet we'll know it when we find it. Finn didn't get screwed up in Duluth. Whatever happened to him, it started right here.'

Fargo was flat. The kind of flat where highways disappeared into the hazy horizon without so much as a bend or an overpass and where only the curve of the earth blocked a view as far as Montana. The kind of flat where Canada would suck in its breath and expel wind across the plains with nothing in the way to slow it down, rocketing walls of black dust, rain, and snow into the city in fierce clouds. The kind of flat where a trickling, muddy stream like the Red River could lazily swell over its banks and drown everything in its path, like a pitcher of water spilling across a table.

Serena and Maggie drove west out of Fargo, passing fields of high corn and sprawling lots of soybeans, barley, and rapeseed. Hot wind and sun beat against the windshield of their rental car. They left the windows open, and as a compromise they kept the radio off. Every few miles, they passed a car on the two-lane highway, but otherwise the land was open and lonely. Serena drove. Maggie had a map on her lap.

They turned south off the county road thirty miles outside the city, and three miles later, they turned again onto an unpaved road and kicked up a hurricane of dirt behind them. Half a mile farther, they

227

parked opposite a well-maintained white farmhouse notched into a huge expanse of leafy fields, like a summer photo from a calendar of rural homes. A ten-year-old girl in a sunflower dress chased a Labrador retriever that barked wildly as it galloped toward them. The girl corralled the dog by its collar and gazed at the car and the two women with open curiosity as she pulled it back toward the house.

'This is where Finn grew up,' Serena said.

She guessed that the house and outbuildings would not have looked much different several decades earlier. There would still have been a dirty pick-up truck parked in the grass. There would still have been muddy tractor ruts leading into the rows of crops. They climbed out of the car and began sweating in the sun. Serena wore blue jeans, a white T-shirt, and sneakers. Her hair was tied back in a ponytail. Maggie wore black jeans, an untucked button-down black shirt, and black boots with steep heels.

'Who wears heels in farm country?' Serena asked.

Maggie pushed her sunglasses to the end of her nose. 'Hello,' she said in a rumbling voice. 'I'm Johnny Cash.'

They crossed the dirt road and trudged up the driveway. Gravel crunched under their feet. The young girl they had seen earlier pushed herself in a swing set in the middle of the lawn. They waved at her, and she stared back at them without smiling. They heard the dog barking inside the house. As they got closer, Serena smelled flowers and the sweet-tart aroma of apples baking.

A thin woman in a summer dress, with dark curly hair, opened the screen door and let it bang behind her. She strolled to the edge of the front porch, watching them. She picked brown leaves from a hanging basket of fuchsias.

'Afternoon,' she said, with mild suspicion in her voice. 'Can I help you?'

They introduced themselves, and Maggie produced her identification. The woman relaxed, but her eyebrows arched with interest. 'Minnesota?' she said. 'What are you two doing out here?'

'Chasing wild geese,' Maggie said.

'We're interested in a family that owned this house a long time ago,' Serena said. 'Their name was Mathisen. This was back in the nineteen sixties and seventies.'

'Mathisen? Well, that's a good North Dakota name. I'm Pamela, by the way. Pamela Anderson. And yes, don't say it, I've heard the jokes. Imagine my horror ten years ago when I realized what my married name would be.' She laughed. 'I got my husband a framed pin-up of the other Pamela as a wedding present.'

'So you've only lived on this property for ten years?' Serena asked.

'Me? Yes, but my husband has been here since he was a boy. This was the family home. I didn't even realize anyone had owned the place before his parents did.'

'How old is your husband?'

'Not old enough to help you, if that's what you're thinking,' Pamela replied. 'He was born in nineteen seventy-three. However, my mother-in-law lives with us. This was her house until her husband died, and then she deeded it to us. Of course, I have no idea whether she knew anything about the people who lived here before she did, but around here, everyone has a way of knowing everyone else's business.' She smiled.

'May we talk to her?' Serena asked.

'Oh, of course, she'll love it. She's in a wheelchair now and mostly blind from diabetes. You'll be the highlight of her day.'

Pamela led them inside. Serena heard George Strait crooning on the stereo, and she grinned at Maggie, who rolled her eyes. The Labrador bounded up to greet them, concluding that they must be friends because they'd been allowed inside the house. Serena got down on her knees and mussed his fur.

'I've got some fresh pie,' Pamela said. 'Would you like some?'

Serena saw Maggie smirk. She knew all about Serena's diet.

'It sounds wonderful, but I better resist,' Serena said.

'I'll take a big piece,' Maggie said. 'With ice cream, if you have it.'

Pamela looked pleased. 'I'll be back. Mary Ann has a room at the rear of the house, so I'll bring her out to meet you.'

She left them alone.

'Warm apple pie,' Maggie said. 'Yum.'

'Bitch,' Serena muttered.

They took seats on the tweed cushions of the sofa. Pamela returned with a large slice of pie, adorned with two scoops of vanilla ice cream and a glass of milk. Cinnamon wafted from the plate. She put it on the oval coffee table in front of Maggie, who thanked her profusely.

She picked up the plate, shoved a large forkful in her mouth, and chewed loudly.

'Wow, is this good,' she said with her mouth full.

'If you choke, I am not giving you the Heimlich,' Serena said.

Pamela came back, pushing a wheelchair in front of her. The woman in the chair had snow-white hair that framed her head like a halo. Her sun-browned skin was wizened and flecked with black spots, and sunglasses shielded her eyes. She had a crocheted blanket spread over her lap, and below it, there was nothing at all. Her legs had been amputated below the knees.

'Mary Ann, these ladies are here to see you,' Pamela said.

'To see me? Well, isn't that lovely.' Her voice crackled like Rice Krispies, but her demeanor was warm and sunny. Her dry lips curled into a smile. 'I smell pie. Pamela uses my recipe. Four-time blue-ribbon winner at the North Dakota State Fair. Darling, I don't suppose I could have a small piece?'

'Mary Ann,' Pamela chided her gently. 'You know better.'

The old woman sighed. She put a finger to the side of her nose. 'I can still tell when a pie is done just by the smell,' she said.

Pamela turned off the music and sat down in the armchair next to her mother-in-law, who slid her hands under the blanket to warm them. Serena and Maggie introduced themselves again.

'Minnesota?' Mary Ann said. 'My husband and I had a favorite fishing resort near Brainerd. It's a beautiful area. All those lakes and trees. Out here, it's just miles and miles of corn.'

'Your daughter-in-law says you've lived in this house since the nineteen seventies,' Serena said.

'Oh, yes, Henry and I bought a small parcel of land near Minot shortly after we got married, with some money we got from his grandfather. Henry did very well with it. He had a degree, you know. He was very scientific.'

'Near Minot? How did you end up here?'

'Well, my family was from Minot, and Henry's family was from Fargo, and that caused difficulties at the holidays. Relatives always want you to be in two places at the same time. So eventually, Henry's father told him about the Mathisen place going up for sale, and we moved down here. My parents were ready to retire anyway, and they got a small home in Casselton. So it all worked out well, you see.'

'Did you know the Mathisen family?' Maggie asked.

'Know them? Oh, no. As I said, we weren't from around here. Henry's parents knew them quite well, however. His parents had a farm about five miles east of here.'

'I wonder if your in-laws ever told you any stories about the Mathisens,' Serena said.

'Stories?'

'We're trying to find out whatever we can about the family. Particularly their children.'

'I'm not sure if I can help you,' Mary Ann said. She tilted her head back, and her left hand darted from under the blanket to scratch her neck. 'I don't recall hearing very much about their children. They only had one, didn't they? A boy? No, that's right, the girl was older. She didn't live here.'

'Did you hear anything unusual about the boy?'

'Unusual? I don't think so. It's just sad how it happened.'

'How what happened?' Maggie asked.

'Well, a teenage boy losing both of his parents. I hate to see it.'

'I heard the father died in a car accident,' Serena said.

'Yes, I think you're right about that,' Mary Ann said. 'It wasn't easy to survive back then without a man in the house. It's a wonder they made it at all. And then the mother – oh, how awful that was. I have to tell you, Henry and I weren't sure we wanted to move into this house after that. I didn't know if I'd ever be able to sleep here.'

'Why?' Serena asked. 'What happened to Inger Mathisen?'

'Oh, don't you know? Being police, I just thought you would know. An intruder killed her. Murdered her in her bedroom. They said it was probably some drifter, looking for jewelry or cash. I just can't believe anyone could do such a horrid thing. It's bad enough to kill another human being, but how he did it – oh, dear, I still don't like to think about it.'

'How was she killed?' Maggie asked.

'She was beaten to death,' Mary Ann whispered, tugging on her blanket. 'Can you imagine? Beaten to death with a baseball bat.'

Twenty-seven

Stride bought a Chicago dog and staked out a seat near the British Airways gate in Terminal 5. He propped his legs on the opposite row of chairs. Outside the window, the international gates of O'Hare were like a parking lot for 747 jets sporting multicolored logos from airlines around the world. Inside, in the departure concourse, thousands of passengers streamed beneath overhead skylights and miles of white piping. He watched the bustle of people and planes while he finished his hot dog.

He was behind the international security checkpoint, thanks to an emergency call to a friend on the Chicago Police. Dada – if it was Dada – would be arriving in the next hour from one of the airport's three domestic terminals. Stride guessed that Dada was flying in from Missouri on his way to Johannesburg. The man he had found on the web, Hubert Jones, was a professor of African Studies at Washington University in St Louis.

The school's website included a faculty photo. Stride had stared long and hard at the picture to make a mental connection to the young drifter by the railroad tracks thirty years earlier. All he could say for sure was that Hubert Jones *might* be Dada. His dreadlocks were gone, replaced by a buzz cut of steel-gray hair. His devil eyebrows had grown out thick and bushy. His broad, jowly face showed a man much heavier than the fit giant who had overpowered Stride. The eyes could have been Dada's eyes – black and intense – but in the end, too much time had passed, and too much age was written in the man's skin.

Stride swigged a large bottle of Coke to wash down the hot dog. He re-read the dog-eared sheaf of paper on Hubert Jones that he had printed at his office before the sun came up. Jones was fifty-two years old, with undergraduate and graduate degrees from Berkeley. He had traveled and lectured extensively in Europe, and the visiting professorship he had accepted in South Africa was his third academic stint on the African continent. As a scholar, Hubert Jones was a star.

He had also written a book.

More than anything else, the book made Stride believe that Hubert Jones was Dada. It was called *Dandelion Men*, and it told the story of three years that Jones had spent living with itinerant laborers around the South and Midwest after he dropped out of college in his early twenties. Over time, he had become one of those wanderers, part of a community of people who came and went as easily as seeds traveling on the wind. They hiked. They hitched. They hopped trains. They worked, stole, got drunk, went to jail, and never knew any area long enough to call it home.

Stride found an excerpt from the book on the web:

These were not the men that you would call homeless, not the mentally ill deposited onto our city streets in later years when our tax dollars discovered the limits of our compassion. This was a time and era when men chose this lifestyle because it made them free. It was predominantly a rural, not an urban, phenomenon. These men were children of our roots, children of our soil, who lived at the mercy of weather, food, and water. On most days they knew violence. Sometimes it was from those among them, but more often it was from outside, from men who wore uniforms. You could beat Dandelion Men, you could even kill them, but you could never strip them of their dignity and of their primal humanness. I think sometimes that the people who were most violent toward them, who were most afraid, were those who envied them their freedom.

To Stride, the book sounded like Dada's story, including its time frame, which spanned the years from 1976 to 1978. When he ran an online search inside the book, however, he found no references to

Duluth or Minnesota or to the events that summer. No mention of murder in the park. No mention of escaping by coal train. If Hubert Jones had lived those events, he had left them out of his journal.

Stride eyed the terminal escalators. In his mind, he relived the events by the railroad tracks and felt Dada swatting him away like a fly. He remembered the panicked wheezing in his lungs as he struggled for air and the wet misery of the mud and rain. He heard the crack of Ray's wild shots. Saw Dada, on the train, growing smaller.

That girl had secrets.

Thirty yards away, Stride spotted Hubert Jones on the escalator.

The noise of the airport became a muffled roar in his brain, crowding out everything but the man gliding down the steps. He was huge, at least six feet six, and round like the mammoth trunk of an ageing tree. He wore a dark suit, a starched white shirt with jeweled cufflinks, and a bright tie. The colors of the tie, Stride realized, were the Rasta colors of green, gold, and red, just like in the beret that Dada had worn. Stride wondered if it was an inside joke, a little signal for him to recognize. When Jones swiveled his head, their eyes met across the concourse, and the big man's thick lips curled upward into a broad smile.

At that moment, Stride knew. He knew for sure.

It was Dada.

For a heavy man, he moved with grace and quickness. At the bottom of the escalator, he reviewed the people pushing around him, as if he were wondering whether Stride had arranged a welcoming party of police and security. When he saw that he was safe, he stepped nimbly through the crowd, which parted for the giant man. Stride got out of his chair to meet him. He didn't like looking up to other men, and Jones was as intimidating as an ogre at the top of the beanstalk. Jones extended his hand, and Stride shook it. He felt intense strength in the man's grip.

'I see you still have the scar,' Jones said, pointing at Stride's face with a meaty finger. 'I'm sorry about that.'

'My wife always said it was sexy,' Stride replied.

Jones laughed. It was the same booming laugh from long ago, like the villain on an old radio show.

Stride recognized the man's voice. 'You called me last night,' he said. 'Not a friend of a friend.'

'Yes, I did.'

'Why the ruse?'

'I didn't know what kind of man you were, Lieutenant. For all I knew, you would clap me in leg irons if you got the chance. I wanted to hear your voice. I've always believed I could take the measure of a man by how he talks to me.'

'I passed the test?' Stride asked.

'Oh, I still wasn't entirely sure whether you would surround me with a posse of Chicago's finest. But I figured that the boy who stood up to me by the railroad tracks would consider it a point of pride to meet me alone. You haven't changed, Lieutenant.'

Stride hated to admit it, but Jones was right. It would have been smarter to bring backup, but he had wound up making the same arrogant mistake he had made as a boy. Taking on this man by himself. 'If I wanted to have you arrested, I could,' he said.

'You could, but I hope enough time has passed that you now believe again what you believed as a boy. I didn't kill anyone. Wisdom comes with innocence and experience, Lieutenant; it's only the in-between time that causes us problems.'

Jones sat down on the opposite row of chairs and laid his fists on his knees. Stride took an unopened bottle of spring water by the cap from the seat next to him. He handed it to Jones, who grabbed it in his big hand.

'You must be dry after your flight,' Stride said.

'In fact, I am.' Jones undid the cap and drank down half the bottle. He recapped it and then said, 'May I keep this until I finish it, or would you like your fingerprint sample back right now?'

Stride actually felt himself blushing. 'Keep it,' he snapped.

Jones grinned and put the bottle on the floor.

'Why contact me after so long?' Stride asked. 'Do you know about Tish Verdure and the book she's writing about the murder?'

'I still have friends in the Rasta community,' Jones explained. 'As you know, there was an article in the Duluth paper recently that rehashed the crime and mentioned that a Rasta vagrant was a suspect. It made the rounds on our websites, and someone finally sent me the article with a note that said, "Was this you?"'

'But why come forward now? I assumed you were dead. You were safe.'

'I thought long and hard, believe me, but I decided it was time to put that part of the past behind me. I confess I was also a little curious about you. The article mentioned that you were a Duluth detective, and I was surprised to find out that you were the same boy I confronted that night.'

'I looked up *Dandelion Men* on the web,' Stride said. 'You didn't mention what happened to you in Duluth.'

Jones eased back into the chair. His girth filled the space, and his waist squeezed against the armrests. 'Oh, I wanted to talk about Duluth, but I knew that people were still looking for me. It's like being a bear loose in the city streets. They don't just put it in a cage when they find it. They shoot it dead.'

'The cop who shot at you back then,' Stride said. 'He was dirty. I thought you should know.'

'That was a dirty time.'

'Why did you choose that life?' Stride asked. 'Why be a drifter?'

'I guess you could say I was appalled by modern life,' Jones said. 'I felt disconnected. Only a boy can be quite so naïve. Still, the community I found in the shadows was deeper and stronger than any I have found since. It was hard to leave it behind. Every now and then, I try to find the dandelion men again, but they're an endangered species. Like feral animals whose habitat has been destroyed. They scamper away when I come close. I'm no longer from their world, you see.'

'You sound like you miss it,' Stride said.

Jones tugged at the lapels on his suit with a bemused smile. 'I do. Sometimes I fantasize about disappearing again. It's only a fantasy.'

'Tell me about Laura.'

'Laura?'

'The girl who was murdered.'

Jones folded his hands over his chest. 'Yes, of course. I never knew her name until I saw that newspaper article. She was just a girl in the park.'

'All these years, I thought you killed her,' Stride said.

Jones nodded. 'And now?'

'Now I'm not so sure. We have a new witness. Someone who says you rescued Laura instead of attacking her.'

'A witness,' Jones said. 'Yes, someone else was in the woods that night. I never saw him, but I knew he was there. I smelled the cannabis he was smoking.'

Finn, Stride thought.

'There was another boy in the softball field,' Jones added. 'He was the one who attacked Laura. I stopped him from harming her.'

Stride nodded. 'After the fight, Laura ran toward the north beach.'

'Yes, I know. I followed her.'

'Did you go all the way to the beach? Did you see her there?'

'I did,' Dada said.

'What did you see?'

Dada smiled. 'I already told you, Lieutenant. That girl had secrets.'

Twenty-eight

'We're never going to make it back to Minnesota tonight,' Maggie said.

They were an hour west of Fargo, seated on top of a park bench overlooking a boat launch that dipped into the waters of Lake Ashtabula. Immediately to their left was the concrete wall of the Baldhill Dam, which held back the Sheyenne River and created a narrow stretch of manmade lake. It was late afternoon. The air smelled of boat fuel and hamburgers. Jet ski riders left wakes in the water. Nearby, in the camping area, children splashed and squealed along a strip of sand beach.

'Peter wants his plane back,' Serena replied.

'Yeah, but this guy could be out there fishing until the sun goes down.'

After leaving the Mathisen farm, they had stopped at police head-quarters in Fargo, where their North Dakota colleagues helped them identify the man who had served as lead detective investigating the murder of Finn's mother, Inger Mathisen. The detective, Oscar Schmidt, had retired from the force more than a decade earlier and relocated with his wife to a town called Valley City. Serena and Maggie tracked down the Schmidt home, where his wife pointed them north to Lake Ashtabula, Oscar's favorite spot for fishing.

'You want to go in the water?' Serena asked.

Maggie tented her sunglasses and squinted at the park. 'You mean skinny dipping?'

'I mean, it's hot. Let's roll up our pants and dip our feet.'

'You're on.'

They left their shoes on top of the bench and folded the legs of their jeans above their calves. The sand on the beach was scorching, but the lake was cold when they stuck in their toes. They shuffled a few feet out until they were standing in eight inches of water.

'So is it a coincidence?' Serena asked. 'Finn's mother was beaten to death – just like Laura?'

'No.'

'Do you believe the intruder story?'

'No.'

'Neither do I. I wonder why Oscar did.'

'That's what we'll ask him. Assuming he ever gets in off the lake.'

Serena lifted her chin toward the warm sun. Maggie finished a can of Diet Coke while they waited, checking her watch impatiently as half an hour passed. Finally, a fifteen-foot aluminum boat that had obviously seen many years of service put-putted toward the boat landing. At the stern, an old man with shaggy gray hair and a mustache that curled over his upper lip cut off the Evinrude motor and let the boat drift into the shallow water. He wore navy blue swimming trunks with white vertical stripes and no shirt. His belly bulged like a basketball, but the rest of his skin was loose and leathery. He was small, no more than five feet five, and wore sunglasses. As Serena and Maggie watched, Oscar Schmidt climbed into the water, dragged the prow until it was nearly beached on the concrete ramp, and then tramped toward his red Chevy truck in flip-flops.

'Mr Schmidt?' Maggie called. They splashed out of the water toward the boat landing.

He stopped with his hands on his hips. 'That's me,' he replied gruffly. 'Who are you?'

Maggie introduced herself and Serena. 'We'd like to take five minutes to talk about an old case of yours,' she said.

'Which case?'

'Inger Mathisen.'

Schmidt folded his sunglasses and shoved them in the pocket of his swimsuit. 'I wondered if that one would ever come back and bite me in the ass.' He sighed and added, 'Let me get the boat out, then we'll talk.'

Ten minutes later, the boat dripped in the parking lot, and Schmidt

239

sat opposite Maggie and Serena on the park bench. His bushy hair was damp, and they smelled beer on his breath.

Serena angled her head toward the water. 'How'd you do?'

'Finished off a six-pack, took a swim, didn't catch a damn thing. Typical day. Tell you the truth, I don't like fish much. Never have. Most of the time, I just throw them back, because otherwise my wife would want to cook them.'

'Nice place to retire,' Maggie said.

'Yeah, it's not so bad, huh? We've got a trailer in Texas where we go during the winter. I'd stick around here if it were up to me, but my wife hates snow.'

'Tell us about the Mathisen case,' Serena said.

'Not much to tell. Isolated farm. Saturday night. Woman was asleep in bed. Somebody bludgeoned her to death.'

'You never caught the guy?'

Schmidt shook his head. 'Nah, we had nothing. Figured it was some bastard who got off the interstate and was looking for cash. Probably surprised to find anybody in the house.'

'The farm was five miles off the freeway,' Serena said. 'And not easy to find.'

Schmidt shrugged and chewed on a fingernail.

'Did you find reports of any similar incidents along the interstate route?' Maggie asked. 'Maybe out of Montana or Minnesota? You can usually track these guys like pins on a map.'

'There were no other incidents that looked like a pattern crime,' Schmidt said. 'We figured the guy got spooked.'

'Any sign of forced entry?' Serena asked.

'Out here? Nobody locks their doors.'

'Did anyone see or hear anything?' Serena asked.

'You saw the place. Not a neighbor for miles.'

'What about the boy?'

Schmidt rubbed his mustache. 'Boy?'

'Finn Mathisen. Inger's son.'

'He wasn't home.'

Maggie leaned across the park bench. 'No offense, Mr Schmidt, but you're not a farmer, so why don't you quit shoveling the shit?'

Schmidt's mustache twitched as he grinned. 'I like you. Never

240

much liked Orientals, but you're smart. Easy on the eyes, too. You both are.'

'Why'd you think this case would bite you in the ass?' Maggie asked.

Schmidt glanced at his truck, and Serena thought he wanted to be home eating dinner. 'Look, ladies, why cause problems for good people after so many years? Who the hell cares?'

'A few years after Inger was killed, a teenage girl was murdered in Duluth,' Serena said. 'She was beaten with a baseball bat. Finn is a suspect.'

Schmidt frowned. 'Well, shit.'

'So you want to give us the real story?'

'Hey, there was no evidence to prove that an intruder *didn't* kill her.'

'But you didn't believe it.'

Schmidt jabbed a callused finger at them. 'Sometimes you have to decide whether you're a cop or a human being, OK? Maybe it's not that way in the big city, but it sure as hell works like that in a small town. The way I figure, Inger Mathisen's murder was an act of mercy.'

'What do you mean by that?' Maggie asked.

'Inger was a mean fucking bitch. Why do you think her husband got drunk every night and finally wound up on the business end of a semi? He hated being in that house. He was weak. He didn't stop it.'

'Stop what?'

Schmidt sighed with disgust. 'The word in town was that Inger did stuff to her kids,' he said. 'Sick stuff. Back then, you knew about that kind of thing, but you didn't talk about it. A lot of fucked-up kids came out of those farms.'

'Go on.'

Schmidt coughed and spat on the ground. 'The boy, Finn, was fourteen or fifteen. Already messed up. Into drugs. The way we figure it, he got stoned and decided he was done with his mother once and for all. It was his bat. His fingerprints were on it.'

'You said he wasn't home,' Serena said.

'That's what his sister told us.'

'Rikke?'

Schmidt nodded. 'She got out of that hell-hole when she went off to

NDSU and got her teaching license. She was working in Fargo and living in an apartment there. She swore that Finn was with her that weekend.'

'Were there any witnesses near her apartment to back that up?'

'A couple people remembered seeing the boy,' he said. 'They couldn't be sure if it was Saturday or Sunday.'

'You think it was Sunday,' Maggie said.

'Yeah, I figure Finn killed Inger on Saturday night and then called his sister. She came out to get him and take him back to Fargo to sober him up and get their stories straight. No one saw a thing, though, so there was no way we could prove it. Rikke took Finn home on Tuesday, and that's when they claim they found the body smelling up the house. She called us, and I came over.'

'Did you interrogate them?'

'Interrogate kids whose mother had just been killed? Yeah, not so much.'

'Except you didn't believe them, did you?'

'Let's just say I didn't push too hard, OK? None of us did. We talked about it. Everybody in town was going to be happier if it was just some stranger who killed her. The kids had suffered enough, so we figured, let them get on with their lives.'

'An act of mercy,' Serena said.

'Exactly right.'

242

Twenty-nine

Tish parked on a dirt road two blocks from Finn's house, sheltered by the sagging branches of a weeping willow. She dangled a cigarette outside the open window of the Civic while she waited. She knew she should quit, but she had spent most of her life alone and anxious since she left Duluth, and smoking was like morphine in her bloodstream, dulling the pain. Her cigarettes were always there with her. On a sailboat in the harbor in Dubrovnik, after the war ended and the tourists started coming back. In a mud and stone hut halfway up a Tibetan mountain. In Atlanta, crying in the parking lot of a Borders bookstore in Snellville, after the break-up with Katja. In Duluth, when Laura ran away and shut Tish out of her life.

If only she had stayed. Things would have been so different.

She felt the car shiver as a train snaked its way toward her from the harbor. The engine came slowly, snorting like an animal and cutting off her view of Finn's house. Coal dust blew off the overflowing boxcars and settled in a grainy film across her windshield. The clattering, rattling, squealing thunder made her clap her free hand over her ear. When the last of the freight cars passed, she saw Rikke, in a navy blue dress, marching down the front steps of her house. It was the first time she had seen Rikke since coming back to Duluth. The years hadn't been kind. Her austere beauty and her Amazon physique had both flown away with age. Even from a distance, she could see a lifetime of unhappiness in her face. Rikke clutched an umbrella in her hand and cut across the lawn to a tan Impala. She drove out of the weeds onto the dirt road and across the maze of railroad tracks, not far from the car where Tish was waiting.

Tish ducked low so that Rikke wouldn't see her. She waited until the Impala was gone, then climbed out of her car and headed for Finn's house. She picked her way through the bed of rocks between the tracks. Her T-shirt clung to her skin in the sticky air. Looking around, she felt as if time had stood still in places like this. The town, the dirt roads, the house, and the trains were like a snapshot from her childhood. It made her think of old things. Cold, sweating bottles of Mountain Dew. Wham-O Frisbees. Black and white television. It made her think of a time when people she loved were still alive.

She knocked on the door. When no one answered, she peered through the cream-colored lace on the window. She wondered if Finn was sleeping.

Tish turned the door handle, but the front door was locked. When she checked each of the window frames, she found one where the inside latch was undone. She slid the window open and climbed through the flimsy curtains into the living room. The house was silent and close. When she felt something brush against her leg, she jumped, then realized it was a cat pushing past her feet. She closed the window behind her.

'Hello?' she called. 'Finn?'

No one answered.

She did a nervous survey of the downstairs space. The kitchen was small, with avocado appliances that hadn't been replaced in years. The screen door to the backyard was tattered, its mesh hanging down from the corner. She pushed open a door and found a small toilet, no bigger than a closet, with a bare bulb hanging overhead for light and an empty pill bottle on the ledge of the sink. Tamoxifen. She felt a stab of sympathy for Rikke.

Back in the living room, she saw the narrow steps near the front door that led to the first floor. She hesitated at the base of the stairway.

'Finn?' she called again.

Tish climbed the stairs, wincing at the noise as her feet pushed down on the warped slabs of wood. Upstairs, she was faced with a closed door immediately in front of her. Without knowing why, she knew Finn was inside. She didn't knock. She nudged the door with her foot and waited in the doorway while it swung open.

The room was dark, the curtains drawn, letting only cracks of daylight knife through the gloom in narrow, dusty streams. Her eyes adjusted. She saw Finn on the floor, sitting with his back against the bed, his arms hugging his knees. His forearms were swaddled in white bandages. He wore underwear but nothing else.

'It's me, Finn,' she said. 'Tish.'

His eyes were lost in the shadows. He didn't look at her, and she wasn't sure if he knew she was there. Then he spoke in a tired voice. 'You should go, she'll be back soon.'

'I don't care.'

'She won't want to see you.'

'I'm here to see you. How are you?'

'How am I?' Finn said. 'I wish I was dead.'

'Don't say that. You're lucky.'

'Yeah. People see me, they say, there goes a lucky man.'

Tish sat down on the floor next to Finn and slid an arm around his shoulder. His bare skin was clammy. 'Maybe you should be in bed.'

'I've been in bed for days. I pretended to be asleep so Rikke would finally leave me alone. She's afraid of what I'll do.'

'Does she have reason to be afraid?'

'You mean, will I do it again? I want to, but I'm a coward. How pathetic is that?'

'I feel guilty,' Tish told him. 'Like I did this to you by coming back.'

'It's not your fault.'

'Then why did you do it?' she asked. 'Was it because of Laura's murder? Did you remember something more?'

Finn squeezed his eyes shut. A tear bloomed like a rose out of the corner of his eye and trickled past his nose to the corner of his mouth. 'Everyone wants me to remember, but I don't.'

'I think you do.'

Finn shook his head. 'I never should have gone to the park that night.'

'Then why did you?'

'Because I can't stop!' Finn exclaimed. 'Don't you get it? I've never been able to stop.'

'Stop what?'

He clenched his fists. 'Watching. That's who I am. I'm a watcher.'

'You mean the young girls in their bedrooms?' Tish asked. 'That was you?'

He put his face in his hands and nodded.

'Why, Finn?'

'You think it's my choice? You think I want to be like this?' He stared at the floor and added, 'Mom made me watch. I didn't even know what was going on, but she made me watch. I hated her for that.'

Tish stared at the bed and began to understand. 'Did you watch Laura?' she asked.

'Yes.'

'Where?'

'Here. I would watch her in bed when she stayed with us.'

'Did she know?'

'No. Not at first.'

'You said you were in love with her, Finn. How could you do that to someone you loved?'

'I told you. I can't stop. I wish I could gouge my eyes out.'

'Did you know Laura was going to be in the park that night?'

Finn's head bobbed.

'How did you know?' Tish asked.

'She told me. I knew she was running away. It was my fault. I scared her.'

'Did she find out you were spying on her?'

'Yes. I told her everything. I had to. But it was a mistake. She didn't understand.'

'You kept following her after the fight with Peter, didn't you? You followed her all the way to the beach.'

'I don't know. Maybe I did.'

Tish felt as if she were being suffocated. 'What happened?'

'I don't remember,' he said.

'Finn, you have to tell me.'

'I don't remember.'

Tish closed her eyes and leaned close to him, smelling his sweat and fear, murmuring in his ears, 'You're so close. What did you see?'

'Nothing.'

'Do you ever dream about it?' she asked.

'No. I don't dream.'

'I bet you do, Finn.'

'Go. Just go. Get away from me.'

'Tell me about your dreams.'

Finn shook his head mutely. She knew he was ready to break.

'Tell me,' she repeated.

'I have nightmares,' he whispered. 'I've had them for years.'

'About what? What do you see?'

'Blood.'

Tish waited.

'There's so much blood,' he said. 'It's all over her.'

'What else?'

'Noise. Like something sucking. Gurgling. And the wind. Except it's not the wind. It whooshes. Like a bird's wings.'

'What is it?' Tish asked. But she knew.

Finn's eyes grew wide, and his mouth opened into a hole like the entrance to a cave. 'It's the bat. I can see it going up and down. Up and down. I can't make it stop. Somebody make it stop!'

He stared at his hands. His bandaged hands.

'I killed her,' he said. 'Don't you understand? *I killed her.*'

Thirty

'Who killed her?' Stride asked Hubert Jones.

'I have no idea.'

Stride shook his head in frustration. 'Then why are we here?'

Jones tilted his bottle of beer and drained it, then dabbed at his puffy lips with a napkin. They had relocated to a quiet table in the rear of a bar in Terminal 5.

'I never said I knew who killed that girl,' Jones said. 'I only know that it wasn't me. When I last saw her, she was alive. I was shocked when word spread at the tracks that she had been murdered.'

'Why not come forward?'

Jones chuckled and shook his head. 'When a white girl gets murdered, the first question the police ask is, who was the nearest black man? You said yourself, the cop on the case was dirty. I knew what was coming. I knew I had to get out of town.'

'You said Laura had secrets,' Stride said.

'Yes, she did. I knew it the moment I saw this girl.'

'When was that?' Stride asked.

'In the woods. I saw her pass me no further away than you are now, but she didn't even see me. She was determined. She had a destination in her heart. It was in her walk and how she held her backpack. I looked at her and I thought to myself, tomorrow this girl will be gone. Not gone as in dead, mind you. Gone as in somewhere else. Gone as in starting a new life.'

Stride wasn't convinced. 'Tell me about the fight in the softball field.'

'I heard the girl scream. I came upon the two of them in the long grass. The boy had her pinned. He was kissing her, tearing at her clothes, and she was fighting back, beating at him.'

Stride waited.

'I became enraged,' Jones continued. 'To me, rape is the ultimate disrespect. It's the barbarian who strips a woman of her soul.'

'Exactly what did you do?'

'I saw something in the grass. A baseball bat. I picked it up and struck the boy in the back. I jabbed it like a spear and heard his ribs breaking. He let go of the girl, and I picked him up bodily and threw him into the weeds. When I bent over to see to the girl, the boy launched himself at me again. I hit him in the face then. He fell backward. He was unconscious.'

'What about the girl?'

'She ran into the woods.'

'The boy who attacked her – was this the same person you heard near you? The one who was smoking marijuana?'

Jones thought about it. 'No.'

'You're sure?'

'I'm sure. You know what that park was like in the summer, Lieutenant. There were lurkers everywhere.'

'What about Laura?' Stride asked. 'Did you go after her when she ran?'

'Of course. I wanted to see if she was all right. That was foolish of me, I know. In her state, she probably didn't even realize who had attacked her. She could easily have assumed it was me. Not many white teenage girls like to find a large black man chasing them through the woods anyway.'

'Did you take the baseball bat with you?'

'No, I left it behind.'

'Weren't you afraid the boy would come after you with it?'

'He wasn't in much shape to follow me.'

'You're certain you didn't take the bat,' Stride repeated.

'Yes.'

'The police matched your fingerprints to it.'

'Like I told you, I picked it up. I hit the boy.'

'Laura was killed with that bat,' Stride said. 'The police found it near her body on the beach almost a mile away. How did it get there?'

'Obviously, someone carried it, but not me.'

'Do you have any idea who could have done that?'

'No, but I already told you that someone else was in the woods.'

'Could Laura have taken the bat with her?'

'No, she just ran.'

'You said you followed her,' Stride said. 'What happened then?'

Jones steepled his fingers under the folds of his chin. 'First, let me ask you something. Do you still consider me a suspect?'

'Yes.'

'At least you're honest.'

'You were there. Your fingerprints are on the murder weapon. You fled the city.'

'I've explained all of those things.'

'Except I have no way of knowing if you're telling the truth,' Stride said. 'Keep going. Tell me about Laura.'

Jones settled into the plastic and steel airport chair, which groaned in protest under his weight. 'At first, I thought I had lost her. I thought she had made her way out of the park.'

'Did you find her?'

'Yes, the trail wound along the lake to another beach. I saw her there.'

'Did you speak to her?' Stride asked.

'Oh, no, she had no idea I was there.'

'Was this the beach where her body was found?'

'I assume so.'

'But she was alive?'

'Very much so.'

'Did she have the bat with her?'

'I told you, no.'

'Then what happened?'

'I left.'

'Just like that?' Stride asked.

'The girl was safe. There was nothing else I could do. I wasn't going to help her by announcing myself.'

'We found semen at the edge of the clearing near the beach. Was it yours?'

His eyebrows arched. 'Semen? No.'

'Did you go back to the softball field?'

'No, I took a different trail and left the park.'

'Did you meet anyone else? Did you see the other person you thought was in the woods?'

'No, I didn't.'

'Is that it?' Stride asked. 'Is there anything else you want to tell me?'

'There's nothing else.'

Stride leaned across the small table and stared at Jones until the big man blinked uncomfortably. 'You're lying,' he said. 'Why bring me all the way out here if you're not going to tell me the whole story?'

'Everything I've said is the truth,' Jones insisted.

'The question is what you're leaving out.'

'What makes you think I'm leaving anything out?'

'*The girl had secrets*,' Stride said. 'That's what you keep saying. I think you know something else about Laura. Something *specific*. I want to know what it is and why you're covering it up. Until you tell me, you're not getting on that plane.'

Jones ran his tongue across his white teeth and smiled.

'You saw something, didn't you?' Stride asked.

'Yes, I did.'

'What was it? What did you see when you found Laura on the beach?'

'I'm not sure it will help anyone if I tell you. Least of all the girl who was killed.'

'Let me decide that,' Stride said.

'What I saw was innocent and beautiful. There was no violence.'

'Tell me.'

Jones sighed. 'Laura wasn't alone.'

'*Who was she with?*'

'I don't know. It was no one who would have killed her. They were kissing. They were in love. You can understand why I didn't bother intervening at that point. They didn't want me around.'

'What did he look like?' Stride asked. 'Laura's lover.'

Jones shook his head. 'Laura had the kind of lover you didn't talk about back then. It wasn't a boy, Lieutenant. It was another girl. Laura was on the beach with a blonde girl about the same age. They were holding each other as if they never wanted to let go.'

251

Thirty-one

Tish studied the framed photographs on the credenza in Jonathan Stride's office in City Hall. She saw a photo of Stride with his arm around Serena, taken somewhere with a view across the Strip in Las Vegas. Beside it, she saw a picture of Cindy, with the Vancouver harbor behind her. Her hair was dark and straight. Her eyes teased the camera. Over time, Tish's memories of Cindy had dimmed to the point where she couldn't hear her voice in her head and couldn't call up a picture of her face. Then a photo like this brought it all back.

She felt her eyes misting. Behind her, she heard the sound of someone approaching, and she quickly put the photograph down, wiped her face, and pasted a smile on her lips. Stride came into the office, and she didn't think she had fooled him. His eyes strayed to the line of photographs, and she thought they lingered on Cindy.

He pointed at the chair in front of his desk and then took his own chair and leaned back, his jaw tight and hard. His hair was unruly, and he looked as if he hadn't slept. Tish sat down uncomfortably. She heard the office door close and turned around to see the tiny Chinese cop, Maggie Bei, leaning against the door. She wasn't smiling.

'Is something wrong?' Tish asked.

'What did you want to see me about?' Stride said.

Tish took a deep breath. 'He confessed.'

'Who?'

'Finn,' Tish said. 'I went to see him yesterday.'

'I thought I told you not to play cop,' Stride snapped.

'I felt responsible for his suicide attempt. I wanted to find out why

252

he did it. We wound up talking about Laura's murder, and that's when he blurted it out.'

'Exactly what did he say?'

'He talked about dreams he has. About seeing the blood all over her and about the bat going up and down. And then he just said it. He said it flat out. I killed her.'

'Is that all?'

'Isn't that enough?' Tish asked.

'Did he use Laura's name?' Stride asked.

'I don't know what you mean.'

'It's a simple question, Tish. Did Finn say he killed *Laura*?'

'No, but who else would he mean?' Tish said. 'What is going on?'

'I think we're done here,' Stride said. 'Thanks for coming in.'

Behind her, Maggie opened the office door and stood beside it.

'We're done? That's it?'

'That's it.'

'Are you going to arrest him?' Tish asked.

'No.'

'No? What more do you need? I mean, look, this isn't what I expected. I admit that I was wrong. I was convinced Peter Stanhope was involved. But now you can match Finn's DNA to the crime scene. He told me he was there. He told me that he killed her. This is the break we've needed.'

'For your book?'

'Not just for the book. To solve the case.'

'The confession is useless,' Stride told her.

'Useless? How can you say that?'

Stride held up his hand and counted on his fingers. 'One, Rikke hired a lawyer. The law says we can't talk to Finn anymore without his lawyer present. Because I was stupid enough to talk to you about this case, a defense attorney can make a persuasive argument that you were acting as an instrument of the police in questioning Finn. Result? The confession gets tossed. Two, Finn was recently discharged from the hospital and was almost certainly under the influence of painkillers when you talked to him. So his attorneys will argue that he was not within his faculties. The confession gets tossed. Three, the fact that Finn did not use Laura's name leaves doubt about who he was talking about. The confession gets tossed.'

'That's crazy.'

Stride gestured to Maggie. 'Tell her.'

Maggie closed the door again and sat on the edge of Stride's desk. 'Serena and I did some digging into Finn's past. His mother abused him. The cops think Finn snapped and bludgeoned his mother to death. With a baseball bat. They let him walk because they couldn't prove it and, frankly, no one wanted to see him put away. Getting rid of that woman was a community service, they figured.'

'Poor Finn,' Tish said softly.

'You get the picture?' Maggie said. 'Regardless of whether Finn said Laura's name or not, his attorney will argue that it's memory transference from the death of his mother. I mean, hell, he said this came to him in a dream? Who knows what his brain has concocted after years of drug and alcohol abuse?'

'The confession gets tossed,' Stride repeated.

Tish thought furiously. 'I was there,' she insisted. 'Finn wasn't hopped up on drugs. He wasn't talking about his mother. He was back there. In the park. With Laura.'

'You didn't let me continue,' Stride said. 'Four, we recovered the murder weapon. The baseball bat.'

'*What?*'

'Peter Stanhope had it. Ray Wallace gave it to him as a little gift. We tested the bat, and Finn's fingerprints are *not* on it.'

'That's not possible.'

'There are fingerprints we can't identify, but they don't belong to Finn,' Stride said.

'So maybe he wore gloves.'

'In July?'

'What about DNA? Test the semen.'

'Even if it matches, all that proves is that he jerked off near the murder scene.'

'Damn it, Jonathan, he told me he killed her.'

'*Five,*' Stride continued, holding up his last finger, 'the confession gets tossed because the only two people who heard it are you and Finn.'

Tish shrugged and held up her hands. 'So what? What difference does that make?'

'No one will believe you. You have no credibility.'

'Excuse me?'

'No one will believe you because you are a manipulative, self-serving *liar.*'

Tish shot to her feet. 'How dare you! What the hell are you talking about?'

Stride stood up too. 'Don't play games with me, Tish. I don't appreciate it when someone twists me around her finger. I don't appreciate it when someone toys with people who are close to me. I don't appreciate it when someone uses me and lies to me in order to further some secret goal. What's your motive, Tish? Why are you really here?'

'I don't know what you're talking about,' Tish said.

But she did. She saw it in his face. He knew.

'I'm talking about the fact that I have one more suspect to add to the list,' Stride said. 'Finn, Peter, Dada, take your pick. And now you.'

Tish looked down at his desk. She wilted back into the chair. 'No, Jonathan, you're wrong.'

'I found Dada. Or rather, he found me. He told me that he followed Laura to the beach that night.'

'It's not what you think,' she said.

'He saw you, Tish. He saw you and Laura together. You were there.'

Thirty-two

Stride waited for her to deny it, but she didn't.

'OK, you're right,' Tish said, looking like a flower that had been left out of water. 'Yes, I was there that night. I should have told you long before now, but I never wanted anyone to know. It was private. It was something for me and her. But you can't possibly believe I would ever harm her. I *loved* her.'

His voice was hoarse with anger. 'You've lied to me over and over. You lied about where you were that night and what you were doing. You lied about remembering the fight between you and Laura. You were at the crime scene when Laura was murdered, and you never said a word about what you saw. You've deceived me from the outset.'

'I know. I'm sorry.'

'You've irreparably compromised this investigation.'

'Without me, there would *be* no investigation,' Tish reminded him. 'I'm the only reason anyone cares. If I made mistakes, they weren't with any malice. You have to understand—'

Stride sliced the air with his hand, cutting her off. She stared at him, scared and silent. Maggie studied the floor with her arms folded. He shoved his chair back and paced in the small space of the office, wrestling with his fury. He stared at the photographs on his credenza.

'Did Cindy know you were there?' he asked.

'Yes,' Tish admitted.

'That's why she wanted you to do the book, isn't it? That's why she went to you, not me.'

256

'Yes.'

He shook his head in disbelief. He felt as if he now had to question all the years they had spent together. His wife had lied to him and kept him in the dark. He wasn't just angry at Tish. He was angry at Cindy, too.

'Start at the beginning,' Stride told her. 'Tell me everything.'

Tish took a slow breath. 'It was a different world. You know that.'

'Meaning what?'

'Meaning there were things you didn't talk about. Not to anyone. Look, it's hard enough being a gay teenager today, even when most schools have resources and counselors. All you want to do is fit in, and you don't. Back then, it was a secret you kept to save your life. I struggled with it, but at least I knew who I was. It was much harder for Laura. She resisted. She was scared. She was desperate to be normal.'

'Did Laura know you were gay?' Maggie asked.

Tish's fingers twitched. Stride knew she needed a cigarette.

'Not at first,' she said. 'We were just friends. I was attracted to her, but I didn't do anything about it for months, because I didn't know how Laura felt, and I didn't want to scare her off. I mean, on some level, I was pretty sure she felt the way I did, but she was so deep in the closet that she wasn't ready to admit it to herself. A lot of people never do.'

'At some point you told her,' Stride concluded.

'Yes.'

'Is that what the fight was about?' he guessed. 'Is that what split you up?'

'Yes,' Tish acknowledged. 'Things were changing between us. We were touching more. It was casual, but it meant something. We'd do homework on her bed, and we'd drape our legs over each other and sort of idly caress and pretend it was nothing. We'd give each other massages after we went running. We'd sleep together, not doing anything, but sharing the same bed. It was like we were circling each other, groping toward both of us admitting what was going on.'

'What happened next?'

'Laura was getting very anxious about her feelings,' Tish said. 'She started going out on dates with boys. Like she was trying to convince herself she was straight. I didn't like it. I was really upset and jealous, but I didn't let on. Most of the dates were disasters. She froze up. Peter Stanhope was the worst. He kept pressuring her for sex, and Laura didn't want that at all, but she didn't really understand why. It came to a point where I couldn't stand by and do nothing. I loved her too much, and I was sure she loved me. So finally, in May of our senior year, I suggested we go camping on a Saturday night. It was just the two of us. We shared a sleeping bag, and we were talking and laughing, and my heart was just aching for her. I don't even remember how it happened, but I kissed her. She kissed me back. Romantic kisses, not like friends. I told her I loved her. And things – happened.'

'What went wrong?' Maggie asked.

'It was a mistake. We went too far, too fast. Laura wasn't ready to accept that she was gay. She rebelled against it. She rebelled against me. The next day, she hardly said a word to me. She began avoiding me. She was never home. She just shut me out of her life. I was devastated.'

'What did you do?'

'I had never felt so totally alone. When school was over, I ran away. I moved down to the Cities, and I tried to forget about Laura, but I couldn't. I was still completely in love with her.'

'Did you contact her?'

'Yes, I wrote to her and told her where I was. I told her I was sorry. I asked if we could just be friends, nothing else, nothing physical. That wasn't what I wanted, and I was kidding myself to think I could be around her at that point without needing to be with her. But I would have done anything to have her back in my life.'

'Did Laura write back?'

'Yes. A few days later, she sent me this long, long letter. About how scared she had been. About how ashamed she was for running away from me. She said she had finally accepted the truth about who she was, and she loved me and wanted to be with me. I don't have to tell you, I was over the moon. Ecstatic. This was going to be the real deal, our whole lives. Sure, we were naïve. We were teenagers. But I've never loved anyone like that, ever again.'

'Tell us about the night in the park,' Stride said.

Tish closed her eyes. 'I try not to think about that night. I've pushed it out of my mind.'

'You have to tell us.'

'It's too awful. It was the best night of my life, and then just like that, it became the worst night of my life. I couldn't believe God would be so cruel. So heartless.'

'What happened?' Stride asked.

'Laura and I talked on the phone every night. We made plans to run away. I had an old car, so I told her I would come up to Duluth and meet her. She picked the fourth of July. She said it was her independence day. We said we'd meet on the north beach. It was going to be magical.' Tish gave a sad smile. 'And for a little while, it was.'

'She found you there?' Maggie asked.

'Yes, I came early to wait for her. She came running out of the trees. She told me what had happened in the field, that someone had attacked her. I knew all about the person who had been stalking her, and I knew how scared she was. I thought we should leave right away, but Laura didn't want to go back into the woods yet. So we waited. And the longer we were there, the more we forgot about anything else, because we were so happy to be together again. I can't remember how many times we said we loved each other. Being there on the beach, in the wake of the storm, was like a cocoon. We kissed. We made love. We fell asleep for a little while in the sand in each other's arms. We never wanted to leave.'

Stride remembered being on the opposite side of the lake on that same night, with Cindy, and feeling the same way.

'It didn't last,' he murmured.

Tish blinked. Her voice was so low he could barely hear it. 'No.'

Tish lay awake, naked, and stared at the sky. The clouds had broken up into a patchwork of dark islands, and she could see open spaces crowded with stars. Near her feet, the lake slurped at the shore. Tufts of cottonwood blew like snow out of the forest and drifted to the ground beside wet masses of heart-shaped leaves. The two of them were on their backs, sand rubbing their skin. Their fingers were laced together, their legs apart, like two dolls in a paper chain. She propped herself on one elbow and watched Laura sleep beside her. She saw a

259

teardrop of rain land on Laura's breast, and she bent over and tasted it with her tongue and then closed her lips over the nub of a hardened nipple. She was rewarded with a sigh of pleasure, a stirring, a rumbling in Laura's throat.

'Do you want to swim?' she whispered.

'Mmm, you go.'

Laura barely came out of her dream, and then she was sleeping again. A spider no bigger than the head of a pin scampered over Laura's shoulder, and Tish pursed her lips and blew it off. Laura murmured and turned over, balancing her head on the down of her forearm. Hair tumbled like a wild mask over her face. Her curving back was slick with sand. Her tattoo fluttered its wings at her.

Tish got up, glorying in the night wind on her body. She glided to the wet beach, where an inch of water pooled between her toes, and then stepped over moss and rocks as she dipped lower into the lake like a mermaid. As she got further from the beach, the bottom fell away, and the deep water lifted her off her feet. She stroked lazily with her arms, floating. She turned over on her back, feeling cold fingers on her scalp. Her feet kicked and barely stirred a splash, nudging her body out toward the far center of the lake. The water was silk on her naked skin.

She wanted to shout for Laura to join her, but the beach was far away and black, and the silence felt sacred, as if she were in church. She let her feet dangle below her, swishing her arms to keep her face above the surface. When a mosquito whined in her ear, she allowed herself to sink. The lake enveloped her and roared in her ears. She drifted down, and when her chest demanded air, she sprang up with a flutter kick. Water dripped from her eyelashes, nose and chin, and ran from her hair down the middle of her back like the tickling caress of fingertips. She couldn't hear, except for her own breath. She could barely see the angry ripples of the lake where she had disturbed it. A swampy dankness filled her nose. She was cut off from all of her senses, and she didn't care. Out in the center of the lake, in a nether land between past and future, she realized she was happy. This was a moment unlike any other in her life. A moment without worry, only bliss.

And as quickly as it had come, it wriggled through her fingers like a sea creature and never returned to her again.

Back on land, where the trees and water intersected invisibly on the half-moon of shoreline, she heard a noise. It radiated across the lake and landed in her ears and traveled through her body like shudders of thunder. Her head cocked in confusion. The noise repeated itself, dull and wet, a noise that had no business here in the woods. Her body became indescribably cold. She knew, without any glimmer of how she knew, that the noise was very, very bad.

Breaking the cathedral silence, she screamed

'Laura! Are you OK?'

There was no response, and somehow she knew there would never be a response. No musical voice. No laughter. No call from the shore, 'I'm fine, silly, what's the problem?'

Just a beating, pounding, thumping drumbeat. A killing beat.

She swam. She put her face in the water and clawed with her arms and kicked up waves behind her. She swam so far and so fast that her body scraped on the sand before she even realized she had scissored into shallow water. Panting, she stood up, wiping water from her eyes. Her mouth fell open, and when she tried to scream again, she couldn't make a sound. She saw Laura's body where it had been before, but nothing else was the same. Her limbs were sprawled and twisted. She smelled of copper and death. Beside her, thrown carelessly to the ground, was a silver bat.

Tish dived across the sand, crying, and wrapped her arms around the girl on the beach, rocking her like a baby, bathing herself in her blood, whispering in her ear, telling her to wake up, telling her how much she loved her.

Over and over.

Until they were both cold.

Tish wept silently into her hands. Maggie squeezed her shoulder while Stride opened his office door and signaled for a bottle of water. Tish took labored breaths and then straightened up and wiped her face.

'I didn't expect it to hit me so hard,' she said. 'I've held it in for a long time.'

Stride nodded. One of the secretaries brought in a bottle of water, and he twisted off the cap and handed it to Tish. She sipped it slowly.

'How did Cindy know you were there that night?' he asked.

'I was still on the beach when she arrived,' Tish murmured. 'I hid in the woods, but she heard me behind her. I told her what had happened. I told her the truth about me and Laura.'

'Cindy never told anyone that she saw you there. Why did she protect you?'

'She knew I didn't kill Laura.'

'That's not a reason to keep quiet. You were a witness.'

Tish shook her head. 'I didn't see anything. Besides, Cindy wasn't just protecting me. She was protecting her father, too. If people knew the truth about me and Laura, it would have killed him.'

'You should have talked to the police.'

'And say what?' Tish demanded. 'For God's sake, I was *eighteen*. I was scared out of my mind. I thought whoever killed her might think I could identify them. I thought people would blame me. To be gay back then meant you were a deviant, a child molester. I had already lost Laura, and I couldn't bring her back. I didn't know who had done this. I didn't have any information that would help the police. I just wanted to escape.'

'Did you touch the bat?' Maggie asked. 'Will we find your fingerprints on it?'

Tish's eyes flashed with anger. 'You see? Even now, you're wondering if I did it.'

'You were the last person to see her alive,' Stride told her.

'I never touched the bat,' Tish said. 'I don't care what you think of me now, but I'm telling you the truth. Finn confessed. He must have followed Laura that night and seen us making love. He must have been crazy with jealousy. So when I went into the lake, he lost control. For all I know, he was stoned and had no idea what he was doing.'

'I'd like to tell you that this changes things, but it doesn't,' Stride said. 'Maybe you can put this in a book, but Finn is never going to see the inside of a courtroom.'

'Is this because I lied?' Tish asked.

Stride nodded. 'I happen to believe you, but a jury could easily conclude that you and Laura had a fight. That Laura met you to say goodbye and you couldn't deal with it. That's what a defense attorney will say. Or maybe Peter woke up, took the bat, and followed the trail. He was stalking Laura, we know that. He had the bat all these years.

262

Who knows what he was capable of? There's also Dada. He fled the scene. His prints are on the murder weapon. Don't you see? We may know what happened, but we'll never *prove* what happened. You're going to have to be satisfied with that.'

Tish stood up. She put the half-finished bottle of water on Stride's desk and smoothed her clothes. Stiffly, she extended a hand for him to shake. Her grip was weak and unconvincing. 'I'm sorry I lied to you,' she said.

She slipped out of the office and closed the door behind her.

Maggie looked at Stride. 'What do you think?'

Stride frowned. 'She's still lying about something.'

Thirty-three

Clark Biggs sat in a bar on the main street in Gary, with his big fingers laced around a bottle of beer. Donna nursed a Diet Coke beside him, but they had hardly talked. When she put her hand tentatively on his shoulder, he couldn't even turn his head to look at her. She laid her head against his arm, and he knew she was crying, but he didn't feel anything. He couldn't comfort her when he was numb all over. He wanted to cry, and he couldn't. He wanted to get angry, and he couldn't. It was like being in a dream where you wanted to run, and your legs wouldn't go.

He knew what Donna wanted – to see if they could rebuild a life, to put their marriage back together after Mary had forced them apart. She wanted something to fill the emptiness, but it was never going to happen. Without Mary, he had no life and didn't want one.

'I wish you'd let me in,' Donna murmured.

Clark didn't reply. He drank his beer. The bar was crowded, but the cacophony of voices created a bubble of privacy around the two of them. He would have been happier being alone. He didn't want Donna or anyone else to share his grief.

'Do you still blame me?' she asked.

Clark hesitated and then shook his head. He had given up the anger he felt for Donna. She had no way of knowing that a monster was in the woods. It was just that life was so damn fragile, and there were so many predators out there. A girl goes to a store to buy a graduation gift and winds up kidnapped and strangled. A girl goes to a Halloween party and gets beaten to death in the backyard. A girl goes to an island

264

resort and disappears forever. Fragile. There and gone in the time it takes to cry. And no one was ever to blame, and no one ever seemed to pay the price.

'It wasn't you,' he told her. 'It could just as easily have been me with her when it happened.'

'Thank you, Clark. I needed to hear that.'

Clark realized that his hands were wrapped so tightly around the mug of beer that his knuckles were white. The truth was that he wasn't numb at all. He was holding his emotions down like a bathtub toy under the water, because he was afraid of them popping up. Afraid that his grief and fury would be like a tidal wave washing him away if he stared them in the face. He didn't know how to deal with any of it. He could be hollow and dead, or he could open the locked door in his heart and go insane.

Behind him, wind and heat blew through the smoky air as the door opened. He heard a chorus of teenage chatter, and both he and Donna turned around as the players from a girls' softball team squeezed into the bar, dressed in white jerseys and shorts, their long hair tumbling and blowing as they peeled off their caps. Their faces glowed with pinkness and sweat. They laughed and shoved each other; it was a post-game victory celebration. They dropped bats, gloves, and balls in a corner near the door, and one of the softballs rolled across the wooden floor and wound up at Clark's feet. He leaned down and scooped it up. It was dirty and solid. A girl about Mary's age, stocky and strong, with chestnut hair, clapped her hands and waved at him. Clark tossed the ball to her underhanded. She caught it with a big grin and juggled it in her hands as she slouched into a chair.

'Do you ever wish that Mary had been like that?' Donna asked. 'Just an ordinary girl?'

'She was who she was,' Clark said.

'Yes, but she missed so much. Getting crushes. Getting her first kiss. Having a best friend. It could have been her on that team, Clark. She could have been any one of those girls.'

'She was happy,' Clark insisted.

Donna stared wistfully at the girls on the other side of the bar. 'She was only happy because she didn't understand what she couldn't have.'

'What are you saying?' Clark asked.

'I don't know. We always said it was God's will, but did God really want her to be like that? Did God want us to split up because we couldn't handle it? I don't think God was watching us at all when He let it happen.'

'Are you saying Mary is better off dead?'

'No.' Then she said, 'I don't know. I can hardly put it into words, but yes, on some level, don't you think she's better off?'

Clark swung back to the bar. He didn't want to look at the girls' team anymore. He couldn't bear their sweetness and young noise. 'Mary's not better off,' he said. 'I'm not better off. Maybe you are.'

'That's not what I mean. You know it's not. I just need to find some meaning in this. Some explanation. Some purpose.'

'There's no purpose at all.' He waved at the bartender. 'Another beer over here.'

'Getting drunk won't bring her back,' Donna said.

'What do you care? I'm not your husband anymore, so just leave me alone.'

Donna sniffled and took a sip from her cola. Clark was impatient as the bartender poured his beer, and he drank a third of it in the first swallow when the man put it down in front of him. The more he drank, the more the wall began to crack. Emotions slipped out. He felt his eyes burning with tears.

'Oh, no,' Donna murmured.

'What?'

She pointed at the television screen over the bar. Clark saw a press conference underway live on the nine o'clock news. The St Louis County Attorney, Pat Burns, stood in front of a battery of microphones in the lobby of the courthouse. Behind her, he saw the two Minnesota detectives he knew. Maggie Bei and Jonathan Stride. He caught the last few words of a crawl on the bottom of the screen.

NO CHARGES TO BE FILED.

'Hey!' Clark shouted at the bartender. 'Turn that up, OK?'

The bartender aimed a remote control at the television. Clark leaned forward, straining to hear. Some of the conversation in the bar dwindled as faces turned toward the screen. It was a small town. They all knew Clark and Donna.

266

'. . . substantial speculation about the murder of Laura Starr that occurred in Duluth in nineteen seventy-seven,' Pat Burns said. 'Recent reports in the media have suggested that we have a suspect in custody and that charges in that case are imminent. Unfortunately, these reports are not accurate. We have made no arrests to date, and we do not have sufficient evidence at this time to put before a grand jury. We will continue to investigate any leads that emerge in this terrible crime, but it isn't appropriate to raise false hopes in a community that wants justice.'

'What the hell does that mean?' Clark asked.

Donna wiped her eyes. 'They're giving up. That's how lawyers talk.'

Clark heard one of the reporters ask a question. 'Is it true that a suspect in the crime attempted suicide following interrogation by Duluth police?'

A photo appeared in the upper right corner of the television screen, and Clark saw the face of the man in the photo array that Maggie had shown him. He saw the name. Finn Mathisen.

'I can't comment on that,' Burns replied.

'. . . heard there might be a confession in the case,' another reporter said over the chorus of voices.

Burns shook her head. 'We've conducted numerous interviews with witnesses, and we're still evaluating them. At this point, the police do not have any statement in hand from anyone claiming responsibility for the murder.'

'Has Peter Stanhope been cleared of involvement in the murder?'

'I'm not going to discuss anyone's guilt or innocence.'

'Do you think this case will ever be solved?'

'I very much hope so.'

Clark didn't look at Pat Burns. He studied Maggie's face behind her. What he saw there turned the hope in his heart to dust. When she looked at the camera, it was if she were looking directly at him, admitting she had failed, apologizing.

Another voice. '. . . is reporting that the suspect is a Superior resident named Finn Mathisen, and that Mathisen is also a suspect in the recent string of peeping incidents involving teenage girls?'

Clark held his breath. Donna clung to his arm.

'We are gathering evidence with regard to the so-called peeping

267

Tom cases,' Burns said. 'Mr Mathisen is a person of interest in that investigation, but he has not been charged. That's all I'll say.'

'Is it true that one of the peeping incidents led to a girl's death?'

'We are investigating whether the death by drowning of a mentally retarded girl in Fond du Lac is in any way related to a peeping incident involving the same girl. It's too early to draw any conclusions.'

'Turn it off,' Clark told the bartender.

The bartender looked back at him with his arms crossed. 'You sure, Clark?'

'Turn it off,' he repeated.

The man switched channels.

'Too early to draw any conclusions?' Clark asked.

Donna stroked his bare arm. 'They have to say that. It doesn't mean he won't be charged. You can't obsess about it, Clark. Let them do their jobs.'

'He's going to get away with it.'

'You don't know that.'

Clark closed his eyes. His drunken mind was like a dam, cracking and growing fissures under the relentless pressure of a swollen river. Each time one of the girls behind him squealed with laughter, he heard Mary's laugh. It was as if she were still alive, holding out her hand and calling for him. When he tried to picture her face, however, he couldn't see it. Another face intervened in his mind.

The sallow, leering face of Finn Mathisen.

'Clark?'

He heard Donna, but she was far away.

'Clark?' she asked again.

'I'm here,' he said hoarsely.

'I'm going to take you home,' she told him.

Clark nodded.

'Let me run to the ladies' room, and then I'll drive us back to the house. I'll stay there, OK? I won't leave you alone. I'll stay with you tonight.'

'OK.'

'I'll be right back,' Donna said. She hesitated and added, 'I need to tell you something, but not here. When it's just the two of us, we can talk.'

268

She nudged past him, but he grabbed her arm. They were surrounded by people pushing and shoving against them, smelling of smoke and stale beer, screeching a jumble of words that made his head spin. He pulled her face close, so that he could inhale her lilac perfume. He saw yearning and despair in her eyes. The down on her neck felt soft and familiar under his fingers. Her chest rose and fell like a scared bird.

'Mary was lucky to have you,' he said.

Her face twisted with emotion. She put a hand on his face, and her skin was warm. He thought he would be able to feel that touch all night.

'I'll be right back,' she said.

Clark nodded. He watched his ex-wife as she navigated the crowd and disappeared through the oak door into the restroom. This could have been a night like so many they had spent in their early years. He could imagine Donna as she had been at twenty-one years old, when their bodies were fit and their hormones racing. Before their dreams grew up, got old, and died.

He shoved a tip into the bartender's jar and got off the bar stool, swaying as he tried to walk. No one paid any attention to him. He balanced himself against strange shoulders until his head cleared. Through the sea of drinkers, he saw the two tables of teenage girls, sipping Coke, laughing with mouths full of white teeth and braces, their innocent giggles like music. Some had dirt on their faces; others had their baseball caps turned backwards. Under the table, they were all bare legs and white socks. Clark felt as if he had been stabbed in the heart.

He made his way to the bar door. The girls had piled their softball equipment in the corner there. He opened the door into the night, but before he left, he grabbed one of the wooden baseball bats by its knob handle and took it with him.

Thirty-four

Tish sat with the manuscript of her book open on the laptop screen. Her fingers lingered over the keyboard, but no words came. She was at the point where she had to decide. Lie or tell the truth. She had postponed the decision in the belief that, by the time she reached this crossroads, it would be easy. But it wasn't. She was nearly done, but she wasn't sure now if she wanted to finish it at all.

She reached for a cigarette, but even the solace of smoking didn't appeal to her tonight. Angrily, she slapped the cover of the laptop shut.

When she had first opened the door to the past, it had felt right, as if the time had finally come in her life to flush out the bats from their hiding places. To fulfill her promise to Cindy. To come home. Now she wondered if it would have been better for everyone if she had stayed away.

She crossed to the glass door that led to the porch, built high above the slashing waters of the lake. She opened the door and took a tentative step onto the deck without looking down. Fear of heights was an odd thing. People who didn't have it didn't understand it. They could shimmy up cliff faces, or stand on rooftops, or dangle their feet from ski lifts, and feel nothing at all. For her, just thinking about those things made her flinch and sweat. It wasn't the height that scared her. It was her own lack of self-control that brought terror. What frightened her was the idea that some foreign, desperate part of her soul would cause her to fling herself over the edge whenever she was faced with a sharp drop. It didn't matter where she was. An escalator. A mountain. A bridge. She had to hold on tight and clench her fists to make sure she didn't panic. It was bad enough to die, but she didn't want to die by falling.

Her breath fluttered in her chest.

She went back into the apartment and shut the door. In the bedroom, she saw her suitcase lying open on the floor, mostly packed. There was no reason to stay in the city any longer. She had the answers she needed, and she would be happy to do what she had done years ago. Escape. Get away. Put as many miles between herself and Duluth as she possibly could.

Tish went into the bedroom and sat cross-legged on the floor in front of her suitcase. Her clothes were neatly folded. She reached across the main compartment to the zipped pouch at the back and tugged it open. The envelope was inside, faded and wrinkled with time. She pulled it out and let it sit in her hands. She had caressed it so many times that the paper was shiny. The ink on the envelope was thin and black.

The handwriting was Cindy's.

Tish read the words again: *For Jonny.*

She had held on to the letter ever since Cindy died. It wasn't right to leave town without giving it to him. On the other hand, she wondered if it was fair to stir up his life any more than she already had, to reawaken the past when he had managed to lay it to rest. Let him go on with Serena and not think about Cindy anymore.

Lie or tell the truth.

There was no need to protect William Starr. He had never earned an ounce of her compassion. She didn't need to protect herself, either. Not anymore. It was time to let go of the shame she had felt when Cindy told her the truth.

Tish slipped her hand inside the suitcase pouch again and extracted the plastic zip-top bag in which she kept the clipping. She removed it delicately, careful not to rip the yellowed newspaper. It was a fragment from another era. A lifetime ago. She unfolded the creases and held it at its edge with the tips of her fingers.

The headline screamed at her. Tore at her heart.

She read it for the thousandth time and then carefully refolded it and slid it back inside the plastic bag. As if, by putting it away, it didn't exist. She got angry all over again to think of William Starr hiding this clipping in the pages of his Bible. Until Cindy found it.

The phone rang in the other room. Tish secured the envelope inside her suitcase and went to answer it.

'This is Tish,' she said.

'This is Peter Stanhope.'

She thought about hanging up, but she didn't. 'What do you want?'

'First, I want to apologize.'

'Oh?'

'I know you had ulterior motives during our rendezvous the other night, but I shouldn't have done what I did. It was wrong. I'm sorry.'

'If you expect me to apologize too, you can forget it.'

'I understand. I'm not asking for anything in return.' He added, 'I saw the press conference tonight. The authorities are essentially walking away from the case. I was wondering what that means for your book.'

'What I write in my book, and what the police and prosecutors do, are two different things,' Tish told him.

'So what are you going to write?' Peter asked.

'You'll have to read it and find out.'

'You don't still think I'm guilty, do you? I heard that Finn admitted to you that he killed Laura. I also heard about his mother and her murder. It's a tragic story.'

'Yes, it is.'

'I'm sure you're disappointed that no one is going to answer for Laura's death,' he said. 'All I can tell you, as a lawyer, is that getting to a courtroom doesn't mean that you'll find justice. Don't judge yourself a failure because you couldn't convince prosecutors to file charges in a thirty-year-old murder.'

'I know that. I feel sorry for Finn, but not for you, Peter. At least Finn had an excuse. He grew up in an abusive family. You were a stalker and an attempted rapist, and your only excuse was arrogance and money.'

'As to being rich and arrogant, I plead guilty.' He laughed.

Tish hated the fact that he was so smooth. So unflappable. Even now, with the truth coming from Finn's mouth, she was reluctant to give up the idea that Peter had been the one to swing the bat.

'Tell me something, did you know Finn was in the woods that night?' Tish asked. 'Did you see him there?'

'No.'

'What about his family background?'

Peter responded with an exaggerated sigh. 'What is this about?'

'It just occurred to me that Finn makes a very convenient fall guy,' Tish told him. 'Particularly if you knew about his mother's murder.'

'I didn't.'

'So why were you so quick to hire a detective to look into his past?'

'That's how lawyers win cases,' Peter said. 'We dig up secrets.'

'I just wonder if you already knew what Serena would find.'

'I didn't. Don't go looking for conspiracy theories, Tish. I had no idea Finn was in the park, and I didn't know a thing about his past.'

Tish said nothing.

'You may hate me, but wishing I was guilty doesn't make it true,' Peter added.

'Ray Wallace thought you were guilty. So did your father.'

'They didn't know about Finn.'

'If you were innocent, why did you let the police hide and destroy evidence for you?'

'Because plenty of innocent men have gone to jail,' Peter snapped. 'I'm getting tired of this, Tish. People like you assume that being rich makes you guilty.'

He sounded defensive. Nervous. As if she had struck a chord.

'Pat Burns may be done with you, but I'm not,' Tish said. 'I was planning to leave town, Peter, but now I'm not so sure. Maybe Finn only thinks he killed Laura, because he saw who did. Maybe he saw you.'

Maggie was almost asleep when she heard what sounded like the angry chatter of an insect somewhere in her bedroom. Her eyes sprang open. Disoriented, she fumbled for the lamp on her nightstand and blinked at the bright light. The buzzing sounded like a June bug, one of those brown summer beetles that flies blindly into screen doors and then drops like a rock and beats its wings in agitation. She realized, however, that the muffled noise was too melodic. When it continued into a third chorus, she remembered that she had switched her cell phone to vibrate mode during the press conference and then left her phone in the pocket of her black slacks draped over a chair.

The phone was ringing.

She glanced at the clock and saw that it was midnight. She climbed out of bed and retrieved the phone. The bedroom curtains billowed like sails in the lake breeze.

'Maggie Bei.'

'Ms Bei, I'm sorry to be calling you so late. This is Donna Biggs.'

Maggie wandered to the window with the phone in her hand. Outside, the night clouds were black. She smelled a storm. 'What can I do for you, Donna? Is something wrong?'

She heard hesitation in the woman's voice. 'I don't know. I think so.'

'What is it?'

'Clark and I were together at a bar in Gary this evening. We saw the press conference that Ms Burns held.'

'I'm sorry about that,' Maggie said. 'I tried to reach both of you to tell you what you were going to hear, but I couldn't connect with you in time.'

'I understand.'

'I hope you realize that I'm still chasing the peeping incidents aggressively. I'm not giving up on this case. I only wish I could be more encouraging about charges related to Mary's death.'

'It's not your fault,' Donna replied. 'I'm just afraid that Clark is very upset. I could see it in his eyes tonight. He's devastated.'

'I know this has been terrible for both of you,' Maggie said.

'Clark disappeared from the bar, Ms Bei. He left, and he didn't tell me where he was going. He was drinking heavily. I went to his house to find him, and I've been here for several hours now. I was hoping he'd come home, but he hasn't. I've tried his cell phone, but he must have it turned off.'

'Did he say anything to you?' Maggie asked.

'Nothing. I went to the restroom, and when I came back, he was gone.'

274

'Have you called 911?'

'No, I wanted to talk to you first. I'm not sure what I should do.'

'I'll put out an alert for Clark and his truck,' Maggie told her. 'Don't worry, we'll find him.'

'I'm afraid of what he might do,' Donna added.

Maggie thought about Clark's face when she had come upon him in the woods where Mary died. 'Does Clark own a gun?' she asked softly.

'He owns hunting rifles, but they're all still here at the house. I checked. He doesn't own a handgun.'

'That's good news,' Maggie told her. She waited a beat and then added, 'I know that Clark has been depressed, but has he talked at all about harming himself? Are you afraid he might commit suicide?'

'No, that's not it,' Donna said. 'I'm not worried about Clark killing himself. I'm worried that he might kill someone else.'

'Someone else? Like who?'

'They talked about that man on the news tonight. The one you've been investigating. Clark knows his name now. He knows where he lives.'

'You mean Finn Mathisen?'

'Yes. I think Clark might try to do what you can't. Get justice for Mary.'

Maggie swore under her breath. 'I'll be there in half an hour.'

'Ms Bei, you have to find him. You can't let Clark do this.'

'I understand.'

'No, you don't. I don't care about this other man. He deserves whatever happens to him. But I don't want Clark throwing away his life. He can't. Not now.'

Maggie heard the pleading in Donna's voice. 'What are you saying?'

'Clark doesn't know,' Donna told her. 'He doesn't know I'm pregnant.'

Thirty-five

Midnight in the rural neighborhoods of Superior was quiet. The media trucks that had surrounded Finn's house for the ten o'clock news were gone. The house was dark and silent. Even so, Clark knew that Finn was hiding there, sitting in some room with the lights off. The silver Rav sat like a ghost truck in the driveway. He hoped that the man who had killed his daughter couldn't sleep.

He thought about breaking in. Kick down the door or smash a window. He told himself that all he wanted to do was confront Finn and look for the guilt in his face, and tell him that he had robbed two lives when he set his sights on Mary. But that was a lie. Clark had darker things in his heart.

He squirmed in his seat because he needed to piss. He opened the door of his pick-up and climbed down to the dirt. Overhead, there were no stars, only angry clouds growing blacker and more threatening as he stared at them. Wind drummed on his back. He stood between the steel rails of the tracks and unzipped and drained a clear stream of urine into the crushed rock. When he was done, he went back to the truck and reached across the seat to grab the baseball bat he had stolen. It was heavy and satisfying in his hand, like an instrument of justice.

Before he could close the truck door, he heard a voice over the howl of the wind, whispering in his ear.

'No, Daddy.'

Clark spun around. 'Mary?'

He looked for her spirit in the darkness, but he was alone. His mind was playing games with him. Even so, the memory of his daughter's voice, which was as clear and familiar as if she had been standing next to him, softened the fury in his heart. Clark stood for a long moment, hesitating. The storm was close and violent. The brittle air felt as if it would snap.

He wondered if Mary had come back to stop him. To tell him that what he was doing was wrong.

He threw the bat back into the truck, where it banged against the far door. He pulled himself up into the driver's seat and held tightly to the steering wheel. The gales rattled the pick-up. He took out his wallet and removed the photograph he kept of himself and Mary on the beach. The picture had been taken two summers ago. After staring at it silently and remembering the perfect Sunday afternoon they had spent together, he craned his neck back until his skull bumped against the headrest. His mouth hung open, gulping air. The tears he had been waiting for finally came. They were a silent army, marching out of his eyes, streaking his stubbled chin. He didn't move or react, or feel his shoulders clench with sobs. It was just his grief letting go in a calm rain.

When it was over, Clark straightened up and wiped his face. He couldn't do what he had been planning. He couldn't kill in cold blood. He reached for the key, wanting to be away from this terrible place. He hoped that Donna was waiting for him at home. Maybe she was right. Maybe something could be salvaged between them. There had been an old yearning in her eyes at the bar, like an ember in a fire that could be coaxed back to life with a warm breath.

Before he could start the engine of his truck, however, he saw a ripple of movement on the front porch of the house across the tracks.

The door opened like the lips of a black monster, and someone tall and skinny sneaked out into the night. It was Finn, nearly invisible in dark clothes. He took each step awkwardly, like a sick man. He stopped at the bottom step, and his head swiveled, surveying the neighborhood. Clark held his breath as Finn's eyes lingered on his pick-up, but the darkness protected him. When Finn thought he was alone, he crept beside the towering lilacs in the front yard and made his way stealthily to his Rav.

Clark knew exactly what Finn was doing. It was the watching hour.

It didn't matter that a sweet girl had died. It didn't matter that his face had been exposed to the city as a suspect. He was off to find another window, another girl.

That was something Clark couldn't allow.

He shoved the photo of Mary into his front pocket. He apologized to Donna in his mind. He waited until Finn's Rav pulled out of the gravel driveway, then started his own truck and left the lights off. He hung back several blocks, but the tail lights of Finn's vehicle were easy to follow. Finn led him on a criss-cross path through the neighborhood, past unlit houses and oak trees slumping like giants over the road. On Stinson Avenue, Finn turned diagonally toward the northeast, heading into wasteland behind the municipal airport. The road cut through corn fields and past the stinking smokestacks of the oil refinery. Clark felt the bump of railroad tracks under his tires.

After several miles, the road led into the East End neighborhood, not far from the main highway and the harbor basin. Clusters of houses built on open lots dotted both sides of the road. The blocks here were laid out in neat squares. Clark noticed the red lights on the Rav grow larger as Finn slowed down, and he braked, not wanting to get too close. Finn turned, and the lights disappeared. Clark cruised past the intersection and eyed the street on his right. He did a U-turn and swung into the street, driving slowly and peering at the road ahead. There were more trees here, like parkland. He saw a playground and an old fence surrounding twin tennis courts.

Two blocks ahead, he spotted brake lights. Clark slowed to a crawl. When he arrived at the intersection, he saw that the Rav had vanished. He drove several more blocks and then retraced his steps and turned onto the side street where he had last noticed the brake lights. There were a handful of cars parked on the street and in driveways, but no Rav. No Finn. He had been gathered up by the night.

'Where are you?' Clark murmured.

He followed the checkerboard of streets like a rat through a maze. Once, he noticed a Rav parked adjacent to a detached garage, but when he got closer, he realized the color was wrong. Sand, not silver. He kept driving, wondering how Finn had managed to lose him and whether the detour through the East End had been a ruse to throw off anyone who might be behind him. Clark worried that Finn had

278

escaped to the highway and turned north or south, heading for a completely different destination.

But no.

There he was.

Clark eased around the next corner and saw Finn's silver Rav shunted off the shoulder of the road under the umbrella shade of an elm tree. The lot was vacant and overgrown. Clark stopped, put the pick-up truck in reverse, and backed around the corner. He turned off his engine and got out, leaving the baseball bat inside the truck. To the northwest, the sky lit up for an instant and then went dark. Lightning. Clark counted until the bass drum of thunder reached his ears, but he didn't have to wait long. The storm was drawing near.

He used the closest house as cover, ducking in and out of the trees. When he was opposite the Rav, he crossed the open lot and approached the passenger side. The truck was empty. Finn was gone. Clark examined the neighborhood in every direction. He didn't see Finn and didn't hear anything other than the whoosh of quaking elm leaves and another, louder peal of thunder.

Clark pulled on the passenger door of the Rav. It was open. The overhead dome light stayed dark. He smelled the man inside the car; there was an odor of sweat and a stale aroma of fried food. He looked for street maps, photos, or notes, but the garbage on the floor mats of the truck didn't help him. The glove compartment was locked, and Clark dug in his pants and yanked out a pocket knife and forced it open. He found the sports section of the local newspaper inside, folded to reveal a photo of three girls on the Superior High School swim team. One girl's face was circled in blue marker. A pretty blonde. He remembered what Maggie had told him, that this man didn't simply happen on his victims by accident. He identified them. Studied them. Stalked them. He had a destination in mind, a specific house, a specific girl.

Clark read the caption with the girl's name. Angela Tjornhom. But where did she live?

He closed the door and studied the nearby homes. He looked for squares of light, but the neighborhood was dark. He shifted away from the Rav, off the street and back into the shelter of the houses. For a big man, he moved quickly and quietly in the spongy grass. At the

279

corner of each house, he looked for Finn crouching in the earth near a ground-floor window. He used the lightning to illuminate the way.

Rain began a frenzied beating in the trees over his head. Where he came into open space, water slapped his skin and soaked him. In seconds, he was drenched, wiping his eyes so he could see. At the end of the street, he stood under the downpour, debating which way to turn. With each bursting floodlight in the sky, he tried to penetrate the gray sheets of rain protecting each backyard. Finn was nowhere to be found. Clark chose to go right, jogging now. He made his way to the end of the next block without coming upon Finn.

Then, through the blaze of another jagged track of lightning, he saw him. Finn was fifty yards away, standing in the cover of a shaggy evergreen, only steps from the rear corner window of a modest rambler. Clark crept closer, staying out of sight. Once, as if he could feel eyes upon him, Finn spun around. Had the lightning struck then, Clark would have been exposed, but instead, he stood stock still, invisible in the darkness. Finn stared right at him and didn't see him. When he turned away, Clark took cover behind a row of skinny pines and followed a winding route that brought him within ten yards of Finn's back.

The window in the rear of the house was dark. Finn brought a hand to his head, and Clark realized that Finn had a cell phone. He was making a phone call. A few seconds later, the window flashed with light, and Clark understood. Finn was calling the girl. Waking her up.

Clark could see through the vertical blinds on the window. The girl in the photo, no more than sixteen, climbed out of bed and padded in her gray half-shirt and pajama bottoms to a white desk. She picked up the phone. Spoke into it. Hung up. She headed back to bed, but before she could turn off the light, Finn called again, and Clark saw the girl answer, her face cross with annoyance.

She hung up again, but she was awake now. She approached the window to stare at the storm and the rain pelting down. Finn was enraptured, staring at the girl framed in the bright square, with her flimsy shirt and her flat expanse of midriff. She was awkwardly beautiful, stroking her messy hair, biting a fingernail. Unaware that she was vulnerable and on display. Clark took advantage of Finn's obsession to come up behind him. All he wanted was for the girl to turn away.

For almost a full minute, all three actors in the play were motionless. The girl, inside, staring with huge blue eyes at the rain and the night. Finn, watching from beside the evergreen. Clark, so close he thought Finn might smell his breath.

Then the blonde girl wheeled around abruptly, and a moment later the window went black again.

Before Finn could move, Clark was on him. His huge forearm encircled Finn's neck with the crushing grip of a snake, and he lifted the man bodily off the ground. Finn couldn't breathe. He struggled, kicking his legs spastically, landing harmless blows on Clark with his fists. Clark thought about choking him, feeling the life drain out of his body, but instead he dropped Finn and backhanded his skull with a swift blow of his fist. Finn collapsed onto the wet ground, unconscious.

Clark slipped off his belt and tied Finn's ankles, then grabbed the man's shoulders and pulled him up in a fireman's carry over his shoulder. He didn't notice Finn's weight. Through the swirl of the storm, he hauled Finn toward his pick-up.

Thirty-six

'Donna's right,' Maggie said unhappily. 'Clark must be going after Finn Mathisen.'

Stride took his eyes off the road. 'Do you think Clark would throw his life away over a nothing like Finn?'

'To get vengeance for his daughter? Yeah, I do.'

'Add Finn's silver Rav to the ATL on both sides of the border. Let's hope Rikke can tell us where Finn went.'

'That would mean admitting he's guilty.'

'To save his life,' Stride said.

Maggie punched the buttons on her cell phone while Stride drove.

As they sped through the driving rain, the St Louis River twisted like a dragon on their right. Walls of water sprayed from under his tires as Stride shot through deep, fast-moving streams that poured off the hills and flooded across the highway. He skidded onto the railway bridge that crossed from Minnesota into Wisconsin over the marshy river lands. Wind howled through the canyon and an ore train thundered the opposite way on the trestle above him. He hung on to the wheel. The entire superstructure of the bridge shuddered as if it would come apart in pieces.

Stride braked at the sharp curve on the far side of the bridge and then flew past the block-long town of Oliver onto the lonely highway leading into Superior. Through the sheeting water on his windshield, he saw miles of birch trees growing parallel to the two-lane road. Cattails swayed in the ditch like spinning toys. He drove through a long stretch of nothingness before arriving at the southernmost end of the city. It was one in the morning. Superior was dead. Silver rain blew diagonally through the glow of street lights.

He followed the chain of streets until he was at the end of the developed land near Finn Mathisen's house, which was ablaze with light. A squad car from the Superior Police was parked out front.

Stride pulled up behind the police car, and he and Maggie both got out. A blonde policewoman with matted wet hair jogged from the porch to meet them. The three of them shook hands while the rain pricked at them like needles.

'Lynn Ristau, Superior Police,' the woman said. She wasn't tall but had a tough, strong physique that would make larger men think twice before messing with her.

'I'm Lieutenant Stride. This is Senior Sergeant Maggie Bei.'

'You guys from Duluth know how to pick the right weather for losing suspects,' Ristau said with a smile.

'Any hits on the ATL?' Stride asked.

Ristau shook her head. Water sprayed from her blonde hair. 'Nobody's spotted your guy.'

'Did you talk to the woman inside?'

'Yeah, but she's not saying much. She says she didn't know that her brother had left the house until I knocked on her door. She has no idea where he went.'

'All right, we'll see if we can pry anything else out of her,' Stride said. 'Can you hang out and keep us posted? We may need some help.'

'You bet.'

Stride and Maggie climbed the front porch and passed through a curtain of water streaming from the roof. Rikke yanked open the door before they could ring the bell. She wore a yellow cotton robe that draped to her ankles, and her face was pinched into a frown.

'What the hell is going on?' she demanded.

'May we come in?' Stride asked.

Silently, the tall, husky woman stood aside. Stride and Maggie shook off as much as water as they could and entered the house, where they dripped on the throw rug. The walls shook as gusts of wind assaulted the frame from the west. Rikke closed the door behind them and folded her arms.

'Well?' she asked.

283

Stride studied the empty living room. Rikke had been sitting on the sofa with a cup of coffee in a china mug. 'Where is Finn?'

'I have no idea. You didn't answer my question. What is going on?'

'We think someone may be hunting for Finn.'

'Who?'

'It's the man whose daughter died in the river.'

Rikke paled and turned away. 'That's ridiculous.'

'We know Finn was at the river that day,' Maggie told her. 'He was stalking that girl. She drowned because of him.'

'If you could prove that, Finn would be in prison right now,' Rikke snapped. She turned back and jabbed a finger in Stride's face. 'This is your fault. You won't quit until my brother is dead.'

'We're trying to protect him,' Stride replied.

'It's a little late after everything you've done. Plaster his face all over the television. Reporters banging on our door all night. It's no wonder some animal decided to come after him. You couldn't arrest him, so you hung him out in the media and let someone else do your dirty work.'

'I'm sorry about the reporters,' Stride said. 'They have their sources, and it's hard to stop them. None of this changes the fact that we need to find Finn before Clark Biggs does.'

'I can't help you.'

'Can't or won't?' Maggie asked.

'I can't tell you what I don't know. I have no idea where Finn went. I told the officer outside that I didn't even know he had left the house. I was sleeping.'

'Do you know what time he left?'

Rikke shrugged. 'It must have been after midnight. Finn was down-stairs when I went to bed.'

'So he's been gone for less than an hour,' Stride said. 'How is Finn's physical condition?'

'Weak. He shouldn't be out.'

'Did he say anything to you about leaving the house?'

'No. He's not strong enough to go anywhere.'

Stride leaned closer to Rikke's face. 'There's only one thing Finn would be doing after midnight. We both know what that is.'

He saw it in her eyes. She knew.

284

'I have no idea what you're talking about,' Rikke protested, looking down at the floor.

'I know you want to protect him, but right now, all you're doing is putting him in harm's way by lying. Let's not play games, Rikke. Finn is sick. He went out to stalk a teenage girl, and if we're right, Clark Biggs followed him. This is a man who believes that Finn is responsible for his daughter's death. If he finds Finn standing outside another girl's window, what the hell do you think he's going to do?'

Rikke swelled her chest with a deep breath. Her jaw hardened like concrete, and Stride saw her hands curl into fists. She marched over to the sofa and sat near the cold fireplace. Water dripped down the chimney onto the grate. She took her cup of coffee in her hand, but she didn't drink from it.

'We know what happened to your mother,' Maggie told her. 'I talked to the police in North Dakota. Finn needs help.'

Rikke rolled her eyes, as if she were a teacher again and one of her students had made a stupid mistake. 'Help? You think I haven't tried to get him help? He's been in and out of therapy for years.' She added, 'I protected him all these years, because I felt responsible.'

'Finn's an adult,' Stride said.

Rikke shook her head. 'You didn't grow up in our house. You don't know what we went through.'

'The police told me there were rumors that Finn was abused,' Maggie said.

'Rumors? Yes, that's all they were. Rumors. Let's keep it hush-hush so our nice little farm town doesn't have to face something ugly.' Rikke's voice was bitter. 'Our neighbors, our teachers, our pastor, they all knew. They pretended everything was fine. Inger baked cookies and pies. She had it so hard after her husband died, the poor soul. Who cares about her kids? Who cares if she's really a wad of phlegm that the devil spat up from hell?'

'You got out of that house,' Maggie said.

'Yes, but I left Finn behind.'

'You couldn't have brought him with you,' Stride told her. 'Not at your age.'

'No? Then how stupid I am to beat myself up over it for thirty-five years. I knew what was going to happen to Finn after I left. Inger started with me. I was her little piece of cherry pie. It wasn't so bad during the day, but Finn and I hated the nights. The farm felt like we were on the moon. Just the three of us in that twisted triangle. She used to make Finn watch, you know. Pretty picture, isn't it? She made Finn watch as she went down on me. Made him watch as she held my head to make me go down on her. He's still watching. He can't stop.'

'Where is he?' Stride asked her.

'I told you, I have no idea.'

'We've sent cops to the homes of all the girls who were involved in the peeping incidents,' Stride said. 'There's no sign of Finn or Clark at any of them. So he probably found someone new. A girl we don't know about yet.'

'We know you sanitized his room before we searched it,' Maggie added. 'We need to know if you found anything.'

Rikke put the cup down and folded her hands as if she were praying. 'If you find him, you'll put him in jail.'

'If we don't find him tonight, he may be dead,' Stride said.

'There were pictures,' Rikke murmured. 'Lots of them. Teenage girls. Some naked, some not. Taken through bedroom windows.'

'Did you destroy the photos?'

She nodded.

'Did you recognize any of the girls?' Maggie asked.

'Yes, I had seen some of them on the news,' Rikke admitted. 'Including the retarded girl. The one who died.'

'Was there anyone recent? Someone he might have found since Mary?'

'Yes, he had new pictures. They were still on his camera. Another blonde. She looked young, maybe fifteen or sixteen. She looked a little like Laura did back then.'

'Do you know who this girl is?' Stride asked.

'I don't.'

'Do you have any idea how he found her?'

'No.' Rikke thought about it and said, 'She probably goes to Superior High School. In one of the photos, she was wearing a Spartans T-shirt.'

Stride turned to Maggie. 'Talk to Ristau outside. See if we can track down a current yearbook from Superior High ASAP. Rikke might recognize this girl in the class photos.'

Maggie was already halfway to the door. 'I'm on it.'

Thirty-seven

Less than an hour later, Stride and Maggie sat in the East End living room of a frightened teenager named Angela Tjornhom. Her parents sat on either side of her. Angela wore a gray Spartans T-shirt and pajama bottoms, with bare feet. Her hands were folded tightly in her lap. She was as waif-like as a model, with a pretty face and tiny frame. Stride could see that Rikke was right. If he looked for it in her face, he could see that Angela bore a faint resemblance to Laura.

'So this guy had *pictures* of me?' Angela asked.

'I'm sorry, but yes, we think so,' Maggie told her.

'That is so creepy. I mean, like, nude pictures even?'

'We don't know.'

'I am never opening my blinds again, you know? I can't believe this.' She nestled her head against her mother's shoulder.

'Where the hell is this bastard?' Angela's father demanded. He was small, with a thin ring of black hair around his bald head. His cheeks flushed red with rage. 'Is this the pervert who was on the news?'

'We're trying to locate him right now,' Stride said. 'We'd like your permission to search your backyard.'

'Do it,' he told them. 'Do whatever you have to.'

Stride nodded. 'Angela, can you tell us if anything happened tonight?'

The girl had been crying. She tugged at her shirt and wiped her nose with the back of her hand. 'I got a couple hang-up calls on my cell phone.'

'When was this?'

'I don't know. Sometime after midnight.'

'What did you do?'

'I turned on the light. The calls woke me up. I looked out the window, but I didn't see anybody. It's not like I could really see anything with all the rain, though.'

'Has this happened before?' Maggie asked.

Angela nodded. 'Yeah, two or three times. Always at night. I just figured it was somebody with a wrong number, you know? I knew one of the other girls at school who got peeped, but I never thought about it happening to me.'

'Someone will come by tomorrow to take a full statement from you,' Stride said.

Maggie put a hand on the girl's knee. 'You should talk to someone, Angela. Girls who experience something like this often react the way rape victims do. It's invasive, and it's scary. You shouldn't deal with it alone.'

Angela shrugged and hid a little deeper inside her mother's arms.

'We'll get her help,' her father said.

Stride and Maggie left the family and returned to the pounding rain outside the house. Both of them switched on flashlights and swept the beams like searchlights ahead of them as they made their way to the backyard. The grass was sodden under their feet. Streams poured out of the swollen gutters. Behind the house, the lot was large and flat and dotted with evergreens. Stride could see the next street more than a hundred feet away. As he shone his flashlight through the grass, pools of standing water glistened back at him.

The room on the corner was Angela's bedroom. The light was on, and the blinds were shut. Stride examined the grass underneath her window.

'Nothing,' he said.

'Maybe the rain washed away his footprints,' Maggie replied.

Stride shook his head. 'He can't have been this close. If he was standing here, she would have seen him.'

He examined the rest of the yard. Lightning turned the night to day for an instant. Stride saw disarray in the wet ground, twenty feet from Angela's window. He used the flashlight to guide his footsteps to a soggy patch of mud and lawn beneath one of the fir trees, where tree roots bulged from the wet soil. In the cone of light, he saw a mess of footprints and crushed grass.

Maggie bent down and studied the overlapping tread marks. 'Two different sets,' she said. 'Looks like a fight.'

Stride spotted a single line of tracks leading away from the scene toward the street. He followed them with his flashlight. Where they passed through a bare patch of dirt, the prints in the mud were deep and clear.

'He was carrying someone,' Stride said, pointing to where the heel marks sank like weights into the soft earth.

'I think we're running out of time, boss,' Maggie said.

They followed the footprints to the street, where they disappeared. Water overflowed from the sewers and poured along the curb in a river. Stride wiped rain from his eyes. He jogged to the vacant lot on the opposite side of the block to see if the footprints started again, but he couldn't find the trail. Clark and Finn had both vanished.

Stride gestured to Maggie, pointing her to the south, while he followed the street to the north, running down the middle where the flooding was lightest. Twin rivers surged through the gutters. He used intermittent bursts of lightning to see between the houses and down the long stretches of asphalt. Each subsequent drumbeat of thunder was closer and longer. The storm was getting worse, not better, and the atmosphere felt violent around him, as if the pressure in the air were building toward an explosion. Wet cold worked its way inside his bones. Trees bowed over his head with the rotating winds, and when he stopped in the dead center of an intersection where two wide streets met, he felt small.

Another branch of lightning cut open the sky, looking like a hangman drawn by a child. Right then and there, Stride saw it. Three blocks away, glinting in the white light, was a silver Rav, parked under the sagging branches of an elm tree. He splashed through deep water. His feet sloshed inside his boots. As he got closer, he saw Maggie, sprinting for the Rav from the opposite direction. They arrived at almost the same time and slowed to study the ground around the truck. Both of them shot their flashlight beams inside the Rav, expecting to see Finn's body slumped in back. Instead, the truck was empty.

'Finn never made it back here,' Maggie said.

'Did you spot Clark's truck?'

She shook her head and got down on her knees. 'Hang on, there's something caught under the tire.'

289

Stride saw it too. Maggie reached around beneath the chassis of the Rav and extracted something white from under the rubber of the tire. When she held it up, they saw that it was a wallet-sized photograph, dirty and wet. She illuminated it with the beam of her flashlight.

'It's Clark and Mary Biggs,' she said.

'Do you think he left it there for us?'

Maggie shook her head. 'It probably fell out of his pocket.'

'If Clark grabbed Finn, where would he take him?' Stride asked.

'I don't know. Unless he already killed Finn and dumped the body somewhere else.'

Stride put himself in the shoes of a despondent father, confronting the man who had driven his daughter to her death. 'I think if he was going to kill him, he'd have done it outside Angela's window.'

'I'll get more cars on the street, but we're at a dead end.'

'What about Perch Lake Park?' Stride asked. 'That's where the girl died.'

'That was my first thought, but the parking lot was empty,' Maggie said. 'I've got a car waiting in case he shows up.'

'What about Donna? She might know where Clark would go.'

Maggie nodded. 'I'll call her.'

She reached into her pocket for her phone, then stopped. 'Wait a minute,' she said, shining a light on the picture again. 'Where do you think this photograph was taken?'

Stride leaned closer. 'It's a beach somewhere around here. Probably along the Point. You can see the lake in the background.'

'We're not too far from the Wisconsin Point, are we?'

'It's just a few miles to the south.'

Maggie shoved the photograph in her pocket. 'Clark told me that he used to take Mary out to the Point. It was one of their favorite places.'

'You think that's where he took Finn?'

'It's isolated, it's close by, it reminds him of Mary.'

'That sounds like our best bet,' Stride said.

'How fast can you go?' Maggie asked.

Thirty-eight

Clark dragged Finn's body one-handed through the wet sand by the belt tied around the man's ankles. In his other hand, he dangled the baseball bat over his shoulder. As the uneven ground jolted Finn's body, the bound man woke up and began to struggle, clawing at the mud for traction with his fingers. He spat out grass and dirt from his mouth and screamed. Clark ignored his cries, which were drowned out by the ferocious wailing of the wind and the beating of lake waves against the shore.

The beach was a long, lonely strip of sand and trees. The sky belched out rain and blinded him with a near-continuous chain of lightning flashes. Somewhere, he could smell wood burning, where electricity had blasted through bark and roots. The thunder was so near and loud that he felt the earth tremble under his feet. If he had believed in God, Clark would have believed that God was angry, but he had given up his faith long ago. He had stopped believing on that day when Mary first went into the water and came out a ghost of who she had once been.

There was no God, he realized then. No mercy.

Clark was not prepared to show any mercy tonight.

He dropped Finn in the empty center of the beach, where a fat, bleached tree trunk had washed up after months rolling and floating on the surface of the lake. It was bare and white, pockmarked with insect holes drilled into its wood. He grabbed a fistful of Finn's shirt and propped him with his back against the tree trunk. Blood trickled down Finn's face where brambles and rocks had scraped open his skin, but the rain quickly washed it away. Finn's ankles strained at the belt that secured them, and his muscles twitched with fear.

'Who are you?' Finn asked. He was practically screaming, but his voice was a whisper.

'You killed my daughter,' Clark said.

Finn gazed in horror at Clark, who was as big and broad as a bear. He read the hardness in Clark's face and knew immediately who Clark was and what Clark planned to do. Finn's torso slid off the tree trunk, and he crawled away, dragging his feet behind him, his body flopping like a fish on the bottom of a boat. Clark took two steps and yanked him back by the collar of his shirt. When Finn was upright again, Clark drove the head of the bat like a spear into Finn's stomach, so hard that blood and stomach juices spewed from Finn's mouth. When Finn took a breath, there was nothing in his lungs, and his fingers clutched the sand in panic as he gasped for air. Tears mingled with the rain on his face.

Clark thought he would take more satisfaction in Finn's pain, but he didn't. He was as lifeless as the huge piece of driftwood where Finn sat.

Thirty feet away, sweeping waves broke across a black mirror of surf and slid almost to Clark's boots. Foam flew up in a white curtain that was as tall as he was. When the water receded across the slick sand, he saw glints of quartz. If he looked hard enough, he could see Mary here as a young girl, her feet slapping through the pools and streams. He could watch the summer sun as it kissed her hair. Hear her squeals of delight. Feel the strength of her damp arms as she hugged him.

'No, Daddy,' she whispered to him again. Urgently.

Clark forced her ghost away. There were some things a child didn't understand. There were some things a father had to do. *I'm sorry, baby.*

He clutched the bat with both hands and held it the way a baseball player would, with tight, thick fingers on the grainy wood. Finn's lips formed the word *No,* but nothing came out of his chest. Clark unleashed the bat in a fierce arc and whipped it into the meat of Finn's shoulder. Bones cracked. Muscle tore. Finn's body rose off the sand and landed in a sprawl four feet away. He curled his limbs together like a baby. His eyes were closed. He wailed.

Clark still felt nothing. He was impervious. Dead.

He retrieved Finn and propped him up again. The man's collar-bone jutted out from his neck like a chicken bone snapped in half. Finn's skin was white.

'Stop,' he begged Clark. 'Please stop. I'm so sorry.'

'You don't deserve to live.'

'I know.'

Clark squatted down inches from Finn's face. 'You took away my whole life. Everything I am, everything I've done, it was all for that little girl. When you killed her, I died. Understand? I'm dead right now because of what you did. And what was she to you? Tell me, what right did you have to be a part of her life?'

Mucus dripped out of Finn's nose. His lips trembled. 'I never meant for anything to happen. I'm so sorry she died. I only wanted to talk to her. I never touched her.'

'You stood outside my little girl's window,' Clark said. 'Did you see her naked?'

Finn was silent.

'Answer me.'

'Yes.'

'Did you take pictures of her?'

'Yes.'

'What else?'

Finn shut his mouth again.

'Goddamn it, what else? Did you jerk off? Is that what you did while staring at my little girl?'

'Yes. Oh, Jesus, I'm sorry, yes.'

Clark stood up again with terrible purpose.

'No, no, no,' Finn screamed, but it was too late. Clark swung again, connecting with the soft side of Finn's knee, hearing it pop as the femur and tibia tore apart. Finn held on to his leg as if he could make the pain stop by covering it up. The sounds from his throat were guttural, like an animal's. He writhed on the ground. Clark took a heavy breath and walked away, letting the rain and wind pour over him. He wandered into the surf and let the waves pummel his legs, so fiercely that they almost toppled him. God was definitely angry now. The lightning was a white strobe light, flashing in his face, knifing across half the sky.

Finn shouted. 'Kill me! For God's sake, just *kill me*.'

Clark heard Mary again, as if she were right there, tugging at his arm, pleading for attention. 'No, Daddy, no.'

I'm sorry, baby. No mercy.

Except now the merciful thing would be to end it. There was that time when his truck had sideswiped a huge buck, and he found it in the deep weeds on the shoulder of the highway, twitching, in agony, dying slowly. He couldn't drive away and leave it there. Donna was in the truck, and he made her stay inside and not watch. Then he retrieved a rifle from the tailgate and shot the deer in the brain.

An act of mercy.

Clark marched out of the surf. He came up behind Finn, not in front. Finn felt him there but didn't try to turn around. Clark could see the man's chest heaving in and out. The bald pate of Finn's skull was like a melon balanced on the tree trunk. Clark knew it would take one swing of the bat to end it. To end both their lives. One millisecond of pain and light to put Finn, Mary, and himself out of their shared agony.

'Just do it,' Finn shouted.

Clark wrapped his fingers around the wet grip of the bat. His eyes found a misshapen mole on the back of Finn's head and focused on it. His target. His sweet spot. He wound up and prepared to swing.

Thirty-nine

The Wisconsin Point was a twin sister to the Minnesota Point, separating Lake Superior from Allouez Bay with a needle of land that suffered the pummeling of waves and gales. Only an inlet of open water not even a thousand feet across separated the two splinters of beach. Unlike its Minnesota sibling, where Stride and Serena lived, the Wisconsin Point was largely undeveloped parkland, so narrow in most places that there was no room to sink a foundation. The only road leading out to the Point was a country lane called Moccasin Mike at the southeastern edge of Superior.

Stride shot through the storm on Moccasin Mike at seventy miles an hour. His windshield wipers sluiced aside the hammering rain. The road was arrow-straight, but it was a roller coaster of shallow hills and dips. He didn't see the worst of the water-filled depressions in the road until the truck was airborne and he and Maggie rose out of their seats. His breath expelled as he landed back down in moving water with a sharp jolt in his back. The truck groaned through the flooded valley and threatened to stall and float, but then the tires chewed back onto solid ground and roared up the opposite slope, cascading spray behind them.

At high speed, the truck gobbled up the two-mile stretch of highway, and Stride nearly missed the left turn to the Point. He braked hard and overcorrected, sending the rear of the Expedition into a fishtail, and then he accelerated again onto the broken asphalt. The truck lurched through a moonscape of potholes. Evergreens leaned in from the shoulders of the road, and he sheared off branches as he drove. His high beams stabbed the darkness, but all he could see was silver rain and black forest, until suddenly the truck burst free from the wilderness onto the slim peninsula and the bay opened up on his left. A roar of wind rattled the truck and threatened to spill it onto its side.

He slowed down. The thunder was a tin can banging in their ears.

'I don't like this storm,' Stride said. 'The lightning is right on top of us.'

They rocked along the uneven road for half a mile, and then Stride caught a reflection of metal in his headlights. A 1990s-era pick-up truck was parked in the long grass on the right-hand shoulder by the slope that led to the lakeside beach. Clark's truck.

He stopped the Expedition askew on the Point road. He and Maggie piled out of both sides. Maggie ran to Clark's truck and pressed her face against the window.

'It's empty,' she called. 'They must be on the beach.'

'Call for backup.'

Stride unholstered his Glock. Maggie grabbed her phone and shouted instructions.

A muddy path only a foot wide wound between the long grass and sagging birch trees to the top of the slope. The wet ground sucked at Stride's boots, and he slipped as he climbed, falling to his knees and nearly losing his gun. He had to sink his free hand in the dirt to push himself up. Maggie followed behind him, swearing as her heels got trapped. She kicked them off, leaving herself in bare feet.

They reached the crown of the hill, where the expanse of beach and lake opened up below them. Superior was a living thing, violent and huge, invading the puny finger of sand. Around them, the trees yawed and spun. Lightning popped in their eyes, and the circling beam of the Superior lighthouse flashed through the darkness out on the water.

At first, the beach looked empty.

'Where are they?' Maggie screamed, cupping her hand beside her mouth.

'I don't see them!' The lightning broke again, and Stride pointed. 'Wait, there they are!'

Fifty yards away, looking no larger than dolls, Clark Biggs and Finn Mathisen were on opposite sides of a giant trunk of driftwood.

Finn lay sprawled on the ground, half his torso propped against the tree. Clark stood behind him. When the next flash of lightning illuminated the beach, they realized that Clark held a baseball bat in his hands and was preparing to swing with deadly intent at the back of Finn's head.

'Stop!' Maggie shouted.

She may as well have been mute. Clark couldn't hear a thing.

'Clark! Stop!'

Stride aimed his Glock into the sky and squeezed off a round. To him, with the gun by his ear, the report sounded loud, but he wasn't sure if the shot could be heard over the wind, rain, thunder, and surf. For a few long seconds, the beach was dark, and they were blind. When they could see through the next streak of light, they saw Clark, stopped, the bat poised high above his head, as he stared directly at them on top of the hill. Stride half expected him to swing, but Clark froze, hesitating at the brink.

Finn's face was turned toward them. He was alive.

Stride stumbled down the slope to the flat stretch of wet sand and rye grass. He splashed through pooled water with Maggie on his heels and stopped ten feet from the slab of driftwood. Stride pointed his Glock at the ground, but he held it out from his body where Clark could see it. He studied Finn and saw that the man was badly hurt, his shoulder broken, his left hand pressed frantically on his disjointed knee, his face twisted in agony. He had bitten his lip so hard that it was bleeding.

'Son of a bitch,' Maggie murmured. Then she said loudly, 'Clark! Don't do this! Put the bat down!'

Clark's face was hard as stone. His eyes were black. He shook his head.

'This is your *life*,' Maggie told him. 'Don't destroy it. Mary wouldn't want you to do that.'

'Mary's dead,' Clark said.

'Listen to me, Clark. I know the kind of man you are. You're not a murderer.'

Finn grimaced and pushed himself higher off the ground. He shouted at Clark behind him. 'Be a man and swing the fucking bat!'

Stride watched Clark tighten his grip. The big man's elbows bent as he twisted the bat back behind his shoulders. Stride straightened and stretched out his arms, steadying his Glock with both hands and aiming straight at Clark's head. The wind buffeted him. Rain poured over his face and body.

'Put the bat down, Clark,' Stride said.

'You won't kill me,' Clark said. 'Not to protect a piece of shit like this.'

They played a game of chicken, staring each other down.

'Please, Clark,' Maggie pleaded with him.

Clark's eyes flicked to Maggie. 'You know what this man did to Mary. He deserves to die.'

'That's not up to you or me.'

The storm swooped down off the hills like the invasion of an army. Wind shrieked and drove their bodies backward. Over the furious lake, veins of lightning tore across the entire sky. The world snapped from black to white to black. Stride felt the pressure and temperature dropping. An explosion was coming.

'We have to go right now,' Stride told Clark. 'It's not safe here.'

'So go. Leave me alone.'

'Put down the bat.'

'I can't do that.'

'Clark, Donna called me,' Maggie told him. 'She doesn't want to lose you. She's scared to death.'

Clark hesitated.

'She still loves you,' Maggie said.

'Do it!' Finn screamed.

Clark's eyes burned into the back of Finn's skull, as if he could see the bat landing there. Hear the awful crack. Watch the blood and brain fly. Stride knew what was going through the man's head. Clark wanted to feel something again. Anything.

'This won't give you what you want,' Stride said.

'Look at me, Clark!' Maggie implored him. 'Listen! There's something Donna didn't tell you. She's pregnant. The two of you are having another baby.'

Clark's eyes wrenched away from Finn. 'You're lying to me.'

'I'm not.'

'She can't be pregnant,' Clark said.

'It's true. I swear. This is your second chance, Clark. Don't give it up.'

Stride thought Clark was crying, but in the rain, he couldn't be sure.

'Mary's dead!' Clark shouted. 'Someone should pay!'

'Yes, someone should,' Maggie agreed. 'But not you. Not now.'

Clark took a step backwards. The fight had fled from him. His head sank, and his chin disappeared into his neck. One hand dropped away from the bat and fell to his side. The fingers on his other hand spread open, and the bat tumbled end over end to the sand. Clark backed away and raised his hands in the air in surrender.

'Thank God,' Stride murmured. His own gun hand sagged. Beside him, Maggie holstered her gun and crouched down in front of Finn.

Clark stumbled toward the surf. He was twenty feet away, ankle deep in lake water, his hands still high in the air.

'Make sure there's an ambulance—' Stride began, but he never finished.

The ground under his feet suddenly felt strange, as if every particle of sand clinging to his wet skin were alive.

The hairs on his head and arms defied gravity and stood at attention like soldiers. His flesh tingled. He tasted hot metal in his mouth. Stride knew what was coming. Death was hurtling through the ground.

Lightning.

Billions of ions searching for a bridge to the sky. Like a body.

He shouted a warning at Maggie, threw his gun down, and fell into a crouch, propping himself up on the balls of his feet. He squeezed his eyes shut and clapped his hands over his ears so tightly that the storm was sucked into a vacuum of silence. It didn't last. Less than a second later, a concussion bomb cracked inside his brain, as if tacks were blowing outward into bone and tissue. His feet left the ground as he was jolted backward, lofted like a javelin. He saw a white flash through his closed eyes, felt the cold air melt into heat, and smelled the char of flesh burning.

He wondered if it was his own.

Forty

The tingling in Stride's flesh disappeared as quickly as it had come.

He lay on his back, eyes open, tasting the rain that spilled out of the sky into his mouth. The world was oddly quiet. No wind. No thunder. No slap of waves and surf. He heard himself call Maggie's name, but the sound was muffled, as if it came from someone else at the end of a long tunnel. He heard the roar a child hears in a seashell.

His head throbbed. His limbs felt like jelly. He patted his face, chest, and legs, and felt no tenderness and no burns. The soles of his shoes were intact, without any signs of melting or scorched entry and exit holes from the electricity. His clothes were wet but untorn. When he felt his neck for his pulse, he found that the beating of his heart was fast but even. However close the lightning bolt had been, and whatever path it had taken up to the cloud, it hadn't gone through his body.

He pushed himself up on his elbows, and the beach spun like a carousel. The sound wave had scrambled his sense of balance. He closed his eyes, letting his brain right itself. When he tried to stand, his legs bent like rubber, and he fell down onto all fours in a slurry of sand. The disorientation made him nauseous, and he swallowed down bile at the back of his mouth.

He tried standing again, and the dizziness made him stagger, but he was able to stay on his feet. The air around him smelled burnt. Lightning continued to flicker like a loose bulb over the lake. Each flash made his eyes tighten. Somewhere in his head, he sensed that the rain that had drilled into his body was gentler now. The wind was dying.

300

When he took a step, his knee buckled. He felt a hand on his arm, steadying him.

'Shit, that hurt,' Maggie said. Her voice sounded as if she were underwater.

'Yeah.'

'Are you OK?'

'I think so,' Stride said. 'How about you?'

'I have the mother of all headaches, but I don't think I was hit.'

Twenty feet away, Finn groaned. Stride and Maggie held on to each other as they limped over and dropped to their knees on either side of him. He sat in a pool of water by the slab of driftwood. His fingers clawed over and over into fists, and his head swung rhythmically back and forth. His eyes were closed. Red blood trickled along his jawline from his ears.

'Finn!' Stride shouted.

He grabbed the man's face with both hands, and Finn's eyes sprang open. The whites were shot through with red, and his pupils were black and wide with panic.

'Can you hear me?' Stride yelled, but his own voice was distant.

Finn pummeled Stride with his hands. Stride fought to gain control of the man's wrists and restrain him as he squirmed in confusion and fear. Finn's chest heaved with frantic, open-mouthed breaths. Stride found a pulse and felt no irregularities. His eyes flicked over Finn's body and saw no burns, but the man's eardrums had obviously burst when the thunder exploded over them, and Stride knew the torrent of pain had to be excruciating.

Maggie rose up on her knees beside him. 'Where's Clark?'

Stride studied the beach where he had last seen Clark standing in the water. He was gone. Stride looked in the shadows of rye grass and down the stretch of sand and didn't see him anywhere.

Maggie stood up, swaying. 'Clark!'

Stride let go of Finn, who twisted restlessly and crawled away, dragging himself with one arm. The effort overwhelmed Finn, and he stopped, panting and gulping down rain. Stride got to his feet and circled slowly. He didn't think Clark could have gone far, but it was as if the man had been sucked into a cloud. The beach was empty.

'Where the hell is he?'

Maggie pointed. A violent wave drew back down toward the lake, and as the sheet of water slid off the sand, Stride saw a body prone in the surf, nearly thirty feet from where Clark had been standing. It was almost invisible, just a darker shadow against the black shoreline. The body didn't move as another wave surged in and completely submerged him.

They stumbled over the driftwood and ran. Maggie spilled onto her face as her legs became tangled, and Stride stopped and helped her up. She waved him on as she waited for her head to clear. Stride splashed down to the edge of the lake and found Clark's body, which was ashen white. Each wave buried the big man in almost eight inches of water and foam. Stride dug his hands under Clark's shoulders and dragged him higher onto the beach, away from the reach of the waves.

Maggie arrived at his side. 'Oh, my God.'

Clark's clothes were shredded, as if they had exploded off his body. His chest was laced with a massive spider web of burns. His shoes appeared to be melted onto his feet, and when Stride checked the soles, he saw two circular black holes. Entry and exit wounds from the massive electricity of the lightning. They were still warm when he fingered them. He picked up Clark's wrist, which was limp and cold, and felt no pulse. He checked again at the carotid and still found nothing. When he pushed open Clark's eyelids, the man's eyes stared back, dead and unmoving.

'There's an AED in the back of my truck,' Stride said.

Maggie took off at a sprint. Stride mentally took stock of the time that had passed and concluded that Clark had been lying in the sand, his heart stopped, for at least five minutes. Way too long. Stride tilted Clark's head back and lifted his chin. He pried open Clark's mouth, pinched his nose shut, and covered Clark's cold lips with his own. He exhaled two slow breaths and watched Clark's chest rise and fall as the air filled his lungs.

Stride repositioned himself and placed the heel of his right hand in the middle of Clark's chest and laced the fingers of both hands together. He rose up for more leverage and shoved down hard and fast, counting to thirty in his head. When he was done, he moved back and swelled the man's chest with two more slow breaths and then frantically pumped against his ribcage thirty more times. He repeated the process

302

again, his mind oblivious to anything around him except the time passing. Then again. And again. When he had completed the cycle five times, he pressed two fingers against Clark's neck.

Nothing.

The clock in his head was at nearly eight minutes.

He continued applying CPR and was vaguely conscious of Maggie arriving next to him with the small AED box, which began to chirp instructions as she unpacked it. He alternated between breaths and chest massage as Maggie worked around him to dry Clark's skin with a towel she had brought from the truck and then position the two electrodes of the defibrillator on his chest. She hovered over him, trying to block the rain.

'It's too fucking wet,' she said.

'I know.'

Maggie turned on the machine. 'Clear,' she told him.

Stride stopped and removed his hands from Clark's body. Maggie pushed the analyze button on the defibrillator, which measured Clark's heart activity and responded aloud with a discouraging message. 'No charge.'

There was nothing to shock. No fibrillation.

'Goddamn it,' Stride said. He checked for a pulse and still found nothing. He bent over and continued several more cycles of CPR and then backed away as Maggie stabbed the button one more time.

'No charge.'

Ten minutes had passed.

Stride tried again. And again. And again. Two minutes later, there was still no pulse. No heart activity. Nothing for the defibrillator to regulate. He assaulted Clark's chest with his fists, harder and faster, and then he heard Maggie's soft voice at the end of the wind tunnel.

'Boss.'

He hammered and breathed, hammered and breathed, hammered and breathed. Clark's body endured the punishment without moving. Two more minutes passed.

'Boss.'

He counted to thirty. Counted to two. Counted to thirty. Counted to two.

'Jonathan, it's over.'

Maggie's hand took hold of his shoulder in a grip that was gentle but unyielding. Midway through the final series of chest compressions, Stride finally stopped and sat back on his haunches. His arms dangled at his side. He could hardly lift them now. He had known from the beginning that Clark was dead, that the electricity had savaged his heart, but it was only when he gave up, when there was nothing else to do, that the reality sank in. His head fell forward against his chest.

'Where's the damn ambulance?'

'It wouldn't have made any difference, boss. You did everything you could do.'

He knew that was true, but it didn't bring Clark back to life. He stared at the body and leaned over and closed the man's eyes again. Like that, Clark looked more at peace, free of his despair.

Stride got up slowly. His wet, cold muscles complained. His hearing was coming back, and he heard a distant whine of police sirens growing closer. He could see fireworks out on the lake where the storm had slouched to the east. A few lingering drops of rain splashed on his skin. The air behind the front was steamy and warm, and his clothes clung to his body.

He needed to get away. 'I'm going to check on Finn,' he said.

Maggie nodded.

Down the beach, Stride saw Finn pawing in the sand and pushing aside the long grass with his good arm. He looked like a scuttling crab with one claw stripped from his body. Stride cocked his head, confused, and took a few tentative steps in Finn's direction. 'What is he doing?'

Maggie looked. 'I don't know.'

'Finn!' Stride called, but he couldn't hear him.

Stride walked faster in the deep sand back toward the driftwood. Maggie lingered behind him with Clark's body. Stride felt a formless sense of unease.

'Finn!'

Without hearing him, Finn sensed Stride approaching. Their eyes met across the dark beach, and an unspoken hostility passed between them. With increasing desperation, Finn turned his attention back to the ground surrounding the huge tree trunk. Stride suddenly understood.

304

He became aware of a lightness under his shoulder and when he tapped his chest, he realized that his holster was empty. His Glock wasn't in it. As the ground current streaked toward him, he had ditched his gun in the sand.

Where Finn was now searching.

Stride broke into a run across the remaining distance. Before he could dive past the driftwood, Finn's left arm broke free of the mud with Stride's gun in his palm. He curled his hand round the grip, shoved his finger against the trigger, and pointed it at Stride ten feet away.

Stride stopped. He held up his hands. The sirens he had heard were close now. Police cars streaked down the Point.

'Put the gun down, Finn.'

Finn ignored him and trained the barrel of the Glock at the center of Stride's chest.

Stride felt an old, sharp pain reawaken in his shoulder. It was a wound from years earlier, where a bullet had torn through skin and muscle and driven him to the floor. A bullet from Ray Wallace's gun. When Stride looked at Finn, he saw Ray Wallace's face, the same agony, the same desperation, the same intent. They were both men with nothing to lose.

'Don't do this, Finn.'

When Stride took a tentative step, Finn jerked, waving the gun to stop him. Finn's muscles were spastic. Stride watched his index finger and worried that it would twitch on the trigger and unleash a bullet into his heart. He edged sideways, but Finn's arm followed him.

'Put it down.' Stride motioned toward the ground with his palm.

Finn flipped the barrel up, waving Stride away.

They stared at each other just the way he and Ray had. A stand-off over the barrel of a gun. Stride thought about Ray coming to grips with his disgrace at the hands of his own protégé. Ray, who planted a memory in Stride's brain of bone, hair, blood, and brain oozing in streaks down the white wall. Ray, his best friend.

Ray, who had pulled the trigger.

Stride reminded himself that this was Finn, not Ray. This stand-off could end the right way, but he was running out of time. Maggie called to him, and she was close. Over Finn's shoulder, he spied the reflected glow of red revolving beacons from a squad car's light bar. Police would soon be spilling over the hill. All of them converging on Finn like a pack. Making him panic. Making him shoot.

'Maggie, stay back,' he called and hoped she could hear him.

Finn cringed. Beads of sweat and rain dripped down his skull. His eyes darted back and forth. Stride watched his anxiety shoot up like a needle on a pressure gauge.

'Take it easy,' Stride told him, his voice calm and steady. 'You're OK.'

Behind Finn, Stride saw two silhouettes crossing the peak of the dune and stumbling to the flat sand and tall grass. Police. With his fingers spread and his arms already in the air, Stride held one hand higher than the other, hoping they could read his body language. Stop.

One of the figures saw his gesture and froze, but the other kept coming. The shadow who had stopped shouted a warning. 'Wait!'

Stride recognized the voice of the policewoman from Superior they had met earlier. He also recognized the other woman, who ignored the warning and ran toward Finn, screaming his name.

It was Rikke.

'He can't hear you,' Stride called to her. He added, 'Finn has a gun.'

Rikke stopped in her tracks. She stood behind Finn, twenty feet away. She wore an untucked, mis-buttoned white shirt and navy shorts. Her once-sleek long legs were lumpy like tree trunks.

'*Finn!*' she shouted, but her brother didn't react.

Stride pointed behind Finn, gesturing toward Rikke. When Finn didn't move, Stride took two careful steps backward, giving him space. He pointed and gestured again. Finally, with a painful flick of his head, Finn turned and saw his sister.

'Everybody stay where they are,' Stride called.

Finn swung the barrel of the gun to his left, and Stride understood. Finn wanted him and Rikke both in his line of sight. He debated standing still, but then took slow sideways steps down the beach until Finn could watch the two of them without turning his head.

Rikke's eyes were locked on Finn. When she took a step toward him, Finn immediately raised the Glock and jammed the barrel into the side of his own head. His finger was tight on the trigger.

'Easy,' Stride told her.

'This is between him and me, Lieutenant,' Rikke said. She took another step, and Finn shook his head violently and shoved the barrel harder against his skin.

'He's not kidding,' Stride warned her.

'I know what he needs,' Rikke said.

Her fingers came together, meeting at the first button on her shirt, which she undid. Finn's eyes followed, wide and staring. She separated another button and pulled the flaps of her shirt apart, revealing a V of white skin. Finn inhaled loudly through his nose. His entire body trembled, as if he were wracked with chills. His mouth fell open, and he drew the gun slowly away from his head.

'I'm sorry for what she did to us,' Rikke told Finn. 'I'm sorry for what we became.'

Rikke undid the rest of the buttons, letting the flaps dangle, and then used her fingernails to push the collar back off her shoulders until the shirt slid off her arms and fluttered to the ground. Her stomach bulged over the waist of her shorts. Her left breast drooped like an underfilled water balloon, its nipple flat and pale pink. Her other breast was a wrinkled cross of scars.

She sank to her knees and spread her arms wide, beckoning Finn to her bare skin. She was crying. He was crying. Finn made a mewling noise like a trapped kitten and sloughed his body toward her.

They were almost touching when another wrenching, involuntary spasm shuddered through his body. His finger twitched on the trigger.

The gun was still pointed at the meat of his skull.

Finn's expression turned to glass as the bullet tunneled through his brain. Fire and noise cracked open the beach. Rikke wailed, and Stride saw one last flashback of Ray Wallace's face before he was jolted back to the present, where Finn slumped forward, lifeless and free.

PART FIVE

FEAR OF HEIGHTS

Forty-one

Serena stood apart from the cluster of mourners while they prepared to bury Finn Mathisen in the Riverside Cemetery. She tugged her trench coat tighter. Her black hair swished around her face. They were beyond the southern edge of Superior, out past the railroad tracks and landfill, in sloping fields dotted with pines whose branches reached for the gray sky like praying angels. Water gurgled over stones in a creek beside the path. The lawn was lush and neatly trimmed.

She stood fifty feet away from the ceremony, beside one of the larger marble headstones on the wooded slope. Finn didn't have a large crowd. Rikke was there, ramrod straight, her face a severe mask. Everyone kept their distance from her. Serena didn't recognize the dozen or so strangers, but she saw Jonny, Maggie, and Tish standing in a trio. She knew she should be at Jonny's side, but she had never met Finn or Rikke and didn't want to intrude on anyone's grief. The truth was that it gave her a convenient excuse to be far away. She liked cemeteries but hated funerals. She didn't mind death but hated dying. If something had to end, she simply wanted it to be over.

Serena heard footsteps behind her and was surprised to see Peter Stanhope. The lawyer's mane of silver hair barely moved in the wind. His lip showed a reddened scar.

'I didn't expect to see you here,' Serena told him.

Peter stood beside her and made no effort to get any closer to the funeral. 'I suppose I feel responsible.'

'Why?'

'Because I sent you off to expose Finn's secrets, and now he's dead.'

311

'Don't blame yourself,' Serena told him. 'Finn's probably better off this way.'

'That's true.'

Serena turned and met his eyes with her own. 'That doesn't mean you walk away with a clean conscience, Peter. There's still Laura and what you did to her.'

'You mean the stalking? I already told you that I was a crass, stupid kid.'

'Don't make it sound like you were a boy stealing gum from a drugstore. You tried to rape that girl.'

Peter rubbed the scar on his lip. 'So that's it? You've decided I'm a monster?'

'I don't know what you are.'

'And that means you can't work with me?' he asked. 'You're turning down the job because of a mistake I made as a teenager?'

Serena looked up at the profiles of the trees, which were like spiny bottlebrushes. She heard the murmur of solemn voices near the grave. 'I'm sorry. It doesn't matter if it was yesterday or nineteen seventy-seven. The answer is no. Keep your job, Peter. I don't want it.'

'You're walking away from a lot of money.'

'It's not about the money,' Serena said.

'I thought you were different. I expected better from you.'

Serena shrugged. 'Well, don't let me spoil your moment.'

'What do you mean?'

'This is your independence day,' Serena said. 'With Finn dead, Laura's case dies with him.'

Peter nodded. 'OK, yes, it worked out fine for me, but I'm not getting a free ride. I didn't kill anyone.'

'No?' Her voice betrayed her suspicion.

'You sound as paranoid as Tish,' Peter said.

'Your own father didn't believe you,' Serena told him.

Peter's eyes turned black. 'He was never my biggest fan. I told Randall I didn't kill her, but he knew what had happened between me and Laura in the softball field. I suppose he figured I was a liar. Or maybe it was all about protecting the Stanhope name. Anyway, it doesn't matter. The easiest thing for Stride and Pat Burns and everyone else in Duluth is to believe that Finn swung that bat. Just like it was the easy thing back in nineteen seventy-seven to assume that Dada killed her. We believe whatever makes us feel safe.'

'Aren't you afraid of what Tish will say in her book?' Serena asked.

Peter studied Tish, who stood next to Stride among the people near the wooden coffin. It was as if she could feel eyes on her back, because she turned and saw Serena and Peter standing together up the hill. Her lips folded into a frown.

'Tish can write what she wants,' Peter said. 'I don't care. Sometimes the easy explanation is the right one, Serena. Finn was in love with Laura, and Laura didn't want him. So he decided that no one else was going to have her either.'

'Except some people might think you felt the same way,' Serena said.

'Maybe I did, but Laura's big mistake wasn't saying no to me.'

'Then what was it?'

'It was letting Rikke get her tangled up with Finn. That was like buying a ticket to a house of horrors.'

He nodded his head toward Finn's sister, who stood with her hand resting on the coffin, but with her face turned toward Tish. Serena could see fury in the woman's taut skin. Her eyes never left Tish, and Tish stared at the ground rather than look at her.

'Rikke knows what Finn did,' Peter said.

Serena pursed her lips and thought about the macabre striptease that Stride had described on the beach between Finn and his sister.

'Finn and Rikke were a strange family,' she agreed.

'You're right, but don't forget one thing,' Peter told her.

'What's that?'

'Back in nineteen seventy-seven, Laura was in the middle of that family.'

Forty-two

Stride and Serena led a parade of cars away from the cemetery. They headed north on Tower Avenue and turned into the parking lot of a bookstore and café where they often stopped for soup and coffee when they were on the east side of the twin ports. Maggie followed them into the lot, and so did Tish. The four of them went inside together, where nutmeg and blueberries wafted in the air. Amanda, who ran the store, waved at them and broke off from the stacks of books long enough to get a hug from Stride.

They took chairs in the café at a table by the window. Stride leaned his head against the wall. The sky through the glass was gray and burgundy, as dusk sped quickly into night.

'What can I get everyone?' Maggie asked.

Stride shrugged. 'Coffee.'

'You, boss? Plain old coffee? I figured you for a moka-loco apple fritter latte.'

Stride gave her a withering stare.

'How about you, Serena?' Maggie asked. 'You want to join me in a chai tea?'

'I'd love one, but you may as well take a hypo and shoot it into my thighs. Get me a bottled water.'

Maggie rolled her eyes. 'Tish?'

'Nothing, thanks. I have to head to the airport soon.'.

Maggie sighed and went to the café register. She placed their order and wandered over to the books counter to chat with Amanda.

'How's the book coming?' Serena asked Tish.

314

'It's almost done.' Tish tugged nervously at the sleeves of her burgundy blouse. Her blonde hair was pulled back away from her face and pinned behind her head.

'Do you leave tonight?'

Tish nodded. 'My suitcase is in the car.' She added, 'I suppose you'll both be happy to see me go.'

Stride and Serena didn't say anything.

'When I came here, I didn't really think about what would happen,' Tish went on. 'I was naïve. I should have listened to you.'

She waited, but the silence stretched out.

'I know you feel bad about Clark Biggs,' Tish told Stride. 'And Finn, too.'

'I don't think you know how I feel at all,' Stride replied.

He saw the café manager put their drinks on the counter. He picked up his mug of coffee and Serena's bottle of water and sat down again. When he took a sip, the coffee was smoky and hot. Over Tish's shoulder, he spotted movement in the foyer and was surprised to see Rikke Mathisen enter the store from the parking lot. Her upper lip was sucked between her teeth. She saw them in the corner, and her stare lingered with venom before she disappeared into a row of biographies in the bookstore.

They sat in silence.

'Maybe I should go,' Tish said finally.

Stride shrugged. 'Then go.'

'I know you blame me,' Tish said. 'I get it.'

'No, you don't.'

'Then explain it to me.'

Stride put his coffee down and leaned forward with his elbows on the table. 'Do I think things might have been different if you had been honest with me? Yes. Do I think things might have been different if you had come forward when Laura was murdered? Yes. But I don't know any of that for sure. The truth is, I had no idea Finn was involved until you came to town. I didn't know anything about the murder of his mother. He was sick. He was desperate. A combination like that can leave someone dead. So no, I don't blame you for what happened to Finn. And Clark Biggs? That's a tragedy, but he put himself on that beach. I didn't. You didn't.'

315

Tish folded her arms. 'So what is it then?'

'Oh, come on, Tish,' Serena murmured.

Tish looked at her and understood. 'Cindy.'

'I'd like to know why she never told me about you,' Stride said.

'I'm sorry. I don't know what else to say.'

Stride scowled and stared at the night sky outside. 'I deserve more than that.'

'I know you do.' He watched the struggle in her face. 'Look, please don't blame Cindy. Blame me. When we reconnected, I asked her not to tell you about me. I knew you'd find out that I was in Duluth that night. Cindy didn't want to leave you out of it, but you weren't just her husband. You were a cop. She couldn't ask you to ignore it if you knew. You'd have to be on my doorstep the next day, and I wasn't ready for that. It was something I needed to come to in my own time.'

'And that's it?'

'That's it.' Tish clutched her purse and stood up. 'I really have to go to the airport. I'm grateful to you, Jon. You could have shut me out. I would have understood if you did.'

She turned for the door, and Stride got up and walked beside her. His hands were in his pockets. He escorted her as far as the outer door that led to the parking lot and opened it so she could pass him. The warm air spilled in with the breeze.

'We're alone,' Stride said. 'Is there anything else you want to tell me?'

'There's nothing,' she replied.

'Are you sure?'

'I'm sure.'

Stride frowned. 'Goodbye, Tish.'

She took a step closer. Her eyes reminded him of Cindy's eyes again. She laid a soft hand on his face. 'You know that Cindy loved you, don't you?'

'Of course.'

'Then nothing else matters, does it?'

Tish backed up awkwardly, tucked her head into her neck, and marched toward her car. Stride let the door swing shut and returned to the interior of the bookstore. Serena was watching him, but he didn't go back to their table. Instead, he wandered idly down the aisles of the store, occasionally reaching out and touching the spines of books without really seeing them. He tried to understand what he was feeling and decided it was loss. He remembered telling Tish that the one thing he feared in life was endings, and this was a door shutting in his soul.

Maybe, on some level, he had wanted Laura's murder to remain unsolved. As long as the case was out there, open, then Cindy would be there too. She would be young. They would be first-time lovers. Ray would be incorruptible. Life would be a mystery. Now that he had the answers, they didn't give him peace. They simply left him mourning another ending.

Or was it something more than that?

He spied Rikke near the lobby of the bookstore. She stared at him defiantly before she left the shop. He turned a corner and found himself face to face with Maggie and Amanda, who were poring over a book on child rearing. Maggie looked up and read his face.

'You OK?' she asked.

Stride shrugged and shook his head. Maggie squeezed his shoulder.

He pointed at the book she was holding. 'What's this about?'

Maggie shared a secret glance with Amanda. 'Think I should tell him?'

Amanda laughed. 'Oh, why not.'

'I'm going for it,' Maggie told Stride. 'I've decided to pursue the adoption thing all the way. I don't care what it takes. I want a kid.'

Stride smiled. 'Good for you, Mags. I couldn't be happier for you. Really.'

'I just hope it's a boy.'

'Why is that?' he asked.

'Are you kidding? Me with a little girl? That poor kid would be scarred for life having a parent like me. I couldn't do that to a child.'

Amanda rolled her eyes. 'He's a man, darling,' she said, with an English accent full of exasperation. 'He doesn't understand the curse we women face and the terrible legacy we pass on to our daughters.'

'Curse?' Stride asked.

Maggie spread her hands, as if it were obvious.

'Sooner or later, we're all destined to become our mothers,' Amanda whispered in his ear.

Stride grunted and decided this was a conversation that didn't need a man in it. He turned away to let Maggie and Amanda continue talking about mothers and daughters, and then he froze in his tracks. He spun round so quickly that both women jumped.

'*What did you say?*'

Tish reached behind her head and undid her ponytail, letting her blonde hair blow loosely in the warm wind. Her leather purse dangled from her shoulder. She was angry at herself and felt guilty for walking away. When she gazed at the back-and-forth parade of traffic on the street, she almost turned around and went back inside the store. The letter from Cindy was inside her purse, and she knew she should give it to Stride. She owed it to both of them, but she felt as if she were on a high bridge, paralyzed as she looked down. She couldn't face the truth.

She unlocked her car and got inside. She threw her purse on the opposite seat and put the key in the ignition, but she sat there without moving or starting the car, wrestling with whether she should stay. If she went to the airport and got on the flight to Minneapolis, she knew she would never come back to Duluth. Not ever.

Maybe it had been a huge mistake to come back in the first place.

Tish turned the key, and the engine fired. She put the Civic in reverse, but when she backed up, she heard metal grinding on asphalt and felt the car lurch as if it were bouncing over something heavy. She stopped, shut off the engine again, and climbed out, leaving the driver's door open. When she went round to the front of the car, she cursed, seeing the hood slumped to one side. Through the glare of the headlights, she saw that the right front tire was flat on the ground.

'Oh, hell,' she murmured.

She squatted by the tire and checked her watch. She knew nothing about changing tires, and she had no idea if there was a service station nearby. The answer was obvious. Go get Stride. Even so, she hesitated to see him again when she had just shut the door in his face.

Tish got up, turned round, and screamed.

Rikke Mathisen stood directly behind her, so close that their bodies were nearly touching.

'Are you having problems?' Rikke asked.

Tish backed up to give herself space. 'Flat tire,' she said.

Rikke towered over her by nearly a foot. Her eyes flicked to the disabled tire, and her face was impassive. 'Do you need to be somewhere?'

'I'm heading to the airport.'

'Leaving town?'

Tish nodded.

'I can drive you,' Rikke told her. 'Put your things in my car.'

Tish attempted a smile. 'You don't have to do that. I can get the tire changed.'

'It will give us a chance to talk,' Rikke said. 'Don't you think we should talk, Tish?'

Tish rubbed the skin on her forearms. She was cold. 'Sure, but it's a rental car. I can't just leave it.'

'This isn't the big city. You can call them. They'll send someone to get the car.'

'I have friends inside,' Tish said, glancing at the entrance to the bookstore and suddenly wishing she could see Stride's face. 'I'm sure one of them can drive me. You probably want to be alone.'

'I said I would drive you, so let's go.'

Tish hesitated for another second. Rikke was angry about the death of her brother, but if she wanted an opportunity to vent her poison at Tish, so be it. Tish didn't care. On some level, she deserved it.

'Sure, OK,' Tish said. 'Why not?'

She retrieved her purse, turned off the lights on the Civic, and popped the trunk. She removed her suitcase and relocated it to the trunk of Rikke's tan Impala, which was parked next to her. Rikke made no move to help. She waited until Tish had closed the trunk and then climbed inside and started the engine.

Tish got into the Impala and went to put on her seat belt. The strap was broken.

'Sorry, I've been meaning to get that fixed,' Rikke said.

She drove out of the parking lot, leaving Tish's stranded Civic behind them.

'Which bridge do you want me to take?' Rikke asked.

'Whichever is lower,' Tish said. 'I hate heights.'

Forty-three

Stride leaned closer to Maggie and Serena across the table at the café. 'How did Finn get home?' he asked them.

Maggie sipped from her cream-colored mug of chai tea and raised an eyebrow at him. 'What are you talking about?'

'On the night Laura was killed, Finn was in the park watching her. How did he get back home to Superior?'

Serena shrugged. 'By car.'

'Yes, except Rikke never let Finn drive himself,' Stride said.

'Well, Rikke swore that Finn wasn't in the park at all, but we know he was there,' Maggie said. 'So he must have had a car.'

'Or maybe Rikke picked him up,' Stride said.

As soon as he said it out loud, he realized that was what had happened.

After Amanda's offhand comment about mothers and daughters, Stride had found himself looking at the circumstances of Laura's murder from an entirely new perspective. In a case with too many suspects already, he had overlooked one other person who must have been in the park that night.

'Does that really change our theory of the crime?' Serena asked. 'If Rikke picked him up, that means she must have suspected all along that Finn killed Laura. So she lied to give him an alibi.'

Stride leaned back in his chair. 'That's what I thought, but it works both ways. By giving Finn an alibi, she also gives herself one.'

Maggie shook her head. 'What are you saying, boss?'

'I'm saying if Rikke went to the park to pick up Finn, maybe she came upon the baseball bat lying in the field.'

320

'Or maybe Elvis found it,' Maggie suggested. 'Maybe he was so wracked with guilt about killing Laura that he OD'd a month later.'

Stride nodded. 'Yeah, I could be crazy, but Finn's prints *aren't* on the baseball bat. We've got prints from Peter, Dada, and Cindy, but not Finn. If he killed her, why wouldn't his prints be on the bat? Instead, we've got a set of prints that we can't identify.'

'Why would Rikke kill Laura?' Maggie asked.

'That depends on what was really going on between the two of them,' Stride told her. 'Amanda said that every daughter becomes her mother sooner or later. We see it all the time in abusive relationships, right? Abuse begets abuse. Rikke admitted to us that her mother sexually molested her. The question is, did Rikke take after her mother and become an abuser herself?'

'You think that Rikke had a sexual relationship with Laura?' Maggie asked.

'I think it's not impossible. Laura spent a lot of time there when she was struggling with her sexuality. After her break-up with Tish, maybe she was confused and vulnerable and needed someone to confide in. So she went to her favorite teacher for help. What if Rikke took advantage of her trust? We already know she got kicked out of the school district later for an affair with a student. We've been saying all along that Finn was insanely jealous of Laura's relationship with Tish, but maybe we've got it backwards. Maybe Rikke was the one who was jealous.'

Maggie took time to think about it, but then shook her head. 'Even if Rikke did seduce Laura, why would she kill her?'

'If she was abusive and obsessed, who knows what she would have done when she found out Laura was running away from her?' Stride replied. 'You're talking about a brother and sister who were raised on violence and incest. We know what it did to Finn. Do you think Rikke doesn't have demons too?'

'Except we know that Finn is the one who's capable of murder,' Maggie said.

Stride had a vision of a lonely North Dakota farm, glowing faintly in the center of miles of night-time fields. It was like being on the moon, Rikke said. His eyes grew hard.

'Wait a minute,' he said. 'Do we?'

Maggie opened her mouth to protest and then clamped it shut.

'Son of a bitch,' Serena gasped. 'No, we don't.'

'I want to talk to Rikke,' Stride said, standing up. 'I want to get her prints to match to the murder weapon, and I want to know what was really going on in that house.' He stood up and looked around the bookstore. 'Is she still here?'

Serena shook her head. 'Rikke left right after Tish. I saw her go.'

'All right, let's see if we can catch her,' Stride said.

The three of them headed for the exit. In the parking lot, Stride turned left on the sidewalk toward his Expedition, which was parked next to Maggie's yellow Avalanche, but he stopped when Serena took hold of his shoulder.

'Wait a minute, Jonny,' she said, pointing. 'That's Tish's car.'

Stride recognized the Civic on the far side of the parking lot and immediately spotted the odd angle of the chassis caused by the car's flat tire. He frowned as he studied the rest of the lot. 'Where's Tish?' he asked.

Maggie jogged over to the Civic and got down on her knees to examine the tire with a penlight on her key chain. 'This was cut,' she called to them. 'Somebody slashed it.'

Stride looked at Serena. 'Rikke.'

The Blatnik Bridge loomed ahead of them beyond the sweeping curve of the highway, its arch illuminated against the night with blurred rows of white lights. Tish grew nervous as they neared the span, anticipating the rope of fear that would twist around her insides as they made the crossing. She wanted to look away, but she couldn't; instead, she stared at the hump of steel as if it were a sea monster arching its giant back over the water. Her tension broadcast itself through the car.

'Is something wrong?' Rikke asked. Her voice was cool.

'It's just bridges,' Tish said. 'They scare me.'

The windows on both sides were wide open, ushering in a fierce breeze that rattled the frame of the car. They climbed the sharp angle toward the summit of the bridge, and the criss-cross steel of the span rose ahead of them like the tracks of a roller coaster. Rikke drove slowly. Traffic soared up behind them, filling the car with their headlights and then passing impatiently on their left at almost twice their speed. On either side of them, far below, industrial lights marked the edge of the land, and the blackness signaled the channel of Superior Bay. Tish wrapped her arms tightly across her chest. Her breathing was fast.

Rikke reached out and rested a warm hand on Tish's thigh, and Tish flinched.

'The view is amazing,' Rikke said. 'You should look.'

'I don't want to see it.'

Rikke slowed even further as they crept skyward. Tish felt sweat on her hands, and her left arm twitched involuntarily.

'Can't we go faster?' she asked.

'No, I love it up here,' Rikke told her. 'Sometimes I think that's the best way to die. Just let yourself drive off the edge of a bridge.'

'Don't talk like that, it scares me.'

The car drifted toward the right shoulder, grinding on loose gravel. Tish was conscious of the three-foot high ribbon of concrete stretching along the bridge deck, which was the only barrier between the car and one hundred feet of air dropping toward the water. It was inches from her window.

'It's hard not to think about death when you know you're dying,' Rikke said.

'Dying?'

Rikke nodded calmly. 'The doctors tell me the cancer has come back. Metastasized, they call it. That's an ugly word. I only have a few months.'

'I'm sorry,' Tish said.

'So you see, it's a choice I have to think about. That's what I face. A death that's fast and free, or one that's slow and painful. What would you do?'

'I don't know.'

Rikke's hand tightened on her thigh. She squeezed hard, her nails cutting into skin. 'I never understood what Laura saw in you. I know you were beautiful, but you never understood her like I did. I was the one she came to for comfort. I was the one who helped her understand who she was.'

'You're hurting me.'

'Good. You deserve to be hurt.' She took her eyes off the road. 'Look at you, you're still so attractive. Me, I've gotten old. My body is a joke now. My breasts are ruined. My thighs are all pebbled over with cellulite. I can hardly bear to look at myself. I was beautiful then, do you remember? My students all wanted me.'

Tish sat frozen, saying nothing.

'Laura wanted me too,' Rikke said. 'Did you know that?'

'That's not true.'

'Oh, but it is,' Rikke went on. 'Laura told me about your affair. She told me how she ran away from you. She came to me because she needed a friend. A mother. She was so scared, so lonely. I was there for her when you weren't. I spent hours letting her cry in my arms. We became close. And one night, when I knew she was ready for it, I showed her that I could love her in a special way.'

'Oh, my God,' Tish said. 'No, you're lying.'

Steel cables dropped from the span around them as they neared the summit. Ghosts of fog drifted around the car and reflected back in the headlights. She could hardly see the road. Overhead, the diamonds of steel looked like spiders viewed through a gauzy web.

'There was nothing evil about it,' Rikke said. 'Laura never should have run away from me. Not to you.'

Rikke spun the wheel and jammed her foot on the brake, turning the nose of the car until it bumped against the concrete shoulder. The car jerked to a stop at the peak of the highway. They were at an angle, with barely two feet of rock and dirt outside the door between Tish and the long drop. Other cars buzzed by like hornets, their horns squealing.

'What are you doing?' Tish held on to herself, trembling. 'Keep going, keep going!'

'It was always you, wasn't it?' Rikke snarled. 'Laura didn't care about me. Or Finn. It was you she wanted.'

'Drive, drive!' Tish screamed. 'Please!'

Rikke turned off the car engine.

Tish felt herself hyperventilating. She squirmed away from the car door. She couldn't stop looking at the steel overhead and the shining rows of white lights. She felt the pull of heights again, the insane urge to leap from the car, to jump.

'Are you crazy? Go, go now, please! I'll do anything!'

'Why did you come back here?' Rikke asked. 'Was it revenge? Is that what you wanted? I tried to scare you away, and you stayed.'

Tish shook her head mutely. Panic and terror ripped through her nerve ends.

Rikke slid the keys out of the ignition and opened the driver's door and got out, slamming it behind her. Traffic wheeled around her through the fog and night. She walked round the back of the car and came up to the open window on Tish's side of the car. Inside, Tish cowered near the opposite door. Rikke sucked in a lungful of the whipping breeze and peered over the barrier at the inky blackness of the channel. Then she reached her upper body in through the window, grabbed Tish's wrist, and yanked her bodily across the car.

Tish wailed. 'Don't do this!'

'Look at me!' Rikke insisted. When Tish buried her face in her chest, Rikke grabbed Tish's chin and wrenched it up until their eyes met. Tish's stare was glazed with tears. She saw violence and desire fighting in Rikke's face. 'This is what you deserve for coming back to torture me. For driving Finn crazy. You killed him, do you know that? It was you. You may as well have been the one to put the bullet in his brain.'

'I'm sorry, I'm sorry.'

Rikke took Tish's skull in both hands, twisted her face, and forced her mouth up, where she bent down and covered her lips in a fierce kiss. 'Is that so horrible? Does it scare you? Laura was afraid of me after we made love. Afraid! That was Finn's fault. He never should have interfered, but he was jealous that I was the one she chose.'

Tish wiped her mouth. 'Stop this!'

'Finn watched us make love in his bed that night. I knew he was there. But the next day, he went and told Laura what happened in Fargo. It was our secret, his and mine. He had no right to tell her. He just wanted to split us apart. To scare her away.'

Rikke's face was black. Horror descended on it like a shadow off the bridge.

'Finn never told Laura that I did it for him. For him! I knew what our mother was doing. I had to put a stop to it, and I knew Finn would never lift a finger to protect himself. He just crawled into his little hole and let her keep coming back for more. So I was the one who had to be strong. I was the one who had to save him.'

If Dad were abusing me, could you kill him? Do you have to be insane to do it?

Tish finally understood. Laura wasn't talking about her father. She was talking about Rikke. About her secret.

'I came back to our farm,' Rikke went on, 'and I took that bat, and I beat our mother until she was nothing but mush and pulp. Finn watched me do it. He knew I didn't have a choice. No one was ever supposed to know. But then he went and spilled his guts to Laura. I heard him. The stupid, jealous bastard! Laura should have let me explain, but she ran away. What was I supposed to think? If she had stayed, I would never have hurt her, but she *left*.'

Tish's eyes were wild. 'She never told me.'

'Oh, but she would have told you eventually,' Rikke said. 'I don't blame her. I don't blame Finn, either. We could all have worked it out if it weren't for you. You're the one who destroyed us. Now it's my turn.'

Rikke let the car keys dangle from her finger in front of Tish's face.

'This is the end for both of us.'

As Tish screamed, Rikke casually flicked the keys out over the side of the bridge, where they fell in a silver flash.

Forty-four

As Stride and Serena drew closer to the glowing white arch of the Blatnik Bridge, brake lights turned red, and traffic around them ground to a dead stop. The bridge lights over their heads were bathed in fog. Ahead of them, horns blared in a sing-song whine as cars trickled forward, slowly merging into a convoy over the span. He lowered the window of his truck and leaned out to study the highway, but he couldn't make out the summit of the bridge through the white cloud.

'Is it an accident?' Serena asked.

'I don't know. Every time the fog rolls in, people start running into each other.'

Serena peered over the edge. 'Long way down.'

'One hundred and twenty feet to the water.'

On the opposite side of the center barrier, traffic streamed toward them out of the haze. In the westbound lane, people jostled for position and cut each other off as they merged. He didn't like the speed or impatience of the other drivers. He reached behind his seat for an emergency flasher and slapped it magnetically to the top of his Expedition. The red light turned and shot a beam around them. He turned on his four-ways and shut off the engine.

'You want to come?' he said to Serena.

'Out on the bridge?'

'You can stay here if you want.'

'Hell, no, I'm with you.'

He opened the door and stepped out onto the bridge deck. Serena did the same on the other side of the truck. She was closer to the

327

edge, where the dirt and gravel of the narrow shoulder bumped against the concrete barrier.

'Be careful,' he said.

'Now you tell me.'

He waved his hands to alert drivers around him and walked up the highway, following the white paint marking the two lanes. Serena veered away from the shoulder and marched beside him. They could only see a few cars at a time in the swirling fog. On their right, steel girders sloped upward toward the semi-circle of the bridge arch. Lights came and went over their heads as the mist drifted in pockets. He slapped the metal frame of each car they approached, so the driver knew they were there. He didn't want anyone bolting across the lane as they came up from behind.

Inside his pocket, his phone rang. He flipped it up. 'What's up, Mags?'

'I'm at Rikke's house. No sign of her there.'

'Get an ATL out on the tan Impala.'

'Already done. Where are you?'

Stride shook his head. 'You don't want to know. We're hiking up the bridge deck on the Blatnik.'

'Hiking?'

'Yeah, traffic is almost stopped. Something's going on.'

'Watch your ass, boss. That's a mean bridge.'

Stride hung up. He and Serena threaded their way through traffic, but the fog grew thicker as they increased their altitude over the water. Cars pushed and shoved around them as if they were trapped in an amusement park ride.

'Let's get back to the shoulder,' he told Serena. 'I don't like being in the middle of traffic.'

'Great,' she said without enthusiasm.

He held up his hands and crossed in front of a Chevy minivan that was angling toward the left lane. When they reached the shoulder, he increased his pace, marching faster.

'Watch your step, the gravel's loose here,' he told her.

'You, too.'

He passed the first of the thick girders that sprouted upward like an erector set into a tree of beams and rivets. Circular holes allowed

328

the wind to pass through the steel. Twin sets of cables hung elegantly from the top of the span like piano strings, suspending the roadbed on which they walked. From the lake, gusts pummeled them, dancing around the towers like sprites. He steadied himself against the concrete barrier, but the sensation of height briefly took his breath away. He could feel the rocking sway of the bridge up here.

Traffic accelerated around them. Cars that had merged into the left lane squealed and left rubber on the asphalt as they roared out of the clogged pipeline of vehicles. Stride made a frantic downward motion with his palms, trying to slow them down. No one paid attention. They sped by like giants.

He heard something. Not the howl of the wind. This was a scream.

An updraft separated the fog like a curtain. Thirty yards away, he spotted a tan Impala, half blocking the right lane of traffic at the very peak of the bridge. A trail of restless cars sped around it, sailing down the open space of the highway toward Duluth. A tall woman stood outside the car, buffeted by the wind. She was dressed in black, and she came and went in the cloud like a witch.

Rikke.

'Son of a bitch,' he said.

Serena saw her too. 'What do you want to do?'

Stride grabbed his cell phone and pushed it in her hand. 'Call Maggie and get Duluth cops up here from the other side of the bridge. Then see if you can stop these goddamned idiots and shut down the traffic.'

He jogged away from her, then turned back and shouted, 'Tell Maggie to get hold of the Coast Guard, too. I want them under the bridge right now in case we need a rescue operation in the water.'

He pulled his gun. He ran.

Rikke gazed downward into the windy stretch of air leading to the bay. 'Fast and free,' she murmured.

A wild impulse almost made Tish bolt from the car and push her, but the roadbed vibrated, and the Impala began to move, inching along the highway. Tish screamed, scrambled across the seat, and jammed the emergency brake with her foot.

Rikke ripped open the passenger door and yanked her across the

329

torn vinyl. Tish clutched the steering wheel, but Rikke was stronger, and when Tish felt her fingers torn away from the wheel, the two of them lurched backward. Tish spilled out of the car onto the bridge deck. Rikke cursed and lost her balance, nearly tumbling over the edge.

Tish flattened herself face down on the ground and covered her head with her hands. She heard a roaring noise from the wind and traffic. Every muscle in her body tightened like a spring. Her fear of heights thumped in her head, shooting panicked impulses to her brain. The voice was seductive, like a Pied Piper telling her to get up, run, and leap for the water. Jump. Make the terror stop.

Rikke squatted beside her. She took a fistful of Tish's coat and wrenched her up, propping her back against the side of the car. Tish closed her eyes, but Rikke pushed them open with her fingers, and Tish saw the concrete barrier and the open air beyond it, beckoning her with open, breezy arms.

Rikke clutched her face with both hands. 'All these years, I wondered if you knew. If you'd seen me. If Laura had told you what I did. I kept waiting for you to come back and expose me. And then, after all these years, you did.'

'I didn't know,' Tish said. 'Please let me go. I can't take this.'

'I went to pick Finn up in the park that night. He was stoned out of his head, babbling about Laura, about the two of you in the woods. I found the baseball bat in the field, and I knew what I had to do. Silence Laura. And pay her back for leaving me.'

'I loved her!' Tish screamed. She beat her hands ferociously on Rikke's chest, driving her back toward the edge of the bridge. 'You goddamned bitch, how could you!'

Rikke recovered and stumbled forward on her knees. She bunched the lapels of Tish's jacket in her fists. Their faces were an inch apart. 'What about you? I spent my whole life looking over my shoulder because of you. You ruined my life. You ruined Finn's life.'

Tish slapped her hard. 'You took Laura away!'

Rikke pushed herself to her feet, swaying and towering over Tish. 'Get up.'

Tish wrapped her hands around Rikke's ankles and pulled violently. Rikke shouted and tumbled like a tree, landing in the gravel. Tish crawled away toward the speeding cars on the highway, but Rikke threw herself onto Tish's back and drove her to the asphalt. Rikke rolled her over. Sharp rocks sliced into Tish's skin. The older woman's face was blood-red and twisted with fury.

Rikke's fingers curled like talons and seized Tish's neck. Her thumbs drove into Tish's windpipe, making her gag and choke. She couldn't breathe. Her body spasmed. She tore at Rikke's hands, but they were two blocks of granite.

'*Rikke!*'

They both heard the voice.

Rikke let go of Tish's neck and peered through the fog on the bridge deck. Tish gasped for breath and twisted away. Behind her, she saw Stride, his gun out, sprinting toward them. Tish tried to wriggle free, but Rikke came off her knees and stood up, wrapping another choke-hold round her neck and dragging her to her feet. Tish struggled and kicked, her eyes growing white and wide as Rikke inched toward the edge of the bridge. Tish clawed for the safety of the car, but Rikke held her tight, forcing her to stare into the black abyss below them.

Tish could see it clearly. In her head, she was already falling. Her breath left her chest, and she thought her heart would burst.

'Stop!' Rikke shouted at Stride. 'I'll kill us both.'

Stride stopped. He holstered his gun and held up his hands. 'Let her go, Rikke.'

Tish squirmed like a frightened animal in Rikke's arms. Her fingers tore at Rikke's clothes.

'If I let her go, she'll jump,' Rikke said. 'She's out of her head.'

'Put her back in the car.'

Rikke's legs nudged against the concrete barrier on the edge of the bridge deck. The height of the barrier barely came up past her knees. She leaned into the wind, carrying Tish's torso with her. Tish wailed, a noise so primal and terrified that it made Stride flinch.

'I'll do it,' Rikke said. 'I'll take her with me. I don't care.'

Stride's mind shut out the world. Distractions fell away. He didn't notice the wind or the height or the thumping of the highway under his feet. He took two steps closer to Rikke. She was six feet away.

'Stay back,' she warned him.

He was conscious of the fact that Serena was behind him, stopping

331

the flow of cars heading west. On the opposite side of the bridge, he heard the siren of a squad car speeding from Duluth. The squad car stopped twenty yards away at an angle across both eastbound lanes, and a young policewoman bolted out of the car, her gun drawn. He slowly brought up his hand, keeping her where she was. The cop held her ground, and traffic from the Duluth side bled away to nothing as cars backed up behind her car.

They were alone up here.

'I want you both to get back in the car,' he told Rikke.

Wisps of fog floated lazily between them. The bridge was in and out of the flow of clouds. Far below, Stride heard a boat whistle. He recognized it as the call of a Coast Guard rescue cutter, churning toward the span of the bridge and positioning itself in the bay. He had been on that boat many times. Most jumpers didn't come out of the water alive.

He took another step.

'Let her go,' he told Rikke. 'Give her to me.'

Rikke's eyes were like blue stones. 'Don't move,' she said.

Stride put his hands up. 'I'm not moving.'

One of the twin sets of vertical cables supporting the roadbed was immediately behind Rikke. She slid her left arm round the cables to brace herself and hoisted Tish bodily off the ground with her other arm. Tish's legs kicked madly, and her blonde hair twirled around her head in the back-and-forth of the wind.

'Go ahead,' Rikke told Stride with scorn. 'Come get me.'

'Tish never did a thing to you,' Stride said. 'Whatever happened between you and Laura has been over for years.'

'Then she should have stayed away.'

Stride saw the policewoman on the opposite side of the bridge climb silently over the barrier between the lanes and sidle into his line of vision. She was thirty feet behind Rikke. She signaled Stride with her left hand, then pointed at herself and aimed her gun where it would fire harmlessly over the water. She looked at him with a question in her eyes.

Fire or not fire. Create a diversion.

Almost imperceptibly, Stride nodded.

The policewoman held up her left hand and lifted one finger into the air. Then two. As she lifted the third, her finger depressed the trigger on her gun, and a sharp report cracked on the bridge.

Rikke flinched, and at the same instant, Stride dove. He wasn't fast enough. Rikke launched Tish violently against the concrete guardrail, where she lost her balance and toppled forward. Rikke turned and ran. Stride clawed for Tish and nearly had her, but her torso slipped through his grasp, and she kept falling. His right hand grazed her thigh, and his left hand caught behind her knee, but she stripped past him, picking up speed on her drop toward the bay. She was sliding, falling, and wailing, until his hands locked around her thin calf and her right foot caught on his clenched fingers, and she finally jerked to a stop.

Tish hung suspended over one hundred and twenty feet of air between the bridge and the water.

Her weight pinned Stride against the concrete barrier. He felt her squirming, fighting him, almost as if she wanted to fall. His upper body was bent over the bridge; he was being pulled, dragged down. He couldn't lift her up. All he could do was hold on to her ankle, but the muscles in his arms groaned and weakened.

'*Serena!*' he shouted. He could hear her running behind him.

'Hold on!'

Stride tried to make time stop. He tried to clear his mind of everything except the lock-hold of his hands round Tish's ankle. They were like handcuffs. Tight. Not giving up.

'Hold on, Jonny, I'm here.'

Serena leaned over the edge, stared down at the dark water, and cursed. 'Oh, son of a bitch, I don't know if I can do this.'

'You have to. I'm losing my grip.'

Serena bent over and hunted for a hold on Tish's body. She bunched Tish's blouse between her fingers, but the fabric tore away when she pulled, and Serena gasped and fell against Stride. He staggered, and the vise he kept around Tish's ankle nearly broke apart.

'Your hand, give me your hand!' Serena shouted at Tish, whose arms made a Y below her head, reaching toward the bay.

'No, no, no, I can't!'

'Reach back, Tish, you can do it.'

'*No!*'

333

Stride's fingers grew numb and sweaty, and pain screamed along the nerve ends in his shoulders and neck.

'See if you can get her other ankle,' he said. They were running out of time.

Tish's leg spun along with her body. The wind played with her like a toy, pushing her back and forth in circles. Serena grasped for her flying ankle, missed it, and tried again, and finally she shouted.

'Got it! Pull! Pull!'

Stride yanked upward with a shout, scraping backward from the edge of the bridge. Serena was beside him, doing the same thing. Inch by inch, they fought their way from the concrete barrier, and Tish came with them. They saw her knees, then her thighs, and when they saw her waist clear the bridge, Serena took one hand, grabbed Tish's belt, and spilled her back onto the highway, where she twitched like a fish pulled from the water.

Stride let go and fell backward against the Impala. His chest heaved. Pins and needles assailed his arms.

Tish was incoherent, moaning and crying.

'Get her in the back of the Impala, make her lie down,' he mumbled to Serena. 'She's going to need to be sedated before we can move her to our truck.'

'Lieutenant!'

Stride's head snapped up.

Thirty feet away, the policewoman who had fired the warning shot lay on her back on the asphalt, entwined in a violent struggle with Rikke. The two bodies rolled and fought, and as he watched, the gun skidded away across the lane, out of reach. Rikke reared back and chopped the officer's face with a crack of her elbow. The cop's head snapped against the pavement, and she went limp.

Stride swore, pushed himself off the car, and ran. His legs felt like gelatin. Beside him, he was stunned to see cars whipping down the slope of the bridge deck toward the Duluth side as if it were a racetrack. The fog made him almost invisible, and he dodged cars that began to merge into the right lane before they saw him. He charged down the shoulder, making ground on Rikke, who staggered to her feet. When he thrust out his tired arms to stop her, she swung wildly at him with both fists. She connected with his jaw, and there was surprising strength in the blow. He grabbed for her wrists, but she shoved his chest, and he skidded backward, losing his balance.

Rikke bolted away.

Stride heard horns and saw dazzling white lights. Cars stampeded like blind elephants. He sprinted after Rikke, but she weaved away from him and darted to his left out into traffic. He shouted a warning, but she didn't stop. Like a cannon barrel coming out of the fog, a huge black Escalade rocketed down the highway in the left lane, and Rikke stumbled directly into its path. Stride saw the red flash of brake lights. Tires screeched and burned. Rikke screamed, but her cry was chopped short as the SUV hammered her torso and nearly cut her in two.

Rikke's crushed body spun off the grille of the truck and rolled to a stop twenty yards away. She didn't move.

Before Stride could react, he felt the presence of something giant and dangerous behind him. He turned to see a white sedan sail like a pirate ship out of the fog. When the driver saw the Escalade stopped in the left lane, he swerved right, coming directly at Stride, who leaped and rolled onto the hood as the sedan struck him. His body bounced on the metal. The windshield hit his chest. He felt air burst from his lungs. He hung onto the hood with his fingertips as the car slammed into the concrete barrier on the side of the bridge, and then his hold gave way.

Stride flew.

He was a bird in the air, shot from the hood of the sedan, launched out over the side of the bridge into nothingness.

Then he was falling.

Forty-five

Time stretches out on a long fall.

In Stride's brain, he knew that it was one hundred and twenty feet to the black water and that he would plummet through that distance in about three seconds. Even so, his thoughts accelerated like shooting stars, giving him enough time to watch himself fall and be acutely aware of his sensations. He had no time at all to be afraid.

As he was thrown into mid-air, he thought he heard Serena cry, but her voice was gone instantaneously, and the only noise around him was the deafening roar of the wind. Air hurtled against his body, cold and fierce, as fast as a bullet. Its wail sounded like a scream, shouting out from his chest. He hoped it wasn't. He didn't want to die screaming.

He caught a last glimpse of the bridge as it disappeared above him. Its lights were a half-moon of blurry white, and then the lights blinked out, and he was enveloped in blackness. He saw nothing below him, no water, no light, and he realized he had squeezed his eyes shut. He forced himself to open his eyes, to take advantage of the strange elongated sensation of time to orient himself. When he did, he could see the lights of the Point, where he lived, and something about that glimmer on the narrow strip of land made him want to see it again.

He tried to breathe, but he couldn't. His lungs had been hammered by the impact of the hood of the car, and they refused to swell to take in the speeding oxygen around him. He felt light-headed, swimming, dreaming, as if he were already underwater.

Three seconds.

He had time to think about the fact that he wasn't seeing his life pass before his eyes. No clickety roll of images like film on an old movie projector. No recollections of Cindy, Maggie, or Serena. No voices, sounds, memories. No angel caressing his arm and showing him the loved ones who had gone before him. He was in a vacuum filled with air, about to hit water, and he would not hit it like a knife cutting through butter; the water was not soft, it was solid like concrete and it would savage his bones and tissue and kill him instantly, the flicking of a switch from alive to dead.

That was the first conscious thought to penetrate his mind in that first long second.

He was about to die.

He thought about people jumping from towers. People in planes about to crash. They must have had that same brilliant moment of clarity. You are alive now, and in another moment, you will be dead. He was almost curious about what it would be like, and he realized that death had a strange seduction to it.

But he had time enough to realize that he didn't want to die, not now, not for a long time, and he had time enough to remember that the Golden Gate Bridge was a lot taller than the Blatnik Bridge, and people had been known to survive the big drop into San Francisco Bay, even when they didn't want to. Not a lot. But a few.

And those that did went in feet first.

Feet first.

His brain began screaming at him. *Feet first.*

If he hit the water with his head or his shoulder or his chest, he would die hitting the water as if it were made of brick. His only hope was to cut a little tear in the liquid concrete and slip through. With his eyes open, and that odd, elastic time stretching out like a pink roll of taffy, Stride uncurled his body into the straightest line he could make it, pointed his toes toward the water, lifted his arms straight over his head, and tilted his chin toward the sky. In the lightning span of less than a second, he twisted himself into an arrow heading for a bullseye.

Don't tense. Let it happen.

You're going to die.

No, you're not.

He exhaled the last gasp of breath that was left in his chest and let his muscles go soft. He closed his eyes again and just as he did, time finally caught up with him. His toes parted the seas. His body fired through the water like a rocket. He was conscious of pain, bones breaking, clothes ripped from his skin, water flooding his lungs. He saw the lights of the world wink out into night. He felt hot agony turn cold, felt himself descending and descending and descending, as if he could travel right through the earth and wind up in hell.

Except the deep channel was not bottomless, and after he had gone down as far as he could go, he hung suspended, a moth enrobed in a cocoon, before his body began to coil and climb. The bay that sucked him in found him hard to swallow and decided to spit him out.

Later, he would remember none of it. His last memory would be of running toward Rikke Mathisen on the bridge. There, the film ended. He would have no recollection of the car that hit him and drove him from the bridge, of falling, of time stretching out, of the impact that broke his left leg and collapsed both lungs, of bobbing to the surface on his back, of the searchlight of the Coast Guard boat bathing like a warm glow over his body. No recollection of ever thinking to himself that if he had made it this far, he was going to live.

Forty-six

When Stride saw the glass door open, he realized that the woman who had stepped out onto the restaurant patio was his late wife, Cindy.

For an instant, he felt as if he were falling again, long and hard toward the water. The enigmatic smile he remembered from years ago was the same. When she lifted her sunglasses, her brown eyes stared back at him with a familiar glint over the heads of the others in the restaurant.

It wasn't her, of course. It was Tish.

She joined them at the same table where she had met them for the first time three months earlier. Stride sat with Serena and Maggie on either side of him. The heat of summer had yielded to September evenings, when darkness ate away the daylight. As he watched, the last sliver of sun dipped below the western hillside, and the lake grew gray and unsettled. Tish shivered as she sat down.

'How are you?' Stride asked her.

Tish sized up his condition. 'Shouldn't I be asking you that?'

Stride's right leg was encased in a cast. His crutches were balanced against the railing of the patio. He fingered the brace on his neck. 'Physical wounds heal,' he said. 'Yours may be a little harder to deal with.'

Tish put on a brave face and smiled. 'You know how they say you have to face your fears to overcome them? That's a load of crap. I never want to cross a bridge again in my entire life.' She reached out and took Stride's and Serena's hands. 'I haven't had a chance to thank you both properly. I should be dead now. You saved me.'

'It's over,' Stride said. 'Try not to think about it anymore.'

But it wasn't really over, not for any of them. Serena had nightmares where she relived his fall from the bridge. She would wake up in a sweat and hold on to him. For himself, he was surprised and a little anxious that he had felt no emotional response to his own near-death experience. He felt strangely empty, as if the fall had happened to someone else. He feared that the emotions would build silently like an avalanche and someday overtake him with a roar.

'Seriously, how are you?' Tish asked him.

'It's going to take me a few months to fully recover,' he admitted. 'The doctors don't want me to come back until the end of the year, but I'm not going to wait that long.'

Maggie winked. 'I'm the interim head of the Detective Bureau. He's afraid I'll take over.'

'Be my guest,' Stride said.

'I already gave away your chair,' Maggie told him. 'It was too big for my ass.'

'Go away, Mags.'

She laughed.

'Did you finish the book?' Stride asked Tish.

'I'm on the last chapter.' Tish tugged nervously at her hair. 'I feel guilty writing it. Like it was partly my fault. I drove Laura into Rikke's arms back then.'

Stride shook his head. 'Rikke knew how to manipulate young girls. She was responsible, not you.'

'I know, but maybe if I had been more patient with her, Laura would have stayed with me all along. She would never have fallen into Rikke's trap. I wish she had told me what happened between them.'

'She was scared,' Serena said. 'Laura found out that Rikke was a murderer, and she ran away.'

'And when I came back for her, she died,' Tish said.

'Don't blame yourself for surviving,' Stride said.

Tish's eyes pierced him. 'That's good advice.'

An electronic alert chirruped under the table. Stride automatically reached for his belt, but he wasn't wearing a pager. Maggie pulled out her own pager and studied it. 'That's me, boss,' she said. 'We've got an armed robbery at a gas station on the south end of Michigan Street.'

340

'You want me to come with you?' Stride asked. 'Unofficially, that is.'

Maggie sighed and looked at Serena. 'Do something about him, will you?'

'I'll try.'

Maggie pushed her chair back and got up. She waved at the three of them and headed for the restaurant door.

'I should be going too,' Tish said.

Tish stood up from the table, but she didn't leave. Her mouth became frozen and sad. Her eyes grew glassy, and she blinked back tears. She sat down again, but when she tried to speak, the words caught in her throat.

'There's something more,' she admitted finally.

Stride felt a sense of uneasiness. He knew without Tish saying anything that whatever she had to share with him involved Cindy. All along, there had been a missing piece. A secret. He wasn't sure anymore that he wanted to know what it was.

'I have something for you,' Tish told him. 'I feel bad that it took me so long to give it to you, but I hope you'll understand when I explain.'

She slipped an envelope out of her purse and pushed it across the table to Stride. He saw the words written on the outside in black ink. *For Jonny*. He had no trouble recognizing the tight, precise handwriting he had known for years.

'Cindy gave this to me the last time we were together,' Tish said. 'She told me if I ever came back here and decided to be upfront about my past, I should give this to you. I never opened it. I never read it.'

Stride didn't pick up the envelope.

'Your past?' he asked.

'Yes. Before Cindy's father died, he told her something about me. Something important. That's why Cindy reached out to me. I didn't think I ever wanted anyone else to know, but I guess the two of you deserve to know the truth.'

Stride waited.

'Cindy's father knew about me and Laura,' Tish continued. 'He overheard Laura on the phone, and he knew we were planning to run away together. He went berserk.'

'I knew William Starr,' Stride said. 'The idea of his daughter being gay would have been horrifying to him.'

341

'It was worse than that,' Tish said. 'It wasn't just Laura being gay. It was me. It was the two of us being in love.'

'You?'

Tish slid something else from her purse. A fragile piece of newspaper. When she unfolded it carefully, Stride saw the headline. So did Serena, who caught Tish's eye. Tish nodded at her, embarrassed.

'I didn't lie to you, Serena, not really,' she said. 'The robbery where my mother was killed had nothing to do with Laura's death. Cindy found this clipping in her father's Bible shortly before he died. He had kept it for years. She asked him why, and he finally told her the truth. He finally admitted the affair.' Tish shook her head with fierce bitterness. 'That selfish, hypocritical son of a bitch. I hate him. Nothing will ever change that.'

'Your mother?' Serena guessed.

Tish nodded. Tears pooled on her eyelids and ran over to her cheeks. 'She was the honorable one. More honorable than he ever deserved. She never told a soul. Not even when she was fired from her job at the store. Not even when she was drummed out of their church. She never admitted that he was the father.'

Stride closed his eyes. He had never liked William Starr. He didn't like him now.

'All those years, he never acknowledged me,' Tish said. 'Even when my mother died, he was too gutless to admit who I was. I'm glad he thought he was being punished by God for everything that happened.' She wiped her cheek with the back of her hand. 'Cindy told me, and I begged her to keep it between the two of us. Can you imagine what it did to me? I found out I had a sister. A half-sister. I also found out that the great love of my life was something terrible. Something immoral. Me and Laura. I was in love with—'

Tish stopped. Her voice seized again.

'You didn't know,' Serena murmured.

'No. We didn't know. Even after Cindy told me, I tried to pretend to myself that it wasn't true. I still loved Laura. I still ached for her. I wanted it to be the way I remembered it. I didn't want to give up what we had.'

Tish fingered the note that lay in front of Stride.

'Cindy wanted me to tell you,' she said. 'She hated the idea of keeping part of her life hidden from you, but I insisted. When she knew she was dying, she made me promise to come back here. She wanted me to do it for Laura, but I think she also wanted me not to be alone. She thought maybe I could find some kind of family here.'

Her eyes formed a question.

'You do have family here,' Stride said.

'Thank you. To both of you.' She stood up. 'I really do need to go.'

'Don't stay away forever, Tish.'

She came around the table and bent down to wrap her arms around Stride's neck. She embraced him and whispered in his ear, 'I keep part of her with me, even though I lost her.'

Stride didn't say anything. Tish gave Serena a brief hug and then slung her purse over her shoulder. The wind mussed her hair, and she fixed it. She gave Stride a broken smile and left the way she had come. Stride followed her with his eyes until she was gone. From the back, she looked like Cindy again, walking away, leaving him.

Stride held the envelope in his hands and thought about letting it go and losing it in the wind. He didn't need a message in a bottle washing ashore right now. He didn't need a resurrection.

He and Serena sat together, not talking, as the evening grew darker around them. Most of the other tables were empty; it was too cold now to be outside. Out on the Point, beyond the lift bridge, white caps crested and lapped at the sand. The air smelled like fall.

After a space of silence, Serena got up and kissed his cheek and put her cool fingers on his bare arm. 'I'm going to walk on the board-walk for a while,' she told him.

Their eyes met, and he nodded. She left him there, and he was alone with Cindy.

Stride traced the sides of the envelope with his fingertips and wondered how long he could wait without opening it. He wasn't sure if he was ready for Cindy to be alive again, even for a moment. Not when his grief was over.

When he couldn't hold back anymore, he used a knife from the table to slit the envelope at the top and slide out the single sheet of paper inside. It was ordinary typing paper, and when he unfolded it, he found a few handwritten lines inside.

343

Dear Jonny,

If you're reading this letter, it means Tish finally told you the truth, and you know why I kept you in the dark for so long. It also means I lost the battle with cancer. I'm so sorry, my love, for leaving you earlier than we had planned.

Stride took a labored breath. His eyes burned, and the words blurred on the paper as he tried to read.

Not a day went by that I didn't long to tell you about Tish, but it was never my secret to share. It was hers. My sister's. And it was a secret born in too much blood and pain for anyone else to reveal. I hope you can forgive me.

I'm gone now, so tell me that it didn't take too long to let go of me. I know what kind of man you are, Jonny. When you hit upon a brick wall, you beat your head against it with your suffering. I hope you didn't do that for me. Tell me you're not alone and that you're in love again. That would give me peace.

I don't really know what else to say. God may not have given me all the time I wanted, but how can I complain? For the time I had, I had you.

With all my love,
Cindy

Stride folded up the note and slid it inside his pocket. He made a pyramid with his hands and buried his face inside, and he no longer felt empty or dead. He cried one last time for his wife, and then he stared up at the heavens hidden behind the charcoal sky, and he exhaled a ragged breath, and he let go. When he turned and watched the quiet boardwalk on the lakeshore below him, he saw Serena sitting on the rocks amid the long shadows, her back to him, her black hair flying. Seagulls soared and cried around her, floating on the wind with their wings spread. He knew it was time to go. She was waiting for him.